Journey Across Time

By
K.D. Richardson

Journey Across Time
Copyright 2009
Kent Richardson
All Rights reserved
First Printing May 2009

ISBN   0-9815845-9-4
        978-0-9815845-9-1

Written by Kent Richardson

Cover by K.D. Richardson
Cover art 'Into the Fire' Courtesy of Todd Price
www.Nightowlstudio.net

Published by Dailey Swan Publishing, Inc.

No part of this book may be copied
or duplicated except with prior written
permission from the publisher. Small
excerpts may be taken for review
purposes with proper credits given.

Dailey Swan Publishing, Inc.
2644 Appian Way #101
Pinole Ca. 94564
www.Daileyswanpublishing.com

Dedication

*To Wanda: You taught me that
through faith, I
could touch what I once
only dreamed of.*

TABLE OF CONTENTS

Chapter 1	In the Beginning...	7
Chapter 2	Window of Opportunity	28
Chapter 3	From Theory to Reality	53
Chapter 4	Eternal Exodus	81
Chapter 5	It's about Time	108
Chapter 6	Point of No Return	150
Chapter 7	Opening Old Wounds	187
Chapter 8	The Second Assault	227
Chapter 9	Trading Allegiance	264
Chapter 10	Farewell and Salutations	307
Chapter 11	A Time to Live...	345

Chapter One
In the Beginning

*"The philosophies of one age
have become the absurdities of the next,
and the foolishness of yesterday
has become the wisdom of tomorrow."*
SIR WILLIAM OSLER

The day was October 25, 1999, and Dr. Welles was preparing dinner at the usual hour, but this evening would turn out to be anything but ordinary. Dr. Henry Welles, a scientist involved in Project Sundial, a restricted-access government project that was studying the possibility of transdimensional access, or time travel as the layman might refer to it, had just scooted up to the table when there was a knock at the door. When he answered it, he found two men standing in the doorway holding badges.

"Dr. Henry Welles?"

"Yes, and you are..."

"I'm Edward Holbach. This is Donald Bloch. We're agents from the United States Defense Intelligence Agency. May we come in?"

"I suppose so. What's this in reference to?"

"You have been working on Project Sundial for nearly three years now, correct?"

"Correct. We last met as a group in June of this year, and are expecting to gather once again in December. Why, what's going on?"

"That's what we thought we'd ask you. It's come to our attention that you have made some positive inroads into the process of time regression.

Perhaps a little more than you've let on at these so-called gatherings?"

"Well, I have been doing a little work is my spare time on this project," he replied in a modest tone. "You see, in my notes I found..."

"Get them."

"I beg your pardon?"

"I said your notes, get them."

Dr. Welles was a bit stunned at this point, but had some idea what was occurring. "Oh, O.K., but I don't have all of them here. I have a few folders at my office."

Edward Holbach spoke up, "Then get your coat as well. It might be a long night."

"What the hell is this, some sort of a shakedown?"

"Dr. Welles, this is a government sponsored project. We own this intellectual property. You're here to give ol' Uncle Sam what he wants. After all, you volunteered for this project. Nobody forced you," Holbach declared.

"But you're apparently going to force me now. Suppose I refuse to cooperate?"

"Oh, I don't think we'll have any problem there. It just depends on how much you enjoy your tenure at Penn State."

"You can't take that from me. No one can," a defiant Welles proclaimed.

Donald Bloch looked over at Agent Holbach and smirked. "Just get your coat."

The trio took the ten minute drive over to the campus of Penn State University and entered the Davey Lab. Dr. Welles produced the requested folders.

"Don, did you see a copy machine anywhere in the area?"

"Yep, there's one just at the end of the corridor."

"Fine, then let's get busy. As soon as we get what we're looking for, the sooner we can get Dr. Zhivago here back home."

The deed was done and the ball was rolling. Unfortunately, that same ball was in the government's court, and they made all of the rules.

That was back in 1999, and it's only now that I can freely discuss what happened during that following year.

We were three years into Project Sundial when Dr. Henry Welles came up with 'The Theory.' A special meeting was called in early November to allow Dr. Welles to showcase his ideas. We all knew something was up. The usual meeting times for Project Sundial were slated for the first two weeks in December and June, and this was neither of those times. A special meeting is something that had never occurred during the three-year history of Project Sundial, and no one was quite sure why the day's unscheduled session was called. I surmised that somebody developed a breakthrough of some kind or another. Perhaps they found a flaw with Einstein's 'speed of light' theory, or it was possible that evidence proving such a concept had surfaced.

A carefully chosen panel of the leading nuclear physicists and micro-electronic specialists was assembled to address this question in the late 1990s. The secrecy of this project didn't rival that of the Manhattan Project a half century earlier, but unlike the Manhattan Project, no real answer was expected from these sessions. That would be, perhaps, beyond realistic thinking. Yet, all of the input and data collected could go a long way for future generations with respect to this concept. And as everyone knows, intense study into any one area of technology often spawns many other innovations for use elsewhere. Therefore, the government felt that one way or another they could collect a dividend from this investment. For that reason, the people involved with Project Sundial understood that information gathered within those walls would not leave the room.

Another reason for the secrecy of this gathering was that the Federal Government was bankrolling the project. That's where I came in. My degree is in finance with a minor in American History. So how did I end up as a financial coordinator at Penn State? Everything else seemed too much like work. I was in charge of dispersing governmental monies that came to the university for projects the feds deemed worthy of study. I also had to beg for such funds from the governing bodies as Penn State deemed necessary. Yes, I was a middleman.

While not a scientist myself, briefings from those involved usually enabled me to evaluate the feasibility of a study and inform the General Accounting Office in Washington, DC how much of a given project we would be able to handle here at PSU. At the end of the fiscal year, our departmental coffers were usually at or near zero. The University wasn't too happy with that, but apparently the government liked our 'no frills' approach. They kept coming back. I'm guessing that's why I was chosen to be the financial overseer of Project Sundial. Since much of the project would be researched at Penn State, I guess it was natural that I'd be a good fit.

At least I wouldn't be a detriment.

I was given a long leash within the project by granting me clearance to sit in on research and related discussions. I was never barred from any area during the sessions. I suppose the government had no reason not to trust me, but I was under the same restrictions as the research members.

Still, the government disavowed any knowledge of Project Sundial. I guess they had no concern that the project could turn into another 'Area 51' type of situation. If the feds played Project Sundial off as just another independent study and research group, many in scientific circles regarded these sessions as nothing more than pointless government expenditure.

Dr. Henry Welles was chosen to participate in this project because of his renowned ability to work mathematical theories and algorithms from beginning to end at a rate that astounded his peers. He was also quite learned in the field of cosmology, a branch of metaphysics that deals with the nature of the universe.

He was a nice enough man, even tempered. I'd say he was in his middle to late sixties, balding on top and white on the sides. He certainly put his time in when it came to research and development. He received his doctorate in physics from Purdue University, yet his research of late focused mainly in religious theology. I guess it was only natural that a man, interested in the origins and operation of the universe, would gravitate towards such a field of study. I think he regarded his time in this plane finite, so he wanted to absorb every possible morsel of knowledge before graduating to another level of existence.

Those in attendance for this special session included two men from the Defense Department, two NASA scientists, and a dozen others from the scholastic world. Included were Dr. William Lawrence and Dr. David Butler, both highly regarded men in their field of study. From what we were about to hear, Dr. Lawrence and Dr. Butler's level of expertise may have proven to be more of a hindrance than help. Their minds were somewhat closed to possibilities beyond the physical.

We were all assembled in a conference room in the Davey Lab around ten AM. Dr. Welles entered from the right accompanied by two men who I've never witnessed at any of the previous meetings. Dr. Welles approached the podium, adjusted the light and microphone, and then proceeded to open his notebook. As financial coordinator of this project, one would think that I would have been informed of the content of this special meeting. Judging from the buzz around the room prior to our start, everyone else was in the dark as well.

Dr. Welles introduced the two men who entered the room with him as security from the Department of Defense. The department had been our overseer, and I believe the money to fund Project Sundial trickled down from their coffers.

Anyway, Dr. Welles ended the preliminaries by thanking all of us for attending on short notice during such an inclement day.

"Gentlemen, a German poet once wrote, "As people used to be wrong about the motion of the sun, so they are still wrong about the motion of the future. The future stands still; it is we who move in infinite space." Remember these words when you have time to mull over what will be presented here today. For the last year and a half I have been combining our Project Sundial research on violating time's barriers with my own field of specialty, religious theology. While we'd all like to think of our research as earth-based, set in concrete concepts, more exists, much more. Sometimes a dreamer's dreams force us to expand our intellectual horizons to make the impossible possible, as they say. I believe it was Stephen Hawking who once stated that when theory and observation come together, science often takes a giant leap forward. Let's hope he's right today."

"For the last several years, we've been looking into the possibility of trans-dimensional travel. While many out there, even a few in this room I'm afraid, think this study to be an exercise in futility, remember that around the year 1900, physicists said that if one traveled faster that sixty miles per hour, the air would be sucked out of your lungs and you'd die."

"Time, as we all know, is nonexistent except in concept form. I guess our notion of time is actually man's ability to measure the distance between events. Our units of measurement are generally arbitrary. They mean nothing to anything other than man. I believe we're all acquainted with Einstein's theory of Similarity. That is, if it takes the same amount of time to perform a task as it does for a clock to move the distance of one hour, then our idea of time is based on the intervals we perceive between events. That gives us the impression that time has a beginning, middle, and an end. Believe if you will, gentlemen, that we've been going about this all wrong. What would happen if we found out that there is no beginning, middle, or end to time? That is to say, suppose all events in history are occurring at the same time."

"Speaking in the broadest terms, time is one continuous circle - no beginning, middle, or end. Time, I believe, is cyclical, or better put, cylindrical. Like a cylinder, time has no beginning, middle, or end. Yet, it can travel very deep, right to left, or up and down, based on how one views the so-called cylinder of time. Therefore, it's my contention that we've been wasting our time trying to formulate a route back to something that's already occurred. We can, it is my theory, make a lateral move through time."

"Our mission should be to find a way to divaricate the sequence of events of our planet's history, not how to reverse a calendar on the wall."

"But Dr. Welles," Dr. Lawrence interrupted, "if that is so, we're still left with the obstacle of transcending time's cylinder, regardless if it has a beginning, middle, or end."

"Precisely Bill. That's why this special gathering was called, if you'll allow me to continue. I was able to employ my extensive background in religious theology to include the possibility that our universe operates from a higher power. Like I stated previously, one needn't think of that as a 'god.' Perhaps man needs to rethink his idea of God as a white-haired, bearded man sitting high upon a golden throne. We have a cultural bias with regard to our religious beliefs I think most educated people will agree. We have incorporated our own cultural beliefs into what we'd like religion to be, not necessarily what it was originally supposed to stand for. Who knows, our 'higher power' may end up being nothing more than an electrical spark, which jump-started all of life and its forces. But, I digress. I breach this aspect because, if our ideas of man's existence can change, a whole new door to possibilities concerning the entire systematic whole of the universe can be born."

"Perhaps in our own lives there is no beginning or end. Perhaps the self or soul, a real life force mind you, remains constant. The soul's vessel or era may be the only things that change. With man, I believe there are transitions with the soul from pre-existence, to birth, then death. Time itself progresses from one second to the next, one day to another, one year to another..."

"Dr. Welles, where are you going with all of this?" Dr. Butler interrupted.

"David, if time is a 'thing', then what is it?" Most in the room looked lost or disinterested. Answering his own question, Dr. Welles replied, "Time is a vibration. Time, my friends, is motion. More specifically, everything around us, including ourselves, is a collection of particles vibrating at different rates," he proclaimed while spidering his fingers. "Our rate of vibration is so low that it's nearly immeasurable to the human eye without the use of photographs to document the changes. And change is merely the constant interaction of physical particles with one another. Through archaeology, we know that some mountains were once only small hills, or in extreme cases, ocean bottoms. Hence, the ability to find the fossilized remains of ocean-bearing plants and animals on today's mountaintops. Some credit the 'great flood' of Noah's time as an explanation of that phenomenon. The science of plate tectonics suggests otherwise. So, even as a rock looks solid, the molecules within are moving—just too slow for us to observe. You see gentlemen, time's events are cyclical, and not just a period from point A to point B. Time itself is cylindrical. Just as black holes remain a mystery to us, unraveling the cylinder of time has proven to be just as perplexing."

"Henry, how much thought, that is, how certain are you about this, er, theory of yours?" asked Professor Wayne Richmond.

"The more I put two and two together on this idea, the more my answers led to more questions. I kept getting deeper and deeper into unraveling time and its properties. It was as if I was solving a 'who done it' mystery. Everything kept fitting together like a giant jigsaw puzzle. I really doubted my good fortune thinking that this was too easy. If it was this simple, I thought, certainly someone before me would have come up with these answers."

"Perhaps no one thought of looking there", responded professor Richmond.

"Precisely. Sometimes the more complicated the problem, the simpler the solution."

"Also, others didn't have the advantage we have in relationship to the information we've gathered during Project Sundial. Not to mention, Doctor, you took a bit of an unorthodox approach into deciphering the origins of time itself. Please continue you have my interest now."

"As I was saying, one piece of information turned me in the direction I took. Many years ago, while still at Purdue, I came across some information concerning Soviet nuclear experiments during the 1940s and '50s. The Soviets had more than their share of nuclear mishaps. People were killed, towns were wiped out, and environments were destroyed. But, I remember seeing some declassified information from the area of the Cheliabinsk 40 Nuclear Chemical Separation Plant."

"Back then, Stalin gave little priority to environmental safety and health. Apparently, nuclear waste from the plant contaminated over 125,000 people around the Techa waterway which originates from the Ural Mountains. Tens of thousands were evacuated, many unfortunately too late. The Techa River and its flood plains had to be rerouted to minimize additional contamination—8000 hectares or about 20,000 acres in all. What that information didn't tell me, I saw for myself."

"In the early 1980s, after the cold war cooled a bit, I was privileged to be in the Soviet Union—while it was still a union. We were involved in a low-level information exchange, while our Russian counterparts were allowed to enter the U.S. under the same precept. I'm guessing that it was done to further Reagan's trust but verify policy at that time. It was nothing major mind you, but enough to justify the trip. I was anxious to get a tour of the Cheliabinsk 40 area to investigate the accuracy of my declassified information. That request met with a few red faces, a couple of "nyets", and a few flimsy excuses. Apparently they weren't ready to let the world see the destruction they had caused. It was too much of an international embarrassment for the Soviets at a time when they were struggling to hold the union together, I'm sure."

"During our free time, a noted Russian molecular biologist, Uri Sloviniski, showed sympathy towards my inquiries. After hours, he took me to their departmental archives and granted me access to all of the information I wished to see. He was nervous as all get out, but he knew that if the information were to be made public, he could not be the one to do it. I found it all very fascinating, but I wasn't able to categorize that information until recently. He showed me some still-classified photos of that area taken prior to, and at six-month intervals shortly after the plant was shut down. I wasn't sure that the photographs I saw weren't pictures of an area poisoned by excessive radiation."

"My Russian host procured us each a train voucher on a route that would pass as close as possible to the Cheliabinsk 40 site. There's not a lot between the towns of Sverdlovsk and Chelyabinsk, so the train wouldn't be making a scheduled stop near the old plant site. We were able to take a route via Kamensk-Ural'skiy that took us around the lower valley portion of the Urals. I took my camera equipped with a long-range zoom lens to record what I could of the region. From where I was and what I could see, that area still appeared devoid of most of its former major vegetation. However, it was evident that much low level growth was in abundance. There are plenty of trees growing there now, but they're still immature when compared to the old growth forest in the surrounding areas. So I think we can rule out radioactive poisoning as a cause. The land wouldn't have come back as fast if that were the case."

"What is your opinion of what occurred then, Henry?" Dr. Butler inquired.

"I really wasn't sure at the time, but with that visual information, the verbiage from the Russian M.B., and most importantly the photographs, I was only recently able to tie it all together."

"What was so important in those photos?"

"The photos taken during the construction of the Cheliabinsk 40 Nuclear Chemical Separation Plant showed that the surrounding terrain to be as one might expect it to be. Throughout the surrounding area, there appeared to be quite a bit of dense forestation. After the plant shut down, the photos showed how much the area's terrain had changed. The drainage area leading from Cheliabinsk 40 to the Techa River exhibited a startling deviation from the pre-operation snapshots. The area, particularly around the settling ponds, Techa River, and local valley area had been obliterated, free of all vegetation. And, it wasn't the result of a nuclear explosion, per se. It did mimic that in appearance on a small scale, but I found no information to verify such an occurrence. The years-old structures were still intact and in good shape."

"Radiation poisoning," shot back Dr. Richmond.

"Wait, there's more. Official reports described the area as, let me see here," Dr. Welles said as he shuffled through his pile of papers, "leaving no residual indications of any pre-existing forestation." It was as if the trees and low growth vegetation never existed. The land was clean. No brush, no stumps, just the bare earth. And, the affected area was feathered out the farther away from the waterways you got. The reports go on to say that within a year, these areas flourished with all kinds of native foliage. That wouldn't have occurred if the area had been severely damaged by radiation poisoning. If they're correct, the photos taken five years after the fact proved that point. And, I believe that to be so."

"Doctor, you don't think the surrounding area could have been bulldozed to remove the contaminated soil?"

"That's unlikely, Wayne. The lay of the land hadn't changed from what I could see, plus, from what I've read, once the radiation leaks were discovered and the damage determined, the Soviet crews pretty much beat a path out of there. None of the skilled personnel stayed one second longer than they had to. Anybody else who was around, namely prison labor, or as I like to call it, slave labor, wouldn't have the skill or opportunity to operate big equipment such as that," replied Dr. Welles. "Plus, they lacked a motive."

"So, what is your opinion of what occurred there, Doctor?"

"It is my now-educated guess that the area was affected by the nearby experiments. The nuclear fusion material wasn't contained properly in those days. And, that in and of itself led to many Soviet disasters. I believe gentlemen, and all kidding aside, that the trees simply disappeared."

An uneasy laughter encircled the room. Many didn't know if they were being put on or if they were in the presence of one of the most Earth-changing discoveries known to mankind. Dr. Welles seemed so sure of himself.

"Uh, Henry, as you can see, I'm not laughing," retorted Dr. Melvin Goodrich. Dr. Goodrich was a highly regarded man in his own right having worked with renown physicist Dr. Stephen Hawking on such subjects as black holes in relation to time's relativity. Dr. Goodrich was a driven man. He was all business. A staple at MIT, he was not known for his 'fun and games' approach when it came to research-related information.

"Good, Mel, I wouldn't want you to hurt yourself," came the reply from Dr. Welles that nearly brought down the house. "Please allow me to explain. I believe those areas fell victim to molecular displacement. I'll explain more after lunch about the educational portion of this theory, but for right now, Neil if you would, the lights."

I reached over and darkened the room. Dr. Welles turned on the overhead projector and with laser pointer in hand, continued.

"Here is a typical molecule, the smallest particle of a substance, surrounded by atoms. Each atom has its own charged arrangement of electrons. Accelerate or decelerate these electrons by a charge of whatever means, and you've changed the structure of the molecule. Change all of these molecules within the structure, and you've changed the organism itself."

"Now, we know that everything in the universe has movement—everything," Dr. Welles continued. "Even empty outer space has energy from gasses, which implies movement. There is no such thing as nothingness. On the other hand, we also know that nothing is solid. There is space between all matter within itself. Yes, that's even true for something such as this table top, which appears to be wood," Dr. Welles acknowledged, rapping his knuckles loudly on the laminated top.

"Knowing this, we must go back to the beginning of what we refer to as time itself. Here, this next transparency shows that at the start of existence, everything was, perhaps the only time during creation, as close to being a solid as there could be. A black hole is the closest thing we have today which mimics that condition. After the so-called 'big bang' took place, all matter developed a vibration upon separation from the whole. That vibration, while signifying movement within a structure, tends to evolve with time, changing as it goes. All vibration in the universe is decreasing, much like the Doppler Effect. You know, you drop a pebble into a still body of water and the ripples enlarge from the center starting point, yet they decrease in intensity because their force is being spread over a larger area. Therefore, the ripples if you will, are still spreading outward from the 'big bang,' yet the frequency's vibration is slowing down. We tend to define much of that as aging. I know this goes against modern thinking, but stay with me here."

"The object of Project Sundial was to explore ways to transcend the time barrier. To do that, we need to somehow increase an entire organism's rate of vibration, or frequency, or molecular make-up if you will, to mimic that of an earlier point in the history of the universe."

"So what you're saying Henry, is that the nuclear waste from the Cheliabinsk 40 plant was infused into the trees altering their chemistry, so that the trees' vibration mimicked that of trees from another era?"

"Correct, and the same applies to some of the smaller vegetation near the edge of the waterways that wasn't initially poisoned. I'm sure there's a fine line between dose and toxicity. But where those trees and vegetation ended up, I have no idea. Based on the evidence I've come across, it was truly as if the trees never existed. This was an unnatural alteration of a living organism's frequency. Don't get me wrong, it was a million to one shot to be sure, but the numbers and evidence don't lie."

"That's some pretty flimsy evidence to support a rather broad-based theory, isn't that Dr. Welles? I mean, if we could decrease an organism's vibratory pulse, would this lead us to a future time in your opinion?" Dr. Goodrich quizzed.

"Please, one thing at a time. Good God, the implications of it all. Let me put it this way, just as Neanderthal man had a higher vibratory rhythm and a lower intelligent quotient, modern man has a greater capacity for learning, yet a lower vibration. That's the Doppler Effect coming into play once again. The two appear to be synchronized, yet they're proceeding in opposition to one another. To sum up, we see 'today' as 'today' because the entire universe, including our little corner of it, is oscillating at a particular and fixed rate. Each living organization has its own vibration relative to size, energy needed and expelled during its lifetime, and so on. That's one of the many reasons you rarely see interspecies propagation. As all our frequencies decrease through the decades, albeit a scant amount, we eventually cease to exist, at least in an Earthly sense. Physics simply won't permit it."

"So why don't we see remnants of earlier eras?" asked Dr. Butler.

"Who says we don't? We don't 'see' yesterday's action because the audible and physical vibrations don't travel through the vacuum of another era. Some refer to that as the 'time barrier,' I suppose. Just as sound doesn't travel through the vacuum of a bell jar, even though it is indeed occurring, dimensions themselves are separated by a natural partition."

"So if I follow you Henry, running my own theory off of yours, our spirit, or our electrical pulse, lives on after its earthly demise because it has no set position. I'm guessing that it remains constant, correct?" quizzed Dr. Butler.

"David, you've just taken on your next project; proving the existence of an afterlife," Dr. Welles with a laugh. "But, you may not be too far off of the mark. Your future is somebody's past. And, your past was someone else's future—maybe your own if you follow your own hypothesis."

A nod of the head ensued from Dr. Butler.

"With time, and possibly life itself being cyclical, taking Dr. Butler's idea into consideration, perhaps we do live over and over again. Wow! I think we've just come up with the 'theory of existence,' Dr. Welles proclaimed with amusement.

"But," Dr. Lawrence ensued, "how do we know what an organism's frequency, vibration, or whatever is, or for that matter, was?"

"Good question," Dr. Welles went on to explain. "I'm guessing that it would be possible to test a piece of preserved wood from ages ago since trees are one of the most highly carbon-based life forms. Now if we knew specifically what year that wood existed as a living form, we'd be in business. One draw back is that would still only be a ball park figure," he said while scratching his chin.

"But, if you took the carbon dating information from the preserved specimen and compared it to the same type of lumber grown today, one could ascertain the difference of the molecular oscillation between then and now. That numerical difference may or may not apply to all living organisms between those two times. I'm speaking on a percentage basis, of course. We would have to compare samples of many items from a known period and compare them to today. Then we'd know for sure if we had a consistent variation or not."

"With Project Sundial, we were supposed to expand the study of Hawking's 'worm hole' theories as well as Einstein's 'speed of light' concepts pertaining to time travel. Our notion here doesn't concern itself with the speed of an object to create a difference in time dimensions. The speed, gentlemen, is within the organism itself as well as its surrounding environment. Instead of merely studying the question and coming forth with suggestions to be used for future generations, we were able to come up with a solution to the problem."

"Whoa, hold on a minute Henry," Dr. Goodrich interrupted. "We don't have any answers yet, just theories. And, some pretty far out theories, if you ask me."

"Mel, were you the one who was quoted as saying that everything had already been invented? I think Charles H. Duell said that around the early 1900s. With some of the ideas bouncing around here today, that may have indeed been your spirit during another time," Dr. Welles sarcastically shot back. "I know that our profession deals with hard, cold facts and numbers. But let's not become wrapped up with surface-level thinking. Perhaps man's greatest adventures lie ahead. If this project can be brought to a reality, we'd not only be traversing time's barriers, we'd be breaking the finite limits of man's knowledge."

"Henry, do you know what you're saying? You're attempting to change reality as we know it," added Dr. Butler.

"*As we know it* is the key phrase. I'll be soliciting input from all of you on bringing this undertaking to an actuality. With all of us working together on this, and I think our colleagues from NASA would agree, Project Sundial would be on a parallel with the Friendship 7 undertaking with respect to the moon landing. This is merely the first step on the journey of a thousand miles. Gentlemen, I'll see you all back here after lunch. Thank-you all for attending."

As we all rose from our chairs, the room was abuzz with disbelief, comments, and stunned looks. Just as I picked up my folder and began descending the risers, Dr. Welles called out, "Oh Neil, how about grabbing a bite with me over at the HUB?"

"Sure, I'd be honored," I answered. What in the world would Dr. Henry Welles want with me, I wondered. He may soon be the most famous man in the world and he wants to have lunch with me?

Chapter Two
In the Beginning

"The price one pays for pursuing any profession, or calling, is an intimate knowledge of its ugly side."
JAMES BALDWIN

    I grabbed my coat and went across the street to the Hetzel Union Building, or HUB, to get a bite of lunch. I was a bit stunned after hearing what just went on at the meeting, so my choice of food wasn't a top priority. I grabbed a seat next to the aquarium and within eyeshot of the staircase so I could motion to Dr. Welles as to my whereabouts.
    I thought that it hardly seemed possible that we could actually be near a solution to transdimensional travel. My God, the uses for such a device could change all we know and do for the rest of eternity. I was staring off into the fish tank thinking of all of the implications of this discovery when someone came up from behind and said, "BOO!" I nearly fell out of my chair. I turned around to see Dr. Welles.
    "I thought I'd catch you coming down the stairs from here," I told him.
    "Your detective work was incomplete," replied Dr. Welles. "I came in from the other side. I had to grab some stamps at the post office. I'll be right back. I've worked up quite an appetite."
    Dr. Welles went up to the counter, grabbed some food, and proceeded over to another table.

With a wave of his head, he motioned for me to join him.

"Dr. Welles, it's quite an honor for me to be able to converse like this with you, but I'm not real sure why you chose me to speak with."

"To be honest with you, I just wanted to get away from those eggheads for a while. I thought by conversing with you I'd be able to put my mind on hold for a bit."

"Oh, well thank-you, I guess," I replied sounding as if I had just received a backhanded compliment.

With that, Dr. Welles started laughing and slapped me on the shoulder. "Of course I'm just kidding. But really, I did want to get away from the others for a while. There is a rhyme and a reason for our visit. I'm sure you noticed the two men who entered the meeting with me."

"Yes, I was wondering who they were. Their faces didn't ring a bell."

"They're from the Department of Defense."

"I thought Bill Johnson and Lieutenant Samuels were the Defense Department's representatives?"

"They are, but they're with the Research and Development Division. Edward Holbach and Donald Bloch are with the DIA, the Defense Intelligence Agency, a branch of the CIA. They're in charge of, well, figure it out. Apparently, they were alerted to the progress I had made on deciphering the conundrum of a trans-dimensional alteration."

"Who tipped them off?" I asked. "Do you know?"

"No I don't. For all I know they may have

found out on their own. I may have said a little more than I should have within earshot of Johnson or Samuels. They may have taken that information back to Washington after our June meeting. So at the end of last month I received a nice visit from two fine gentlemen from the Department of Defense Security. They wanted to see my research material from Project Sundial. They let it be known that I didn't have much of a choice. Since the government is footing the bill for this study, the data basically belongs to the federal government. That's when they determined that I had made substantial progress—much more than they ever expected."

"Yes, they really weren't expecting a solution to the question from this project, were they?" I asked.

"Maybe they were, but there's not one yet. I'm not sure about their motives, but I'm certain they were willing to accept anything we could come up with. Either way, the federal government would come out an intellectual or financial winner. Anyway, when they saw what I had accomplished, they told me I'd be presenting this information to all of you today. I wasn't asked to do this, mind you. I suppose they figured that if I was that close, all of us together could 'push it over the top,' so to speak."

"Doctor, I was wondering..."

"First of all call me Henry. Now proceed."

"O.K., Henry, how close are you really to solving this question?"

"A hell of a lot closer than I'd like to tell them," he said, motioning his head in the direction of the Davey Lab.

"Why are you telling me all of this. Why not

tell someone like Dr. Butler or Dr. Lawrence about your fears?"

Dr. Welles looked me square in the eyes and said, "Because I can't trust them." Relaxing his attitude a bit he continued, "Oh, don't get me wrong, they're great guys, good researchers and all. In fact, I worked with David on an earlier long-term project right before I left Purdue. But I'm not sure who would say what to whom. I can't take that chance. So, I figured I could confide in you. When it comes to your job, you're no slouch. Your spotless record speaks for itself. Yes, even I do some snooping around," he said with a good-natured wink.

"But" I continued, "what are you afraid of? If what you say about your theory is true, then sure, the government will have the rights to it, but you'll be the most famous man, maybe in all modern time. Think of how much society will benefit from your breakthrough."

"That's just it. If my theory comes to fruition, as you put it, I'm afraid that it will never see the light of day; at least, not in our life times it won't."

"What, are you afraid of ending up like that guy who supposedly invented a pill that turned water into gasoline? And, later he was found floating face down in a swimming pool that he didn't have, and in his home he didn't own?" I returned.

"Actually, I hadn't thought of that. Thanks a lot, now I've got some real worries," Dr. Welles said returning the sarcasm. "Anyway, what I'm afraid of is that the feds will stop the project altogether, or they'll get hold of the information before it becomes public and allow the CIA to use it for their own selfish interests. You know Neil, he who controls time controls the world. It's true. Could you imagine what would happen if the CIA would be able to go back in time and correct past mistakes? Its one thing to upset the balance of time, but what would possession of a device such as this do to the balance of world power? I love my country, I served during the Korean War, but an imbalance such as this would be unhealthy."

"It would probably put us over the top though."

"But we're not always right, you know. What would that do to our present if the political, military, or financial mistakes of our past were wiped out? We learn from our mistakes. I guess that's why they're there. Things are the way they are for a reason. By correcting past errors, there would be no mistakes in the past from which to learn. And what good would that do for the society of that era? Without any consequences from their actions, that society would learn nothing from their circumstances. And, what would we learn today? Nothing. We as a people have never learned too much from our perfection. How would mankind function?"

"Oh, I don't know. Maybe someone from a future generation would come back to the past and help us out."

In his best Jack Benny voice, Dr. Welles replied, "Now cut that out!" He did manage to keep his sense of humor despite the current circumstances. Continuing on he explained, "I'm confused enough already without that kind of logic. Don't add to my problems."

"I see what you're saying. But again I have to ask you Henry, why me? About all I remember from the obligatory one year of physics I muddled through is the definition of the subject itself. Let me see if I remember correctly; Physics: An understanding of our universe and the ultimate structure and conversion of matter, or something along those lines. How did I do?"

"I'll give you an 'A' for the day," replied Dr. Welles. He quieted his voice, hunkered down towards his tray and asked, "Neil, with your job, you have connections in DC, correct?"

"Sure, yeah I guess so. They're not considered higher ups, though."

"Yes, but they would have connections—those above them, right?"

"Sure, I'm positive most of them have the run of the place and could acquire access to some fairly sensitive information if they set their minds to it."

"Good, good."

"Henry, exactly what would I be looking for?"

"Keep an eye and an ear open to see if the feds plan to shut Project Sundial down. That's when I'll know that they're planning to confiscate the material we've worked so hard on. I dare say it just depends on how far they think we can go with it. I believe that they'll give us as much leash as we need. Once they feel that they have enough info to 'take it from there,' they just might."

"Doctor, are you sure that they'd do something like that?" I asked.

"You can bet on it. I've watched them do that with smaller projects in the past. Money was the impetus then. God only knows what their motivation would be for this concept, but I suppose that's part of doing government work. They own the product *and* you. Money's always the bottom line. Oh Neil, if you could have been there when those two guys came knocking at my door," he said shaking his head. "It scared the living hell out of me, and in America of all places."

"Vee have veys of making you talk, olt mon," I said using a stereotypical German accent.

"Uh close, very close. Although they were fair in their demeanor, I knew they meant business. That's why I chose this table for us to talk. No one's close enough to eavesdrop."

"Henry, do you think we're under surveillance now?"

"Naw, the material I'm presenting is just in theory form, at least in their minds anyway. Now if the pieces of the puzzle start to come together, well that will make for a whole different ball game. Then, we'll have to be very clandestine concerning our meetings. Neil, I need you. You're my ace in the hole."

"Henry, you're not going paranoid on me now are you?"

"No!" he replied in a mild shout. Lowering his voice back down, Dr. Welles explained, "Hey look, you don't know how those guys operate. I do, I've seen it before. Never on a project this sensitive before, but I've never been involved in an undertaking with such potential societal ramifications. None of us have since World War Two. I know that you may be dumb as a box of rocks when it comes to physics, but..."

"Thanks a hell of a lot."

Following a laugh, Dr. Welles continued, "What I'm trying to say is that I'm going to try and describe all of the details of my theory, step by step, so you'll get a full understanding of what we're about to embark upon. I just hope the others won't be bored by my 'Physics 101' approach, so keep your ears open. I won't be able to repeat myself."

Checking his watch Dr. Welles summed up, "Well, I've got to pick up some additional papers for the afternoon portion of my talk. Uh, you will be there, won't you?" Dr. Welles said more as a statement rather than a question.

"Oh, I don't know. I was going to go upstairs and watch some TV. I don't like to miss my stories, you know."

Dr. Welles just glared at me.

"Yes, of course I'll be there! I was just kidding. See, I have a sense of humor too."

"Yeah, you're awful funny. Anyway, see you over there."

"Uh, Henry, just what will you do if the government plans on seizing your material?"

"I'll cross that bridge when I come to it. Later."

After Dr. Welles headed for the exit, I found myself looking around to see if anyone had been spying on us. Now I had myself doing the 'paranoid shtick.'

With that, I finished off my mystery meal and grabbed my coat. I didn't have time to go back to my office to pick up the additional supplies needed for the upcoming session. My car was parked behind the Osmond Lab, and I always kept enough papers, pens, and folders inside for just such an emergency. And, I guess this situation qualified as much as any.

As I crossed Pollock Road, I caught a biting blast of cold, frigid wind to the side of my face.

People probably thought that it would be a cold day in Hell before something like this would occur, I thought while contemplating the revelations about to take place. I guess they were right.

After retrieving my needed provisions, I started back towards the lab. There was one of those gray federal cars parked not too far from the rear of the building. I'm sure it belonged to our two security buddies who made their appearance this morning. They sure don't try too hard to conceal their presence, I thought.

I went back into the lecture room and took my usual seat. I thought it would be best if I separated myself a bit since I would be acting the part of an observer. I also took into account that those who were here, were so not only learn but also to put in their two cents worth. They would best be served if they sat front and center.

Dr. Welles was already at the podium sifting through his two-inch thick binder as he waited for the others to return. When it appeared that everyone was in their places, including our Department of Defense friends, Dr. Welles asked me to shut the door so that he could begin.

"Gentlemen, let us refresh our memories. If I'm being a bit redundant in the presentation of this material, please bear with me. I want to make sure everything's understood. The more you comprehend, the more ideas we'll be able to float here today. And, I will need all of the input you can give me. I'm close here, very close to our goal. But, many refinements are still needed to bring this project a reality—even on an experimental level."

"I know when Project Sundial was put together, they only expected some new ideas that would aid industry and science, or perhaps the Department of Defense," he said snapping a glance towards Holbach and Bloch. "Well, they're going to receive a bit more than that. It was said of Christopher Columbus when he set sail for the new world, that he didn't know where he was going. When he got there they said he didn't know where he was, and when he got back, he didn't know where he had been. Let's hope that we have a bit more direction than that."

"What we are attempting to do is access another dimension. We hope to go, to sound a bit cliché, where no man has gone before. I guess, better said, going where man *has* gone before. We'll be keying off the research of several theorists and their works. Amongst those will be Albert Einstein, of course, and Edwin Hubble, just to toss out a couple."

"Like I stated earlier, Albert Einstein's theory of time's relativity focused on the physical velocity of an object reaching the speed of light, approximately 186,000 miles per second. Since we're not yet able to achieve those means, it would actually be difficult to tell if ol' Al was right or not. Concepts from that theory have only held water in relation to stellar light waves themselves."

But," he continued, "Einstein was probably right to a degree judging from the analysis we're able to do from pictures taken of distant galaxies by the Hubble telescope. We mustn't forget, however, that Einstein's theory primarily dealt with future travel, not necessarily a lateral shift to the past. I'm guessing that many of his concepts may not be relevant to today's topic."

"What we will be attempting to do is to alter the organism itself so that its molecular make-up will mimic that of another era. A radio can only receive a signal if it's tuned to the right frequency. That receiver merely converts energy back to its original vibratory structure, and as we've stated earlier, energy is a physical mass. The radio is the instrument that exhibits this particular re-conversion. Like I stated earlier, thanks to his particular molecular make-up, a man is tuned to receive the signals of the present, his present. What we'll be attempting to accomplish will be an adjustment in the speed of the atoms' mass throughout the body to a great enough degree that it will be able to escape its inborn grip on a particular era. We're not concerned with the fleetness of the organism itself."

"We know that electromagnetic waves, such as X-rays, light, and radio waves are transmitted through space, and now possibly time, as waves of energy. Now, the trick is to change the body's electrical field wavelength to the speed it would have possessed at a given time in history. Virtually all of these waves travel at the speed of light. Therefore, they're easy to work with, theoretically speaking."

"Doctor, it sounds as if you're saying that we're not unlike a radio receiver, and we're trying to discover a way to receive another station," suggested Edward Holbach.

"Yes sir, exactly. Take another citation out of petty cash for that insight. That's precisely what I'm saying, gentlemen. That's why I suggested earlier that all of history is happening at once. If one's mind, soul, and body weren't tuned to that particular era, it would be analogous to a radio being tuned to the wrong station. The rest of the 'wasted' broadcasts from other stations wouldn't be perceived by us and thus have no effect on our lives. Therefore, those stations wouldn't become a reality as far as we were concerned, at least to our senses. Good. Nice way of putting it."

"If that's true Dr. Welles, for the sake of argument, why don't we see today what happened, say, yesterday? Forget about another era," asked the lieutenant.

"As I stated earlier, time is cyclical. And, again, like a clock, the hands of time, or in this case the vibration of the universe's mass, shall progress. It's always progresses and never stays the same."

"When looking in a mirror, the image one sees isn't the actual object itself. It is, however, a visual resemblance of the arrangement of points, or atoms, interacting and producing energy waves in a particular pattern. In other words, if you don't see it, it ain't there. I'm speaking visually, of course. We're the actual physical manifestation of that make-up."

"Henry," Dr. Richmond asked, "That still doesn't explain how things in history can be occurring at the same time and at the same place, yet we can't perceive them. Could you be a bit more scientific than the radio receiver scenario?"

"Yes, yes, let me finish. I don't want to get too far off on this tangent, but a Serb-Croat physicist from the late 1700s named Roger

Boscovich went on to explain that there are two modes of existence. There's the temporal mode and the local mode. The 'local' is where the event takes place. The 'temporal' mode refers to the time when the action takes place. The points he referred to join up to form what we call energy and those in turn go on to produce a physical reality. One point can join with a group, but a group can't join another group. Yes, even points have a capacity, and that capacity becomes their boundary. Now, it's the modes of existence that define when and where the points of matter become united. Points of different modes can't coexist. Therefore, we end up with masses of energy becoming a reality at only one place and one time."

"Dr. Welles," Wayne spoke up again, "If Boscovich was right, that would mean that the possibilities for matter and events to manifest would be infinite."

"Precisely, Wayne, and that, as they say, is why time marches on. Now, how it marches on has as much to do with the so-called Big Bang Theory as much as anything else. The vibrations of the Earth and the universe progress like the ripples produced when a pebble is dropped into the water. This progression is referred to by some as evolution. A similar situation occurs with the points of matter. They too evolve with time. And, like all life forms in the universe, all compounds created by the union of two or more points of matter will eventually break down or cease to exist as a unit. We tend to refer to that process as disintegration, death, erosion, decay, corrosion, or what have you. Those terms all refer to the same physical activity. This process frees up the points of matter to conjoin with other random points to create new compounds. Examples of this process would be vegetation to soil, soil to rock, rock back to soil, and us, I suppose, as food for the worms."

"So now we have defined time and how we measure it. The question remains, how do we access events of the past. Actually, my theory incorporates a two-step process. First, we'll have to determine the actual frequency of the Earth's vibration, or electrical field, from a given era. Next, we have to ordain the difference in frequency of an organism between then and now."

"You make it all sound so easy, Doctor," Donald Bloch remarked.

"Hardly, this is just theory. The proof will be evidenced in the result. The real trick here will be to change the organism's electrical field from within. It would have to coincide with that of another era."

"Henry, sorry to interrupt, but is this what you think happened to those trees around the Cheliabinsk 40 area?" asked Dr. Goodrich.

"Absolutely," affirmed Dr. Welles. "That's what got me started in this direction. Like I stated earlier, that happening was certainly a million to one shot. But, this century is probably the first time man has dealt with substances that could bring about such a severe change within an organism."

"Amazing."

"Now comes the hard part. We'll have to be meticulous in determining the frequency of an organism's electromagnetic field."

"And you have that ability to do so now?" asked Dr. Lawrence.

"Just about, give me a month or so. Anyway,

once we can determine an organism's electrical pattern of oscillation over say a twenty-four hour period, week, month, or year, we'll have a rough base number with which to work. If this formula proves itself out in the long run, we could have our multiplier. We would then use that base number to establish the organism's electrical pattern for any given era."

"Dr. Welles, are we talking about 'biorhythms' here," asked Dr. Lawrence.

"Well," Dr. Welles started, followed by a light laugh, "it's a bit more complicated than that, although that's a nice descriptive term seeing how we're dealing with the body's entire electrical and cellular system. I like that. So in layman's terms, that's how we'll refer to the body's electromagnetic field. It's easier to remember anyway," he said while glancing my way.

"Doctor," Bill Johnson finally spoke up, "getting back to determining one's bio-vibration, if you will. How would we go about determining how much an individual's electrical field should be slowed to mimic that of another era?"

"Like I stated earlier, if we have an object from a known time, say a sliver of wood from a log cabin known to have been erected during the time period you wished to visit, we would measure its electrical field and compare those readings to the same species of tree growing today. The difference in that charge would at least give us some idea of the percentage of change in the Earth's electrical magnetic field. And yes, even old wood still has an electrical charge. That charge is energy. To see that energy released, just set it on fire. The energy would transfer from structure to heat."

"While I like to work with wood, being one of the highest carbon life forms, several samples of different objects would be needed to determine if the percentage of change is identical across the board. It is my contention that it will be."

"What about metals or iron, Henry?"

"Good question. From the testing I've already completed, many metallic compounds won't be of much help to us. Since fusible alloys were forged at different times and by different methods, there's no way to guarantee their accuracy. They're what I refer to as a 'new life form.'"

"The Earth's core is, amongst other things, molten magnetic iron. And, that substance is what keeps the Earth's electrical field in operation. From studying lava flows, we can map the changing positions of the magnetic poles with great accuracy. It's my contention that the Earth's vibration evolves and changes at the same rate as most other living organisms."

"But Henry, back to the subject of metals, didn't you say that everything on the Earth is or was living?"

"No, I said that everything on Earth and the universe is changing. Sure, everything gives off some energy waves, but it's an organism whose earthly life has a beginning, middle, and end that we're concerned with. Those benchmarks, or periods of existence, will give us our points of reference with regards to our measurement, or as some might put it, our Concept of Simultaneity."

"That brings me to another point, Doctor. If living or once living objects are era-specific, how are we able to have objects still around from, say, Colonial times? What about the pyramid's treasures?" Johnson asked.

"Well, a piece of leather, for example, begins to break down and deteriorate immediately after becoming detached from its living host. The organism is no longer replacing dead cells with new. Time and the elements will continue to take its toll upon the object. We may make a concerted effort to preserve that article, an unnatural intervention if you will, but all we're really doing is delaying the inevitable. So, as with any formerly living specimen, all we're observing is the remains, or carcass of what the object once was. This is not unlike examining a corpse. The progression of the electrical make up within the sample ceased when the host expired. The object is now in a state of regression. Change is still occurring within until the item's eventual dissolution as a unit."

"Henry," Dr. Butler asked, "You keep talking about this bio-rhythm vibration thing. Assuming that we're all vibrating," he said in a mocking tone, "where does the buzz come from? Is it from the Earth's magnetic core?"

"David, you're half right. Yes, our electrical field's rate is determined, I believe, from the magnetic properties from within our own Earth. And along those same lines, our universe controls the Earth in a similar manner. And, in a comparable way, some would say, as the soul controls the body."

"And what controls the universe's speed of change? A stellar collapse, then discharge known as the Big Bang, which supposedly took place over fifteen billion years prior?"

"Bingo," replied Dr. Welles. You hit the nail right on the head. Um, let me see. Uh, well, to put it into layman's terms, imagine if our sun were the center of the universe."

"Oh god," Dr. Butler was heard muttering under his breath as he rested his chin on his palm.

Dr. Welles shot Dr. Butler a glance. "Now, remember the analogy I gave earlier this morning about the pebble dropping into the still water? Remember how the rings grew weaker and devitalized the farther they ventured from the drop zone? The same situation occurs in the universe. The rate isn't the same for any two galaxies. There's too much room for variation with respect to those galaxies' position within the universe. Just as the energy from the Big Bang established the frequency for the entire universe, the energy from our Earth's center emanates outward."

"I suppose I can take much of my inspiration for this theory from George Lemaitre, a Belgian physicist, who was one of the first to propose the 'Big Bang.' I got the chance to meet him one time while I was still a student at Purdue. I think reading about him and learning how he was able to combine religion with physics became my early inspiration."

"Henry, enough of your life history, get on with it," moaned Dr. Butler as he glanced once again at his watch.

Dr. Welles was acutely aware of Dr. Butler's irritability. "Uh huh. Anyway, it was Lemaitre's contention that with the universe expanding, all matter is in motion, thus constantly changing its electrical vibration as time progresses. Changing positions of the universe point to a different place on the light spectrum, or in this case, a different frequency."

"Do you see what I'm saying? It all boils down to energy waves. That's all matter really is. That's all that we are. You could say that we're a symphony of vibrating points of energy. Sight, sound, and the physical; all matter is made up of energy waves."

"To sum up this part of my text, just as Hubble theorized that there was no middle of the universe, per se, I theorize that there is no middle of time. I'm certainly not the first to venture down that path. Mel, didn't Hawking preach a school of thought known as 'imaginary time'?"

"Absolutely. Stephen Hawking theorized that since the universe had no beginning, middle, or boundaries, the same holds true concerning time. "It simply exists, he said," answered Dr. Goodrich with his cupped hands extended.

"I couldn't have put it better myself. Some concepts we can explain the whats and the wherefores. The whys still elude us on occasion," concluded Dr. Welles.

"Henry, the ideas you're presenting here today are going to be nearly impossible to prove. I mean, theories are fine, they're what future breakthroughs are built upon," proclaimed Dr. Lawrence.

"Exactly," Dr. Welles continued. "To paraphrase Otto Bismarck, "Theory is a simple piece of paper. The main thing, still, is to make history, not to write it". So get comfortable while I bore you with a bit more nuclear physics. We'll see if we can remove the obstacles between theory and reality."

"Our question at hand is how to increase the frequency of an organism's electrical field within the cellular structure itself," he said as he drew a diagram of a simple molecule on the board.

"We need to raise its electrons into a higher vacancy to an orbit of higher vibration. A higher vibration, of course, means an acceleration of the speed of matter within. The increase of radiation in the form of photon energy results in that molecule increasing its speed. More speed means more energy. And that means a higher vibration which, in essence, puts us on par with a cell's operational frequency from yesteryear."

"If we can accomplish that task, our only roadblock would be to achieve this feat not just molecule-wide or cell-wide, but to realize that process throughout the entire body. That is to say, without damaging the organism or its cellular operation. When that reality is met gentlemen, our goal will be realized," he said slamming his piece of chalk into the tray.

"And, suppose we meet that goal. Just what will happen to our specimen? Will it simply disappear like magic?" a mocking Dr. Butler asked.

"Hell David, how would I know? To be honest, no one knows yet."

"Well your reasoning sounds a bit spacey if you ask me," Dr. Butler returned, his tone now becoming a bit caustic.

Dr. Welles' face reddened as he came up with one last quote in an attempt to soothe Dr. Butler. "It's been said that the farther and farther we get from the familiar, the stranger things become. This concept goes well beyond the familiar, I'll grant you that. Look David, we're amongst the elite. We've been chosen out of all others to attempt to bring this project to a reality. This isn't only an opportunity, it's a privilege. You should feel honored to..."

A smirk and a roll of the eyes crossed Dr. Butler's face. "Henry," he said as he waved his hand side-to-side, "don't talk down to me. I'm here because I was asked, not because I volunteered."

"Hey, come on now, David. We have a real opportunity to do something big here. It's going to take a lot of gray matter. If your heart and mind isn't into it," Dr. Welles said with a pause while taking a deep breath, "then I suggest you get your ass the hell out of here!"

"I've had about as much of this sci-fi shit as I can take for one day," Dr. Butler said while throwing his folders into his briefcase. "This entire project flies in the face of common logic. Gentlemen," he said while scanning the occupants of the room, "it's my opinion that you're all wasting your time."

The tension in the room was running a bit high after that exchange. Dr. Butler exited the room, and Dr. Welles, trying to compose himself, cleared his throat and endeavored to continue. "Okay, now where was I?"

"Increasing an electron's speed I believe," came a voice from across the room.

"Oh yes," Dr. Welles said while clearing his throat for a second time. "Actually, in a negatively charged electron, it's not the charge of the orbitals we want to change. Most atoms are neutral anyway containing one positive and one negative electron."

"Then what exactly are we trying to change?"

"The speed, man!" Dr. Welles shot back. Grabbing his chalk and diagramming like the frustrated man he was, he continued with a rapid, forceful delivery, "To simplify things, the electrons move around the nucleus at a high rate of speed, follow me?" he declared while making numerous circles over the same area with the chalk. "When negatively charged electrons move from atom to atom, the energy released is electricity. That becomes the electrical field within our bodies. And, the electrical cycles under which the body performs determines our mode of physical existence," he said with emphasis as he struck the board with the chalk on each word. "Mode, time! Better said, that determines *when* we exist as a physical and intellectual reality."

"What about the rest of the atom's substance?" Dr. Goodrich asked.

"What about it?" Dr. Welles asked.

"What about the properties of sub-atomic particles? What about the exotic mesons that were discovered recently at Brookhaven? Would those affect the structure of the atom and its properties?" asked Dr. Goodrich. "Are you going to side-step important information like that?"

After some time to contemplate the substance of the question, Dr. Welles looked up and answered, "Yes." Those in the room stared back at him. "Look Mel, this is a very broad theory. We don't need to worry about things like that until we find out how much, if any, a cell's structure is affected by such a molecular change. Hell, until recently we weren't even aware of mesons, and that didn't stop us from splitting the atom, did it?"

"We will rely heavily on our quantum theory when we attempt this undertaking. The regressive transformation will take place on a molecular scale, and will be our focus for the next twelve weeks or so. Now, how to accomplish this quantum leap will be another matter entirely. We'll have to figure a mathematical formula based on the electrical interactions within a cell's molecules. Hopefully, once we come up with that integer, it will become our multiplier for that subject. And, that multiplier will become our quantum number. It will indicate the magnitude of the electrical charge within the entity. That number, gentlemen, will become our map to the past."

"This same process will have to be duplicated through multiple samples until we arrive upon a satisfactory medium. The difference between our medium number from the past and the charge of our electrical field today should open the door to a process of 'devolution,' if you will."

"The math part; that's yours, Henry," declared Dr. Lawrence followed by a laugh.

"Yeah, yeah, don't remind me. Actually, to be honest, I'm well into that process already. I've performed analysis upon several plant samples as well as a few wood specimens. So far, so good, the process has thus far proven itself out."

"In the next few months I hope to come up with an acceptable multiplier for a small animal."

"Dr. Welles, are you saying that you're ready to try this process out on a living creature?" asked Edward Holbach.

"Oh Lord no, not yet anyway. If our tests on an organism's electrical field reveal no physical damage to the subject, that would certainly be our next step, agreed?"

"Well, I suppose so. It sounds as if you're a bit on the fast track on this aspect of the project."

"Well, you never know what will happen in the near future," Dr. Welles said glancing slightly my way, "no pun intended. So if you'll mark your calendars for three months from today, say Valentine's Day, with any luck we'll have something to show for our efforts. For those of you who can volunteer a couple weeks of your time, it would be much appreciated. See me after our adjournment. Any questions?"

"Yes. Uh Henry, are you actually planning to bring time recession to a reality within the year?" asked Dr. Richmond.

"Or sooner if possible, Wayne. It depends on the help I receive from all of you, and the progress we make. Our task at hand will be to bring all of our ideas together. If it works, great; if it doesn't, well, we'll have to adjust our research until we reach a satisfying conclusion. Gentlemen, the physics are there. Now is the time for action, any more questions?"

The room was silent. "Okay, well then, I guess I'll see most of you back here or next door at the Osmond Lab sometime around Valentine's Day. To those of you who can contribute some hands-on time, come on up and we'll set a schedule. Thank-you."

Chapter Three
From Theory to Reality

*"If we like a man's dream,
we call him a reformer;
if we don't like his dream,
we call him a crank."*
WILLIAM DEAN HOWELLS

Six to eight weeks went by with barely a word from Dr. Welles. I sent him a memo about two weeks earlier informing him that I checked my sources at the General Accounting Office and the Office of Management and Budget concerning the financing the university was receiving for Project Sundial. So far so good. No news was good news, especially in this case.

Shortly thereafter, I received a notice on my e-mail thanking me for the report. It was from Dr. Welles, and as usual it was brief and to the point. I assumed his crew was hard at it in the Osmond Lab. The ground level lights were always on no matter what time of the day or night I passed by. That typically wasn't the status quo.

Finally, going into the third week of January, I ran into Dr. Welles at, of all places, the campus book store over on East College.

"How goes it, Doc?" I asked him. He spun around with a wide look in his eyes. "Oh, I'm sorry. Henry. I didn't mean to startle you."

"Oh," he said with a relieved grin, "that's O.K.

I'm sorry; I'm a little on edge. I've been living on caffeine for the last month or so. I just stopped down here to buy a shirt for my niece for her birthday. I can't forget that. Sorry I haven't gotten back to you earlier; it's just that we've been putting in so many hours over at the lab. I'm to the point where I don't know whether I'm coming or going half of the time."

"Oh hey, I understand. I noticed that the place was lit up almost every night I've cruised by. How are things coming? Any luck?"

"Geeze Neil, you wouldn't believe our good fortune. So far everything's falling right into place like the pieces to a puzzle. That's my baby," he glowed. "You wouldn't believe how proud I am."

"Oh yes I would, I can see it in your eyes. That is, when I get through all of the blood shot whites."

"I love you too," Dr. Welles shot back. "On Monday the fourteenth we're going to have a very important meeting of all those involved. I want you there. I think we're about ready for a breakthrough, at least I am. It seems to me that everyone else is dragging their feet. I guess they're not quite seasoned for success, at least not to this magnitude. Well, I sure don't plan to fail."

"So long as you don't fail to plan," I commented. "Is anyone from the fed looking in your bedroom windows yet?"

"No, I don't think so, but then again we haven't done anything yet. If we do come close however, keep your eyes and ears open." After a contemplative pause, Dr. Welles declared, "Well, I've got to get going." As he paid the cashier, he asked, "See you on the fourteenth at eight o'clock?"

"My place or yours?" I joked. "Of course I'll be there."

"Good, I'll fill you in on all of the intricacies at the meeting. You're going to be impressed," he said with his back to me and his right hand in the air as he exited the store.

Hell, that wouldn't take much, I thought as I watched him cross the street on his way back up to the lab.

The next few weeks seemed to drag on forever. I was waiting to see something unusual—something out of the ordinary—anything. After all, this would be a first for me. In a job where you shuffle papers, write out expenditure reports, and prioritize purchase orders, there is so little that deviates from the norm.

Finally, Monday the fourteenth rolled around. My mind had been on little else. We assembled back at the Davey, same room as before, for a briefing on the doings of the last couple of months. Looking around the room, we had a full house. Nearly everyone from the first meeting was there. The mood of this group appeared to take on a more serious tone. The room became hushed as Dr. Welles approached the speaker's table.

"First of all I'd like to welcome everybody back," Dr. Welles began. "Just about all of you have participated in the research phase of our project next door at the Osmond. Since all of you were here at different periods, I'd like to summarize just what's been accomplished."

"We're happy to report that we've made extensive progress towards our goal of acquiring trans-dimensional access. Dr. Goodrich, fill us in on your developments."

"Very well," he replied as he made his way over to the microphone. "We thought the best approach to this query would be to adapt our knowledge of high energy physics using our computerized techniques to analyze the light spectrum of a given specimen. We believe this method will run circles around any information a carbon dating process could give us. We found that it would be to our advantage to measure the energy waves, not just the age of an object. We would then measure those waves, or vibration given off from the substance, using a magnetic analyzer and scintilization counter."

As Dr. Goodrich placed a transparency on the projector, he went on to explain, "A beam of extremely energetic electrons directed from the electron microscope, strike the object scattering its electrons." The illuminated sketch illustrated the quintessential electron being bombarded with many arrows from all angles. "The amount of scattering that has occurred can now be calculated. Actually, what we're attempting to measure is the weight, if you will, of the electron within a given substance."

Switching transparencies to side-by-side electron comparisons, Dr. Goodrich continued, "Now, once we have that number established, we compare that quantity using the same technique on our modern day version. We were hoping to come up with a difference, across the board, relative to the creation of all objects depending, of course, on their year of origin and their year of harvest. Your turn, Henry."

"And, we accomplished just that," joined

in Dr. Welles. "In fact, we were so accurate with our formula that even without verification we could probably tell you when the tree was felled to manufacture the baseball bat your child uses. I'm talking to within the day, gentlemen."

"Henry" asked Dr. Lawrence, "If that's true and the formula proves itself out, this could be a major hurdle out of the way in our hopes of traversing time's barrier."

"Absolutely," Dr. Welles answered in a matter of fact. "Once we worked out the numbers, the rest of the blueprint just fell into place. Let me show you briefly what this equation involves."

Dr. Welles went to the blackboard and took chalk in hand. He scrubbed the board down the best that he could with the blocky felt eraser. He was having a difficult time by my observation. You could still see the imprint from the writings of our heated meeting months prior even though the board had been cleaned numerous times.

"O.K. now, we know that the Earth has a magnetic field equal to seven cycles per second, give or take." He then wrote the numeral '7' on the board. "That's a good starting point anyway. Actually the Earth's magnetic vibration is 7.8 Hz, but as long as we don't deviate from our even quantity throughout any of our calculations, we'll be O.K. It's all relative."

"We tested a sliver of wood taken from a portrait's frame that was installed here on campus around the turn of the century. We then compared that with the same type of wood, in this case an Acer Saccharum, or a typical sugar maple, being grown today. The frequency, or amount of electrical cycles emitted per second, varied only twenty billionths of a cycle."

"Why, that's virtually an immeasurable amount," added Dr. Lawrence.

"Nearly. We also took a sample from the limb that we used as a doorstop when the boiler wouldn't shut off last year around Groundhog Day. Those of you who were around here then remember how stifling it got next door. We could barely breathe. Anyway, last week we took a sample from that same tree, one year later, and compared the two readings."

"And what did you find," asked Dr. Goodrich, knowing full well the answer.

"We came up with a variance of point twenty billionths of a cycle; exactly one one-hundredths of the variance we surmised in doing our one hundred year study. When we repeated the study on the same tree on a twenty-four hour interval, the number of increased cycles turned out to be .000000000005479," Dr. Welles said as he chalked that number on the board. "That," he said as he snapped off his chalk underlining the number, "is a perfect fit."

"That is, if you're a maple," was Donald Bloch's response.

"So far, that number has held constant throughout other species of plants," joined in Dr. Hayes, a microbiologist currently working with the people at the Buckhout Greenhouse.

"Henry, that's terrific," shouted Dr. Richmond. "Hell, that means that we're half way home."

"How much luck did you have in breaking that number down to hours, minutes, or seconds? Was that all relative as well?" asked Bill Johnson.

"Actually, we didn't go there. We could take our number out four additional digits for minutes and seconds, but we found that there just wasn't enough variance between the shorter periods to bring us a workable number. Maybe some day, but we're so strung out now. Hell, even breaking our calculated entity down to a yearly number left us about point-eight percent short of the true sum. And, we're slightly over that quantity if we bring leap years in to the formula. Our numbers seemed to prove themselves best over the long run rather than in terms of an hour or day regression."

Bill Johnson once again spoke. "So then the numbers are useless to us for this project, you're saying?"

"Oh no, quite to the contrary, those figures are incredibly useful. They're our backbone as of now. I just meant that it was impractical to break the numbers down any farther at this point. There was just too much variance."

"Now let's get into the 'nuts and bolts' of this machinery which will hopefully allow us to journey to another dimension. As we covered a few months back, our senses respond to certain wavelengths. An organism of a certain period is tuned to only experience events or wavelengths of that similarly charged era. What we'll be attempting to do is extend that vision, much the same as a telescope allows us to see distant galaxies—galaxies, mind you, that may no longer exist at this time. We need the events to stimulate the receiver, and a receiver to pick up that stimulus. Of course, that's the crux of our entire project. The two shall become one."

"Over the last three weeks we have been exposing plants of several varieties to very low-grade electro-magnetic waves. We're trying to see how much is too much. It's very important to find the breaking point of an organism, when devolution carries the potential of becoming mutation."

"We subjected our specimens to a variety of waves, amongst them were low grade X-rays as well as microwaves, but they yielded inferior results."

"What do you mean inferior results?" inquired Dr. Welles.

"The plants looked satisfactory to the eyes, but under the scope we could see clusters of lifeless cells in irregular patterns throughout the leaves. Not so on our control specimens. That leads us to believe that while low concentrations of these waves may not kill a subject, I wouldn't want to take that chance on a larger scale. Something such as that could produce genetic mutations or cancers within an individual. I wouldn't recommend the risk."

"I agree," Dr. Welles chimed in. "Our challenge still is to temporarily modify an individual's electron speed without damaging our subject. Did you attempt larger doses of energy in any of your experiments?"

"Not necessary," replied Dr. Hayes. "Electrons are so much lighter than protons, or other particles for that matter, that so little voltage was required for our current experiments. We didn't want to harm the other elements of the organism. A subject on a larger scale would of course need a larger, more sustained charge."

"Now we also used alpha, beta, gamma pulses, as well as light waves, just to name a few. As of now, no real short-term injury has been indicated from our observations. Solar light waves brought about its typical reaction. While the plants thrived on it, I'm not real sure those particular waves will help us much in this endeavor. But, we needed a control group. The other tests looked promising."

"How about the tests with beta waves?" asked Dr. Welles.

"Fine, fine, no problems so far, why do you ask?" returned Dr. Richmond.

"I already have a preliminary sketch of an electron transducer utilizing beta waves. It's modeled after an old-fashioned betatron particle accelerator. I believe that's what we'll be looking at for an experimental model for a transdimensional transfer." Dr. Welles passed out a handful of printouts to each row. I'm hoping that together we can make this our working model."

A copy ended up in my lap and I took a look-see. While I couldn't make heads nor tails out of it, I'm sure the others understood.

"And when do you plan to have a working model ready for testing, doctor?" asked Edward Holbach.

"Uh, yes," Dr. Welles started with a bit of trepidation based on the inquiring party. "Larry Stokes over at Hammond has fashioned a preliminary test vehicle for our effort. We'll have to provide the guts to the craft. That should be no problem. What we have already in small scale may prove to be acceptable."

"Good God, Welles! You didn't tell Stokes what we needed it for did you?" asked Donald Bloch.

"Do I look dense to you? Hell no I didn't tell him what we were doing with it. He didn't even ask. I gave him my rough sketch and mumbled something about electrical experiments or something."

"Uh, Henry," reminded Dr. Goodrich, "even if that vehicle is sound, we're nowhere near fashioning an attempt of a transdimensional junket."

"Correct," echoed Dr. Richmond. "We can't just blast something with beta waves and hope and pray that it arrives in a different era."

"Hey, hey, hold on. Don't get ahead of me here. I'm not done explaining how our work and theories can and hopefully will pan out. We're still in the planning stages, folks."

"Anyway, getting back to the beginning," Dr. Welles continued, "the entire process must begin by prepping the subject for the electron molecular conversion. Ours is a two-tiered process. The first element consists of an ionization procedure. When the ionizer neutralizes the electrons within the individual, the accelerator moves energy across the body's electrical field. That action causes the waves within the body's atomic electrical field to contract. Shorter waves mean a higher frequency. If all goes as planned, voila! The body's electrical field now mimics that of another era. The individual is now in tune with the frequency of another time and able to experience all that the era has to offer—sight, sound, touch, and so on. The body is only a vehicle, remember? The soul, or whatever you would call the self, is the true entity."

"We're playing God here. And what happens after that, the body just disappears?" asked Bill Johnson.

"No, it's still here. You just can't perceive it,

and the subject can't sense you either. It's responding to and receiving the stimulus from another era. Remember when I said that everything is happening at the same time? The subject is now tuned into another station, if you will. Like on a television set, your antenna may be bombarded with signals from channel seven, but if you're tuned to channel two, channel seven means nothing to your receiver."

Dr. Lawrence spoke up. "Dr. Welles, that's a splendid theory. But, have you given any thought about how we'll fill all of the gaps in between?"

"I'm way ahead of you, Bill. Actually yes, we have filled in almost all of the voids already. It was certainly not too difficult to scrounge up the makings for an old Cockroft-Walton accelerator tube to accomplish much of the task."

"A bit primitive, eh doc?"

"In its former form, yes, but the technology is sound. George, how are you coming on the electrical end of things?"

George Ebbing's specialty was microelectronics. He was one of the 'loans' from NASA. "Splendid actually, I agree with both of you. It's crude and primitive but the technology is indeed sound. Within our power feed, as long as we keep our positive on top and negative on the bottom, we'll be under way. The body, you see, acts as a ground. It will represent the center point of the operation. The heart of the electrical aggregate, if you will. The entire electrical process passes through the body before it completes the circuit."

"Of course we would use advanced microcircuitry to replace the old X-ray style tube. That goes without saying. This unit will use a modern type of rectifier here," he said as he pointed towards his copy of the schematic. "It will follow the distribution terminal and act as a one way valve. That unit will keep the ionization process at a steady current. That's very important."

"We will use a low but steady electrical source, so we'll have to find a suitable power generating supply. The voltage/ion transfer takes place at a rapid pace to prevent particles from being lost during the shift. The complete process will take only seconds, I'm guessing, due to the amount of voltage we'll be using. Nothing like the millionth of a second the original process takes under lab conditions, but we're dealing with an unknown here. What we suspect is that a lower current will account for the longer period of exposure. We want to transform the body at its own pace."

"Ah, precisely," responded Dr. Welles. "so much for the ionization process. Thank-you, George, that's what makes the whole ball of wax roll. That's why a person can receive an electrical shock or be struck by lightning and not be transferred to another time. The electrons haven't been neutralized first."

"Correct, Henry, and that generally doesn't occur naturally. An exception may have been when you came upon the information from the Russian nuclear refinement plant. Apparently, the absorption of the nuclear waste run-off may have somehow neutralized the electrons within the vegetation. I'm still not sure what the catalyst was that propelled the flora into another dimension."

"What about a nearby lightning strike? That area was mountainous from what I understand,

and something of that nature isn't unheard of. Or, perhaps it was the Earth's own electrical field in which the plants were rooted that provided the charge," suggested Dr. Hayes. "It's possible that the Russians are farther along in this field than we could ever imagine."

"Good guesses, all of them, but guesses none-the-less. We'll probably never know, at least not until our technology in this field becomes far more advanced," surmised Dr. Ebbing. "That most likely also explains why not all of the growth disappeared from that area. Some of the vegetation just plain died off from radiation exposure before it had a chance encounter with an electrical catalyst. I'm guessing that the trees that vanished were likely on death's door as well if their electrons had already been neutralized. Like you stated, a million to one shot, but as they say, even a blind squirrel occasionally trips over a nut. Anyway, what does the second part of this process entail?"

"O.K.," Dr. Welles continued, "part two has to be just as precise as the first. This portion of the process, as we stated, is based upon the old betatron concept. Our accelerator can regulate how far across time the subject can go based on the amount of current distributed. Plenteous exposure to current and one could travel as far back as we could accurately calculate. Given a scant amount and the subject would be able to traverse smaller fractions of time, say, a day or a week perhaps. That's where the mathematical formula comes into play," added Dr. Welles. "That blueprint will tell us the amount of charge that's required to change the body's electrical field to that of another time in history. What else do you have, George?"

"Continuing, a weak electrical field must first be introduced to allow the electrons the chance to build up speed without a distortion to their intended purpose. The more energy we give an electron, the greater its speed. That action increases its mass. We have discovered, however, that we do have limits. Attempt to exceed those limits and you create a whole new set of problems without accomplishing your original objective."

"Doctor, your concept doesn't sound like it's very far from quantum teleportation, true?" asked Bill Johnson.

"Yes and no. Yes, it's a similar concept in that it deals with the transportation and replication of photon waves. But, with Q.T., that move is only from *point* 'A' to *point* 'B'. And that branch of study is still in its infancy as well. Our idea deals more with the transportation of an entire being from *time* 'A' to *time* 'B'. When all of the processes are activated, our subject will emerge with a particle energy field equivalent to the applied inputs," Dr. Welles concluded.

"Marvelous!" applauded Dr. Lawrence, both vocally and physically. The others joined in.

"Henry," interrupted Dr. Goodrich, "how about the inner workings of the actual mechanism? How far have we gotten in that respect?"

"Actually, we're doing O.K. During the ongoing plant experiments we used a weak magnetic core that I believe will be fine for our small percentage gains. Those small percentage gains will necessitate our increasing the current in steps. However, that actually becomes a plus on our side because that measure will ease any possible shock to our subject's system. That arrangement will also allow for the correction of any missed electron conversions within the individual. Not to mention that our process will also allow the electrons to dampen, or slow back down, when the time is right for a return trip."

"Henry, if time's barrier is broken..."

"If?" asked Dr. Welles.

"When time's barrier is broken," continued a corrected Edward Holbach, "will that activity produce an equal and opposite reaction? You know, like when man breaks the sound barrier, a sonic boom is produced."

"Well, I doubt it, probably not. I hope not," replied Dr. Welles, "but you bring up a good point. Like we've mentioned before, we're dealing with a lot of unknowns."

"When can we expect a working model to be in the testing stage, Doctor? You avoided that question when asked earlier," Holbach shot back.

"Right, well we ought to have something ready to go within four to five weeks..."

"Four to five weeks?!" shouted Donald Bloch in amazement. "You can't be serious!"

"Yes, four to five weeks. Is that too late?" Dr. Welles asked sarcastically. He knew full well that the agent was astounded at the velocity with which the concepts were emerging from their theory stage to the realm of reality.

"What, did you think that the research into this concept would go on forever with no conclusion? With every project there has to be a beginning, middle, and end. Yes, even a government sponsored venture. Unlike your wars of the past, here we have an objective and a target. We intend on meeting our goals," Dr. Welles came back stating the fact.

"I just never expected any results until the end of the year at the earliest. I believe that this thing is moving a bit too fast," Bloch concluded. "You yourself said that we're dealing with an unknown here."

"Don, when the technology is there, we see no need to ignore it or drag our heels. The only way to make an unknown a known is to do. I'm curious, why do you ask? Do your cronies in DC want to shelve the project before history can be made public, or even accomplished for that matter?"

Agent Bloch barely looked up from his notes to acknowledge Dr. Welle's comments. "Project Sundial stays under wraps until we say otherwise."

"OK. We'll take a break. Get a cup of coffee, stretch your legs a bit. I'll meet all of you over at the Osmond in say, forty-five minutes," Dr. Welles said as he beat a hasty retreat towards the door.

I grabbed my files and followed Dr. Welles out into the hall. He seemed to be getting more uptight with every step.

"Neil, keep an eye on those sons of bitches!" he angrily remarked.

"Uh, yes sir," was the only comeback I could think of. I didn't know what he expected me to do, but I was willing to do my part.

"Oh, I'm sorry, Neil," said Dr. Welles apologetically as we cleared the steps. "It's just that I've sunk my heart, mind, and soul into this undertaking. You'd think that in every person's life there's one act that defines a person's contribution to mankind. I've done some good work, yes, but no more or less than any other Joe in my field. This can be my defining contribution," Dr. Welles continued as we made our way across Pollock to the HUB. Once inside, we grabbed a cup of thin coffee and took a seat.

"Better go light on that stuff, doc," I said referring to the cup of caffeine in his hand.

"Hah, this stuff! There's not enough caffeine in this crap to give a mouse a buzz." Then, with his fist resting against the side of his face, Dr. Welles lamented, "Oh hell, Neil, maybe I'm just kidding myself. This project will never see the light of day. Even if it turns out successful and the results are forwarded to the Joint Chiefs of Staff, or whoever those clowns' superior happens to be, they'd probably have somebody like the Brookings Institute kill the entire idea because of the 'cultural impact'," Dr. Welles stated making quotation marks with his fingers, "it would have on our society. Those in charge would tell us, in a condescending tone, that the world just isn't ready for trans-dimensional access at this time or some other bullshit like that. Meanwhile, the CIA or whoever would use the technology for their own purposes. And, I'm sure those purposes wouldn't be virtuous. Oh God, what am I doing?" he lamented with a depressing sigh.

"Hey come on Henry, there's nothing to suggest that they will do anything like that. Besides, if they do, there are enough qualified people in that room to verify that time travel had become a reality. The government can't hide facts like that forever."

"Oh yeah, right, I'll end up on one of those tabloid-style T V shows ten years from now looking like one of those retired Air Force generals who 'saw' the UFO aliens at Roswell. Yes, I can see it all now. And the viewers will think me to be one of the biggest idiots who ever lived. I don't want to leave that as my legacy."

"Henry, I'll do what I can. Tell you what, I'll put in a call to Washington and check on the funding status of Project Sundial."

"It will probably be intact for now, but I'm more concerned about later. Anything will do my old nerves some good right now. Thanks," Henry said as he threw down the remaining portion in his cup. "I've got to go and get set up. Be there," he said as he excused himself.

I had enough time to burn, so I proceeded over to my office in the Hammand Building to place a few calls. I phoned the Office of Management and Budget and talked to short time friend and budget officer Ellen. We exchanged our usual greetings and banter, and then got down to business.

"So, how's things over in the land of the Nittany Lion?" she asked.

"Same as. Cold as hell," I responded "How go things in our nation's crapitol? Are you holding down the fort?"

"As always. Of course we're busy as all get out seeing how we're at mid term of the current budget. It seems as if everyone's slamming us with end of year fiscal requests. Can you believe it? Some people are always late. That doesn't take into account that those same people are already hard at it on next year's spending spree. What can I do you for, Neil?" she asked.

"I need to check on the funding of a university project number, let's see, J-316-G. I need to see if we'll have enough gas to complete the job. I was just wondering if the disbursement schedule will allow us enough time to continue until the project's scheduled conclusion," I gave as my reason for requesting such information.

"Hold on a second, let me get you up on my screen here." About ten to fifteen seconds went by when she returned. "Budget number PS12-1999, which is your project number J-316-G, um, no change in status. You're right on schedule. Just curious, are you running short on funds? Would you like to request an increase of the aggregate, because if you do I can put you in touch with..."

"Oh no, no that's O.K.," I interrupted. "So long as everything's intact, we'll survive. You know us, we're an 'eat what you kill' operation. That's all I really needed to know. Our, uh, project is taking a bit longer than anticipated. I just wanted to make sure that we'd have enough funding to see us through."

"You're looking good at this end."

"Likewise, I'm sure," I said back to her in a flirtatious manner.

"You guys are all alike. For a little money you'll say anything!"

"Absolutely," I shot back followed with a laugh. "Hey, Ellen, take care. We'll talk later."

"Uh huh. Bye-bye."

Well, at least that takes care of the university's grant for now, I surmised. As far as the military funding goes, I'm afraid that at this point and time I wouldn't be able to dig up much on that aspect. It was then that I realized I had better get moving if I wanted to get back in time to view the activities.

As I pulled into the back parking lot of the lab, there was that gray government car parked near the rear entrance to the building. I was starting to sense how Dr. Welles felt. Every time I saw that car, I instinctively looked over my shoulder to see if I was being watched. One can never be sure, I suppose.

Inside the Osmond Lab everything was set up. Things were just beginning as I walked in. Resting on the table top in front of Dr. Welles was an odd-looking contraption. The best way to describe it would be to compare it to a skeletal roll cage from a sprint car, except smaller.

"So doctor, is this your model of a time machine?" asked Bill Johnson, R & D man with the Department of Defense.

"It's not a damn time machine!" Dr. Welles shouted back. Apparently his dislike for the governmental types, mixed with a caffeine buzz, still had him in high gear. "This device merely aids in the migratory process of one's molecular make up. It's probably better referred to as a synchronized matter exchanger. A time machine," he muttered under his breath in disgust.

Resuming his lecture, Dr. Welles went on to explain, "The structure of this unit is constructed from pure aluminum. We shouldn't try to mix and match alloys within the body itself. Their quality couldn't be assured during transformation and reentry. We wouldn't know what we'd be dealing with due to their difference in weights and molecular make up. We don't want the whole thing falling apart due to a lack of cohesiveness between the alloys. We believe that aluminum will conduct electricity the best while not being of any real magnetic properties. That is important, for when we alter the electrons within an individual, we have to execute the same procedure throughout the craft itself."

"Why a craft at all, Doctor?" Johnson spoke again. "Why not just connect an individual up to a portable unit. That would seem to me to be a more convenient solution."

"Well, we don't know how much a given terrain has changed between then and now. We'll have to choose our departure sites very carefully. If you alter the body's electrical chemistry and it's transported to another time, do you just want the person to crash land on their ass? Or worse yet, they could find themselves chest deep in the ground. They wouldn't survive something such as that. As a result, the individual is going to need some protection. Aside from the framework, we'll try to have some type of shock absorbing system on the bottom surface just in case. I do, however, have some ideas on your portable unit which I'll elaborate on later."

"I also have a glass-like covering arriving in a couple of days. The coating isn't dissimilar to what you'd see on a lightly tinted windshield, except the reflective alloy is impregnated within the glass itself. The function of that cowling will be to reflect all internal electrical activity back into the craft itself. That's another reason a portable unit wouldn't suit our needs as well."

"What about a timing apparatus, Henry? With all of the electrical activity going on within the structure, how will it be possible to keep an accurate synchronized time with the present," asked Agent Holbach.

"Good question," conceded Dr. Welles. "What we believe will work best is a model of an atomic clock that will be synchronized with the U.S. Atomic Clock based at The Natural Institute of Standards and Technology in Boulder, Colorado. It's accurate to within one second per every million years. I don't think we can do better than that. We'll have a standard digital read out that will work fine for our purposes. As you can see over here," Dr. Welles said as he strolled over to a small panel containing several regulators and switches, "it fits in nicely on the panel. Let's see, we have the clock, the dials here for frequency requested, an ignition switch as I refer to it, and an outlet for the electrodes."

"Electrodes? And what will electrodes be used for?" Bill Johnson asked.

"The frame and the entire craft are all united to form a single electrical system. That's why the unit's entire composition is of one reflective alloy. The structure and the subject within are on the same system. They both receive the same electrical charge. They must act as one. The craft receives its load from the electrical contacts throughout the structure, while the subject receives his charge through the electrodes."

"Now, there will be a series of eight bodily contacts. That series consists of two electrodes to the temples, two to the hands, one at the base of the skull, a complementary terminal at the base of the spine, and one for each foot or ankle."

"Those will encompass the body's entire electrical field," added Dr. Goodrich.

"Precisely."

"What about everything else in the craft? What about the switches, diodes, and power source? How about the person's clothing? Will they be able to travel?" Dr. Goodrich inquired.

"From what we can tell, all of that will go along for the ride. That's pretty much the same deal as a person riding along in an automobile. In a car, one doesn't go forty miles per hour and leave the car's interior on the ground behind them. From all indications, I believe that same principle will hold true here. That's the main reason for the reflective glass covering. At any rate, I'm sure we'll find out eventually. That's part of the reason for testing this structure."

"Based on that principle, Doctor, why would the subject need to be attatched to electrodes at all? Why couldn't he just 'go along for the ride,' as you said?" asked Johnson.

"Would you be willing to take that risk? I mean come on Bill, it's one thing to dispatch and return a craft from another plane. If that craft were to develop checks in its armor or acquire a weakened structure due to a deficient reintegration of its molecular make-up, we would be able to deal with that. But, if the same thing happens to a living creature, they may not make it back alive. Worse yet, if they did survive, they could develop any number of cancers or chromosomal damage over time. Would you want that on your conscience? No, the craft and the passenger must act as one."

"Hey whatever, you're the doctor," was his reply.

"Have we decided on a power source yet, Henry?" asked Dr. Goodrich.

"Ah yes, that has been a thorn in my side. Whatever we end up using will have to be shielded from any electrical interference. The constancy of a power flow will be of major importance. The uniform delivery of a U-238 source would be excellent. I'm not sure we can get our hands on any of that though. As a back up plan, we'd be able to fashion a block of lithium sodium dioxide cells courtesy of NASA. Those tend to do great under very harsh conditions."

"The only flaw in that idea is that connecting these cells in a series would prove to be a bit cumbersome. We'd need a bank large enough to handle the job. A unit such as this could produce a great power drain on whatever source we put in place due to the constant uniformity of the charge necessary. I guess we'll find out soon enough during testing. Anything else?"

"Yes, a million questions," exclaimed Dr. Hayes, "but I'm not sure they can all be answered today," he joked.

"I know, I know. We'll probably have an entirely new set of questions, and hopefully answers, by our next session."

"And when will that be, Doctor?" inquired Agent Bloch.

"I don't know, Don," answered Dr. Welles rather deliberately. "Tell you what; let's tentatively set that date for April first, no pun intended. The campus will probably be empty due to the weekend and/or the holidays. That would be best. We ought to have a trial ready to go by then."

"What? You mean that we'd actually be making the first attempt to transcend time's barrier that soon?" asked Bill Johnson. "Aren't we rushing things a bit?"

"I've been asked the question before. What purpose would a delay serve? If we're ready, it's a go. Why, are you going to be in Daytona on spring break that week?" Dr. Welles said with an added laugh. "What would we be waiting for? You never did answer that. That's our tentative date. You can tell your cronies in DC that's when we'll be making our first attempt."

Johnson, with his arms folded asked, "Why do you dislike us so much, Doctor? If it wasn't for the federal government, you wouldn't have a project at all. We're trying to help, not to hinder."

"Ah yes, the old, 'we're from the government and we're here to help you,' adage," he laughed. "You're from the government, so what's not to trust," he said dripping of sarcasm. "You don't need to keep reminding us that you're bankrolling this project. We've been made very aware of those strings," replied Dr. Welles.

"What the hell do you mean by that?" Came the angry response.

Dr. Goodrich stepped in and announced, "O.K., well thank you all for coming today. Those of you who are going to help us finish up today as well as the rest of the week, stick around. To the rest of you, see you around April first. We'll let you know exactly when."

The meeting broke up with people milling around and looking over the strange contraption that could soon become the first time craft. Dr. Goodrich was over to the side trying to cool Henry down a bit. I figured that my work here was done, so I drove back over to my office. I thought I'd finish up my paper work in about an hour or so, then call it a day.

When I walked past the secretary pool, Donna gave me my messages and said, "Ginny called. She sounded kind of pissed."

"Oh hell, I was supposed to have lunch with her today," I said verbally chastising myself.

"And you forgot? On Valentine's Day?" returned Donna. "Shame."

"Oh geeze, I'll never live this one down."

"Lots of luck."

"Yeah right, I'll need it." I went ahead and phoned Ginny only to receive her voice mail. I left a brief, "I'll get back with you tonight" message as I was sure she was back at work by now.

I drove home with a million things on my mind. I'm about to see world history attempted, and Ginny's not going to be the least bit happy with me. What next?

Around 4:30 I was able to get hold of her. Donna was right, Ginny was a bit upset. I proposed an evening get together and she reluctantly agreed. I picked her up at 6:30 to go to our favorite restaurant. I needed all of the help that I could get.

"How come you have plenty of time for everything in your life except me? Am I that insignificant?" Ginny asked.

"Hey, I said that I was sorry. My meeting went longer than anticipated. I didn't plan that."

"What meeting could you have that would be important enough to forget a lunch date with me? You're a financial officer, not a CEO."

"Oh thanks a lot."

"I'm sorry. I misspoke."

Of course I couldn't tell her the real reason for my tardiness. As much as I was fascinated by this project, I hated keeping secrets from Ginny, but I had no choice in this matter.

"Look, let's just forget all of this and enjoy our evening together. How about it?"

"O.K., but please try and let me know the next time, alright?"

"Let's hope there won't be a next time."

Chapter 4

Eternal Exodus

*"There's much to be said
for challenging fate
instead of ducking behind it."*
DIANA TRILLING

Saturday, April first arrived kicking and screaming it seemed. I guess it's true what they say: A watched clock never moves. After a brief stop off at my office, I drove over to the Osmond Lab. I had no trouble finding a parking spot that day. Being a weekend and a holiday to boot, the campus was fairly empty, relatively speaking.

I met up with Dr. Lawrence as we walked up the short set of steps to the front door of the Davey. We entered the building, descended to the basement via the elevator, then through the tunnel towards the assembly room at the Osmond. I asked Bill, "Do you think you guys will be able to pull this thing off? Do you believe the time barrier can actually be crossed?"

"Well, it looks promising. We'll find out soon enough," he answered.

As we approached the arch leading to the assembly room door, I noticed a man wearing a security badge acting as a picket. He was checking indentifications prior to the entrance of the authorized candidates.

"I haven't been this nervous about my qualifications to enter premises since I tried to get into a bar with my fake draft card back when I was sixteen," Dr. Lawrence chuckled. That comment caused the doorkeeper to glance upward for a brief moment. "Whoops, sorry," the doctor said, realizing that this upgrade in security was there for a reason. Whoever requested such defensive measures went to a lot of trouble. Apparently they meant business.

As Dr. Lawrence made his way through the one-man gauntlet, he waited for me to get checked through. I wasn't sure what was requested of me for permission to enter. I presented my campus photo I D card and waited while the officer checked my name with a list he carried on a clipboard. Now I began to worry. I didn't remember signing up for any meeting. I had to see history being made. I didn't know what I would do if I was refused entry. Finally I was permitted to pass.

When Bill opened the door, I took one step inside, and I was knocked backwards against Dr. Lawrence. "What the hell?" I asked in surprise. "Who let the damn dog in here?"

"Hey Henry, do you know you've got a dog loose in here?" Bill shouted to Dr. Welles who was busy over in the far corner of the lab.

Dr. Welles laughed and jokingly replied, "No, but if you hum a few bars..."

It was then that I recognized the mutt. "Tramp ol' buddy, what's up, pup?" I said as I buffed up his stubby coat. Tramp, I guess you could say, was the campus mascot. He was probably abandoned by a fraternity when they left one summer. From the long, tan hair on his front to the salt and pepper coat on his pit bull style back, the pooch was a real mess. We used to joke that he was built out of spare parts.

"Why the heck do you have a dog in here, Henry? Looking for a new friend?" asked Dr.

Lawrence followed by a chuckle.

"Hey, I need all of the friends I can get at this point. But Tramp here has graciously volunteered to be our test subject."

"Volunteered?" I asked. "How did he pull that one off?"

"I simply asked him if he wanted to go for a ride and he said yes. He hopped into the back seat and I took him home last week."

"Where did you find him? I know he's a busy hound. I always see him around campus somewhere."

"I found him over on Shortlidge, about a block from The Creamery. I guess he was checking to see if the crowds had started forming at the ice cream emporium now that the weather has started to break."

If nothing else, Tramp was resourceful. He managed to stay alive the last couple of years by commuting from the East College area in the winter to the Creamery via Shortlidge Road in the summer. In the winter he lived off fast food handouts and a warm grate. In the summer he made his 'living' by going from table to table using his big 'feed me' eyes to bum the butt end of a cone from the charitable patrons. He usually won those battles, and thus the moniker 'Tramp.'

"Henry, you're not going to use that mangy old mutt in our experiments are you? Hell, he'll probably keel over before the first test begins. How fit can he be?" asked Dr. Lawrence.

"Actually he's fairly healthy. He's had a vet check, and Dr. Hayes took him for a blood work up-the whole enchilada. All in all he's doing O.K. I chose to use him because he's the 'Joe Average' of the animal kingdom. He's not like the lab rabbits. They're bred to be fit and perfect. Chances are, somewhere down the line, we'll never find a human subject as healthy as those lagomorphs. So what would be the point? I want a subject with a few miles on him, like most people in this world, I'd say."

"And he was free," I commented.

"And he was free," echoed Dr. Welles. "If he's free, he's for me."

Just then you could hear voices approaching the door. Dr. Welles said, "Watch him," referring to Tramp.

The dog got down in a crouch and stared at the bottom corner of the door. When the door opened, Tramp sprang at the first unsuspecting victim who crossed the threshold. Unfortunately it happened to be Dr. Goodrich. We all just burst out laughing.

"Good God, what in the hell is that flea bag doing in here?" No dog lover, he.

"Come on in, Mel," Dr. Welles said with a laugh. "We'll explain it all out."

Still laughing, I continued to reminisce. "Hey, last fall, Steve Snyder from accounting and I went to the Penn State/Ohio State game over at the Beav. We were walking around inside near a closed off gate when we saw Tramp outside staring in. We urged him to come on in and enjoy the game. Well, he smelled the hot dogs and popcorn, so he figured that this place couldn't be all that bad."

Dr. Lawrence interrupted, "He's not the dog who was running around on the field during the game was he? I saw that on T.V."

"That was him. We got a real kick out of it.

He even made the sports update on *Sportswatch*. Damn dog was pretty darn fast too. He thought the chasers were playing. They couldn't catch him on that damp turf. The crowd loved it. Most of them knew who he was."

"What's the dog's role in our experiments Henry?" asked Dr. Goodrich, still trying to brush the stray dog hairs from his conservative brown suit.

"Tramp's going to be...come on in, guys," Dr. Welles said while waving to several arriving members as they entered. "He's going to be our test pilot, if you will."

"That thing is what we're going to put our butts on the line for?" asked Dr. Richmond.

"Absolutely. Hey look, the poor thing doesn't have a home, or in some cases food. God forbid that anything would happen to him, but if it did we'd be here to pick up the pieces."

"Yeah, literally," mumbled Dr. Goodrich.

"Look, as I tried to explain before, if one of the lab rabbits checked out physically fine after a time journey, that gives us only half of the picture. If there are additional problems with our subject, they might surface in his personality. How would we be able to detect that in rabbits? What the hell do they do all day? Nothing. How would we be able to tell the difference? Besides, we always have the lab animals to fall back on just in case, so how about it?"

Most people shrugged with indifference while others just mumbled.

"Good, then it's settled," proclaimed Dr. Welles as if he had just won a point in a debate. "O.K., is everybody here? Yes? Well then let's get started."

Walking over to the center of the room, Dr. Welles stated, "Here gentlemen, is the finished version of our first test craft." He lifted the grey cloth off of the vehicle.

"Primitive, but not bad," commented Larry Davis as he looked it over. "It's a lot like the Wright brothers' first craft: crude, clumsy, yet functional."

"Yes, pretty close. What we hope to see today is the positive results of our four plus years of research and development."

"Hold on, Doctor," started Agent Holbach, "I was under the impression that the actual test wasn't until tomorrow."

"You're half right. We're working on a very short-term basis right now. Ol' Tramp here, where is he, will be sent out across time's barrier tomorrow at noon. He will be sent back exactly twenty-four hours. That means if successful, he should arrive in the center of the room at noon today or there about. So I'll tell you what, let's get this unit moved over to the side. Our twenty-four hour target period is still only in theory as of now. Hours are so much harder to hit exactly than a period of days."

The craft, sitting on a dolly, was moved over to the side where it could be explained to the masses.

"O.K. now, this vessel is what we'll refer to as an Alteronic Transformation Module or ATM for short."

Dr. Lawrence grinned. "ATM, huh? Will it spit out money as well?"

"Hah! Well, for somebody perhaps. As for us, I doubt it. But I named it that because it alters the electrons within a subject, transforming their electrical energy field into that of another time. If you'll look up here in the nose cone you'll see the heart of the ATM." Taking hold of the edge, Dr. Welles said, "Mel, grab the other side." As they lifted the hood from the craft, Dr. Welles continued his tour.

"This, of course, is the power plant. As you can see, we had to go with the lithium sodium dioxide cells that George was able to scrounge from NASA."

"Doctor, you said that the power source has to be shielded. What about that?" asked Donald Bloch.

"Right you are, Don. So here," Dr. Welles said reaching over and picking up a metal case about one foot square, "is a lead impregnated casing which will keep out any stray electrical charges. It fits into the lip on the floor. It's not perfect, I know, but I think it will do for our purposes," he informed us as he fit the container back over the power source. "These batteries carry no memory cells. We don't know what a trip would do to something like that."

"In front of that we have the guts for the ionizer," Dr. Welles stated as he pointed out the individual sections of inner workings. "And here is the make-shift betatron."

"Doesn't look like any betatron I've ever seen," observed Bill Johnson. "The one I saw recently at Los Alamos was over one half mile long. This is hardly larger than a bread box."

"Thank-you," replied Dr. Welles in mock gratitude. "We're trying to transform the individual's electrons, not split them. George did most of the electric work on the ATM. We owe him a debt of gratitude. What would we do without your knowledge?" Dr. Welles asked George Ebbing.

"You'd probably still be flipping burgers over at McDonald's."

"Yeah, and feeding Tramp his daily ration," Dr. Welles replied while laughing. "Speaking of which, where is that dog?"

Tramp was walking around amongst the desks and chairs that had been moved to one side of the room. You couldn't see him, but you could see his tail over the top of the obstacles. It stuck straight up like the flagstaff on a dune buggy.

"He's O.K. Now, we have the passenger compartment here in the back. That's where our subject will be anchored. Then we'll cover the exposed area with the cowl, 'locking in all of the freshness'."

"Are you sure you're not going to fry him, Henry?" I asked, startling myself as I spoke. It was the first time I had made my presence known at one of these gathering. I didn't know if that was a mistake and that people would discover my true relationship with Dr. Welles. After all, I wasn't amongst the scholastic elite.

"Oh no, I doubt it. Neither the ionizer nor the betatron by themselves will do him any short term harm as far as we can tell. Not at the doses we'll expose him to, I'm sure. That's why we have so much confidence in this contraption. It's the impending results that we're most concerned with. We're willing to take the risk."

Edward Holbach looked over at me as if it was the first time he laid eyes on me. Perhaps it was. "What the hell is he doing in here?" he asked, knowing that my background had nothing to do with physics.

"Because I wish him to be here," answered Dr. Welles raising his voice a decibel. "He arranged the financing for this project so it could take place here at this university. If he sees that we're getting our money's worth, he might be able to steer some additional funds our way," the doctor added.

Returning to the 'show and tell' portion of our meeting, he continued, "Here we have the instrument panel," Dr. Welles said as he pointed out the particulars. "We have the current time here. Next to that we have the energy input dial. We will set that tomorrow. And lastly, here is the input jack for the electrodes. It's all fairly simple. It all fits together."

"I see how you're going to send the craft out, Doctor, but how are you going to retrieve the unit once it's gone?" asked Dr. Hayes.

"Good question, Fred. The way this test unit is timed, once activated there's a ten second lag until the power kicks in. That allows us time to clear out."

"You mean, run for cover," dropped in Agent Holbach.

"Anyway, that's when the ATM does its stuff. Once the cycle is complete and the craft has hopefully reached its destination, the process will reverse itself after a thirty second period. A shorter flight than the Wright brothers made on their maiden voyage, but our impact could be far greater."

"Absolutely amazing," answered Dr. Hayes while shaking his head in disbelief. "So when the ATM is in the past, it will actually have to travel into the future to get back home, correct?"

"Not necessarily. The craft won't actually be traveling into the future. It will only be returning to its original coordinates. It's a round trip for our subject, if you will. It's all semantics I suppose. Future travel will be studied by those...in the future, I guess."

"So, that's it in a nut shell. It's a fairly simple operation; part energy transformer, part frequency generator. The technology has existed for some time. We've just never been able to find a slot 'B' for the part 'A.' So we'll just have an informal session to go over the ATM to get a better understanding of its inner workings until the big doings occur. We have coffee and do-nuts over there," Dr. Welles said pointing towards the far end of the room, "so go ahead and help yourselves. If nothing else, hang out for the next few hours. Might as well, they won't allow anyone to leave the room until the day's experiments are complete. So go ahead and get comfortable."

I spent the next couple of hours acting the part of a tourist, hands in pockets, just looking. I also passed some time by entertaining Tramp. The best way to keep him interested was to keep feeding him do-nuts. Dr. Welles brought in an old pair of athletic tube socks tied in a knot to be used as a toy. Tramp loved to be beaten about the face with it trying to latch on to the knot. Once he finally caught it, he'd never let go. Even with his 'brakes' applied, he was no match for the slick concrete floor. I would just drag him around. The bout was ruled a standoff.

I noticed it was about a quarter 'til noon. My heart began to pound in my ears as I realized that we're almost at zero hour. Dr. Welles broke my train of thought by saying, "O.K. everybody, if you will, gather your chairs in a semi-circle. Leave plenty of room in the center. Where that piece of tape on the floor is will be the landing zone. We're not sure what to expect here. The video cam is rolling," he announced as he switched a tripod mounted camera on over in the corner.

People reacted silently in anticipation. At the risk of sounding cliché, time literally seemed to stand still. That watched clock still wasn't moving. About three minutes until noon Dr. Welles said to me, "Neil, hold on to that dog. I don't want him wandering into the landing zone and getting hurt. We're really not sure what could happen." At this point, the thought of an explosion entered my mind.

The absolute silence returned and hung around for the next three minutes. About the only sound one could hear was the hum of the vent fans and the click of the clock as it approached, then passed twelve noon. People glanced around, eyebrows raised, and I think everyone was hoping someone would say something, anything. "Why was there no activity?" seemed to be the look of the moment.

At approximately ten seconds past the hour, the silence was broken by a very low, faint thump reminiscent of the commencement of a far distant fireworks display. It was just a very slight yet noticeable thump.

Just then Dr. Goodrich, in an urgent manner, let loose with an, "Ooooh!" while pointing to the center of the room.

People began to rise from their chairs as an unfocussed, translucent vision of the ATM began to appear, followed by a more distinct but foggy image. Finally all was clear and solid. While the process seemed to persist for a stretch, the entire course of action took just seconds.

Shouts of "Oh my God" and a hushed "Yes! Yes!" resounded throughout the room. Many in attendance just appeared slack-jawed and stunned.

Edward Holbach broke the silence by asking, "What's wrong with him? The dog looks ill."

"That's to be expected," replied Dr. Welles, not taking his eyes off of the recent appearance in the center arena. "We plan on sedating him before his trip. How else would we be able to fit him into the ATM and keep him connected to the electrodes?"

The poor hound had the quintessential 'hang dog' look about him. He sported no wagging tail and his perky eyes were now glazed over. While I was holding Tramp by the collar, he took notice of his competition seated in the ATM and started to growl, not realizing of course that the 'other' dog in the ATM was none other than himself.

Before any additional observations could be made, the process that gifted us with his arrival reversed itself leaving a room full of stunned observers.

Finally, Dr. Goodrich spoke out, and with a shaky voice said, "Good God Welles, you did it. You broke the time barrier."

"Hey, hey, *we* did it! Sure it was my concept, but everyone here had a hand in its success—everyone," Dr. Welles proclaimed in his own humble way. "But the process is only half complete. It's like sending a man to the moon. We have to get him back in one piece before we can classify the trip as a success."

"We'll know tomorrow at noon, give or take," answered Dr. Hayes.

"Uh Doctor, a dumb question, but when the dog was there in the ATM, how was he also able to be sitting over here?" Donald Bloch asked, gesturing in my direction. "Can two representations of the same individual be present in the same place at the same time?"

"Why not? Tramp here didn't go anywhere. He's the vision and vibration of today. In the ATM, that was the visual reality of tomorrow's vibration that we were privileged to see today because of the process. Why couldn't they occupy the same room? One is the vibration of today. The other is the vision of tomorrow. Tomorrow's reality has become able to visit today's vibration. They're two different entities," explained the doctor. "You're not the man today that you were yesterday, nor will you look or act the same twenty years from now. What a difference a day makes. And so it goes," Dr. Welles concluded.

"My God, I can see where this could cause some real problems."

The next hour consisted of prep for tomorrow's historic attempt and generally milling around exchanging ideas.

"Henry," I asked, "what do you want to do with Tramp? Do you want me to take him home with me or what?"

"No, he's going to be my roomy for tonight. I want to make sure he doesn't run away or eat anything bad to skew tomorrow's attempt. We have too much invested in him."

"What, you'd think I'd feed him something bad?"

"You already stuffed a handful of do-nuts down him over there. I saw you," Dr. Welles said with a shake of his finger and a chuckle. "Probably bind him up for a week."

I returned the laugh and was permitted to depart the premises to allow the greater minds to do their thing.

By the time I made it outside it was nearly 2:30 PM. I decided to go straight home rather than check on any new work that came in to the office. As far as I knew everything was finished anyway. It was just as well, for at this point I wasn't quite sure what was real. What I needed was some relaxation to cleanse my mental pallet, some TV, then bed. After all, the authenticity of this landmark would be tested tomorrow.

As Sunday arrived, I woke later than the previous day. I didn't have to be at the lab until 10:00 AM. I went out and hauled the Sunday paper in and perused the news. As bad as the shape of the world was in, at least according to *The Times*, no news would be able to top what was just hours from occurring. Yet, other than a privileged few, nobody will know of the historic event, at least not yet.

I showered, shaved, and took care of anything else that needed attention. I then headed over to the lab. I had to go through the same screening process as yesterday. As I approached the door to the assembly room and was cleared to enter, I stopped just before pulling on the door's handle. This time I opened the door very slowly.

When Tramp saw that I was wise to him, he straightened up and went into a full body wag.

Many of those involved were already in place. I didn't want to go over and exchange greetings with Dr. Welles. He appeared to be all business- fairly serious and intense, sometimes rushing around, sometimes just busied with decisions. I did however make my way over to the ATM. As Dr. Welles passed me he said, "Hey Neil." Enough said.

I watched as Henry dialed in the number to the ATMs readouts while making sure the present frequency registered 7.0. Another gauge displayed the atomic clock's time.

Dr. Ebbing had an ammeter on the terminals of the power source, then marked the checklist he had beside him.

After roughly fifteen to twenty minutes of this examination and adjustment, Dr. Welles said, "Neil, bring Tramp over to this table."

As I picked the canine up, his happy demeanor went south. He was about as delighted as a dog that knew he was going to the vet.

I put him on the table and Henry gave Dr. Hayes the go ahead to administer the tranquilizer. The poor mongrel was looking for help from anyone as Dr. Hayes inserted the needle into the scruff of the dog's neck. Shortly after that, our subject didn't really care one way or another.

"I'm also going to administer him a dose of hydrazine sulfate," he said as he screwed another syringe on to the needle, "to stabilize the body's energy. Usually used for cancer patients during treatment some years back, I'm hoping this will aid us greatly during the energy transformation."

The next half hour or so was spent locating

areas on the subject's body for the monitoring electrodes and shaving each region leaving the already disheveled dog with mangy looking bald spots. The wires and electrodes were then glued into position, and the finished product was hoisted into place and strapped down.

I could hear the banter of "You got it?" and "Hold on, hold on" as everything was positioned in its proper place.

"Is that it?" asked Dr. Welles.

"I guess so, yep," came the uneven chorus.

"O.K. then we made it with five minutes to spare. I'll go ahead and set the ignition timer," he said as he reached inside and set the dial for the delay. Dr. Welles placed the cowl and clamped it into place. Henry took a little extra time repositioning the module on the floor, first an inch or two this way then an inch or two that.

"Henry sit down," commanded Dr. Goodrich. "You're acting like an expectant father."

"Yeah, yeah," was his reply. He took one last look at the clock in the ATM and compared it to a readout displayed on the tabletop. "Good, fine," Henry said with satisfaction as he reluctantly took a seat with the rest of us.

We watched the ATM, then the clock on the table. This was it, zero hour. I heard one member muttering, "...eight, seven, six,.."

When the clock hit twelve hundred hours, the process we observed yesterday began to occur. First the craft turned semi-transparent, foggy, then gone. Instead of relief in the room, everyone sat dead silent as if waiting for the other shoe to drop. It was the longest thirty seconds of our lives.

Finally, the clock hit 12:00:30. Everyone's

eyes focused on the now vacant spot in the middle of the room. Nothing.

Dr. Hayes spoke up. "Well, the process does take ten seconds from beginning to end, doesn't it?" trying to justify the delay in our minds.

But by now, we were at fifty seconds past the hour. You could almost hear a collective sigh throughout the room when it was interrupted by a familiar, barely audible thump. First came the foggy image, the translucent vision, and then a completed reality. There in the middle of the room was the ATM with one tail-wagging dog, just happy to be home. With a small bark, he showed it.

A chorus of "Yeah!" echoed throughout the room. Even Dr. Goodrich, in his suit and tie, was jumping up and down like a child who just spotted the ice cream truck. Everyone was whooping, hollering, and celebrating. Everyone, that is, except Dr. Welles. He just stared intently at his creation.

"We did it Henry! We did it!" shouted Dr. Richmond as he slapped Dr. Welles on the back.

Not able to hold back any longer, Dr. Welles exploded. "No! It's wrong, it's all wrong!" he shouted, extinguishing the party atmosphere of the room. Talk about raining on a parade.

"What are you talking about, Henry? The craft is back safe and sound and the dog looks great. Of course we'll have to have him examined, but..."

"That's just it. We sent a 'doped out of his mind' dog out of here only a minute ago, and now he's stone cold sober."

"What gives," a confused Dr. Richmond asked as the celebration in the room cooled.

Dr. Welles angrily pulled the glass covering off of the ATM, shoved Tramp's licking face out of the way, and checked the clock. Then he looked at the synchronized clock on the table.

"Dammit, we're three hours off," he yelled as he thumped the table.

"That explains why the sedative has already worn off," replied Dr. Hayes as he checked Tramp's eyes.

"You mean that we don't have the real dog back?" asked Agent Holbach.

"Oh, he's the real deal O.K. He's just three hours older than he should be. Dammit!" was the only words Dr. Welles could bring forth.

The rest of the day was disorganized. Yes, history had been made, but it wasn't right, not yet. Something about making the outcome correct somehow legitimizes a historic effort.

Dr. Hayes took the dog over to his lab and had a blood chemistry and scan performed. While there were no sickling or cellular abnormalities detected within Tramp's red blood cells, it appeared to be a 'back to the drawing board' type of situation for the entire project. I decided that the best thing I could do was to lay low until I was needed.

Two weeks later I ran into Dr. Welles while leaving the HUB. In a hurried fashion he said to me, "Oh Neil, glad I caught you. Could you be over at the lab at four o'clock this afternoon?"

"Something big?" I asked.

"I hope so. I believe we've gotten all of the glitches ironed out."

"I'll be there."

I finished up early and drove over to the lab. Parking was at a premium this time of day so I had to park down on East College, feed the meter, and hike up the serpentine walkway. I didn't mind though. The weather was starting to become a bit more palatable. A light jacket was all that was required.

When I arrived at the lab, business was as usual. I approached the assembly room and noticed a man in plain clothes sitting in one of those classroom desks at the door. I guess he was trying to look inconspicuous. My ID was checked and I was permitted to enter. Again I opened the door slowly to avoid the canine assault but found that to be unnecessary. As I walked through the room I noticed that the crowd wasn't what it was during the initial test. That reminded me of the old Apollo moon program. After the third trip or so to the moon, it was as if nobody cared anymore. I guess they had been there, done that.

I walked over to Dr. Welles as he readied the craft. Tramp was already inside, doped and ready to go. "We made a few changes to the process," Dr. Welles reported. Our main problem last time, we discovered, was that hydrazine sulfate should not be mixed with a sedative. It's not a good combo. We're guessing that played havoc with Tramp's electrical system. We also found that this stuff doesn't mix well with alcohol or cheese either. Just food for thought."

"So I guess that nixes Tramp's champagne and Mozzarella kibble dinners, huh?" I joked.

"Very funny. We're going to try this run with just a mild tranquilizer. We'd like to keep things as natural as possible. We also have something new we're going to try out that will blow your mind," Dr. Welles said, borrowing a vernacular from the '60s. "We'll be able to control the entire operation from this keyboard."

"How are you going to pull that off? How can you contact the ATM? Won't it be in a different time zone as you say?"

"Correct, but remember what I said before? The object is still here. Its vibration frequency merely makes the subject a reality to that which shares its identical frequency." Walking over to the console, Dr. Welles explained, "You see, we are able to increase the power of the signal without changing the frequency itself. A simple booster did the trick, no big secret. With the increased signal, this transmitter can send, contact, and retrieve the ATM."

"So you're saying that radio signals can cut across the time barrier without any problems?"

"I didn't say that. Yes, we believe they can go across the barrier of time. But from the tests we've done on an empty ATM, our signal board does carry a limited range. So there is some impediment or interference between here and there. We're just not quite certain what we're dealing with at this point. We're not going to try and stretch it, at least not right now; first things first."

"But you know, broadcast signals have always been able to travel across time. Theory says that somewhere in outer space, if you had a powerful enough receiver, you could watch 'live' programming such as a first run Milton Berle show. And you have to take into consideration that it's been a half century since that program originally aired. That's a situation concerning the lack of signal strength due to a magnitude of distance, not one of time. There's more to it than that simple, bare bones explanation, but that's the best I can do for right now."

Dr. Welles was interrupted when Dr. Hayes proclaimed, "We're about ready, Henry."

Getting back into his official mode, Dr. Welles stepped behind the console and questioned, "Is the ATM's panel up yet?"

"Up and running," reported Dr. Goodrich.

"Time synchronized at sixteen hundred hours at...check?"

"Check."

"Input at 7.000000000005479." That was the difference in cycles per second up from the present 7.0.

"Check. All systems go."

"All right, thirty seconds until manual launch," Dr. Welles announced. "Mel, I can feel it in my bones. It just feels right." He proclaimed with a clenched fist. Dr. Goodrich didn't answer back. He, like everyone else, was too keyed up.

Just like in the early days of the space program, Dr. Welles watched the countdown on his screen until the clock hit :03. He then hit 'enter' and let the computer take it from there.

The now familiar 'fade out' procedure began. "How long will he be gone?" I asked.

Rather preoccupied, Dr. Welles answered, "Thirty seconds, same as last time. And coming up on thirty seconds...check, enter."

With that we heard the same low thump as the ATM proceeded to make itself perceivable through its fade back in. At the end of the ten-second period, Dr. Goodrich hurried over to the craft and peered inside. Tramp still looked fairly groggy.

"Mel," Dr. Welles asked, "how about 16:02:00 at...check?"

"Check! Yeah! Now that's what we've been looking for! The clocks are synchronized; the power intensity is set at 7.0 Megahertz even, current frequency. Yes!" Sighs of relief and satisfaction surrounded the room.

For the first time since this entire operation started, Dr. Welles face showed some relief and a fair semblance of a smile. Even his worry lines seemed to fade a bit.

"Hah!" was his version of "Eureka!" Handshakes were the rule of the day.

"Henry, are you up to phase two?"

"What's phase two, Doctor?" I asked.

"I'm going to load the next program," he stated as he scooted the computer's mouse around the desktop, "which will reset the multiples." It took only seconds to bring the new file up. "This attempt will be aiming for a one year regression rather than just one day. By George, I think we've got it now," he claimed in his best British accent.

"Sure, we might as well go for it while we have the pooch still sedated. Less wear and tear on him," replied Dr. Goodrich.

"O.K., the program's loaded. Mel...check?"

"Check. The input reads a cycle increase of .000000001999 up from 7.0 cycles per second."

"Check. Well, hold your collective breaths, guys. Here goes nothing. And, at :05, :04, :03..."

Dr. Welles then hit the 'enter' button. ":02,

:01." Fade out.

The same silence accompanied this launch as the others. A few sighs heard around the room led me to believe that some were becoming impatient. I guess they wanted to see everything happen like, right now, this second.

Dr. Welles once again broke the silence by saying, "...:28, :29, :30, enter". There was nothing but silence. "Give it time, give it a chance," he cautioned. "He's a long way out." We waited.

After a moment, Edward Holbach asked, "Does this mean that we've lost him?"

"No, we haven't lost him! Manual override!" Dr. Welles commanded as he checked his screen once again. For the second time he punched 'input' then 'enter'. Once again there was nothing.

"Henry, you don't suppose..." Just then, Dr. Goodrich was interrupted by the faint, nearly silent 'sonic boom' of reentry. All heads turned towards the room's center.

"Alright, alright. Check readouts. Mel?"

"7.000000 check? 16:06:30...check?"

"Check and check," replied Dr. Welles with a sigh of relief.

"That was a long one. How are you doing, pooch?" asked Dr. Goodrich, waving to Tramp through the lightly tinted glass. The dog just sat there and sighed. He had no idea what was so important.

After doing some checking around, a cocky Dr. Welles queried, "Well, fellows do we go for broke?"

Dr. Hayes answered, "I don't know, Henry, we've done so much already today. Perhaps we should leave it at that. Besides, we've probably used quite a bit of the battery's reserves." They were beginning to sound like someone who wanted to walk away from the roulette wheel with their winnings rather than 'letting it ride.'

"All systems check out fine here. Amperage looks fine. I'm fine. You're fine. Tramp's hanging in there. Where's your sense of adventure? Let's do it. What do you say?"

"Well, it's up to you. You know what you're doing," Dr. Hayes said with little enthusiasm. "I still think we should find out what took so long for his return trip."

"I'm guessing because he was so much farther across the time spectrum. The new file is booted up and ready to go if you are. Shall we?" asked Dr. Welles with delight.

The others seemed less enthusiastic, but agreed.

"Time to break the ten year mark. Mel, 16:10:00...check?"

"Check."

"7.00000001900?"

"Check."

":05, :04, "03..." was the count as Dr. Welles hit 'enter'. Fade out.

Dr. Welles seemed to be sweating a bit. It may have been due to the amount of work that he had performed, or perhaps Henry may have been a bit apprehensive himself by pushing the limit. A mistake at this point could easily snatch defeat from the jaws of victory. The ten-year mark was definitely uncharted territory, but then so was everything else connected to this project.

"Coming up on :30...and check." After a pause, Dr. Welles said, "Wait for it," as he stared intently at the center of the room.

But there was nothing to wait for. Moments turned into periods. Periods became stretches. Some in the group bowed their heads in defeat. Others just looked around the room as if trying to find something else to do. No one wanted to face the inevitable.

Regardless of the amount of time the ATM was sent back, the return period seemed too long. You could just feel it. Finally, Dr. Welles said, "I'm going in," as he switched to a manual override mode. Punching in '7.000000 enter' several times, he tried to bring the craft back himself but to no avail.

Dr. Hayes quietly said, "Doctor, we're losing him."

"Dammit, I know it! I'm doing everything I can to..." Just then, Dr. Welles stopped in mid speech and just stared at the screen. "Dammit," was all that he could say, almost in a cry, as he continued to stare at the numbers with his hand clamped over his mouth.

Dr. Goodrich went over to console Henry when he looked at the screen where Dr. Welles was staring. In a very weak voice, Dr. Welles pointed to the monitor and muttered, "My program is missing a decimal point, right here. I blew it!" Dr. Welles cupped both hands over his face.

"It's O.K. Henry," sympathized Dr. Goodrich.

"Yes Henry," joined in Dr. Hayes. "That's why we do these experiments. Rarely is anything perfect the first time around, you know that. None of us are."

"I don't give a damn about that. It's my fault, it's my entire fault! I broke my own rule. I didn't have someone double check my work. I was so damn intent on doing everything myself..." Dr. Welles replied as he looked around the room at nothing in particular. In a fit of self-anger he slapped the 'off' button on the keyboard. The screen faded to black.

Chapter 5

Its about Time

In aging, one becomes more foolish and more wise."
FRANCOIS DUE de la ROCHEFOUCAULD

    I didn't go back to the lab or even call Dr. Welles for about a month. I'm sure he felt horrible about what happened. He blamed himself. Even though others made excuses concerning the equipment, Dr. Welles said that the true problem lay between his stool and his keyboard. He insisted that perhaps he was taking things a bit too fast. He thought he might not have been checking as close as he should have. Maybe that was the case. I wasn't in a position to say.
    He wasn't satisfied that he and the group had done something that the world, up until now, had believed to be impossible. As Dr. Hayes said, "Nothing's perfect the first time around."
    It was just after the first of June when I passed the lab on my way home one night and noticed the lights on inside. It had been some time since I saw the place all lit up at that hour. I was apprehensive about entering. Perhaps the group was back on track. Would they want me hanging around? Did Dr. Welles even need me tagging along anymore? I decided to get an answer to that question once and for all.
    I went down the steps and through the hallway to the door of the assembly room. Out of habit, I opened the door very slowly until I remembered that I didn't need to do that

anymore. When I entered, I noticed no elaborate experiments in progress. The guard and crowds were absent as well. Dr. Welles was the only person on the premises. He looked like a secluded, lonely figure sitting there on a stool by himself. He heard me come in, glanced up, then resumed his work while tilting his back towards me slightly. It was as if he couldn't face me.

"Uh, Henry, how goes things?" I said with a bit of an unsteady voice. "I see you're still hard at it," I added, trying to put a positive spin on things.

"Hard at it, huh?" he replied as he stopped what he was doing and rested both fists on the table in front of him. "Neil, I'm a failure. I'm sorry, I didn't think things would turn out the way they did. I'm very sorry."

"Oh come on Henry, you did things here that man has only dreamed of since the beginning of time. You'll forever be known as a pioneer in this science."

"Pioneer, huh? Neil, this science will never see the light of day," he declared as he threw his pencil down. "No one will ever know of our accomplishments here. My goal was to see this thing through to human experiments. If those went well, I had planned to pass the torch to a younger, more vital generation of physicists. My mark would have been made. I would then be able to retire and hit the lecture circuit with my history-book legacy intact. Instead, the Department of Defense heard of my debacle and put the brakes on our efforts."

"Yes, but they haven't moth-balled the project like you thought they would," I reminded him.

"They might as well have. You want to see what they have me doing now?" he asked. "I was preparing to run the last test of the day. Watch."

With that, Dr. Welles went over to a cage and retrieved a rabbit. The animal was fairly inactive, but I wasn't sure if it had been sedated or not. It's hard to tell with rabbits, but the critter had already been shaved and prepped for a transfer. Dr. Welles loaded the animal into its harness and fastened him in. After attaching the electrodes, he stepped behind the console, pushed a few buttons and said, "Wait for it."

About thirty seconds later, I heard the thump, or faint sonic boom that I had become familiar with. Over to the side, about twenty feet away, an ATM appeared, equipped with a cotton tail of its own. Dr. Welles went over and removed the furry mammal from the craft and carried it over to the rabbit he had just finished prepping.

"Look at that, a perfect clone in every respect," he said with no real enthusiasm. "It should be, it's the same damn rabbit!" he said as he carried his new arrival over to the former owner's cage. "I'm scheduled to send this one back here tomorrow night," he said holding the white animal up slightly. "Apparently I did. As you can see, it arrived in perfect condition. This one over here, I'll send back in the ATM so it'll end up here last night. I'm sure it'll reach me, believe me. Confused?"

I was. Dr. Welles then took an object that resembled a pager from his table and depressed it into the panel activating the ATM's LEDs. "It's all automatic now." He then replaced the cover and checked the console.

"Give it a couple of seconds." With that, the ATM faded from sight evacuating the cargo with it. "Real impressive, huh?" he said with an 'I don't give a damn' attitude to his voice.

"I'd say it was very impressive. Why, if you told me a year ago that something..."

"You don't know sarcasm when you hear it, do you, boy?" he said in an irritated tone. "Save the congratulations. That's all this thing is ever going to be good for. Geeze, producing clones of rabbits. They're more than copies of the original—they're one in the same. That's all they're going to let me do with it. Big deal, rabbit tricks. I knew it would come to this."

"Henry," I said getting serious with him, "did you become a physicist to discover and enrich man's horizons, or did you get into this game for the accolades?" A legitimate question, I thought. I had a point to make.

"Hey look, you try to sum up your life's work in one project and have it fail. Then you can come and lay that kind of shit on me!" I hadn't seen Dr. Welles this angry since he got into it with Dr. Butler. And this time that anger was aimed at a sympathetic ear.

"Uh, I had better be going," I said trying to excuse myself from this uncomfortable situation.

"Yes, you do that," he angrily shot back.

I left the lab, got in my car, and sat for a moment. I wasn't angry with Dr. Welles, I felt bad for him. The lack of confidence he exhibited in himself had already reared its ugly head. I didn't know what to say to get him to believe in himself again. I drove home, and all of the while tried to come up with a solution to his dilemma, but nothing surfaced.

Two weeks went by. During an idle moment at my desk, I put in a call to Ellen at the OMB.

"Hey Ellen, it's Neil Gates at Penn State. How goes things?"

"Pretty good, how's things shaking with you?"

"Not bad. I need you to check on a project's funding once again for me. We're still running a bit long with it."

"Sure. Number?"

"It's number J-316-G, our number."

After some ticking on the computer keys, Ellen came back and asked, "Are you sure of that number? Right now I'm showing nothing under that listing. Do you have your Federal cross-reference number for that project handy?"

I dug through my paper work. "Just a moment." Finally I found an old sheet in my file that pertained to Project Sundial. "Yes, here we go. Your reference number is PS12-1999."

"Oh great, that will work, one moment."

After quite a while Ellen came back on line. "Neil, I'm not showing anything under either listing. I think that I've checked on that project for you before, haven't I?

"Absolutely."

"Have you been notified of a cancellation by any chance?"

"They haven't informed me of such. That's curious because the project wasn't up for review for several months yet. Hey look Ellen, this is pretty important. I wouldn't ask this of just anybody but..."

"But you're going to ask me, right?"

"Yeah come on, I need your help badly.

Could you trace down and find out where the money for the project went? I mean, where somebody lost funding, namely us, somebody else had to pick it up, right? I was wondering if you could find the destination of those dollars."

"Hey, you're asking for a pretty big favor there, Neil."

"I know, I know, but it's pretty important." Thinking fast on my feet I continued, "It's a situation where, if someone gets a leg up on us concerning this project, it will sink us financially. All of that work down the drain, you know."

"OK. I'll see what I can do. I make no promises though."

"Many thanks, Ellen. I owe you one."

"You keep saying that. I'll dive into it. Take care."

So it's official; they're shutting down Project Sundial. The funding on that project was supposed to be open-ended; at least that's what the original paper work said. I sat there trying to decide whether I should go over and see Dr. Welles and give him the bad news. He wasn't too happy to see me the last time. But the primary reason he befriended me was to protect his intellectual investment. I thought that I could do a 'hit and run' and just leave a message on Henry's email, but that would be too unprofessional. After all, he trusted me enough to allow me to join his elite group so I could witness history being made. What's the worse he could do, I wondered, throw me out? There was only one way to find out.

I drove over to and entered the Osmond Lab for what I figured to be the last time. I went down the steps, through the hall, and into the assembly room. Once again, Dr. Welles was the only one in attendance. He was about half way back in the room tinkering with something. Looking up as I approached, he straightened up and said, "Neil, where have you been hiding?"

Dr. Welles actually had a smile on his face. He looked quite different from the last time I saw him. "Well I've, uh, been around. Look Doc, I was talking to..."

Interrupting me he said, "Hey Neil, I was thinking of what you said the last time that we got together."

Returning the interruption, I said, "Oh yeah. Look I'm real sorry I came across like that but..."

The conversational volley was back in his court. "No, no, you were right. I think I probably was looking more towards having my name up in lights rather than actually performing my craft. Your advice really changed my outlook towards this project. Yes, the gains will be small, but my research will help the overall picture. I'm actually enjoying my work now more than I have in the past year or so."

"Doc, I hate to rain on your parade but I've got bad news for you. Project Sundial is dead. They pulled the plug on it," I reported.

With his voice dropping, he asked, "Oh my God, Neil, are you sure?"

"As sure as I can be. The OMB says that they don't have and never did issue a grant under that listing."

"Wouldn't they just have a note in their files that the funding had been canceled or dried up?"

"One would think so."

"If what you say is true, then it sounds as if they're burying the project or redirecting the funds to the unknown. They're covering their tracks."

"Could be true. I figured that you'd be looking for an explanation so I'm way ahead of you. I have my contacts at the OMB trying to track down the beneficiary of our funds."

"That could tell us a lot, how long until we find out?"

"It's hard to tell. It could take hours or even weeks."

"Damn, that's too long. Neil, my massive ego aside, we've got to do something to safeguard this project."

"I know. I'd like to help but all I'm able to do is ask for additional funding. It's up to Washington to say "yea" or "nay." That could take months or years if ever."

"They're not going to hide this information from the people and bury the evidence like they did with the Philadelphia Project," he said in a loud voice. "I'm not ready to go yet. We may have to take things into our own hands."

"What do you mean *we*? I hope you've got a rabbit in your pocket. What do you plan to do Henry, heist the machinery from the federal government?" I asked.

"That's an excellent thought."

"Henry, you'd get in a hell of a lot of trouble trying to pull something like that off. You could do some big time."

"They wouldn't dare. If it got out that I was doing time for stealing a governmental project for time travel, they'd have a lot of explaining to do. They wouldn't want another Roswell situation on their hands."

"If you couldn't come right out and tell the media about Project Sundial, what good would it do for you to whine from a jail cell?"

"Well, you've got a point there."

"So what do you plan on doing?"

"I'm not sure yet, give me some time. I'll call you tomorrow morning. What time do you get in?"

"About 8-8:30," I answered.

"I'll try and come up with something by morning. Until then, keep tight-lipped about this situation. And Neil," he said as I turned to leave, "thanks for all of your help. I do appreciate it."

"No problem, Doc. Take care and be careful."

The inescapable prospects of the entire situation left me a bit uncomfortable. Going up against the federal government, one would have to realize that they are a bit over-matched. I wasn't sure what Dr. Welles had in mind, but I definitely had an uneasy feeling about it. I also sensed that I'd somehow get pulled into that mess.

I arrived at the office a little bit early the following morning. I was waiting on that all important call from Henry. 9:30 AM rolled around and still no word. I was beginning to get a bit nervous. Henry rarely misses a deadline. A short time later the phone rang. Right on time, I thought.

I answered the phone only to find that it was Ellen from the OMB. After our hellos, Ellen said, "Neil, glad I caught you in. I think I found the answer to your inquiry. Maybe you can make heads or tails out of it."

"Damn girl, you're fast."

"Yeah, so I've been told," she replied with a playful laugh. "With all of my experience with budgets, I haven't come across something such as this too often."

"Great, let's have it," I insisted as I grabbed my pencil and pad.

"I scanned the OMB's records to no avail. I called Linda over at the GAO. She saw a glitch in her records that roughly coincides with the amount missing from your program. But it was a 'here today, gone tomorrow' situation. The funds seemed to leave one program as soon as they came in."

"Somebody was trying to cover their tracks. Where did you go from there?" I asked.

"We did an across the board scan of the budget going from department to department. That, coupled with the relatively small amount of dollars we're talking about here is what took so long. We were looking for any movement of monies from project 'A' to fund 'B.' You know, it's fairly obvious when a senator gets rewarded for his service to the president while another is being scolded. It shows up. Where do you think those rumors come from? Anyway, since a piece of your budget came from the Department of Defense, we dug through their files."

"You can do that?" I asked in amazement.

"We're not supposed to, but hey, if you have the right contacts who can get you passwords, you can look up just about anything. We were able to obtain a United States Appropriations and Expenditures document dating back two weeks ago when your project's fund's dried up. It showed a decrease from the research and development area of the CIA's already inflated general budget of $26 billion, and an increase in the undisclosed area of the Department of Defense's budget of roughly the same amount."

"So, do you know what sector of the defense budget landed our funds?"

"Yes. The money was funneled to a little known, obscure bureau known as the White House Commission on Science and Technology."

"What in the hell is their purpose?"

"No one's really sure," she said with an uneasy laugh. "No, actually it's not much other than a paper commission. As far as I can tell this agency is just a fancy name for a pool of scientists the president calls upon to back up his position in order to get legislation through congress. They try and make it look as if all in the scientific world agrees with the Chief Executive's position."

"Sounds like the President's propaganda cabinet."

"Pretty much, they push for legislation on things such as acid rain regulations, global warming legislation, you know, those 'feel good' programs that benefit a particular congressman's district and make it look as if he's actually doing something."

"What do they need an increase in funding for?"

"I really couldn't say. Maybe the Chief needs a source for some payola. But at any rate, that's where the funds ended up, at least for now. What kind of project are you guys working on anyway, a safer nuclear bomb?"

Kowing that Ellen was unaware of the exact reason for our existence, as few were, I glossed over the whole thing with, "Oh no, but it is defense related. You know how secretive they can be. I'm just surprised they folded us up so soon. Oh well, there will be other projects. Hey Ellen, again thanks. You've been a great help. I know that took some doing."

"That's O.K., I get paid whether I do anything or not," she said, downplaying her efforts. "Hope I was able to shine some light."

"Oh yes, very much so. Take care. Talk later."

Well that settles that, I thought as I replaced the receiver. Now I'll have to pass on the information to Henry. Perhaps he can make heads or tails out of it.

Since I hadn't heard from him, I went ahead and called Dr. Welles down at the lab. I wasn't sure he'd be in yet or not, but he was.

"Henry, I've got some information you might be interested in. Apparently..."

"Uh Neil," Dr. Welles interrupted, "how about if I, uh, buy you a cup of coffee. Tell you what, come on down to the lab. I'll be finishing up here in fifteen to twenty minutes. See you then."

That was a strange conversation, I thought. It was a little one-sided if I might say so myself. Either someone was in the room with Henry who shouldn't be privy to our conversation, or he felt it best if we discussed these things in private. Phones, on occasion, do have ears.

I drove over to the lab and went on in. Dr. Welles did have a guest. A man was running a scan list on items from Project Sundial, boxing them up, then labeling them with printed out UPC bar codes from his hand-held printer.

"Well, that's about it," Dr. Welles said as if being very efficient.

"O.K., well thank-you Doctor, we'll move the unit over in the next day or so," the visitor remarked.

When we all left the room, I asked Dr. Welles on our way across the street, "Who was that guy and what is he doing with your equipment?"

"Oh, that was just a fellow from maintenance. Apparently they need the room at the Osmond for another Defense Department project due in later this month. They're going to need the additional space so they're going to move all of my stuff next door to the Davey. It won't be perfect, but a bit more up-to-date. It will be smaller, however. Perhaps your sources may have been mistaken, Neil. At least it sounds as if they're going to allow me to continue working on the project."

"Did he say that?"

"Well, not exactly. He was just from maintenance, he wouldn't know. Why else would they want to move my equipment next door?"

"Henry, I found the recipient of the Project Sundial money. Some obscure group called The White House Commission on Science and Technology is quite a bit richer."

"What?" he said as he stopped just after entering the doorway leading to the lower level of the HUB. "They don't have a budget to speak of. That group is made up mostly of volunteers. Hell, I even worked with them once or twice during the Reagan Administration. A stipend is paid on occasion, and I'm sure they incur administrative costs, but what in the world would they need additional money like that for?"

"To pay off somebody?"

"Naw, they would get that from some unmarked soft source."

"Well, they were fairly diligent in burying the evidence of the monetary transfer."

Dr. Welles was deep in thought when a look crossed his face conveying that something didn't sit right with him. "You know now that I think about it, that maintenance man wasn't wearing the standard campus uniform, and dammit," he said as he slapped the table, "it didn't even faze me that he knew the names of most of the parts that we were boxing up. He was checking them off before I even handled them. And to think that I was even helping him! What an idiot I am. Dammit Neil, they're making off with all of my work! That White House commission is probably just a cover for our CIA or DIA friends. They will do with my project what they will. And now they're funded! I told you, I told you this would happen!" he said as he jumped up from the table.

"Yes, but what can you do about it?" I asked. "There are more of them than there is of you."

"All night long I thought about the possibility of this happening. I just felt it. I didn't think they'd try and pull it off right under my nose. And to think they almost got away with it!"

"Almost?"

"Neil," Dr. Welles said hushing his voice, "you've got an old pickup truck at home, don't you?"

"Uh oh, why do I get the feeling that I'm in an old 'I Love Lucy' sketch and Lucy just said, Ethel, I've got a plan."

"Neil, I'm dead serious."

"Oh, I'm sure you are. Good choice of words."

"They're not going to hide this technology from the people. I won't let them use this for their own selfish needs."

"Henry, if you're thinking of stealing that equipment, count me out. We could end up in a world of hurt, not to mention, behind bars in a federal facility."

"If they found out it was me who perpetrated the crime, yes."

"Who in the world else would it be? It's not like there are roving gangs of science project thieves working the campus. You'll be the first one they'll come looking for," I reminded him.

"I'm not finished with my research yet, Neil," he said in a depressed tone. "I need more time with this project," he professed as he slammed his napkin down on the table.

"For what, human experiments? Doctor, you can't experiment on yourself. Only a fool would have himself for a patient. If you ended up lost out there somewhere, the world would never know of any of your concepts."

"I know, but I'm still not done with it yet. I'm not ready to give it up. There's still so much to learn. We've only scratched the surface. To be honest with you Neil, I'd rather go down with the ship than to let it fall into the fed's hands. First things first—the truck?"

"Yes, I do own a truck," I said slowly and with much resignation.

"Tonight," he said, "we've got to get that apparatus out of there."

"And do what with it?" I asked. "Where in the world would you store it and not leave a paper trail?"

"How about your place?"

"Are you nuts?" I hollered.

A startled Dr. Welles commanded, "Keep your voice down. Neil face it, yours is the last place they'd check. I really need your help on this one, son. Please don't let me down."

Remembering how far Dr. Welles had fallen emotionally after the failure during the original tests, I couldn't disappoint him again. "Henry, you're really digging me in here on this one, aren't you?" I said as I saw a bit of a smile cross his face. He knew he had me.

"O.K., I can't stand to see a grown man beg. Good God Henry, what have you gotten me into now?" I asked while shaking my head.

With that, Dr. Welles got up from the table and patted me on the shoulder and said, "Thank-you, Neil. Oh, and don't call me. Let me get hold of you. I really can't trust anyone else at this point. They wouldn't think twice about loading the phones if they thought enough to pull the old fake maintenance man trick on me. The higher ups won't give this thing up without a fight, but neither will I. You will be home tonight?" he said more as a statement rather than a question.

"Yes, you know that I'll be there."

"Good. I've got to go back over to the lab to finish packing," Henry said with a smile.

Oh Lord, what have I done now, I thought.

After finishing up my work for the day, I went home to prepare a spot for the equipment storage. The natural place was the basement. I could fold the ping-pong table up and move some chairs against the wall. That opened up all sorts of operating room for Dr. Welles.

As I was looking over the area to make sure it was just right, I noticed the view that the ground level basement windows afforded to the outside world. While trying to figure out what to do about that problem, I looked upward and noticed a couple loose pieces of insulation in the ceiling joists. That will do, I thought. I removed the custom-sized chunks and placed them over both windows to block an outsider's line of sight. They fit perfect. "Why invite trouble?" I muttered.

After dinner I sat back to watch some TV. I was unaware of how or when Dr. Welles would get hold of me. Around 9:30 PM, a van pulled in the driveway. It was one of those lawn maintenance/landscaping vans. I thought, what the...until I saw Dr. Welles get out, thank his driver, then make his way up the walk towards the front door.

"Henry," I said as I opened the door, "what are you doing, midnight fertilizing jobs? Trying to pick up a few extra bucks in your spare time?"

"Can the crap. I had a friend of mine give me a lift over here. I told him my car's battery was dead and that you would give me a new one. I didn't want to tell him that I didn't wish for my car to be spotted in front of your house. And I certainly couldn't ask someone from the faculty to drive me over here. That would link us together, and the powers that be would eventually know."

"You have friends in the blue collar sector? Henry, I'm impressed."

"Actually, he probably makes more than you do. He owns the place. But seriously, I have friends lower than that. So, how have you been, friend?"

"Boy, you are spreading the fertilizer a bit thick tonight, aren't you? You wouldn't want to bite the hand that feeds you," I said correcting the doctor. "Anyway come on in and I'll show you your work area."

We went down to the basement and looked around. "This is fine. It's almost larger than the room they supposedly were going to give me at the Davey Lab," he said with a wry grin.

"I believe it. Well tell me, when are we going to pull off this caper?"

"In a couple of hours. Until then, you can get me a cold one."

"Just make yourself at home, won't you," I said returning the taunt.

Around 11:30 PM, after checking his watch, Dr. Welles proclaimed, "Well, we must be off."

"I couldn't have put it better myself." I couldn't tell if he caught that one or not. Our senses of humor were on different frequencies.

"How will we get in?" I asked, referring to the area around the lab.

"Pull in to the rear parking area. We'll back the truck in the loading dock behind the Osmond. I'll try either the side or back door. We'll know when we get there."

"Henry, you're not going to try and use your key card are you? They'll know you were there for sure," I warned.

"I didn't say *how* I was going to use my card."

We made the short drive over to the lab. My nerves were on edge during the trip over. I thought every car we passed was occupied by a government agent. Dr. Welles didn't seem any worse for wear, but I know his stomach had to be in knots as well. It was only natural as this was a one shot deal for both of us. This was his life.

I pulled the truck in and parked. Dr. Welles went around to the front door. He must have slid his card between the latches and gotten in through there. The plan was that he would pick up the first box and use it as a prop to keep the back door ajar.

Why did I feel like a burglar? I guess it was because we were in the process of stealing government property. "Boy, when you bite off a piece too big to chew, Neil, you don't fool around," I said. "I must be nuts. I'm talking to myself."

I stood by the opened tailgate of my truck when I heard a "click." I looked over and saw Dr. Welles propping open the door. He picked up the second box at his feet and silently motioned for me to come on. As I passed him he said, "It's all clear. Grab anything that's boxed up."

I went through the dimly lit storage room, down the hall, and into the assembly room. There were about ten to twelve boxes sitting there. I grabbed as many of the smaller ones as I could for my first trip. I was a bit on the uneasy side, to say the least, and wanted to make our stay as short as possible. As Dr. Welles and I passed each other on return trips, the only sound to be heard was our shoes creaking against the cool, tile floor. Neither of us said a word until I was on my way back in for what I figured would be the last trip. Dr. Welles was exiting with two boxes in his arms. In a quiet, raspy voice he said, "That's it. Grab the one down by the door." I did, and the door locked behind us. "Let's go."

As the last boxes went in, I leaned into the closed tailgate in an attempt to latch it as quiet as possible. I hopped in the cab, started the truck, and put the vehicle in gear.

"Lights," Dr. Welles said, reminding me to turn on my headlights as the vehicle began to move. We didn't want any suspicion turned our way. "Just act natural," he reminded me in a calm voice.

"Yeah, I always act like this when I rob the government," I answered.

We weren't on the road ten seconds when Dr. Welles said, "Look." Approaching us in their vehicle was Campus Security.

"Oh God, you don't suppose we tripped of a silent alarm do you?"

"No, I don't even think the lab has a silent security system. The guards make their rounds over here at pretty much the same time every night. I'd see them pass by as I took a smoke break."

"Henry, I didn't know you smoked."

"I don't, but it just sounded good," he said with a laugh.

"Man, I'm sure glad you can laugh. I'm still on pins and needles trying to pull off this game of political hide and seek."

"Well why shouldn't I be happy?" he went on to explain. "I have my intellectual property back."

"Yeah, but now what do you do with it?" I inquired.

"Good question. Hopefully with all of the parts we have, I'll be able to perfect things to the point to where we'll be able to do human tests. That's where the real proof is. Animal tests can only tell you so much. A person, verbally, can tell you so much more."

"Where are you going to get a sap crazy enough to volunteer for that task?"

"Hello Sap," he said with a song in his voice.

"Oh no, you'll not get me in that crate. Besides, you wouldn't be able to squeeze my big ass into that tiny little thing anyway."

"Well surprise, surprise!" he bellowed in his best Gomer Pyle voice. "Before, well before all hell broke loose within the project, I had a prototype of a manned craft fashioned by Larry Stokes. He's the same fellow who built the first ATMs. He called to tell me it was finished a few days after, well, after things took a turn for the worse within the project. Hoping for the best in the future, I stored the model over at my place. I can strip the current ATM of its parts and place them in the full sized craft. It's the same electrical process. We can use your truck and go over to pick it up first thing tomorrow morning."

"You're serious aren't you?" I asked in astonishment.

"Absolutely. Hey look Neil, you don't have to be the inaugural passenger. I was only joking."

"Then who will you get? Who would you be able to trust enough?"

"I don't know, maybe me. Yes, I could teach you the board."

"No way. In a crisis, I wouldn't be able to dissect the problem like you could. You know this unit inside and out. I don't want to lose you too, Henry."

As we pulled into my driveway I said, "I'll back it in. That will make for an easier unloading." While we were carrying boxes down to the basement, I recommended, "Henry, why don't you stay here tonight. You can use the couch over there.

You'd be able to guard your 'stash' from there better, and we'd be able to get an early start tomorrow. I don't have to go in until ten AM anyway."

"Sounds good, I've about had it for the night as it is. And Neil, thanks again. I really appreciate all of this."

"No problem. For allowing me to see history being made, I guess I owed you."

Before I went to bed, I sat down with a history encyclopedia. I was actually considering Henry's offer to use me as a guinea pig. I perused every historical subject in the directory from 'A' to 'Z'. While it was all very interesting, nothing really grabbed my attention. I would have no idea where to go in history even if I had the chance. I just couldn't let Dr. Welles use himself in his own experiments. He knew better than anyone else how to run that contraption. But what could I do? I was at a loss for a solution.

Now that we had the equipment over here, we had to use it for something. Stealing it was wrong, but I just couldn't stand idly by while the government railroaded Dr. Welles. Having run that thought through my mind, a light came on in my head. I went and dug out a box containing the old Gates family Bible, along with other related paper work, that my dad passed down to me. I glanced through the old dog-eared sepia-toned photographs and yellowed papers. That's when I made up my mind. I'd tell Henry of my decision tomorrow. I had better sleep on it first to make sure I'm not truly insane.

My alarm went off at five o'clock AM to make sure we could get a fast start on the day. I figured the quicker we could get into Henry's place, the quicker we could get out lessening the chance of anyone spotting us. I opened the door to the basement and yelled down to Dr. Welles to get his rear in gear. He came stumbling up looking like hell.

"Good lord Henry, you look like crap. Looks like you slept in your clothes."

"There's a good reason for that," he answered. "I did. Sorry I didn't have time to pretty myself up for you. I just want to get over to my place as soon as possible then get out. We don't need to leave a trail."

It was already light on our trip over. "The longest day of the year," I said referring to the first day of summer. I thought that this was as good a time as any to finally let Dr. Welles know what was on my mind.

"Uh, Henry, I think I found a passenger for the ATM."

Catching him off guard, he answered, "Who?" in astonishment.

"Me."

"Oh now come on Neil, I was just kidding when I said..."

"Henry," I interrupted, "I thought long and hard about this all last night. It's just the right thing to do. If you need a warm body, I'm your man. I won't take no for an answer."

"Well I'll be damned. What the hell brought this on? What changed your mind?"

"I sat around all last night thinking about a way out of all of our problems. I drew a blank when trying to think of a period I'd like to go and visit, given my choice. All I could think about is how, if caught, the feds could really send you up big time. You could really take a big fall, and for what? Trying to further mankind's knowledge of himself and his place in the universe? For doing what's right? That's when it came to me. My family lore has it that in the battle of Gettysburg during the Civil War, I had a great-great grandfather who was convicted of the friendly fire death of his own brigadier general. The court claimed that the act was deliberate. In talking with him before his sentencing, the family was certain that he was set up. They said that the crime wasn't within his character. He professed his innocence until the end."

I continued, "I remember visiting the battlefield when I was a boy. My dad and I walked over to the spot where the alleged incident was supposed to have occurred. I remember having a strange feeling that day. It felt as if I could almost reach out and touch my great-great grandfather right there, both physically and spiritually. I then flashed back to your lectures."

"And that's when you fell asleep, huh?" he interrupted.

"No, I remembered when you talked about how two events can occur on the same space at different times. That's when I started to think last night that perhaps I did truly experience my great-great grandfather's presence there that day. I'd like to go back and see for myself what really happened, if for nothing else, peace of mind. Anyway I figured that we could kill two birds with one stone, so to speak."

"Neil I don't think you realize what you're saying. I don't think you comprehend what could happen to you. If the actual process of breaking time's barrier doesn't ruin you, the battle could."

"Henry, you have something of worth that you could leave to humanity here. Me, I'm just a paper shuffler, even Ginny said so. I'd like the opportunity to add to mankind's knowledge of his universe. I'm certainly not going to achieve that doing for a living what I'm doing now. How else would I be able to add to man's understanding of the universe, shuffle a few more papers? It's you and me, Henry."

"You and me, huh? Neil," Dr. Welles said with a shake of his head and a mock laugh, "You're one crazy son of a bitch."

"Then it's settled," I said with some satisfaction.

We pulled in to Dr. Welles place a bit before six AM. "Geeze Henry, don't you own a mower? Look at your yard," I commented.

Raising his eyebrows, he exclaimed, "Uh, I've been a little busy lately. I'll have to get Ed on it. He's pretty slow this time of summer." Ed was the man who drove the lawn maintenance van.

We loaded up and drove back over to my place. Dr. Welles also brought along a bag of clothes and toiletries. He was in it for the long haul.

The new, larger version of the skeletonized ATM was surprisingly light yet a little clumsy. It wasn't too difficult to load or unload, and that would be a great asset. We carried it down to the basement and set it next to the dozen or so boxes.

"Henry I've got to get ready for work. The fridge is empty, so bon appetite! You can tinker around down here while I'm gone. Oh, I meant to ask you; won't you be missed at work?"

"Well, after Project Sundial, I hadn't been assigned anything new until the fall classes commence. I just assumed that I would be busy with the ATM until then."

"And so you will."

"Somebody might notice my absence. I just hope it isn't the wrong people."

"You can use the truck if you need to run any errands. Just don't go near the campus. Oh, and don't forget to put some gas in it. Take care," I said as I got ready, then left for work.

The next few days I felt like I was sitting on a powder keg and watching for a match to be struck. I made it a point to take most of my lunches over at the HUB. I wanted to see if there was any unusual activity over at the labs. I didn't note anything out of the ordinary, so I decided not to investigate any further. You know what they say: the criminal always returns to the scene of the crime. I preferred to be the exception to that rule.

After lunch, I went over to the Ritenour Health Center to have a blood draw. I told them that I was feeling a bit run down and hadn't had a physical in years. Of course it was just an excuse. I wanted to have a sample of my blood chemistry in case Henry wanted to compare before and after results from the trans-dimensional trip. All of the tests on the lab animals came back negative for any unusual DNA or genetic deviations. That was fine for them, but man is an entirely different beast.

It was now the twenty-fifth of June, and Henry had completed his record-setting conversion of the manned craft and said that it was ready for a test. He asked if I was up to the task. I told him I hadn't had the chance to study. He wasn't amused.

"Neil, do you know what you're about to do? Just because we were able to launch and retrieve lab animals doesn't mean that the outcome will be the same for a human. It's a completely different ball game I'm afraid. Do you realize that you could return with a mental or physical disorder?"

"As opposed to what I display now?"

"Listen to me," he said while grabbing my shoulders. He wasn't in a joking mood. "After this process, your body could become vulnerable to cancers and chromosomal abnormalities. It may not be possible to pass your genes on to another generation. You may not want to. You might return not as a person but as a scattered mass. We've never tried this process on a human, and this particular module hasn't been tried on anything. Neil this decision shouldn't be entered into lightly."

"I know Doctor, I know, but I want to do this. In your words, "It's my chance to leave a legacy." I mean, I feel bad for those people who leave this plane with nothing to show for their efforts other than being able to put a meal on the table for their family. Many people, unfortunately, end their lives as victims of violent crimes. Senseless. If, God forbid, something terrible would happen to me here and now, at least I would go doing something I wanted to do. Isn't that how you'd want to go? I know you, Henry, and I have confidence in your work. Believe me, I have given this undertaking quite a bit of thought."

"Don't say 'undertaking'."

I pulled a piece of paper from an envelope. "Henry, here's a letter I had notarized. Don't worry, the notary didn't read it. All it says is that, in the case of, well, for lack of a better term, a failure should occur, I hold you totally blameless."

"Oh God, do we have to do this?"

"Yes, it's for your legal protection. People will ask questions. You're the one who said that I could return as a sub-human mass. Anyway, I've done nothing but think about this all week. After all, I don't have a wife, kids, or dog that depend on me. Face it Henry, I'm your perfect subject. Let's do it."

With a sigh, Dr. Welles said, "O.K., if you're sure, I'll school you in the operations of the ATM. Let me show you what you'll be going through."

Walking over to the open craft, Dr. Welles pointed out, "I've replaced all of those clumsy monitoring electrodes with sharp contacts in the back and base of the seat. The excepton are the two that attach to the temples. If you'll look down there," he said pointing to the ship's floor, "you'll notice that there's a contact for each foot that you'll rest your ankles against. Here on the armrests, you'll have to place your wrists against each of these. When a complete bodily circuit is achieved, the green light will illuminate on the panel."

"On the first run," he continued, "I'm going to take you back one year exactly. You didn't have any obstructions in this area back then, did you?"

"No, not that I can recall. I usually don't use this room very often during the summer. It's more of a winter entertainment center," I answered.

"OK. Well, let's get loaded up. Are you ready?"

I just shook my head. I didn't think that we would proceed for an hour or two. This was so sudden.

Dr. Welles showed me where to step and where I shouldn't. I wore a T-shirt and jogging shorts to help rather than hinder our work. We wanted as little resistance for the contacts as possible. A contact to skin connection was a must to ensure the entire body's electrical field was a complete grounded circuit. We wanted everything to be perfect.

Once I was all secured, Dr. Welles gave me my instructions. "On the first trip, you'll only be gone for thirty seconds. I don't want to risk anything more than that. Don't, I repeat, don't leave the ATM. Just remain seated in place. Right now we're concentrating on your exit and reentry, nothing more. Got it?"

"Yes sir."

Henry then placed the Plexiglas dome over me, clamped it into place, then stepped behind the console to begin his routine. "Eleven hundred hours at...check?"

"Check," I affirmed as I gave him the thumbs up.

"Hands down and in place, dammit! Don't move them or I swear..." Wiping his face from top to bottom with one hand, he gained his composure and continued, "Current levels at 7.0 cycles?"

"Correct."

"Destination at 7.000000001999?"

"Yes." My heart was pounding so hard that I

could feel it beating through my kidneys.

"O.K.," Henry said as he took a deep breath, "brace yourself. This is it," he alerted me as he counted down, ":05, :04, :03." Having said that he hit the 'enter' button and yelled, "Good luck!"

Nobody hoped for that more than myself. Just then, I felt a full body hum akin to being electrocuted minus the pain. My head was also filled with a low vibration. It reminded me of becoming one with the lowest note that one could achieve on an old style pipe organ. It wasn't terribly uncomfortable, yet it was all encompassing. I could almost taste it. That sensation was followed by a great flash. It wasn't a flash of light, but one of darkness. Finally, everything subsided just as rapidly as it had begun.

When I cleared my senses, it appeared to me that the procedure either hadn't succeeded, or I had already made the round trip with no recollection of any stop. I was still in the same place at the same time, except it appeared that Dr. Welles had straightened up the basement a bit. Was there a time lag I wasn't aware of? The furniture was back in its place. When I looked over to Dr. Welles to ask why the procedure had failed, he wasn't there. None of his equipment was either. What the hell was going on here? I wondered. I began to think that it was Dr. Welles who was the traveler, not myself. Perhaps he put me in this thing to protect me from his proceedings.

I began to look about and I noticed that a couple of beer signs I installed behind my bar last fall were missing. Oh my God, I thought, could I really be in my basement exactly one year ago? I wondered if I was at home back then to see these goings on. God knows what I would have done in that situation-on both ends.

I noticed that it was very quiet. I continued to look around. My old card table was up against the wall. I threw that old thing out after a rowdy get together this past New Year's Eve. I'll be damned, he pulled it off, I thought. This definitely was my place last summer. I'm a part of history...

Just then, my thought processes were interrupted. The hum started once again. My hands gripped the armrests to the point where the contacts were digging in to my wrists. The flash followed the hum, then everything subsided. I looked around. To my right I saw Dr. Welles smiling from ear to ear. He was as excited as I was confused. I began to attempt my exit from the craft when Dr. Welles cautioned, "Hold on, hold on, readouts please."

I recited back all of the readings with a "check" for each.

"Yee haw!" yelled Dr. Welles with a side I haven't seen from him in months. With his hands in the air, he danced in a 360-degree circle. "We did it! What was it like? What did you experience? Where did you go? What did you see?" came his barrage of questions. "How do you feel?"

"Henry, let me get out of this can first," I said while struggling to free myself from my cramped quarters.

"O.K. O.K., of course," he said as he helped me up then out. "Now first, how do you feel?"

I hadn't had any time to make a proper assessment of my condition, but I told Henry all that I could. "Actually, I feel a little bit hung over,"

I reported as Dr. Welles wrote down everything I said. "I feel a bit fuzz-headed, but other than that, not too bad. I don't know if I went back exactly one year or not, but I was definitely back there sometime last summer. The basement wasn't full of your junk," I said with a laugh.

"Junk!" he yelled good-naturedly. "O.K., you look fine. Can you walk around a bit? Let me look at your eyes first," he said examining the whites for any blood vessel damage. "Do you feel hungry or thirsty or anything?"

"No, I feel O.K. Once my head settles down a bit, I think I'll be a hundred percent." I went into more details concerning my experience. I don't know who was more emotional afterwards—me for what I had been through, or Dr. Welles at having attained his goal.

We headed back upstairs to take a break. "We both have to get something to eat and drink to celebrate." I think that suggestion by Dr. Welles was actually to see if my inner workings were still operating correctly.

"I'll bet you'll regret that if I drink a soda and leak like one of those characters full of buckshot on the cartoons," I said accompanied by a laugh.

After one o'clock PM Henry asked if I was up to taking another shot at it. "Sure, the jet lag has subsided nicely, thank-you. Where are we off to this time, Henry?"

With a little hesitation Dr. Welles, looking away from me said, "Well, I thought we'd try the ten-year mark." The ten-year mark was where we lost it last time. "This house has been here for at least that long hasn't it?"

"Oh yes, I had it built about twelve to thirteen years ago. My dad, God rest his soul, lent me the down payment for it." I was equally as nervous as Dr. Welles but tried not to show it. I'm sure he returned the favor. I knew that the operation would be the same. Only the destination would change.

"We'll have a slight change in procedure on this run. This will prep you for the actual sequence in a week or so. We'll do everything on this run that you'll do next week, except on a smaller, localized scale."

"When you arrive at your destination, I want you to exit the craft and check out your surroundings. Try to verify the time and date. No one knows this house better than you. You'll have exactly five minutes, no more and no less. You don't want to overstay your welcome."

"Why just five minutes? Why not shoot for ten minutes or a half hour. I could collect so much more data during that time frame."

"For the simple reason that we're just testing procedure here. I want you do depart, send the ATM back, explore your surroundings, meet the ATM on cue, then return. Got it?"

"A piece of cake."

"Remove the tether here," he said pulling the mechanism from the panel and showing it to me, "and carry it with you. Get used to it. It's your lifeline, your umbilicus if you will. You'll need it to return home. When you exit the module, push the start button. That will download the return sequence from the tether. When you receive the green light on the panel, remove the tether, replace the cowl, and step away. You'll have ten seconds. The ATM will then return back to me."

"You mean that I'll be stranded ten years back in the past?"

"Not entirely. At exactly five minutes from your departure time, push this button here on the tether," he said as he showed me the fingertip-sized button on the front of the pack. "This will be your receiver. The craft will be the sender. I will be the intermediary. For the ATM to return, the two signals must mate in an electronic handshake in order for the round trip to be a success. Our batteries are limited so don't hold the button down any longer than necessary. And don't press it more than once. One press will be sufficient. Any more and that might cause a double start, and it could end up God knows where. When the module returns, get in, get situated, then replace the tether. If you followed procedure and completed the circuit, the return sequence will commence and the craft will depart on its own in exactly five seconds."

"What's the purpose of the tether deal, Henry?" I inquired.

With some hesitation, he answered, "In the event that something happens to you, I don't want the craft returning with somebody else as its passenger. The ATM will just sit right here if no mating signal comes across. It will be up to you to play an equal part in your return. You could say that it's for both of our protection. We don't want to interfere in somebody else's life, not to mention their potential heirs, because of our thirst for knowledge. Plus, you wouldn't want that craft sitting in a clearing at Gettysburg for three or four days while you're out gallivanting around. The vessel could get taken out by a shell or worse, it could end up being salvaged for its metal. How would you feel if you returned to the ATM only to find it up on concrete blocks?"

"Yes, I see what you mean. It's a bit awkward, but with what we have to work with, it will do for now."

"I'm sorry I have to put so much on you Neil, but with the time and resources we have available, we'll just have to make do. Is that O.K. with you?"

"It will be fine. Like you said, a necessary evil. Shall we?"

A confident smile broke across Dr. Welles' face. "We shall."

I went ahead and climbed aboard the craft. This time Dr. Welles put the cowl in place without clamping it down. "I don't think you'll be hitting any bumps in your landing zone which would dislodge the top. After this test, I'll reverse the clamps and put them on the inside. The passenger within will be able to control that better. They'll have to exit somehow," he said, followed by a laugh.

"Don't I know it."

Henry went over to the console and reviewed the readings that I ratified. Once he announced that everything was in place, I hit the enter button and removed the tether. "Sequence started."

"What? Oh God, no!" Dr. Welles reached over to the console and hit the escape button.

"What the hell did you do that for?"

"Because that's what you told me!"

"No, I said you do that when you send the ATM back to me. Damn! You don't do anything but sit on your ass on the way there. Can you manage that?"

"Yes sir."

"Damn it man, I knew we weren't ready for this." With a deep breath he asked, "Have you got it straight this time?"

"Yes sir. Sorry."

"Sorry don't feed the bulldog." With another deep breath he said, "O.K. let's do it right this time. Is everything in place, up and ready?"

"Check."

The countdown went smoothly and Henry hit the enter button at :03. I looked over at him and he at me as the sequence of events unfolded.

Procedure-wise, everything seemed identical to the preceding trip except the 'black-out' phase appeared to last longer. How I was aware of that I'm not sure. I'm guessing, however, that it was to be expected considering the distance traveled was greater.

When all subsided and my haze cleared, I looked about. Around me was nothing but the bare concrete walls of my basement. There was no paneling, no ceiling tiles, and no carpeting. Only a pile of lumber and a couple of five-gallon paint buckets were present over in the corner. They occupied the same space they did ten years earlier.

Then it hit me that I was to exit the craft and prepare it for its return. It all came back to me rather quickly. Once out and about, I was to confirm the exact time and date from a clock or calendar.

I lifted the cowl and swung one leg over the edge and on to the floor. Yep, it's concrete, I thought. I felt like I was placing man's first footprints on the moon. I got out and stood fully upright. Everything seemed O.K. I almost forgot to start the return sequence and remove the tether. This time I made sure I performed the procedure exactly as Dr. Welles instructed me. I did so and replaced the cover. I stood back and watched my life saver disappear across time's spectrum.

I had never felt so alone in all of my life. I hoped, in the end, that it wouldn't be the case. The world of ten years prior had all it could handle with one Neil Gates. It didn't need two. Plus, what would the junior me think. Who could figure that concept out?

I walked across the floor and up the steps. I had forgotten how much the wooden steps creaked before they were carpeted. Hoping that my younger self wasn't present, I slowly opened the basement door. The room appeared to be dimly lit. I looked over and noticed that the curtains were drawn. I began to realize that I must have been on vacation at that time. That's really the only occasion I close this place up. It may have been when I went to Chicago to see the Cubs at Wrigley. That appeared to be the case.

I looked around the place a bit. The video machine on the T V showed the time and date of June 25, 1:35 PM. I took the tether out and checked it for a comparison. It was a minute short, but my Betamax was never quite right, so I had to take things as they were.

Just then I nearly jumped out of my skin as my telephone went off. Next to the couch was the phone and its answering machine. I had a call. I was curious; do I see who it is? After all, it is my phone. Why did I feel like an outsider in my own home?

The answering machine beat me to the punch telling the caller to leave a message.

"Hi Neil, it's Pop," came the voice on the other

end of the line.

My God, it was Dad. It was so good to hear his voice again. I haven't been able to say that since he passed away eight years ago.

"Hey, when you get home I'll need you to give me a call. I have some lease papers on a new car that I can't make heads or tails out of."

Talking to my dad for the first time in nearly a decade was just twenty-four inches from my hand.

"You understand that crap better than I ever will," he continued. My hand went down to pick up the receiver. "Give me a call so I can get this thing rolling. Love you." Then his silence once again became my memory of him. He sounded so close. In fact he was. I'll bet that I could call him right now. It would be so good to hear him in person once again. I've longed for this moment for so many years.

I picked up the phone. "Dad? Dad?" Nothing. I tried to recall his phone number, then thought better of it. No, let him rest. He isn't in my time anymore, I'm in his. And I don't belong here. In fact, I've got to be going anyway. I replaced the receiver. "Aw, Dad."

Still looking at the phone, I rose from the couch slowly with the knowledge that dad was just a handful of digits away, and there was little or nothing I could do about it.

That's when I snapped back to reality and remembered that I had to find some proof for Dr. Welles of the day's date; something other than a VCR reading, that is. I looked out of the window in the front door. There at the foot of the step were several morning papers. Ah, my souvenir. That damn paper carrier never did heed my hold notices stating that I was going to be away on vacation. For once his incompetence paid off. I opened the door, sifted through the papers locating today's edition, and snapped it up. Just as I began my retreat back into the house, I saw a police car drive by, then suddenly stop.

Oh great, I've been spotted. I usually alerted the police that I'd be out of town on vacation and for them to keep an eye on the place. Wasn't that thoughtful of me? I thought they followed through on those requests about as well as the paperboy.

When he checked his rear view mirror and threw it into reverse, I made a beeline for the basement. I scooted a five-gallon paint bucket over, reached up into the floor joists, and pulled down a piece of insulation. I halved it and placed a piece over each basement window to exclude prying eyes. I went to the middle of the room and pulled out the ATM's electronic tether. I waited for it to count itself down to 13:40:00. I looked over at the windows and saw the insulation's color change from light pink to dark, then light once again. The patrolman was on the move. "Ten seconds to go, come on!" I yelled inside.

Just as I heard the doorbell ring, the clock read zero hour. I pushed the button. "Doctor, don't fail me now!" I begged. Thankfully I heard the familiar thump and the ATM appeared shortly thereafter. I quickly pulled the top off and wasted no time hopping inside and getting situated. Just then I heard a voice say, "Hello?"

In my haste to exit the premises, I probably forgot to rebolt the door. I shoved the tether into the slot in the panel, tossed the cowl in place, and then pushed the start button.

I could hear the steps creak, so whoever it was, was on their way down. No matter what was about to happen I managed to keep a clear head and remember all of Dr. Welles' instructions. I secured all of the contacts, and the panel light showed green. I waited.

What could or would I do if the policeman tried to interfere with my 'get away?' Just at that moment my question was answered. I felt the hum then saw the black flash. As my cerebral buzz subsided, I looked around and saw my paneled basement walls. I quickly looked over to my left and saw Dr. Welles.

As I began to exit, Dr. Welles reminded me, "Readings first, please."

"The hell with that, get me out of here! I was almost arrested in my own house!" He lifted the cowl from the craft, I threw the newspaper at Dr. Welles' feet, then related my story to him. He got a laugh out of it. I went on to exclaim, "Hey, it wasn't funny!" That made him laugh all the harder.

Dr. Welles checked everything out and looked me over. He then asked me to take my shorts off. "We don't know each other that well, Doctor," I responded. "Did you want to see if I mussed myself? I damn near did." Actually he wanted to check to see if the cloth fibers had been weakened. He would do the same check on the newspaper. After the fact, as far as we could tell, everything appeared to be as it should.

"Well, that will have to do. We can't risk any further tests. Were you satisfied with the craft's operation?"

"Everything seemed to go as prescribed;

crude but functional as has been said. I guess we have one shot to do this thing. I say we go for it."

"And so we shall. Get your stuff together. We'll be leaving in less than a week for Gettysburg."

Chapter Six
Point of no Return

> "Experience isn't interesting till it begins to repeat itself—in fact, till it does that, it hardly is experience."
> ELIZABETH BOWEN

It was Friday, June thirtieth, and the day we were to leave for the launch site. To defer any suspicion, I went into work as usual. I stopped off and told Donna that I'd be gone for a few days.

"Oh, a long July fourth weekend?"

"Yes, something like that. I'll have all of the pending accounts on top of the file cabinet if you need to check on anything. The password for my terminal is in my top drawer if you need it. You have the key to that. And if any messages come in that are in need of urgent attention, refer them to..."

"Neil, I know all of that. Geeze, you're going away for a couple days, not an eternity. We'll be O.K. Nothing much will be going on here for another few weeks anyway. Have fun, enjoy."

"Oh O.K., and Donna, thanks." Thinking back on that scene, I must have sounded as if I had an appointment with the firing squad. Donna gave me a strange look as I walked away, but I had to say what I said. There was no guarantee that I would be coming back. I may indeed be gone for an eternity. I was only trying to cover my backside just in case.

I planned to leave work that day around noon and help Dr. Welles get loaded up. Just as I was locking up, Ginny called.

"Hi Neil, are we still on for tonight?"

Oh no, I thought, I had forgotten all about that. I was supposed to take Ginny out clubbing tonight. She loved to dance. I hated it. But for her sake I acquiesced.

"Oh hon I'm sorry, something's come up. I've got to go away for a couple of days."

"Oh yeah, right," came the sarcastic response. "Neil, why don't you just come right out and say that you don't want to spend time with me. It would save us both a lot of time."

"Hey, that isn't it. You know I care for you, it's just that I have to go south for a, er, history seminar. I am getting paid for the trip. I'll make a little extra 'jack,' then we can really go out and do it up right. With any extra luck I should be home by the fourth anyway. We'll be able to catch the fireworks together then."

"Yeah, right." Ginny sounded unconvinced. "Look, I know you are less than thrilled with going out and dancing, but why can't you do something for me once in a while. I don't ask for much."

"Ginny," I returned, "yes, I'll admit I do hate clubbing, but I intend to honor our commitment. But what can I do? This thing just came up."

"I'll tell you what you can do. You can have a nice weekend!" she said while slamming the phone down.

During that conversation, Donna came in with some papers to be filed. She caught part of my conversation.

"History seminar? Whoa boy, you can do better than that. You've got something on the side, don't you?" she said, implying that I had an extra romance in progress.

"No," I said, not taking what she had just suggested. When it finally sank in, I looked up and loudly responded, "No! Get out of here!" I tossed a desk calendar towards the door. She left laughing. I left for home.

Ed's lawn care van was in the driveway when I arrived back at my place. The two rear doors were swung open aiming towards the garage. I looked inside and saw much of Henry's equipment already loaded.

"Henry, are we going to have Ed as our chauffeur for this trip?" I asked.

"Hardly. Ed agreed to lend me his van for a few days. I told him I was going to be doing some moving."

"And you weren't lying."

"Absolutely. Ed drove down to Lake Cumberland for the holiday weekend anyway, so it all works out real nice. We still have a little time to burn. We probably won't leave here until three o'clock or so. Let's go ahead and get loaded up now so we'll be ready."

As logic dictates, the first item out will be the last to be loaded. That just happened to be the ATM. We slid the ship in with little room to spare, and then bolted the doors.

The rest of the time was spent getting our essentials together. I planned to take my 35mm camera along to record the historical events as they actually happened. During the week, Dr. Welles and I fashioned what looked like a small version of an old wooden single plate camera. That type of camera was used most often back in those days. However, our version was a hollow, epoxied plywood box where a camcorder would reside.

That disguise would raise less curiosity and fend off any suspicion. Dr. Welles wanted video evidence for the scientific community to prove that his process was a success. The video camera would provide an undeniable verification that echoes of the past do indeed exist. We glued the video camera's lens frame to the opening and secured an old Minolta sunshade I had to the front to make it look like an extended lens. It would give me something to play with. A nifty little unit ours was. Even famed Civil War photographer Matthew Brady would be fooled.

When all was said and done, we finished up with half an hour to spare before departure. I left Dr. Welles to watch the rest of the Game of the Week so I could secure things outside of the house. I needed some time on my own.

I just strode around my house looking at all that I had done to the place over the years. The trees, whose trunks were once no larger in diameter than my thumb, had grown as large around as my thigh. The shrubs had filled out to conceal the barren strip adjacent to the foundation. As far as my home goes, if the ATM was Dr. Welles' baby, then this was mine. It was my refuge from the cruel world. The ranch was always there to greet me after work no matter what kind of day I had encountered. It kept me warm in the winter and cool in the summer. Certainly a lot had changed over the passage of almost a decade and a half. I took my time looking everything over. It might be the last time I would get that chance.

I'd love to say "good-bye" to Ginny, but of course I couldn't. No one was to know where or what Dr. Welles and I were up to. I felt as if I was leaving behind so many unresolved issues in this period. In my heart I found a parallel to my dad and how he must have felt when he left his earthly existence. Who knows, I might be meeting up with him again soon.

When I walked around to the back yard, I stopped and marveled at the complexity of the vein system found within a Cherry tree's leaf. I was coming to realize that I had never taken the time to notice the fine details of nature. Unfortunately, I rarely took the time to consider many things of real importance in life such as my relationship with Ginny. I took that for granted.

I was absorbed in personal reflection when Dr. Welles broke my train of thought by rapping on the sliding glass patio door. He pointed to his watch reminding me that it was about time to leave.

"I guess this is it," I said as I took one last quick look around the backyard. I returned to the house to get cleaned up and ready to go.

As we were preparing to depart, I turned everything off and closed all of the curtains. That task reminded me of when I went back ten years into the past and found my house all closed up for vacation. I had never been on a vacation like this though.

We grabbed our bags, loaded ourselves into the van, and headed out towards things unknown. I pulled out of the driveway slowly and scanned the exterior of the house and its surrounding yard.

Sensing my hesitation, Dr. Welles asked, "Hey Neil, are you O.K. with this whole thing? I mean, you don't have to go through with it if you don't want to."

"Oh no, it's O.K. There's a time and a place for everything in life. This is my time for a change. And," I said with more confidence, "I'm looking forward to the challenge."

I put the van into drive and motored south from Happy Valley towards Gettysburg via 322. It was a short and fairly quiet ride. Not a lot was said along the route, but Dr. Welles did ask me if I had observed anything out of the ordinary around the labs.

"Nothing that stood out," I reported. "I didn't see anyone following me nor did I hear any strange clicks in my phone either."

"That's what worries me. It's a little too quiet for comfort. You'd think that those involved would raise some suspicion upon finding that their equipment was missing."

"Maybe the man was indeed a campus maintenance man. Or, perhaps the feds thought someone else with jurisdiction moved everything out. Who knows, it's possible they haven't even made it over to the lab to pick the stuff up yet."

"Something this important? What, after they went to all of the trouble to cancel our funding and have everything packed up for shipment? That man wasn't from campus maintenance, believe me. No, this is no time to let down our guard. When you least expect it, things happen. I don't trust them. They're playing it a little too cool."

"And thus, the lawn care van?"

"Sure. Not to mention that we'll raise far less suspicion at Gettysburg in this thing than we would in your average pick-up truck. At least this way we look like we have some business being where we are. Plus, the van is equipped with a generator. I almost forgot that we'd need electricity to get you off the ground."

The rest of the hour and a half long trip was spent enjoying the landscape and retreating into personal contemplation. I guess, all in all, both the doctor and I had our 'game faces' on. We knew this was it, and neither was sure if we could pull it off. If I didn't make it back, would Henry be charged in my disappearance? Would he be able to live with the consequences? And what about me? Would I be able to live with it—both literally and figuratively? No pun intended, but I guessed time would tell.

We just pulled on to State Route Fifteen when Henry said, "Pull in here," pointing to an inn just outside the village of Summerdale. "We'll stop here for the night. I don't want to get too far in towards Gettysburg. If anyone's caught wind of this, that's the first place they'd look. Tomorrow morning we'll have to do a 'get in and get out' to avoid any unwanted attention. This place is fine. We're only about an hour from the battlefield anyway. Tell you what, let me out here," Henry said as we drove up to the lobby. "Go ahead and park the van while I get us a room."

We stored our luggage, cleaned up, and then went next door to the twenty-four hour diner for an evening meal. Dr. Welles ordered the steak while I opted for something a little lighter. My head was a little too full of 'what ifs' and 'what abouts' to enjoy a heavy meal.

To take my mind off some of the matters at hand, I tried some conversation with Dr. Welles.

Most of our dialogue up until then had been business oriented. "Henry, what worries you most about your invention?"

"Oh Neil, there's so much to worry about when it comes to time travel. Let's take for instance, someone could go back in time, rob a bank, then return to modern time with his ill-gotten gains. Theoretically, if enough people did that sort of thing, what do you think would happen to our monetary system? What would that do to the victims of the crime? How would that affect the victims' future generations since that individual was now poor and couldn't provide for their family then?"

"Suppose the CIA goes back and kidnaps President Kennedy just before his fatal tour through downtown Dallas in 1963? What would that do to him? What would that do to that day in history and all of the participants? People would blame the Russians, then there goes World War Three. The list goes on and on."

"Remember what I said when we first started in this final phase of Project Sundial? Your past was somebody else's future. Your future is somebody's past. Everything in time fits together like the pieces of a giant puzzle, and not just from a human stand point."

"Then the question is whether we should be trying to disassemble that puzzle," I added.

"I think we could benefit by seeing *how* it all fits together. It could prove to be quite a learning tool for the purpose of observation. But to tear the fabric of time..." Dr. Welles contemplated without finishing the thought.

"Perhaps the feds were right to try and cover

such a thing up. I doubt mankind is intelligent enough to handle such a reality. But in all fairness, the government shouldn't ask a question when they're not prepared for the answer. You know, they tried that once a half century ago or so with the Philadelphia Experiment."

"I heard something about that once. What was the deal with that?"

"The Philadelphia Experiment, or Project Rainbow as it was called, dealt with time travel. Whether it was intended for that purpose or not, they won't say. So much of that is still classified. It's another one of those projects whose paper trail has been buried by the government. I believe they were dealing with super magnetism, probably for the purpose of throwing explosive mines off a ship's course during war time. You know, some of the great physicists of the time such as Nikola Tesla were involved with that project. Tesla basically walked out on it when the feds wanted to take things in a different direction."

"Some things never change, do they?" I said looking directly at Dr. Welles. "Just out of curiosity Henry, what would be the proper use for an invention such as this?"

"Well, the recording of many of our historic events has often been slanted due to the writers' prejudices. Many incidents in this country's past have now been politically corrected. They've swung the pendulum as far one way as it was to the other. Who knows what really happened during those times? We can only guess that it's somewhere in between, but that's only a guess. Wouldn't it be great to learn the truth sans bias? I mean, that's exactly what you'll be doing starting tomorrow."

"You know, you're right."

"Yes, but whatever mankind does with this technology in the future will be their business. Ours is to go as far as we can with it, then pass that information on to another generation and allow them to make up their own minds. Their destiny will be in their hands," Dr. Welles concluded. "That's the way research goes. A lot like life itself."

"True, but like anything new, it's scary. A brave new world it is, never to be the same again. Like you said, a lot like life itself. I suppose its all relative."

"But Neil, could you imagine the implications of this concept if it got into commercial hands?"

"It could be very profitable."

"For whom? I suppose trips could be sold so that people could go back and make amends with a long-gone relative. While some good could come of that, what would that do to the ancestors themselves? Would they see themselves as a failure? What if the traveler refused to return home? I guess that in life, we're supposed to make our own mistakes so that we can come up with our own solutions. If we had a 'do-over' for everything negative that occurred in our lives, how would we grow as an individual? Doesn't that make sense?"

"Uh, yeah, I see what you mean," I said with an uneasy delivery.

Sensing the change in my tone, Henry stopped eating his bread and asked, "Neil, you didn't do something you shouldn't have when you went back last week did you?"

"No I didn't, but I was this close," I said showing my thumb and index finger about a half of an inch apart. "I had the chance to talk with my dad who passed away about eight years ago. Like every father/son relationship, some issues were left unresolved. He went so suddenly. I was so close to picking up the receiver just to talk with him again, but I realized that I would probably end up trying to make amends to him for my thirty plus years of living in the two minutes I had available there. Pop probably wouldn't know what the hell I was talking about. There just wasn't enough time to tell him everything I wanted to tell him."

"And therein lies the dilemma. I think we've learned a lesson here. I guess the time to make your feelings known is now. We should use it wisely."

"Henry, with ideas like those, you should have been a minister."

"Yeah," he said between laughs, "like I've always said, if you can't impress 'em, B. S. 'em."

"Holier words were never spoken." I laughed in a mock philosophical tone.

Just then our main course arrived. I was quite at ease by that time. With my stomach a bit more settled, I went ahead and ordered a dessert for when we finished our main course. I came to the conclusion that this may end up being my last decent meal for a while.

"Henry," I asked, "Now that we know that there is more than the present dimension, have you given any thought to the possibility that there could be more out there than even you could fathom?"

"Oh, most certainly, I have all sorts of theories about that. I'll never be able to prove any of them though. Pass the salt please. I don't think

I'll live that long, but it's food for thought anyway. You know," Dr. Welles continued as he wiped his mouth between bites, "something like this discovery could open new doors to concepts we once regarded as quackery."

"Such as?"

"Well, take for instance psychic abilities. While I'll grant you that the field has its share of charlatans, the discovery of more than one dimension could lead to more research into the cognitive ability to see into the future, past, or what whatever else exists out there. My theory would be that some of these people can actually tune their mental receiver so that they're able to pick up visions or at least the emotional or physical vibrations from an individual. They may have adapted their auditory and visual abilities to accomplish what we will be doing through a physical means. It certainly isn't out of the realm of possibility, you'd have to admit."

"Do you mean someone like a channeler? You know, someone who works through another and brings forth conversations and ideas from long ago, or from some event that is yet to occur?"

"Absolutely, and, that information may not be coming from some other spiritual entity. It may be coming from the subjects themselves. It's often been theorized that one's bodily cells not only have a cellular memory, or DNA, but also historic retention. Those in the know may want to go as far as to say that one's soul itself carries a true historic recollection. Who knows, one's destiny may be scripted. Remember, one day, your future will be your past."

"So what's your thought about people who

are considered mentally ill? You know, people who reportedly hallucinate and hear voices. Could they be tapping into some other dimension?"

"Well, that may be stretching things a bit. Sometimes a dream is just a dream, as they say. Some things may be just as they appear, nothing more, nothing less. On the other hand, some day it may be discovered that those people are indeed ill. Not mentally, mind you, just ill. That person's receiver, whatever and wherever that is, may be picking up stray signals from any number of other dimensions. Their brains may be unable to separate the 'today' signals from all others, to the annoyance of that individual. I suppose enough of that over a person's lifetime could distract an individual rendering him unable to function. It's something to think about anyway. It's questions like those that drive the scientific fields."

"You may be on to something. I hadn't thought of it that way. There is one thing I was really curious about. I did an extensive amount of reading at the library about tomorrow's destination. I located some books about military ghost sightings. Perfectly sane people hear and see things around battlefields that aren't physically there. Some people also report smells around those grounds such as cigars, a big item on some of the older battlefields, or even worse, the smell of rotting flesh. These reports say that those odors have no apparent physical source. Possible?" I asked.

"I'm not sure about the former. There could always be some type of biological explanation for much of that. Some people see, hear, and smell only what they're open to. They discount all else. However, you have to remember that the universe, while being orderly, isn't perfect. It's merely a system of checks and balances that benefits the majority. Just because the dimensions are divided doesn't mean that some information doesn't leak over into another. Not even time is of a solid property. I've found, theoretically mind you, that time has constant checks and openings. Why should its make-up be any different than that of most other processes in the universe?"

"So why can't part of a past or future event may make it to our eyes or ears? We're all receivers, if you will. We can, on occasion, pick up a stray signal, I'd surmise. Maybe that's what deja vu is—a belch in time from the other side if you will."

"Wow, which makes sense hearing it come from you. Couple that with what I've learned these last couple of months makes me believe that we've only scratched the surface when it comes to learning about the ways and means of the universe."

"Oh, most certainly, but of course I can't prove any of my theories. It's all purely speculation on my part. I'm not really qualified to answer most of those questions. I'll leave that research for others to ponder. I've done my bit. I mean, who knows if the vision of a deceased relative is a moment from another dimension seeping through the boundary of time? If a person is grieving over the loss of a loved one, perhaps that tunes the individual's receiver to the vibration of their dearly departed."

"But, to attempt to answer your question, in your readings you probably came across ghost stories where an entity is observed repeating the same action in the same place, occurrence after occurrence."

"Exactly."

"That moment may have hit a glitch in time's progression and continues to stutter itself across the time spectrum. That particular moment, for whatever natural reason, has no fixed mode of existence. That explanation certainly makes sense, but we'll probably never know for sure. Like I said, the universe is ordered, not perfect."

"Perhaps we'll find out eventually. Maybe someday, whether we're in this plane or not," I said with raised eyebrows. "Sounds as if a lot of things we refer to as weird or imaginational, may indeed have some basis in truth."

"I think that's safe to say. That's one thing my studies in religious theology taught me: Never discount that which you cannot explain."

"Nicely put. That's what helped bring about the success of Project Sundial, no?"

"Sure, despite all of the governmental roadblocks," he said followed by a look over his shoulder at the van just a few hundred feet away. "At least this will be one less thing in life that will have to be explained. We'll know the answer. Well, O.K.," he corrected himself, "we're still in the process of discovering that one."

"As far as my formerly stated concepts go, don't discount the power of the hoax. There's a lot of different phenomenon out there, and many too many occurrences. Also, don't underestimate the power of the bottle," he chuckled.

"Yes, like the UFO people?" I joined in.

"For the most part, but don't necessarily make that out to be a blanket statement."

"How's that?"

"The process we have here," Henry said referring to the ATM, "relies upon electrical activity within the body, right? There have been reports of UFOs being spotted by aircraft. You've heard of them; shortly after the discovery, everything electrical within the plane, including the compass, starts going haywire. Next thing you know, the spotter plane disappears from the radar screen. Now I'll grant you, legitimate reports of this kind are rare, but there may be a few with some credibility. UFOs may be nothing more than airborne ATMs of the future for all we know."

"It all fits."

"Well, fit is only one criteria. A pair of parts may fit, but they may not belong together. What I'm trying to say is don't label me a UFO junkie. I'm far from it. But, those reports do give us something to chew on. Speaking of which, I've about had enough," Henry said as he leaned back in his chair and wedged a thumb between his stomach and his belt.

"Yeah, well I'm going to pack away as much as I can just in case rations on the upcoming trip are less than palatable. So, if the waitress asks if I'm going to eat that second dessert here or take it with me, I'll tell her I intend to do both."

"Speaking of the trip, we had better go up to the room and check the supplies to make sure we have everything we need. If we don't, there's still time to run out and pick up some things. We don't want to scurry around in the morning trying to find a place open. There probably won't be many decent places open at that hour anyway."

"And when is the launch scheduled for?" I

inquired.

"You'll leave by the dawn's first light," he answered.

"How appropriate."

As we walked across the parking lot I asked, "Is the van locked, Henry?"

"Yes, for now. We're too close to victory to let it slip away. I plan to sleep out there over night."

"You're kidding?"

"Would you trust your life to a mechanical device that someone could have tinkered with all night long?"

"Good point. You had better stand guard tonight," I stood corrected.

We entered the motel room and I said, "I'll sit here by the window. I can keep an eye on the van from here. You can stay up in the room until snooze time anyway. We'll see what's on the tube."

Dr. Welles went ahead and took the opportunity to partake of a shower. While he was in the process of drying, he alertly asked, "Neil, have you given any thought of what you're going to wear out there on the battlefield? You can't wear those jeans," he said pointing to my current blue attire. "The South will think that you're from the North. You'd be a sitting duck for their sharp shooters. You can't go with tan or neutral khakis either. You'd look too much like a Southern soldier. You'd lose either way."

"Doc, I'm way ahead of you. While you were monkeying with the ATM all week..."

"Monkeying?!"

"Dickering, toying, fiddling, adjusting, you know what I mean. Anyway, I took it upon myself to put an outfit together. I thought of the same dilemma you just brought up. I went over to the Playhouse Theater and picked up this," I said lifting a black frock coat out of my bag.

"What the hell is that? You'll look like the Wizard of Oz," Dr. Welles said while looking over the knee-length duster.

"I think that's what it's from. Anyway, I'll tell you what it isn't. It isn't gray and it isn't blue. Actually, I picked this one in particular because it looked similar to what a Civil War era photographer would wear out in the field. It will kind of match the camera we built."

"Yes, you're right. Good choice, I like it."

"I'm going to top it off with a pair of dark brown jeans that I haven't worn in years. This will be as good as any opportunity to get rid of them," I affirmed as I continued to dig through my bag. "I also brought a couple of these cheap plastic fold-up ponchos for a dollar just in case. It pours down right after the battle, you know."

"Ah yes, God's tears, as I've heard that referred to."

"I just hope that I'm not there that long. I shouldn't be, but if I am I hope it's raining so hard that no one notices what this thing is made of."

"Good thought. Be on the lookout for that. Have a back up story in case anyone asks."

"Hopefully I won't even be in that situation. If all goes as planned, I'm to leave the morning before. By the way, you will remember to come back and pick me up, won't you?"

"If I'm not otherwise engaged," came a shot from Henry as he looked off into space.

"Boy, you're reassuring. In reality, I'll hang

out until you show. You can't get rid of me that easy."

"I'll be there on the morning of the fourth. You be too. From fireworks there to fireworks here, if you don't show up..." Dr. Welles joking conversation suddenly turned solemn. Henry was thinking of the authentic possibility. "Just show up, OK.?"

"I will if you will," I assured him. "If I'm not there, go up to the Visitor Center and check the roster of Civil War casualties. If I'm on there, well..."

"Not funny."

"No, I know. I'm just trying not to think of any unfortunate outcomes."

"Neil, are you really prepared for what you're about to experience? Are you ready to witness 50,000 casualties' right before your eyes? You'll see the loss of limbs, decapitations, you'll see entire bodies explode into a cloud of red mist, animals maimed and suffering. Worst of all, there isn't anything you can do about it, nor should you try."

"I know, but how can anyone prepare for something like that? I'll just have to convince myself that all of those soldiers have long since passed. They're merely the visual manifestations of what once was. This is their time to live and die, not mine I hope."

"Agreed. That's a very healthy attitude."

"Every time I think of when dad and I were at the spot where great-great grandpa allegedly committed his crime, I can't help but remember how I could almost feel his presence. Henry, I have to know. The still and video cameras will fulfill your part of the trip. I'm going to take care of my part of the trip for my own peace of mind."

"Fine, if you can find out what happened without going into actual battle, so much the better. Don't you dare venture on to the field. You'll be torn to ribbons. Too many were."

"Yes I know. Keep low and out of the way."

We both watched the Pirates/Phillies game until the ten o'clock newscast. With that Dr. Welles said, "Well, I had better hit the van. Three forty-five in the morning comes all too quick. I'm going to take a comforter and a pillow down there to create some semblance of a sleeper, if you don't mind."

"Exit through the back door so the clerk doesn't spot you."

I didn't sleep much that night. When my alarm went off at 3:45 A.M., a tear almost rolled out of my eye. I wasn't ready to get up. It was just too damn early for anything. I realized, however, that there was no compromise with this situation. In my bare feet, I stumbled down to the parking lot, nodded at the night clerk as I went, and pounded on the van to wake up Dr. Welles. After some time, a God-awful looking face emerged to window level. It alarmed me at first. It was too early for that.

"Geeze Henry, don't you ever look good in the morning? You look like a wreck."

"I just got to sleep a little bit ago," he groaned. "Please don't tell me it's quarter 'til four. Now leave me alone!"

"Come on Henry, time to get ready. Come on up to the room and splash some water on your face. You've got all tomorrow, well today, to sleep. I'll finish loading the van."

Dr. Welles performed a quick splash and

dash as I climbed into my photographer's uniform.

"I don't know if they'll mistake me for a photographer or not. I'm unarmed and have a camera, so who could argue?"

"You'll find out. They could take you for a spy from the other side."

"Thanks, I didn't need that. Anyway, photographers pretty much had the run of the place during the Civil War from what I've read. I guess they operated under the Freedom of the Press or something of that nature. No one really gave them much trouble or hampered their efforts to any degree from what I can tell. Yet no photographer that I heard of went into battle armed with a camera. Those box cameras were too impractical for battlefield photography. It took so long to expose a shot that all they'd end up with would be one large blur. Plus, those devices were too damn big and clumsy to carry into combat. I've seen a few photos taken of a battle from a long distance, but those shots were usually obscured by heavy smoke. Not a lot of good action photos made it out of the Civil War, until now that is."

"Uh, let's try and keep it that way. Don't venture in too close. That's why you have a long lens."

We left a little after four AM. The stars were still out so it might as well have been nighttime. We had to do our work as early as possible. We didn't want to draw any unneeded attention, and it was all unneeded. Dr. Welles was doing the driving. He said he knew where he was going. I'm not sure that I could say the same.

"While you were at work last week, I located

the perfect place in which to launch," Dr. Welles stated.

"I wondered where all of those miles came from on that old beat-up truck. You're a trusting fool."

"There's a picnic grove right off Emmitsburg Road on Warfield Ridge. It's part of the tour route. Being tree enshrouded, no one will see us there this time of day," the doctor declared as we drove down State Route Fifteen. "Do you have your info handy? Go over it and remember it."

I reached under my seat and produced a box containing a few files and some old hand written notes. "Geeze, I feel like I'm cramming for an exam."

"Let's hope you pass this one with flying colors. Fate isn't grading on a curve today. What do you have on your great-great grandfather?"

"The family kept fairly good records. Let me see," I said as I produced the file. I clicked on the dome light and began to read "Um, Jonathan Gates...oh here we are. Jonathan Gates was born in 1838 just outside of Lizella, Georgia. He married at the tender young age of nineteen to Christiana Patrick who happened to be eighteen years old at that time. He and his wife had two sons and a daughter. His family, along with his widowed mother, lived in the Lizella area between the Echeconnee and the Tobesofkee Creeks."

"Who-what?"

"I think that's how they're pronounced. That's what it says here anyway. I don't have a rural street name from back then so that's the best I could do there."

"Any photos?"

"Not of Jonathan Gates."

"That will hurt your effort a bit."

"I know. There is one of his widowed wife and children taken when the boys appeared to be in their mid-teens. The taller one is my great grandfather, pretty typical." I said as I showed Henry the faded, sepia toned picture. "I guess photos were so expensive back then, especially to a family as poor as this one, that they were considered a luxury."

Continuing on I read, "It says here that shortly after 1863, with dear Jonathan forever gone, the Gates family became quite destitute. The only real possessions the family owned, other than the property, were their farm animals. They lived off of them, it says here, and sold the rest. That enterprise was wiped out when an offshoot of Sherman's men came through on their march to the sea. Apparently Sherman's men had a need for livestock as well."

Finishing up that file and producing another from the stack, I resumed my recitation. "Anyway, back to great-great grandpa. From what I could gather, Jonathan didn't have to be inducted into the Army of Northern Virginia. He could have claimed either an economic hardship or an exemption due to the fact that he was the sole surviving able-bodied male of his family at that time. On a farm, that's a hardship in and of itself, but he enlisted anyway."

"A patriot?" asked Dr. Welles.

"More than likely he was trying to support his family. There was a lot of that going on at that time. Even the Confederate Army paid Jonathan more than he could make around home."

"Is that it?" Dr. Welles inquired.

"On the Gates' background, yes. It does say that the entire Gates family was well thought of around those parts. It says here that Jonathan was 'a real help to all, an honest and hard working member of the community'."

"Doesn't sound like a man who'd blow away his general."

"True, but I guess war does things to a man."

"By the way, who was it said that he popped?"

"His name was Paul J. Semmes, Brigadier General. He was in charge of some of the Georgia troops. I had a rather difficult time locating information on him as well."

"Oh really? You'd think a brigadier general who served at Gettysburg would garner more type than just a footnote."

"You would. I found more information on his brother Raphael. I guess that man was quite a Confederate navel commander. He supposedly sank seventy union vessels before his 'Alabama' was shot out from under him."

"Bye bye 'Bama."

"About all I could find on Brigadier General Semmes was that after being wounded at Gettysburg, he was shipped back to Martinsburg where he died about a week later."

"Wait a minute, I thought that was Stonewall Jackson."

"You're close. If I remember correctly, Jackson had his shoulder accidentally blown off by friendly fire and died about a week or so later from pleurisy. Come to think of it, that incident did occur almost exactly one month earlier."

"Sounds like deja vu all over again."

"Another one of your theories? Anyway, about all that I located on Semmes was that he was once a prominent businessman in Georgia. He was active in the local militia," I said as I continued to flip through my notes. "He took command in March of 1862, fought in campaigns such as Antietam, Fredericksburg, and Chancellorsville. He performed well in all, it says. Just biographical info."

"That's impressive enough. He sounds like a good guy. So the question remains, why did great-great grand pop rub him out?"

"That's the million dollar question. From what I've read in the family lore, I'm not convinced that he did. That's what I intend to find out. It says here, after the alleged incident, an injured Gates tried to desert. He was captured fleeing confederate troops about seven miles south of Gettysburg. A scuffle ensued," I reported as I read my aged copy. "Gates was captured unarmed, treated for his wounds, and then sent on to the next encampment at Culpeper Court-House where he was handed over to the proper authorities sometime around the end of July. They ended up sending him to Hunter's Chapel, Virginia, where a military court was convened."

"What charges did they bring him up on?"

"Well, he was charged initially with desertion, but it says here that shortly thereafter those charges were upgraded to murder when he reached his military jail. He later was convicted of desertion, conduct prejudicial to good order, and voluntary manslaughter involving a friendly superior officer. He was also dishonorably discharged from the Army of Northern Virginia."

"What was the point of that last move? Didn't they already have enough to send him to the chair?"

"I'm guessing that it was standard operating procedure. What the family did write was that it prevented them from receiving any soldier benefits Jonathan or his heirs would have been entitled to. I'm sure it was a typical army course of action."

"Great, nothing like adding insult to injury."

"Yeah, and if that wasn't enough, his punishment was, let me see, I had it here a second ago," I said sifting through my notes. "Oh yes, here it is. He was ordered to be "shot to death by musket"."

"A firing squad?" Dr. Welles asked.

"Sounds like it. The sentence was carried out on Monday, November thirtieth, at sunrise. Some Thanksgiving that family had."

"Wow Neil, it sounds like your great-great grandfather was something between Benedict Arnold and Charles Manson."

"It sure doesn't sound good. A note here in the family Bible said that the Gates family didn't believe the charges. Jonathan's mother and wife appealed his sentence to President Davis but to no avail."

"So the sentence was carried out?"

"Apparently so. It says that, thanks to the generosity of a Mr. Mueller, I don't know who that was, Jonathan's body was trained home. His remains were interred in the village cemetery on December fourteenth of that year. A stone, also a gift from Mr. Mueller, was ordered to be placed. I'm guessing that he might have been a family friend or neighbor."

"Or perhaps a future suitor."

After that recitation, I needed a mental break. I finished munching down on the do-nuts and orange juice we picked up at the gas station's mini mart. We continued our trip until we hit the town square of Gettysburg around ten minutes past five. A quaint little town: Most of the buildings look as if they were built around Civil War time or thereabouts. They still held up rather well. None of small shops had opened for the business day yet. We exited the town proper coming out on the south side of the city on Steinwehr Avenue. We stayed on that track as Steinwehr branched into Emmitsburg Road.

"Our spot is about a mile up on the left," Dr. Welles reported as he slowed down.

Now my guts were really in an uproar while my palms were turning cold and clammy. I realized that I had reached my Rubicon on this extraordinary journey.

I looked over to my left out Dr. Welles' window. As the sky was lightening for the morning, I could see the field of Pickett's charge and the angle where the few Confederate troops pierced the unions defense. To the right of that area I could see the silhouetted outline of the Copse of Trees, the point of convergence for the Southern troops. Shortly thereafter, we passed the Codori barn so close that one could almost reach out and touch the dark, aging siding. A few moments later we drove by the infamous Peach Orchard and what remained of the old Rose farm. I took a long and hard look at those areas. That's where some of the fiercest fighting went on, where most of the action concerning Jonathan Gates took place, and that was the area I was to concentrate on. In that sector, the battle surged and flowed like the ripples of a flag in the breeze. Land was won, lost, and then won once again. That's where Jonathan Gates' future was decided.

My thought process was interrupted when Dr. Welles said, "O.K., right up here is where we're going."

Spotting the location, I commented, "We're a little close in, aren't we Henry? We're right on the battlefield. I'm liable to get picked off before I even exit the ATM at this distance."

"Naw, don't worry, there should be no fighting in this sector on the day that you'll be arriving. The best-case scenario was to drop you off at the Eisenhower farm. That's out of the line of fire, and yet it's in the vicinity the troop's eventual encampment. Unfortunately, that area is off limits to public traffic. That would make it a bit difficult for us, lawn care van or not. Hopefully, if history has any truth to it, most of the troops will have retreated from this area by the time you're ready to leave as well."

"We're cutting it a bit close."

We took a left turn on to West Confederate Avenue when Dr. Welles let loose with a "Damn!"

"What's wrong, Henry?"

"They have the road gate closed and locked." Indeed a wooden park gate was closed blocking our access to the picnic grove. There didn't appear to be a safe way around the impediment. We drove right up to the gate. I almost thought Henry was going to run it, but instead he stopped and we got out to consider our options.

"It will probably stay locked until sun-up,

or six AM. It's nearly sun-up now," observed Dr. Welles. "We could break through here, but that would draw too much attention. Plus, I'd never be able to return to pick you up."

"Then we don't want to do that," I agreed.

"No," he affirmed. Henry looked around and said, "I guess we'll just have to make do. I don't like being so close to the road. With the crowds of tourists being as heavy as they are on the battle's anniversary, not to mention the July fourth weekend upon us, our cause won't be helped any."

"Well, I guess all we can do is work as fast as we safely can," I suggested. Going around and opening the back doors to the van I said, "Grab the other side of the ATM, Doctor. We'll pull it out and set it...where?"

While gripping the other side of the craft, Dr. Welles made an unrelated observation. "You're going to burn up out there in that outfit," he said referring to a black coat on a ninety plus degree day.

When we had the entire ship out of the van, I steered the conversation back on track. "Henry, will you have any trouble loading and unloading this baby when I'm not here?"

"I don't think so. It's light enough, not to mention that I have Ed's ramps in the back with all of the rest of his junk. I'll tell you what, let's head over to that mowed out area near that stone wall. Try and pick out a registration point that will be easy to find today as well as yesterday. Don't forget that landmark. Remember, the tether has only about a ten foot radius with which it can send out a matching signal to the wireless LAN on the laptop. The laptop will signal the ATM."

As we marched through the damp morning grass I asked, "How about right over here? This area probably hasn't changed since the war. We'll put the ATM parallel to that large boulder over there," I suggested. "I doubt that anyone moved that pebble recently. It will be an excellent benchmark."

We carried the transport over to the wall and I remarked, "Here is fine. I'll check out the reliability of the landscape when I get to the other side."

We spent the next few minutes setting up and looking out for traffic. The cars were few and far between this time of morning. Our only other concern was being discovered by a ranger. So far, so good.

Dr. Welles ran an electrical cord from the van's generator to the boulder housing his console. He connected the base to its power source. "Ah ha," he commented, "we're in business. Now, our readings should hold true throughout the entire trip," Dr. Welles instructed. "Radiation from the sun causes radio waves to change every twenty-five days or so. That change matches the rotation of the sun. I think that we'll be able to make that window, but don't dawdle. Return at the arranged time. We can't risk some sort of quantum fluctuation"

Back at the laptop console Dr. Welles reported, "O.K. now, when I get the readings up to speed here, we'll synchronize the tether with the ATM's board. If both units aren't in synch, neither can act as a sender nor receiver. If that were to occur, nobody would go anywhere. These two together act as a single unit. If there's even a single glitch within the system, you may make it back, but to what time God only knows."

"Then what would we do?"

"Neil, we'll have one shot at it," he continued. "You'll send the ATM back empty. If nothing else, I'll know that you made it safely. When it comes time for you to depart from there, you'll have to hit the tether's button at exactly 05:30:00 hours. I'll be on this end implementing the same procedure. When the signals mate, the ATM will return to you. Don't waste clicks on the tether's button, please. We don't know how much power is left in either unit. Remember, this is a one shot deal."

"That's reassuring," I answered.

"No, that's just the way it is. You know that I can't risk sending the unit back on its own. If you're not in the right place at the right time, the craft could be tampered with or destroyed by whoever comes upon it."

"What happens if I can't get the ship to come back to get me or what if the ATM makes it back but can't return me to modern time?" I asked the legitimate question.

"Call AAA."

"Not funny, Henry."

"Hey look Neil, I've got to get serious with you here," he said as he stopped what he was doing. "You're going into an area of great hostility, we know that. But you're also going farther across time's spectrum than has ever been attempted. You're going to stay there for a couple of days dodging bullets. The longest we've ever had anyone stay at a destination then return was the five minutes you did last week. We don't know if you'll lose a second of modern time for every hour you're gone. We're only guessing here. God forbid that there's a time lag or miscalculation. You know my history on that subject. You could end up in this area on July second rather than the first. You would wind up in the middle of the battle. You could end up losing your life or the use of the ATM forever. This entire journey is uncharted territory. It's so damned rushed!"

"Yes, I understand all too well."

"Let me finish. Your attempt to summon the return module after an absence of fifty to one hundred hours is, well let me put it this way; as much confidence as I have in this undertaking, I'd have to say on a scientific level, the odds of you pulling this off are against you, brother."

"Henry, I know that any number of things could happen to us on this project. Hell, you could be involved in a fender bender accident that could damage the ATM and render it useless. Or, you could be delayed if the van develops engine trouble the day of the return. Anything can happen. Henry, I have confidence in your abilities. This ship is a testament to your fine work."

"Yeah well, I've said that before. Let's just keep our fingers crossed. One thing I have to remind you, when you get there, don't change a thing. You don't partake of the battle. If you shoot someone, even in self-defense, that person would have no future generations. One of those generations may be alive today. What would happen to them? I don't pretend to have all of the answers here. This whole science is still so new to all of us. We're just not sure."

"So what you're saying is, if somebody comes at me with a loaded rifle, I'm a dead man?"

"Let's hope that it doesn't come to that. We

just haven't had the time to sift through all of the ramifications of our actions and reactions. I hate throwing this mission together so darned fast. Damn feds. So to be on the safe side, don't help any of the wounded. That will be a difficult task, I know." Getting a bit more reflective, Dr. Welles looked out over the battlefield and added, "Neil, you're going to see an awful lot of suffering out there."

"I know. And I know that it won't be like in the movies where you hear the ricochet, then a man falls dead virtually unscarred. That's a rarity in real war."

"You've read your history rather well." A half serious and half joking Dr. Welles then exclaimed, "And for God's sake, don't go and tell General Lee of the folly of Pickett's Charge! You're only there to observe. To quote scripture, as you say, "History must speak for itself. A historian is content if he has been able to shed more light." That's your job. Enough said."

I knew exactly what he meant. While almost laughing to relieve my tension, I replied, "Got it. I'll play the part of a loner."

"Well, let's get you loaded up here then. You've got a lot of junk to take along with you. I hope we can cram it all in there."

"Yes, but I tried to limit it to two cameras and a bag of essentials," I reported as I climbed in to the craft and attempted to situate myself.

"Such as?"

"Well for one, I have a small Civil War replica canteen of fresh emergency water. I have the feeling that the water there will probably give me dysentery. I have the folded up ponchos I already showed you. I'm also taking a note pad and a pen to record my personal observations."

"What's that big wallet doing in your pocket?"

"I'm taking a few Confederate dollar bills. They may buy me something essential along the way."

"You're not taking that, are you?" Dr. Welles asked of a candy bar in the bottom of my bag.

"Sure, I'll need that for quick energy, just in case. You know, when I need that sugar buzz."

"It will be melted long before noon, you know."

"I know. That's why I wrapped it up so it won't get all over everything. It won't be too good, just functional. Well, I guess that's everything."

"What's that?"

"A bottle of Jack Daniel's. What money won't buy me, perhaps this will. Hey, whiskey was at a premium back then. A few gulps of this can buy me a lot of information, or perhaps a desperately needed meal. Our fighting boys deserve only the best, I always say."

"Or a bracer for yourself, huh? Look, just remember not to imbibe right before your trip back home. That could play havoc with your body's electrical system. We saw what happened with the hydrazine sulfate." Dr. Welles paused briefly before saying, "Hey, before you leave, I just want to reiterate what I said earlier; you're one crazy S.O.B., you know that?"

"Crazier than this tin can's inventor? Hell, I'm no crazier than Lindberg. No one thought that he'd be able to make it across the ocean in one piece. There's no major difference. His was a journey across an impossible distance while mine is just a journey across time."

"Yes, but Lindy didn't have anybody trying to shoot him down, did he?"

"Henry, I remembered a quote from English class that went something like, "It is good to have an end to a journey towards; but it is the journey that matters in the end." Not bad, huh? I can quote scripture as well. It fits, doesn't it?"

"Well put," Dr. Welles said with a tilt of the head and mock applause. "You've learned your lessons well, I guess, so it's time for your graduation," Dr. Welles said as he passed our remaining time together by looking down at the ground. Neither one of us knew how or when to say good-bye. That statement could, in the end, become a final reality. Our schedule was about to decide that for us.

"Well?"

"Well?"

"Yes, well. By your clock there, we have one minute until launch. Today is Saturday, July first. When you go back to 1863, the day will be Wednesday, same date, just for your info."

Dr. Welles moved the cowl over to the side of the ATM. Before fitting it into place, he concluded his farewell by saying, "You take care of yourself, Neil Gates. I want you back here in one piece. Keep a low profile."

"You do the same," I answered in a barely audible voice.

Then, in a rare display of emotion, Dr. Welles put his arms around my shoulders in a make-shift hug and patted my back while saying, "God speed, son," with his voice cracking slightly. I silently mouthed the words "thank-you" back to him. That's all I could get out.

That was the last either of us spoke. With his hands slightly shaking, Dr. Welles placed the protective covering over the craft, watched me secure it into place, then moved over to the console.

No words were needed during the launch sequence. Everything had been double and triple checked. That's the best we could do under the circumstances. By now we knew the procedure by heart. After attaching the electrodes to my temples, I checked the cycles per second increase as it ended up on 7.00000027216. I watched as the numbers on the panel clock counted down past 05:29:40 on its way to the 05:30:00 mark. One last time I looked at Dr. Welles, and he at me. We both looked a bit worried, both for our own reasons. Dr. Welles gave a thumbs-up to me while all I could muster was a nod of the head in return.

I secured my hands in place and moved the rest of my extremities around making sure that full bodily contact was being made. The green light on the panel proclaimed my actions a success. I stared straight ahead as the countdown moved from :03, :02, then to :01. I felt and heard the all encompassing, low vibratory tone. I gripped the armrest for all I was worth. As the low hum settled after a second or two, I noticed the surrounding landscape beginning to fade from my visual senses. Then with a flash, all faded to black.

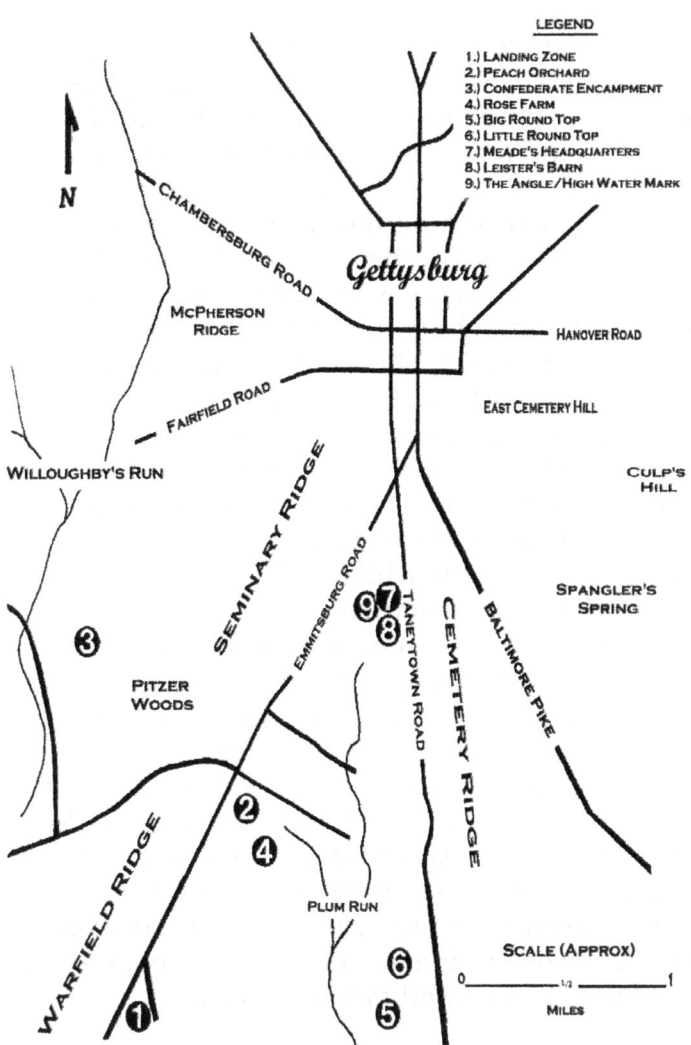

Chapter Seven
Opening Old Wounds

"History is worth reading when it tells us truly what the attitude towards life was in the past."
DOROTHY CANFIELD FISHER

I was surrounded by darkness and an almost euphoric unawareness of my sense of being. The sensation reminded me of that funny feeling one receives when driving over a soft rise in the road. During this period, I felt separated from my body, yet at the same time I knew I was still a complete physical and spiritual being. I'm not sure how long that state lasted. It didn't seem the same as the couple of seconds that appeared accompanied me on my ten-year recess of a week ago, but I couldn't be sure. At this point, it was as if time had become immaterial. That calmness, those thoughts, and my feelings were interrupted by a sudden jolt. I don't know if that impact was of a physical or mental origin. My darkness quickly lifted as I once again became in tune with my physical surroundings. Feeling as if I had just awakened from a deep sleep, I had to take a few moments to reacquaint myself with my situation and whereabouts.

The sense of both excitement and doom hit me all at once as I remembered who I was, where I was, and what purpose I was to fulfill. Recalling what Dr. Welles said about the possibility of the ATM's readings misjudging time and dropping me in the middle of the second rather than the first day of fighting, I quickly checked the panel's readouts followed by a visual scan of the surrounding landscape.

If the numbers were correct, I had arrived at 5:30 AM on July 1, 1863. It had worked. Upon removing the ship's cover and placing it on the ground next to the ATM, I took a deep breath and looked outward over the battlefield. I viewed a scene not too dissimilar from that which I just left. Studying further, I noticed that the tree lines were a bit different, yet not contrary from what they would become. The street that Dr. Welles and I turned down from Emmitsburg Road on our way to the picnic grove was still there, but now it was little more than a rutted dirt and gravel path that seemed to narrow just before my current location.

Directly in front of my line of vision I could just make out the peak of Little Round Top, sight of an almost futile stand off between the two battling foes. It really hadn't changed very much except the monuments that now grace its summit had yet to be awarded. I also noticed that there was no traffic noise to be heard, just the sounds of morning crickets and a few early birds. Could this be the calm before the storm, I wondered. Did the ATM nail it or miss it?

The area seemed so nice and peaceful. The air smelled damp, but country fresh. The scent of manure slipped past my nostrils as did a whiff of the honeysuckle that had woven itself into the rock wall just to my right. It was difficult for me to believe that this beautiful countryside would soon become the scene of carnage of the worst kind.

The Civil War, I thought, where 660,000

casualties resulted from both detonations and disease. Adjusted to the times and population, that would be equivalent to a war of today taking five million of our soldiers—almost one hundred times the number of U.S. casualties from the Viet Nam conflict. In today's climate, that would be akin to a holocaust whose memory would never be allowed to die. I guess that's why we have yet to relinquish the horror of America's War Between the States.

Reality then hit me, and I was reminded that I was to send the ATM back to Dr. Welles. I set all of my belongings out on the ground next to the craft's cowl. I managed to free a leg from its cramped quarters and swing it over the side to its new residence. I braced myself on the sides of the ship and pulled my person out altogether. My feet rested on the still unadulterated Pennsylvanian soil.

"Well, here I am," was all I could think of to say. It was hardly a 'One small step for man' speech.

The earth on which I placed my footing was real, firm, and bona fide. I proceeded to take a personal inventory of myself to make sure that everything was as it should be. I did feel a bit flushed and a little 'fuzz-headed,' but other than that, everything appeared in its appropriate place. The ATM looked none-the-worse for wear either.

Standing back, I noticed that, although some of the trees were differently placed, the boulder and most of the stone wall I was in between were at least in their rightful positions. I gathered my equipment up and set it all to the side of the large rock. I was trying not to think about what I was doing because deep down I knew the ramifications of my actions. I didn't want the opportunity to talk myself out of my intentions. Before I placed the canopy back over the craft, I pulled a prepared note from my pocket and placed it on the seat for Dr. Welles. Simply stated it read, "Don't worry—Neil." That would let Henry know that without a doubt I had successfully completed the first step on the 'journey of a thousand miles,' as he used to put it.

With much apprehension, I hit the button on the panel that would send the ATM back across the vortex of the time spectrum. I removed the tether and placed it in my pocket. It would truly be my lifeline. Having finished that sequence of events, I replaced the canopy and merely stood back.

The same action I observed taking place at my home a week ago was now repeating itself. I continued to stare at the area that the craft once occupied. The grass in that spot was still matted down, so I guessed this wasn't all a dream.

That feeling of doom hit me once again, for I realized that for all intents and purposes, I was alone one hundred and forty years earlier than I should be. At least when I traveled back ten years, if I had become stranded, I would still have been able to function quite well in that world. I would even be able to win a few bar bets on the World Series. But this was different, far different.

Where do I go from here, I wondered. I hadn't planned that far in advance. I guess I would have to wing it for the next several hours until things started to heat up.

Just then I heard a muffled thunder, not dissimilar from the reentry 'thump' of the ATM. I stood back and watched the area where I had just disembarked. Nothing. Then it occurred to me that the rumble's site of origin was of a northeasterly direction from my present position. That was no ATM, I thought. For all I knew, that may have been the beginning to the greatest military battle on American soil.

    I took the rain poncho out of my pack as it was still drizzling a bit this morning. I picked up my things and moved up the hundred or so yards towards Emmitsburg Road. Once there, I wasn't quite sure where I was to go. I did know that the real fighting wouldn't start for a few hours, and it would begin far north of me. I remembered what Dr. Welles said but I wanted to be close enough to the fighting, yet far out enough out to be safe. However I wasn't sure if there was anything such as 'safe' in this town once the lead started flying.

    I stopped at the intersection on Emmitsburg Road and looked for a place to set up for the day. I just stood there for a moment. Now that I was out of the trees I had a much better overall view of the area. To the south I saw nothing but an occasional farm bordered by the muddy road. To my north, I could just barely make out the skyline of the town of Gettysburg. Preceding that municipality by about a mile was the Peach Orchard. It didn't appear to be the same grove I passed on my way in this morning. It was now quite a bit larger. To the right of that area, I could see a bit of the Rose farm, its roofs jutting out from the glen. At this moment of great indecision, I took the road to the right and ventured northward towards the Sherfy farm area. Once again it struck me a bit odd that a place as peaceful as this countryside appeared at the present time would end up as the recipient of a blood bath.

I walked for some time down the mud and gravel road until I was parallel to the Peach Orchard. I paused for a moment, and then decided to go over and inspect one of my future checkpoints. It looked a bit different than when I had visited that site as a child. I estimated that today's acre of trees was once two to three times that size. The Park Service has done a great job in keeping the area in as original shape as possible, though.

Walking up through the orchard, I noted that the grass was much longer than it's allowed to be today. The trunks and the finely manicured branches of my day gave way to a more 'au natural' look. The developing peaches were little more than golf ball sized, green, and not fit to be consumed by anyone other than a desperate, hungry man.

I dug my thumbnail into the skin of one of the fruits and tasted the essence. My thumbnail left an abrasion in the produce and the juice tasted quite bitter. That's when I concluded that all of this was real, I was indeed here, and it wasn't a dream.

I abandoned the corner grove, crossed the fence, and walked west down Wheatfield Road that passed near the Sherfy farm. Even though I was some distance from the farm house, I could hear what appeared to be some day-to-day activities going on in and around the homestead. I thought it was a bit out of place since I was led to believe that most people in the outlying areas had been warned of a possible impending attack. I didn't stop to see if the sounds were those of the residents or of looters. If it was the title holder, how could I approach and inform them that their house was about to be overrun, their possessions destroyed, and their barn burned to the ground.

I continued for about a quarter of a mile down the path which would eventually become Millerstown Road. I stopped for a moment and looked over my surroundings once again. This looks as good as any, I thought, as I veered off of the roadway near a small outbuilding, cleared the fence, and then started north along the ridge through the damp grass. It was the general area where Warfield and Seminary Ridges converged, depending on which map one consulted.

Actually, calling them 'ridges' was a bit of a misnomer. That area was as flat as the rest of the surrounding terrain, but compared to the territory just west of there, they were indeed elevated.

I proceeded past the small building towards a tract that would serve as my temporary post. There was a gap amongst the trees that would offer me protection from the yet to emerge sunshine, however it would still provide me with an opening allowing me to keep an eye the action to my front.

Inside that gap was strewn a hand full of man-sized boulders. This entire region was littered with them. I went over to one, took a seat to plan my future action, and waited for something to happen.

It was now roughly eight AM, and the sun was still in competition with the clouds to see which would be victorious for the day. While having time to think, I began to wonder if I had indeed made it to the right day and the right time. Other than the shot heard earlier, which could have been a hunter's mark for all I knew, I saw or heard no trace of what I had expected. The fact that there was some activity around the Sherfy farm also raised some questions in my mind. Might I be at the right date on the wrong year?

Another thought crossed my mind. I had yet to make any human contact on this my third voyage across time. What happens if I can see into their time but they can't sense me? Dr. Welles and I never considered that possibility. I reached down and pulled at a one and a half foot long blade of grass. It squeaked right out of its base. I looked it over and decided that if I could physically impact a weed, or a peach as I did in the orchard, then I guess I would be a physical reality to humans as well.

I sat on the rock reviewing my historic notes when I heard a muffled, yet thunderous roar. Once again it reminded me of the grand finale during a distant fireworks display. I jumped to my feet and instinctively stared towards that area of town but to no avail. From where I was stationed, I wouldn't be able to see much anyway. Be that as it may, the noise, while five to six miles away, emanated from my northwest. I now knew, according to my notes, that the battle of Gettysburg was officially under way, and it sounded as if there was no end in sight. I'm sure many of the participants felt the same. I was at the right time and day, I deduced. I was pleased to make that conclusion, but nervous none-the-less.

The pounding went on from the McPherson and Herr Ridge areas for some time into the morning. Occasionally, the action would sound louder and more fierce than other times as the conflict would ebb and flow. As I sat under the protection of the trees, my heart pounded right along with the artillery while I listened to history occurring right before my ears. My eyes would soon inherit that privilege.

The unrelenting siege continued into midday as the resonance emanating from the skirmish slowly progressed southeastward towards the town itself. I finally relinquished my perch in the Pitzer Woods and ventured back down to Emmitsburg Road. In sharp contrast to what I had viewed earlier in the day, the road was now a busy thoroughfare funneling the armed assemblages towards the burg itself.

Waiting for an opening in the procession, I crossed the road back into the Peach Orchard, took a seat in the fork of a tree's trunk, and watched what action I could. Sometimes the columns of troop progression would extend for half of an hour, while other times a five-minute parade passing the grove fit the bill. Surprisingly, I only received a handful of glances. Those soldiers were too close to the action to allow their minds to wander. Their thoughts were on one thing and one thing only at this point—self-preservation.

I watched the uniformed men, some smartly attired while others were dressed like little more than common laborers, filed past me towards the Codori farm until their assembly faded from my line of sight. The look on some of those faces was one of grim determination, while others carried a look of resignation to their fate. I pulled out my camera and got a shot of that.

I rose and walked up to the slight summit of the orchard. Even with the booming in the distance, the grove continued to be an oasis from the conflict. I knew that this would quickly change.

I reached down and raised the video camera to my eye to record the the final march for some of the combatants, and the beginning of the end of the South's advancement of secession. I took several still shots as well. They would frame up nicely, I thought, as my viewfinder captured the distant warriors now surrounded by a cloud of dust from the drying lane. I then strolled down Wheatfield Road and took a shot of the Rose house, turned, and exposed a frame of the orchard itself. I turned once more and captured the Pitzer Woods for posterity. All were photos that really don't exist in any number, pre or post war.

After several hours of observing the Army's movements, I thought it would be best if I went back to the safety of the woods. I inconspicuously crossed Emmitsburg Road about ten yards behind a company of northbound troops. With the dust in the air and the humidity now hitting its stride, I thought back to what Dr. Welles said to me right before I left. He was right; I was going to roast in this outfit.

I removed my coat hoping that I wouldn't become a sitting duck on the wooded ridge. I might be mistaken for a spy and be shot. My white shirt would provide an ideal target. I figured that my only options were to sweat bullets or to ingest them. Under the circumstances, I decided to take my chances. I tossed my coat over my shoulder as a compromise.

I didn't dare explore any part of the town proper at this point in time. There were too many areas for a sharpshooter to hide. Currently, they were of the mindset that nothing living should be left standing.

It was around two PM now, and I felt useless just standing around doing nothing. I was beginning to feel like some of the soldiers who would stand around and wait their turn. I spent much of my time pacing, re-reading my notes, and occasionally venturing down in the direction of Hagerstown Road to see if I could get a quick look at the fighting. All that I was able to glimpse through nature's haze was an occasional plume of smoke, yet I could feel the increasing concussions from the distant hostilities.

The fighting continued until sunset. The action had finally made its way down towards me, and troop strength would continue to build until daybreak. I continued to wile away my time by shooting a few frames of the still virgin soil to my west and skipping the occasional stone down towards Millerstown Road. The area wouldn't remain pure much longer.

While I felt as if I had accomplished little or nothing during my first day, so much had really been achieved. I almost forgot that while I hadn't covered a great deal of territory, I had crossed over one hundred and forty years of time. That was a feat unto itself. It was at that point I thought back to my exit scene with Dr. Welles. He, and that time in general, seemed so far removed from my situation here. And to be honest, they were. I guess I was changing and adapting to my surroundings.

While the glow of the sun submerged itself behind the surrounding western hills, I thought it would be best if I looked for a place to settle in for the night. I continued down the ridge towards what is now the old Eisenhower Farm proper in search of shelter. I couldn't trust the situation enough to attempt a stay at the Sherfy Farm. I knew that it was right in the line of fire even though I was sure that the military's 'alarm clock' would have alerted me when it was time to evacuate. I wasn't in a position to take a chance like that, or for that matter stay out in the open like I currently was. Unfortunately I didn't study my history well enough to determine when the ignition would be switched on for the following day's activities. I didn't have enough time. Dr. Welles was right; this entire operation was a bit too rushed.

  I walked through the farm's yard looking for an outbuilding for a secure place to rest. It didn't appear that anyone was around. There was no activity on the farm itself as well as an absence of light within the house. I couldn't imagine that everyone would already be in bed this early on such a beastly evening. The animals residing within the farm's confines appeared as they should. It was my contention that if the family had to flee in a hurry, there was no time to transport the beasts out of harm's way. Everything was eerily quiet except for the occasional cluck from the chickens or a hoof beat from one of the heavier livestock.

  I went over to the water trough and produced one of those little bars of soap that I confiscated from the inn back in Summerdale earlier this morning. I did the best I could to remove a day's worth of sweat and road dust from my person.

  I looked in the carriage house barn only to find it mostly empty. There was no carriage or its accompanying hardware. That pretty much affirmed my suspicions of a rapid evacuation. I opened up a side window and left the door cracked to create some airflow. The temperature and humidity still were a bit on the close side. Any air movement was a relief.

Laying my coat to the side, I pulled loose enough straw to make a bed, used my backpack for an improvised pillow, and then reclined to reflect on the uneventful yet intense day I had just encountered. My God, I thought, I'm back one hundred and forty years before my time. I'm a long way from home. I began to wonder what would happen if I didn't make it back. Would I be robbing my future ancestors of their opportunity for life? Could something that simple disrupt the entire order of our world's operation?

I wondered what those in the modern world were doing right about now. Many in the area were probably finishing up their dinners at one of the various area restaurants, families could be enjoying an end of day ice cream cone, children were probably still running up and down the boulders at Devil's Den, and God only knows where Dr. Welles might be at this moment.

A few booms and an occasional crack from a musket's barrel brought me out of my stupor. That's when I remembered that I had a candy bar stashed in the bottom of my bag. I thought it was strange that I hadn't thought of food all day. That must be a record for me, I mused. I guess the trans-dimensional transfer left my stomach a little queasy. I dug the confection from the bottom of my 'pillow.' Dr. Welles was right. At this point I probably could have eaten it through a straw better than the regular way. I went ahead and did my best, chased it down with a shot of J.D., then cleaned up using some straw as a napkin. I placed the bottle under my 'pillow' for additional support, then laid back to contemplate the enormity of this entire situation. I thought of the history that I would witness in the upcoming day. It then occurred to me that I had been awake nearly nineteen hours. That was my last reflection as I drifted off to sleep.

Despite the crudity of my sleeping arrangements, I slumbered throughout the night oblivious to any occasional gunfire and troop movements that may have occurred. I must have been exhausted. Sometime towards morning I pulled my coat over on to myself for a makeshift blanket.

When my eyes cracked open, I was facing the window and noticed that it was closer to sunrise than not. I thought that I might have rolled into a piece of farm equipment, for I felt something blunt exerting pressure to my kidney region. I shortly realized that it was not a piece of farm paraphernalia because the object proceeded into a jabbing motion. That fully awakened me. I was hoping that I wouldn't roll over to find one of the cows or swine standing over me.

That thought was quashed by the shout of, "Hey boy, up!" I slowly rolled over to see two Confederate soldiers with the barrels of their rifles pointed in my direction. I was shocked not only at the soldier's demands, but this was the first real human contact I had since arriving, and it wasn't a positive one.

"Hey hold on, I didn't do anything," I said trying to talk my way out of the predicament.

"On your feet, boy," the taller one ordered. "What the hell are you doing here?"

"I'm a photographer, I said with a shaky voice. "I'm here to cover the battle."

"Oh yeah? Who you with?"

Trying to think fast to save my skin, I replied, "Um, I'm a freelancer. I'm doing a photo shoot based on the Southern perspective of the war. I'm hoping to sell it to Harper's."

"Yeah, I'm sure. Judging from your accent, you're a Northern boy, none-the-less. What have you got on you?"

"Oh, I have no weapons. I'm not here to fight, I'm only trying to capture the action on film, see?" I said holding up my 35mm. "All I have with me is my camera."

The taller, more talkative soldier took the 35mm camera and looked it over. "This is a camera? Shoot, I can sell something like this for a bundle."

Starting to panic at the prospect of losing my avenue of proof I proclaimed, "Nobody would buy it. No one other than the manufacturer can develop the film. And even then, the owner is registered. It's all experimental equipment. The Pentax people wanted someone to try it out in a combat situation. You see, it has a faster shutter..."

"What else do you have?" he said, speculating that I might be right. He tossed the camera down into the straw.

"Well, nothing really. I have no food and I'm carrying no valuables to speak of."

"What about money?" he demanded, reaching into my breast pocket of my 'blanket'. He pulled out my large billfold containing the Confederate money I had stashed. "Hah, you've just bought your freedom," he announced as he motioned his silent partner towards the exit, and then followed him out.

I just stood there for a while stunned, not knowing what to do. I reached down and picked up my camera. From what I could tell, it was none the worse for wear. I gathered the rest of my stuff up and escaped the confines of the barn.

It was light, but the sun had yet to rise. I could see a dozen or so Rebel soldiers milling about the immediate area. A few were on horseback while the majority were on foot. They were probably scouts sent ahead to check out enemy troop movements and areas of strategic importance.

I went back over to the stagnant water trough and splashed off. During that process, another Confederate soldier on horseback approached me. Oh great, what now, I wondered. He may or may not have been privy to my recent encounter with one of his colleagues.

He rode up to me and turned his steed to the side while announcing, "Sir, I'm going to have to ask you to vacate this sector. You're directly in the line of fire."

"That's O.K. I'm here to cover the battle for the newspaper." My story was changing by the hour. "I'm receiving extra combat pay for this assignment," I answered. "I really need the money, sir."

"Suit yourself, but you've been forewarned," he proclaimed as he turned and galloped back to his comrades.

I walked back up to the edge of the Pitzer Woods to see what action if any had taken place. There were scattered troops from both armies grouping up. However, they were not sufficient enough in number on either side to initiate an attack or to defend against the same.

The ripening morning was accompanied by an increase of Union soldiers into the Peach Orchard. Their build up multiplied at a greater rate than their gray-shirted counterparts across Emmitsburg Road. Even a layman such as myself could see that this flat-topped area would be at the hub of the conflict. As it turned out, that general vicinity nearly became center stage for the entire Gettysburg campaign.

Fighting, north and east, once again broke out and had been in progress for some time since the early AM. With reinforcements from both sides pouring in, the hostilities would only increase from here on out. With my long lens, I snapped a few photographs of the Union build-up in the grove. I bided my time for the remainder of the mid morning awaiting the bulk of the Southern reinforcements. That's where I'd find Jonathan Gates.

There was little traffic on Emmitsburg Road now. A few of the blue troops had spilled from the orchard and lined the pike less than a quarter mile to my front. Aside from the fighting in the Culp's Hill and East Cemetery Hill areas, there was no major action in my sector. In reviewing my notes yesterday, General Longstreet was supposed to have attacked earlier this morning, but the strike never materialized. Longstreet had his own timetable apart from Robert E. Lee's. History hadn't changed that.

Around 11:30 AM, soldiers from an Alabama brigade began to line the tree-covered crown that I presently occupied. Most of the newcomers just looked at me as they filed into place. They were trying to figure out if I was a spy or a misplaced civilian without a lick of sense. I was indeed the latter, so I felt that it was in my best interest if I departed from the line of fire. I picked up my equipment and descended well to the rear. No one said anything to me, but I did receive a few visual votes of no confidence from the surrounding participants.

I walked quite a distance to the west in hopes of meeting up with the incoming troops as they descended upon the region. Nearing noon, I caught up to a massive influx of rebel troops pouring down from the north as well as from the west. This was the major build up I had expected. I made my way westward deeper into the bottomland. After a short span of time there was an unbelievable increase in the number of wagons, horses, and soldiers milling about, all awaiting orders for positioning. They seemed to appear out of nowhere.

Makeshift messes had been set up to feed what men they could in the time available. Some of the battalions awoke over eight hours ago and had been marching ever since. I noticed that quite a few of the soldiers went up to the Willoughby's Run/Pitzer's Run creek area to refill canteens and to loiter around a bit.

In this mass of humanity, I began to wonder how I would be able to locate Jonathan Gates. There were so many soldiers, and for the most part, identically dressed. With each group resembling the other, I decided to conduct a search by the process of elimination. Ideally, the best way to start would be for me to locate a Georgia state flag. From that point, I would try and identify a battalion's banner.

The flags of each unit were displayed in all of their glory from one end of the encampment to the other. I found several Georgia flags, but the brigade banners were more difficult to recognize. The flag bearers were very protective of their colors. To have one's banner confiscated in battle was akin, in their hearts, to losing the battle itself. A piece of themselves went aboard each flagstaff.

A little closer to the Eisenhower Farm was McLaws' Division. Pausing to check my notebook, I discovered that Semmes' brigade was supposed to be contained within that congregation. After walking thirty yards or so, I spotted a couple of Georgia state flags in close proximity to one other. I went over to a soldier who looked as if he didn't really want to be bothered, a Captain Ford as it said on his pouch.

"Excuse me Captain, is this the Fifty-first?" He didn't say a word, he just pointed to the next group down.

I walked over to that gathering and beheld a banner representing the Fifty-first Georgia infantry. I'm almost home, I thought. Right up front was a man in uniform sitting on a crate checking out his equipment. He looks more like he was cooling his tired heels while passing time. I went over to him and introduced myself as a photographer from a Pennsylvanian newspaper. I asked him if I could talk with him for a spell.

"Sure," replied the man who introduced himself as Rueben Langston. "Do you take photographs of just the war or do you shoot portraits as well?"

"I suppose I could do either. Why do you ask?"

"Well, I never did get a chance to get my picture took in uniform to send to my family."

Glancing at my box camera he continued in a good-natured tone, "So if you want to talk to me, that will be my price."

"Sure, I'd be happy to," I replied. I figured this would be a good time to get a little portrait work in anyway. I could get a great 'soldier preparing for battle' type of shot. I took my 35mm camera out of my side bag and retreated ten feet.

"Are you ready?" I asked as I turned towards him and focused.

"Wait a minute, aren't you going to set up this camera?" he asked pointing towards the larger model.

"Oh no, that's just for long shots. This will be fine for portraits."

"Looks like it will make a real small picture," he observed.

"These negatives can be enlarged to any size you'd want," I assured him.

"I'll take your word for it. How about this?" Rueben asked as he sat on the crate, rifle barrel in hand with the stock end planted firmly against the ground.

"That's fine," I replied as I snapped his picture.

"That's it? That was awful fast. I thought it usually took a few seconds of sitting real still."

"Not with this camera. The shutter is set at $1/500$ of a second."

"I don't know how much that is. "

"Yep, small in size yet quick at exposing."

"Could you send a copy to my wife when it's ready?"

Not wanting to lie to him I replied, "Sure, I'll see that your family gets it." I figured that if I was lucky enough to locate his descendants when I got back home, I'd send a copy to them. I suppose that I could sepia-tone it and tell them it was found in some archives somewhere.

"Let me give you my post address," he said while fumbling for a pencil and paper.

"Here you go," I told him as I tore off a piece of paper from my notebook and handed it to him along with my Bic pen.

"What's this?"

"It's a pen. Why?"

"Where's the inkwell for this thing?" he asked.

"Oh, it's all self-contained. Go ahead, it'll write." With that he proceeded to pen the address. After scribbling down a few letters, he stopped and looked at the pen in amazement seeing that it did actually write without a fill up. "Well I'll be," was all he could say. "This sure beats the sharpened piece of bullet lead that I've been using."

Rueben finished with the address and continued to gaze at the pen and tap on its casing. I guess he was trying to figure out how they made the barrel clear-looking.

"Rueben I'll tell you what, you keep the pen. Use it on your letters home. It will probably last the duration of the war."

"Are you kidding me? Thanks Mr., uh..."

"Just call me Neil."

"Thanks Neil." Alternating looks at the pen, then towards the distant wood line Rueben proclaimed, "I'm not looking forward to this fight, I'll tell you. We're not supposed to say that, I guess. They want us to be so brave, the Fifty-first. Well I don't mind telling you that I'm not. I will always follow orders though."

"If you weren't afraid, you probably wouldn't be human," I observed. Reaching into my bag I offered, "Here, this'll stiffen you up a bit."

Accepting my bottle of Jack Daniels, he asked, "What's this?"

"A little bracer. It's Tennessee sipping whiskey. It's the best the South has to offer. Take a draw."

Once he figured out that the stopper screwed off, he took a gulp. "Oh hey, now that's smooth, that's real smooth. I've never heard of this. The last stuff we had was a few weeks back at Williamsport. It would get you drunk but it was tough to keep down. Old home brew I think." He took one more sip from the bottle, 'corked it', and was in the process of handing it back to me when we were abruptly interrupted.

"What the hell are you doing!" a rather loud individual said coming towards me. "You cutting into my business? Give me that!" he said as he made a grab for the Jack Daniels.

I reeled the bottle in and looked at him in surprise. It was then that I recognized him. It was the man who robbed me a few hours before.

"You again? Why you just don't get enough, do you Mr. Pictureman? It takes guts not to get the hell out of here. You must be a glutton for punishment, ain't you?"

Getting angry, I stated, "Hey, this conversation has nothing to do with you. You already took all of my damn money. That's all you're going to get. Now leave me the hell alone!"

He reached over and grabbed a fist full of my hair and said, "You come peddling one more bottle of liquor into this camp and it'll be your last.

Got it?" he proclaimed as he gave my head a shove back.

"Hey Jon, leave him alone. That's his own personal stuff. He ain't selling."

"Make sure you don't neither," he said as he turned and walked away.

"Jesus, has that guy got a problem? What's with him?"

"He's our local whiskey runner. He gets it and sells it. He thought that you were horning in on his territory. Don't mess with him Neil, he's a bad egg. That's also why he's still a private. Colonel Ball reprimanded Jon for his running. He said that it brought a bad element into the camp. Hell, even General Semmes warned him to cease his activities. It didn't work, though. After one hell of an argument between the two, Jon told the general, face to face, that one day his saddle would be emptied. I guess one could take that any way they wished. Problem is, they really can't afford to get rid of him. We're real short of men. So I think that's what caused his demotion. He's got balls, I'll give you that. That's all the brass cares about."

"I hear tell," he continued, "that he was an O.K. fellow when he signed up. He was a liked man until he fell in with some bad fellows. They showed him that there's a lot of money to be made through black market whiskey, cigars, and even whores. I guess, like a lot of folks from our parts, his family was real poor. He needed to send the money home to help out. Since about a year he's not a person you want to be around."

"I'll make it a point to avoid him."

"So what're you doing a story on, Neil?"

"Oh, just the war in general, from the Southern point of view that is," I answered. "Actually I just take the pictures. I leave the writing to the writers."

"Good. Hopefully the folks around these parts will see that we're right."

"Well maybe." Cutting to the chase I said, "I was also here looking for a friend of a friend to interview. Maybe you know him, he's supposed to be in your outfit—Jonathan Gates?"

Upon hearing that, Rueben's eyes got real big. "Jonathan Gates?" Rueben started laughing out loud while slapping his knee and coughing.

"Why do you laugh," I asked.

"Jonathan Gates is the man who robbed you this morning!" He laughed and shook his head in disbelief.

"Him? Mr. Rum Runner? That's Jonathan Gates? You mean my great...uh I mean, my God. Well with friends like I have, who needs enemies huh? I'll be sure and let my buddy know what's happened to him."

"Yeah, you must have some real strange friends."

"Oh, you wouldn't believe some of the things they do," I said cryptically.

While talking with Rueben, I looked around and noticed that the size of the crowd had grown appreciably. I felt a bit out of place amongst of all of the butternut and gray. When I glanced back in Rueben's direction, I noticed that he was digging through his personal effects. He stopped to glance at an old tintype photo.

"Is that your gal?" I inquired.

"Yes, that's my wife Sarah. I haven't seen

her for over half a year now. We write each other all of the time though. I hope she still loves me. She says she does in her letters. I still love her, I'll tell you that. I fear that she'll find company with another man while I'm gone. That can happen when a man's not around, you know. Do you have a girl back home?"

"Yep," I said as I pulled out my wallet. I dug past my credit cards and produced a picture of Ginny. It was one of those 'glamour poses.' Actually, I wasn't sure that I should show that to Rueben. Ginny looked quite alluring there. That's a side of her I probably took far too little time noticing lately what with the job keeping me busy, meetings, 'history workshops,' and what have you. I guess I wasn't around too much either.

"Oh my God, fantastic!" observed Rueben.

"Yeah, she's quite a girl. I hope she's still my girl. She hasn't been too pleased with me lately."

"Where did you get a color photograph? This is amazing. It's so life like." I then realized that his expression was as much for the photo as it was for the subject itself.

"Oh yeah," I humbly agreed. I had almost forgotten what year I was currently residing. "Well," I went on to explain, "I can get my hands on a lot of new experimental equipment from suppliers." As I fumbled for the right words, over Rueben's right shoulder I noticed an officer ride up on horseback, step down, then confer with some of his colleagues.

The man appeared to be in his late forties, displayed a receding hairline, and sported a full beard. From the old unclear photo I found while doing my research, I guessed the man to be

Brigadier General Semmes.

"Uh, excuse me for a minute," I said as I got up, dusted my rump off, then went over to confront the man who gave my great-great grandfather so much grief. I waited for his conversation to hit a lull before introducing myself.

Extending my hand, I said, "General Semmes, I presume?"

Looking as if he were about to receive a court summons, he slowly extended his hand and replied, "Yes, and who do you presume to be?"

"Neil Gates. I'm a photographer with the upstate press. I'm here to capture the Southern prospective on the war."

"I could tell that you weren't a Southern boy yourself," he said with a laugh, alluding to my flat accent. The general appeared to be in relatively good spirits considering the impending task at hand. "I hope you aren't expecting an interview from me. I'm no good at those things, not to mention that I'm a little busy at the present," he explained as he turned to leave.

"Oh no, General. I was just hoping that you'd O.K. me to follow your men into battle. I would be one of the first photographers to capture actual combat scenes on film. And your unit would be featured."

"I won't disapprove. You realize that you're at your own risk."

"Yes sir, I realize that. The only thing that I'll be shooting will be my camera."

"Suit yourself. He turned to leave, then stopped and added, "Gates, huh?"

"Yes General."

"You aren't by any chance related to a

Jonathan Gates, a member of my brigade, are you?"

"Uh, well you can say that we've met."

"I'll bet. That S.O.B.'s a handful. He can't follow orders worth a damn. If you're willing to go into a combat situation without an arm, you're about as crazy a son-a-bitch as he is."

"Uh, thank-you General." I took that as a compliment although I'm not sure he meant it to be so.

"Look, you've probably come quite a distance," he said, not knowing how true those words were. "Tell you what, treat yourself to some grub over there," he said pointing to one of the chow wagons that followed the division. "There's plenty for everyone, but once it's gone, it's gone. And if anyone refuses you service, tell them they'll have to answer to me. Welcome aboard."

"Thank-you, General." He certainly seemed like a nice enough man, I thought as the general mounted up. As he turned to leave, he saw me with my camera trained at him and his steed. He paused for a moment as I snapped the quick shot, then he rode off.

I walked over and got at the end of the chow line waiting to be served. It dawned on me that, other than the liquid candy bar I ingested last night, I hadn't had anything substantial to eat since I left yesterday morning. Once again I guess I was just too busy to notice. It seemed that nearly every brigade had its own curricle on which to prepare and serve whatever food that could be scrounged up. It appeared that all they had to offer today was meat. I couldn't tell if it was pork or beef, but it was probably a little of each. You took what they handed you and were grateful for it. It didn't matter;

any fresh meat was a real treat for the men in gray.

As I stepped to the front, a black server went to slap a chunk of meat on to my plate, but I didn't have a platter to offer. "Um, General Semmes told me to come over and get something to eat. I don't have a mess kit though."

The man thought for a second then said, "Well that's no problem, sir. I got something that will work for you," he said as he reached under his table to a shelf and produced a dish that resembled a metallic bowl more than a plate. Beggars can't be choosers, so I gratefully accepted the receptacle. I knocked the dirt out of it, blew the dust from it, and presented it forward.

"Here's some A-number one vittles fo' your belly, sir," the servant said as he dropped the lump into the bowl.

Being grateful for this bounty I said, "Well thank-you very much, uh…"

"Nate. My name's Nathaniel but yous can call me Nate. At your service, sir," he announced with a mock salute.

"Thank-you very much, Nate."

"Yous ain't army folk is you sir?"

"No, I'm a photographer with an area newspaper. I'm shooting a story for an upcoming issue."

"Yous one of those writer folks too?"

"No, I just do the photography. I leave the writing to the smart folks," I said as my hand was getting a bit tired holding the awkward plate. As I turned to go back to my spot and get down whatever my stomach would hold, I once again thanked Nate and said, "I really appreciate your efforts," tilting my bowl upwards. I was being honest.

"Thankee. Much 'bliged, sir," was his reply.

"What in the hell are you thanking that blackey for?" came the voice of Jonathan Gates who was leaning against a tree just to my right. "Nigger Nate's just doing his job."

"Yes, and being paid a king's ransom for his efforts too I'll bet," I snapped back.

"Hell, without us giving them coloreds a job, they'd probably all starve to death." Looking upwards, and striking an analytical pose while stroking his chin he commented, "Not a half bad idea come to think of it. When we win the war, I may just have to recommend that," he said. With his index finger pointing skyward he proclaimed, "Freedom for the black man and good riddance." The laugh that followed made me wonder how someone could become so evil within his soul.

"You don't have much of a heart when it comes to your fellow man, do you Gates?" I asked.

"If he were a man, I would," he said with a guffaw. The soldiers nearest to him were enjoying the show. "And as for you, you ain't going to be a living man much longer if you don't mind your P's and Q's around here. You ain't never going to be one of us. You can't stand that tall."

"Hey, he was only trying to be nice, Mr. Jon," explained Nate.

Using his best minstrel man voice, Jonathan came back with, "Well 'scuse me, Sergeant Jackass," to the delight of those present.

I turned and went back to sit down with Rueben to gnaw on what I had acquired. After I was seated, I asked him where the army was able to come up with so much fresh meat. Speaking in a very cold tone he replied, "We take what we need."

I looked over to see what put Rueben in such an indignant mood. He just stared back with anger in his eyes. "What's wrong?" I asked.

"Who the hell are you?"

"I don't follow you. What are you talking about?"

"I've got a notion to turn you in. You ain't who you say you are." His face reddening, he continued, "You and your, your fancy writing sticks, your new fangled cameras, your colored pictures. Hell, according to the label on your whiskey bottle, this stuff ain't even going to be made for another three years."

"Rueben, what are you talking about?"

"I knew that these objects just weren't right with today. We don't have anything like those here. Neither does the North."

"Rueben, I've got no idea what you're talking..." With that, Rueben produced a five-dollar bill from my wallet that I left on the ground when I went over to talk to General Semmes. "Oh yeah, that. Look, I can explain that."

"I thought you could. You ain't from this time, are you mister? This dollar has the year 1996 on it. This one says 1999. You have some cards here along with something with your picture on it. Says it's a driver's license. You don't need a license to drive a coach and team. What the hell is your deal Mr. Gates, if that indeed's your real name. Are you some kind of witch or something?"

I sat my food down and decided to come clean. At this point I didn't feel that I had any choice. I figured that if anyone could be trusted with my secret, Rueben could. "You're right, Rueben, I'm not of this time. Perceptive of you to figure that out. To be honest with you, I'm from about one hundred and forty years into your future. But, I am here to photograph the battle from the Southern perspective. I didn't lie about that."

"That's impossible."

"Up until a few months ago, I would have agreed with you. But, recent breakthroughs have allowed me to become a test subject. Here I am."

Rueben just stared at me and looked less than convinced.

"I shouldn't do this, but to prove that I'm not lying to you, take a look at this," I said as I reached into my bag and handed him my camera's operating manual. "See, printed in 1998. And take a look at the scenes in here. These are sights your generation will never see. They're all of today, my today that is."

Rueben flipped slowly through the sample shots that demonstrated good and bad camera operation. "I didn't want to lie to you Rueben, but you see my dilemma here. I couldn't tell anybody. You're the only one who knows. You're the only one I'll be able to trust."

Almost ignoring me from being so transfixed to the strange new images afforded to him, he turned the book towards me and asked, "What's that?"

"It's an automobile, a car. Think of it as a horseless carriage. That's what they were called when they were first invented around the turn of the century. They won't be available in a sellable form for another thirty to forty of your years. That's what I have the driver's license for."

"That's what I want," he said sounding positive. "I want to own a car. If what you say is true, I might still be young enough to get one of those when they come out. Could you imagine me racing down the street at over thirty miles per hour?"

Coming to an image of a woman in a thong bikini nearly silhouetted by the setting sun, Rueben asked, "Why's this woman at the ocean in her under things?"

"That's what some women wear to the beach to get a lot of sun," I tried to explain.

"But it ain't got no back in it!"

"Yes, I know. That outfit is the exception rather than the rule." I laughed cheerfully at his innocence.

"And this, what's this thing?"

"Well, that's called the Space Shuttle. It can carry people in it. It's like a missile that flies into outer space. You know, way out there towards the stars," I said pointing towards the heavens.

"And then it explodes when it comes back down?"

"Oh no, no, it's not really a missile per se. They can stay up there for months at a time if they have to. There's no atmosphere up there to pull it back down towards the ground so it just hangs up there," I said, trying to explain it to him in the simplest of terms.

"What do they do up there?"

"Mostly experiments. They discover things that lead to new medical treatments, innovations for industries, you know. They once had a rocket ship that took men to the moon a while back."

"Come on, now you're funning me. They

cain't do that, not even in your day. When he saw that I didn't change expression he asked, "O.K., what did they find up there then?" he asked in a tone that led me to think that he still didn't believe me.

"Well, as it was, all they found was a lot of rocks and dirt."

"No plants or water?"

"No, it's pretty desolate. Think of it as a freezing cold desert at night and a very bright, hot desert during the day. There's no atmosphere to hold the temperatures in check."

"Wow, it must have been pretty hard to breathe in a place like that." I let that remark slide. I didn't want to get in to that subject too deep.

"A while back they also sent an unmanned craft up to the planet Mars. Now that was exciting."

"It was? What did they find there?" he asked as if I finally had his attention.

"Well, rocks and dirt actually," I replied with a laugh. I saw where he was going with his response.

"Hardly seems worth the trouble. We have plenty of that down here," he said in a disappointed manner as he continued flipping through the remaining pages.

"Well, it really was. We all watched as the TV camera showed us shots of the Martian surface for the first time."

"How did you get a camera up there and the pictures down here so quick?"

"It's a long story," I told him. At that point, I got the feeling that somebody was eavesdropping. I glanced over my shoulder and saw a dirty, fuzzyheaded fellow I thought to be in his mid to late teens staring at me. He started into a soft, almost maniacal laugh then said, "You got funny pictures." He returned to his laugh, got out of his squat, then sauntered back over to his perch about twenty feet away. He'd look over on occasion and chuckle to himself.

"Hey, is he all right?" I asked Rueben.

"Who, Mojo? Yeah, he's O.K. He means no harm."

"What kind of name is Mojo?"

"To be honest with you, nobody's sure of his real name. He won't tell us. Someone said they think his name is Morris Johnson, while others believe that he's actually Maurice Jones. Everybody's always just called him Mojo."

"Is he stable? He doesn't seem to have himself together, mentally I mean."

"Hey look, you folks up north, or where ever you're from, probably have all sorts of men waiting to sign up for the service. Down south, we have to take what's available. If his finger's long enough to reach the trigger, he's in."

"Well, I guess if he's smart enough to sign up..."

"Actually, from what I hear, his mother signed him up. She just couldn't handle him anymore. He didn't have a dad around."

"My God that's sad. Is he all on his own out here?"

"We all take turns looking out for him. He's been hanging around with me since we left Fayetteville."

Looking up, I saw Jonathan Gates heading in our direction. I thought he was returning to continue our argument but he was just passing through. He veered his path over towards Mojo. This caused the young soldier to cower against a tree. Jonathan just laughed and walked away.

"What was that all about?" I inquired.

"Well, ol' Private Gates over there loves to pick on those less than himself. In this case, it was Mojo. Jonny once lent Mojo a dollar knowing full well that the guy didn't have the means to pay him back. After demanding his money back and receiving nothing but a stuttering excuse in return, Gates dragged Mojo over to one of the larger cannons and shoved his head inside the barrel. Jon kept commanding the imaginary cannoneer to fire. When the 'gunner' didn't follow orders, Jon grabbed a large rock and slammed it against the side of the cannon making Mojo think that the cannon was in the process of beheading him."

"Good God that's terrible. What happened?"

"What do you mean what happened? He's still here isn't he?"

"No, I mean was Gates disciplined?"

"Oh of course, but they've done all that they can do with him. He's a certified malcontent. I saw when he and General Semmes got into the shouting match. It wasn't pretty. I couldn't figure how anybody would have the guts to go face to face with his general. He must have some kind of death wish. I thought they were going to go into fisticuffs. Anyway, that's when Semmes demoted Jon from corporal back to private. He's the original Johnny Reb, he is."

"Anyway, we need all of the brave soldiers that we can get, and Gates' one of the bravest, or the craziest; probably a little of both. The brass extract their pound of flesh from Jon by sending him on only the most dangerous missions. I think they're hoping that nature takes its course and Gates, as they say, falls by the wayside."

"Literally," I added.

"Correct." Rueben, in a somber voice, finally asked, "Gates, huh?"

"Yes."

In a quieter tone he asked, "Jonathan Gates is some kin to you, isn't he?"

"Yes, I'm afraid he is," I said in a slow, deliberate inflection. "That's why I'm here."

"Geeze, you have my sympathy. It's good to see that you turned out O.K. I guess there's hope for us all."

After an intermission of some time, Rueben spoke up in a quiet, depressed cadence. "Neil, we're going to lose the war, ain't we?"

"Hell, I couldn't tell you that one way or the another. If I said, "Yeah," you might say, "Well then why should I stay here and put my life on the line. We're going to lose anyway." Or, if I said that the South was going to win, you could answer me with the same line that you wouldn't be needed. I can't tell you, Rueben. Nothing happens until it happens. And this war still has some time to go, unfortunately. In this war, or any event that occurs in life, we all have a role to play. The scenes of history aren't complete if no one participates. It was once said that there is no inevitability in history except as men make it."

"Maybe so, but we're going to lose. I've finally come to realize it."

"Why do you say that?"

He once again reached down and produced

the five-dollar bill. "Only heroes get honored this way. Mr. Lincoln's picture is on this money. If we won the war, you'd never see that happen. You'd see President Davis's face."

"You don't know that. Time has a great way of forgiving."

"Yeah, but the money says 'The United States.' It doesn't say 'The Confederate States of America'."

"I'll grant you that. I will tell you that when this war is over, all of the states will get back together and form one country. Those states will once again be united. That doesn't imply that the South loses at all. Look Rueben, win, lose, or draw, your task is as noble as those who fought for the revolution almost a century before. You have to fight for your beliefs." Almost sounding like Dr. Welles with all of his quotes, I proclaimed, "It's been said that, when liberty is taken by force, it can be restored by force. When it is relinquished voluntarily by default, it can never be recovered."

"Uh huh."

Thinking back to what Henry said a couple of months ago, I added, "Just as individuals learn more from their mistakes, so shall this country. And, we will become one once again some day. Today, what both sides are doing will be for the growth of this nation. Just as pruning injures the branches of a Peach tree, that tree will eventually yield a hundred fold. Look Rueben, I can't change the country's destiny any more than I can change my own. I can, however, change my actions and reactions to the events I encounter. My personal destiny is the result of my reactions. Things just are, that's all."

Rueben briefly contemplated that bit of information. "Still, I wish I lived in your time. When you go back, you'll be at peace. I'll bet there are no wars where you're from. That seems like an impossible concept for me to grasp, that something like that actually exists somewhere."

"We still have our problems."

I was interrupted by a massive volley of shells and twelve pound cannon balls. Someone shouted, "Incoming!" and we all instinctively hit the ground. As the ordinances were fired from quite a distance, they missed most, but took its toll on a few towards our front. People could be heard screaming for help. Everyone was in motion creating quite a dust cloud. Some went up to assist those who were injured while almost everyone began gathering up their equipment. They knew that the orders were about to come down.

The Alabamans who lined the edge of the Pitzer Woods to our front could be heard opening fire and returning the volley. The repayment was steady and long. It must have been effective, for we didn't see anything else like that during the remainder of our time in that locale.

"Well, I guess that ends lunch huh?" I observed, trying to take a nonchalant attitude about the impending clash. Rueben didn't follow that comment up. He had a serious pained look on his face. I hurriedly wolfed down my remaining fare.

Looking around, I could see that Mojo was beginning to lose his composure. He began to cause a scene by crying and hugging the tree next to him. A colonel came over to quiet him.

"Look Mojo," his counseling could be

overheard, "this is just like an exercise. There will be a lot of noise around you but you'll be in no danger."

What a line, I thought. I looked at Rueben and said, "That kid hasn't seen any live action yet, has he?"

"I don't think so. He hasn't been in long. We picked him up at Sperryville several weeks back. I don't know if he's ever even fired a gun before."

"Oh God, and he's walking into a holocaust. If that isn't literally a baptism under fire, I don't know what is."

Hesitating for a second, Rueben then turned to Mojo and shouted, "Hey Mojo, stick with us. You'll be safe with us."

Some relief crossed Mojo's face as he haphazardly gathered his belongings and made his way over to us. "You're nice to me, Rueben."

"Stick close and we'll do our best. Come on, let's go over and put our equipment on the ground pile. All you'll need is your gun, caps, powder, and lead."

"There's going to be some real shooting?" Mojo asked.

Looking towards the ridge, Rueben responded, "Yep. You may want to make some noise yourself."

We walked over to the pile of personal effects and non-essential equipment that was placed under guard. It would be kept safe until the soldiers returned to camp. I put my video camera inside my larger satchel and placed it with the rest of the bedrolls and other gear. I was leery about doing that, but as valuable as that unit was, it was still too bulky to be hauled around in a full sprint. I had plans to use it later.

I knew that Dr. Welles warned me to steer clear of the actual battle, but I'd never find out what happened between Jonathan Gates and the general if I did. This was it.

The battalion marched its way down Black Horse Tavern Road with Kershaw's men in front of our group. We passed by the Eisenhower Farm and headed up the grade towards the Pitzer Woods. As the unit took some semblance of a formation, I called over to Rueben, "Hold up a second." I joined them about ten yards away.

"You're not going into the field unarmed, are you?" he asked.

"I have no choice. I have a job to do," I said while holding up my 35mm camera.

A look of skepticism turned to the best smile Rueben could muster considering the circumstances. "This means that we're going to make it," he said in a hushed voice leaning in towards me. "You wouldn't go into an area where you knew you'd get hurt. I think we'll stick close to you."

If they only knew, I thought as we neared the summit of the ridge.

Chapter Eight
The Second Assault

*Any coward can fight a battle
when he's sure of winning."*
GEORGE ELLIOT

As we settled in on the summit of Seminary Ridge, I was surprised how much wooded cover was available. It's certainly not that way today. Even so, with all of the rebels filing in around us, that area soon became filled to capacity.

Scanning around, I could see that most of the soldiers were preparing their weapons so they would be ready at a moment's notice. Unfortunately, we found that the moment wouldn't be arriving any time soon.

Those of us in McLaws' Division were to be holding down the right flank of the Confederate assault line. To our front was Kershaw's Brigade of around 2000 men. If my history notes were correct, Semmes' Brigade would follow Kershaw's into the scrap. Barksdale's men behind us would bring up the rear.

Brigadier General Joseph B. Kershaw was an interesting man. A lawyer by profession, he was the South's clean-cut version of the Union's General Custer. However, Kershaw was considered a clearer thinker by comparison. Around forty years old or so, it was also said that Kershaw was cut from the same cloth as the South's General Pickett, but not nearly as perfumed or reckless. All in all, he was considered to be quite a competent leader. Between Kershaw and Semmes, one couldn't ask for a more proficient right flank, at least on paper.

McLaw's Division was bordered to the left by the rest of Longstreet's company that extended up towards the town's southern boundary. General Longstreet was considered cautious to a fault. Even though General Lee requested that Longstreet proceed with the attack around mid-morning, no action was forthcoming. Despite an additional direct order from Lee, Longstreet's men didn't even advance to the ridge until mid afternoon. I heard tell that the general was waiting for Pickett's men to come up. Then there was also a rumor floating about that Longstreet was waiting for Law's Brigade to get set. There was always an excuse. Longstreet's entire operation became an unfortunate waiting game as he was playing the part of a reluctant participant.

From what I later learned, Longstreet wasn't sold on this battle from the start. He wasn't keen on the ground on which his troops sat. He preferred to face the enemy on terrain closer to Washington. With the constant delays, I guess the General was hoping that the battle of Gettysburg would amount to nothing more than a skirmish, sparing his group of any serious casualties. That wasn't to be, as General Lee stated that the enemy was here, and here is where he'd fight them.

Despite our delay, there was fighting going on all around us. While waiting, we were hoping that we weren't on anyone's hit list. There would be exceptions to that rule we found out.

I surmised that this would be as good of a

time as any to snap a few pictures. We were all tucked behind the foliage for cover, so I had to move up. I walked in front of Kershaw's men and rested my camera's lens against a tree's trunk. I was using a 500 mm lens that brought the action in the orchard right up close. I was even able to pick off a signalman on the crest of Little Round Top. These were great shots that any photographer would die for, I thought. It was then that I realized that my thinking could end up being prophetic.

I wrapped up my business after a half a dozen shots and made my way back to Rueben and Mojo. During my commute I received quite a few stares but nary a comment. I guess they figured that I knew what I was doing.

Upon arriving back at my starting point, I knew that I'd have to lighten my load. I placed the 500 mm lens down at the base of a tree and installed the shorter, more compact 35-70 zoom lens. I wouldn't even be able to carry the long lens with me. Between my camera, its bag, and canteen, I simply had no more room. The shorter lens was all I needed for now anyway. I hoped that the 500 would be there in one piece when I got back, but I doubted it.

At this point, we were far from being alone. On either side of our group was a half dozen or so twelve pound Napoleon cannons which could hurl a four inch ordinance over a couple of miles with sufficient accuracy. Also, thousands and thousands of men were now packed into the wooded flats. The distance between the right and left flanks was approximately three to four miles. General Lee figured that he'd average 10,000 soldiers per mile. While that may sound impressive, that was far less than the Union's 17,000 per mile. The Confederate lines were more spread out as opposed to the dense groupings of Meade's men in blue. Our portion of the line would concentrate its efforts on the Rose Farm and Peach Orchard, an area of approximately one half mile or so wide.

The target region to our front saw an increase of intensity in the firefight. Even though the action was a half-mile or so straight ahead, the roar of the cannons became deafening. It was no wonder that, in those old photos of Gettysburg military reunions, you could always tell who the cannoneers were. They were usually the ones holding the ear horns attempting to gather enough sound to activate their decimated ear drums.

Believing, and rightfully so, that the woods were full of Rebs, ten and twelve pound Napoleons, probably from Buckley's orchard battery, began to pour forth their charges in our direction. It amazed me that, if you kept your eyes on a particular gun's barrel, you could follow the flight path of an ordinance until it arrived at its destination. Most of the shots didn't make it our way. Perhaps mistakenly, one round fired at a low trajectory had its sights set on our center. People began to scatter when somebody yelled, "Incoming!" Amazingly enough, the conical shell performed a perfect ricochet off the unyielding ground and became airborne once again. The charge cleared our heads by plenty as it ripped through the trees above us. As it passed overhead, we were pelted with limbs and branches causing everyone to cover up. Mojo was trying to pull his jacket up over his head, but the garment wasn't built for that.

Not all of the incoming artillery volleys were

that haphazard. One shot fell short of us by a dozen yards, but this time the ordinance hit the ground and shattered into dozens of pieces. As intended, projectiles from the burst canister flew into the crowd and tore one soldier's arm completely off at the shoulder, spun him around and landed him on his stomach. I was astonished that the man didn't holler out in pain. He did however flop around like a fish out of water gasping for air. I'm sure that shock had already set in, and the man would eventually realize that he'd see no more battle forever. Several others in that same section were hit in the face by flying debris. Those affected scattered to the rear, being careful not to step in the puddles of spurting blood from their downed comrade.

It seemed like forever that we had been bunched up, spread out, then compacted once again. Finally around four PM, Longstreet gave the orders for Hood's men on the far right flank to advance to the Devil's Den area. The line of soldiers he ordered into action extended from the Den itself, half way up to the Rose House.

Despite the present carnage, and the bloodbath yet to occur, most of the surrounding participants were silent or quietly talking amongst themselves in a serious tone. It goes without saying that there wasn't a whole lot of clowning going on. Most were aghast at what they had just witnessed. They knew much worse was yet to come.

I did hear two men from Kershaw's brigade conversing about twenty feet to my front. Being an interested observer, I attempted to eavesdrop on their conversation. To my surprise, I wasn't familiar with their dialect. If I had to hazard a guess, I'd have to say that it was of an eastern European derivation, possibly Hungarian or Polish.

That was a surprise. In all of the old Civil War movies, most of the Southern boys talked with a twang while their northern counterparts carried the flat accent. I guess Hollywood doesn't place a premium on historical correctness. I even caught a mutton-chopped officer barking out his orders while mixing French with his broken English. God only knows if his men were able to decipher their leader's intentions.

I didn't keep a running count of the many different dialects I encountered, but a rough estimate would be in the neighborhood of five or six distinct languages being spoken freely, not to mention the accents. I guess one learns something new every day.

Word had it that McLaws and Longstreet had already established who'd be sent out first and who would follow whom. Apparently all were in agreement, and the stage was set. We knew that our time to act was swiftly approaching.

It was now past 4:30 PM, and the majority of the Confederate assault was well under way. It seemed as if ours was the only division not seeing any action.

When the five o'clock hour rolled around, I'm guessing that we had been in the woods for several hours at least. I suppose that it beat standing out in the open, yet it was far from safe. We could hear the balls of lead snapping their way across the treetops, some coming closer than others. One man took a direct hit to the leg from a minie ball. He fell to the ground yelling in pain.

His fellow soldiers helped him to his feet and checked out the damage. The ball must have been traveling at such a slow velocity that it didn't even perforate the man's skin. He dropped his drawers to reveal a burgundy colored blood bruise about the size of your fist. Some of his brigade members began laughing and joking to the soldier telling him that he should take the rest of the war off. The Rebel was understandably shaken but suited up for more.

The men around us were beginning to become unsettled. While some exhibited nervous and jittery behavior, others acted bored and uninterested. The delay was taking its toll.

A handful of soldiers went as far as to curse the Confederate brass. "Longstreet has waited too long," one remarked. He was probably right.

Around that time, the general himself rode up to our sector and dismounted. Being oblivious to the shelling, he and General Kershaw had a few words as they gestured towards the horizon. After a minute or so, we felt several cannon blasts in succession to our right from the North Carolina artillery. It was at that point General Kershaw turned to his brigade, and with both hands motioning from the ground skyward yelled, "Up men!"

A rebel cheer rang out from those involved causing my heart to beat so fast that it turned my trembling hands to ice. I wondered how I would be able to take photos in that condition. Someone in our brigade, in the spirit of the moment yelled, "Don't give them Yanks nothing! Give them everything!" I guess you had to be there.

Kershaw's men emerged from their shield

of timber, moving about ten deep and several hundred wide, as they ventured eastward towards Emmitsburg Road. They hadn't cleared the underbrush by more than fifty feet when a federal volley greeted them. Several fell before their operation had even commenced. In spite of that, the battalion held its ranks and filled in the gaps. I began to get the same feeling I get when I'm in the dentist's waiting room and the assistant is about to lean out and shout, "Mr. Gates!" I wished all I had to worry about today was an abscessed tooth. What had I gotten myself into, I wondered.

As Kershaw's brigade encountered the Emmitsburg roadway, General Longstreet, still walking out in front, stepped to the side to allow the combatants to clear the fence rails ensuring a clean pathway. When that task was complete, General Longstreet took off his hat, waved it in the air, and shouted encouragement over the sound of the cannon blasts. Without breaking stride, the swarm of gray shirts broke into double time, shrieking and yelling the entire way. We watched as the unit disappeared across the road and down into the dell.

There wasn't enough time to survey those activities as we had developments of our own to worry about. General Semmes was less spirited than the previous leader as he turned, faced his troops and yelled, "Colors up!" The flag bearers jumped front and center. "Places!" he shouted to the rest of us. Those who occupied the ground ascended to the upright position, weapons clicking to the ready. The General removed his saber from its sheath and aimed it skyward capturing everyone's undivided attention. As he struggled to be heard over the detonations, he shouted in a hoarse, gruff voice, "Gentlemen, you're going to experience fighting the likes you've never seen before!" He then turned on his heels 180 degrees and faced his road of destiny. After a slight hesitation, the vertical sword came down and pointed straight ahead as General Semmes turned his head to us yelled, "Forward men, forward," and led the way.

We emerged from the safety of our forested haven and began our journey across 600 yards of unobstructed field, open to any and all elements. General Semmes led a confident charge at a deliberate pace of ninety yards a minute. There was no turning back now. Each moment seemed to take an hour to pass as we trudged across the weeds.

My mind began to wander, wanting to avoid the inevitable. Aside from the smell of gunpowder, I noticed that the grinding action of hundreds of soldiers' feet, mixed with the heat and humidity from a long summer's day, radiated the scent of clover, Queen Ann's Lace, and golden rod upward. It almost brought back a human perspective to an inhuman situation. Despite the fact that many define weeds as plants not worth growing, their aroma satisfied the nostrils of men whose life's worth was considered even less.

I glanced around and was thankful that the sun was over my shoulder making for perfect photographic lighting conditions. Even now I was thinking of photography. That's dedication.

I was brought back to reality when a crashing volley of fire emanated from the cannons to our rear in an attempt to soften up the opposition. The blast was so intense that my heels were actually scooted ahead of my normal gait while my toes barely touched the ground.

Looking around, this entire operation reminded me of one of the Civil War reenactments I've witnessed as we all held rank despite the projectiles flying to and fro. But this was no reenactment. This was the real McCoy as were the ordinances.

For many soldiers, too many, there would be no future waiting for them after this day's work was done. There would be no dreams of heavier than air flight, horseless carriages roaming the streets of their towns, and the opportunity to bounce a child or grandchild upon one's knee would forever be lost.

We finally made it as far as Emmitsburg Road where the procession came to a halt. We were now able to see over the rise and could make out a dozen or so fallen comrades, some of Kershaw's men no doubt, lying still and presumably absent of life. From here we could observe the movement of the troops, both theirs and ours. I was fascinated by the two army's attempts at tactical precision despite the shelling raining in from every direction.

My first instinct was to go into a permanent duck to avoid any flying lead until I realized that maneuver would be futile. I felt useless armed with only a camera, a canteen, and what little nerve I had left.

Other than his rifle, I noticed that Mojo was armed with even less. He was starting to lose his wits again as he resumed his quivering and shrieking when he saw what lay ahead of him. As few faculties as he possessed, Mojo was smart enough to realize that this was no simple drill. He wheeled towards the safety of the Pitzer Woods until grabbed around the collar by Rueben.

"Turn this way dammit or you're going to get hurt. You've got to be a man! It's time to grow up!" That statement was made as a threat as well as a matter of fact. Rueben knew that this was not the time for him to demonstrate compassion.

We had been detained for only about twenty to thirty seconds when, while watching Kershaw's brigade, we saw them up and advance over the rise towards the enemy. As they departed, General Kershaw turned in our direction, rose, then waved his hat furiously in the air. That must have been our signal. This was it. We were all about to experience a horrible clash of arms, some for the first time, some for the last.

In my attempt to stay alive at the road's edge, I almost forgot to take a few combat photos. That was one of the reasons I was here. I managed to click off two frames of Kershaw's advance when General Semmes yelled, "Remember Richmond! Charge!" Being in the middle of the pack, I had no choice but to obey.

We proceeded at almost full gallop down the slight incline towards our destination about three hundred yards away. The center of our advance ran along a tiny glade in the middle of the field. Kershaw's brigade, thankfully, drew much of the fire away from us.

As we scrambled en masse, I was jockeying for position like a participant in the Kentucky Derby as I cut across the grain in an attempt to gain a positional advantage. I wanted to be near Jonathan Gates for the moment of truth. Obeying verbal instructions, our entire line swung out wide to the right, then inward as it tried to achieve the perfect northeast angle as we approached our first stop. There was a slightly wooded tree line, easy to see through, which General Semmes designated as our destination.

About half of the way to our newly vacated position, our flag carrier was gunned down just three rows in front of me spraying those of us behind him with his blood. Any soft tissue wouldn't deter an ounce or two of lead traveling at 900 feet per second. Even bone didn't remain intact upon impact.

After the soldier crumpled in a heap, the banner was immediately picked up by the next in line and held high. I was relieved because from a physical stand point, I was the next in line to the downed carrier. That wasn't my job, and I don't know what would have happened if I refused.

Anyway, to break the moral of a fighting unit, unofficial rules of war stated that a soldier should take out the officers and flag carrier first. Carrying a banner in that fashion seemed too much like advertising a desire to be first in line for the lead, I thought. Many times it was, but such was the ways of war at the time.

Two more fellows felt the devious work of the Union's .58 caliber minie ball before we made it to the safety of the grove. There was a small, natural stone rampart at the front edge of the tree line where we all fell flat for protection. Almost everyone arrived in unison; quite an accomplishment when considering the conditions. This was to be our stop for the next five minutes or so. Our next break would take us eastward towards a steep ravine right into the center of enemy territory. There would be little if any way out once we reached that point.

This lull, if you will, gave me time to look around and see the mess I'd gotten myself into. I could hear drum and bugle calls coming from the area that now housed Kershaw's brigade as they advanced or repulsed a charge. Some of the men amongst our huddled mass would occasionally rise up and take a pot shot at an advancing group of Federals. They would then lie back down, flat on their backs, and attempt to reload. While the enemy troops were within target range, they had their own hands full of Anderson's and Kershaw's boys. That didn't stop the intermittent buck and ball from gracing our heads with a breeze. We were fortunate that since we arrived behind the safety of the stone fence, no additional troops had bought any lead. There were a couple of Kershaw's men lying about in our area. While some were hurt pretty bad, most looked as if they'd make it. One was so close that one of Semmes' men was treating him.

My God, I thought as I watched the carnage to my front, this battle wasn't as orderly as they'd like you to believe when you read the history books. There was a fright and fire in the eyes of these people that no movie or book could give justice to. It was a look of desperation. It was a look of anger. It was a look of hate.

I took the opportunity to snap an additional photo or two, one picture of the Union troops aligning themselves into position, and one of Kershaw's men to our front positioned behind the scattered boulders. At any time I could have taken a bullet through any part of my body, but I found out that once you play the role of soldier in a combat setting, you end up playing the role of the fool. No battle would be fought and no war would claim a victor if that wasn't a fact. I remained low.

Just after Kershaw's men advanced from our line of sight, General Semmes barked out the order to rise up and advance. After we upped and cleared the stone fence, our compact formation grew in size to two to three hundred feet wide and half as deep. Most of us took refuge against a second natural stone formation. Naturally, General Semmes, along with two other junior officers, was towards the front and huddled against a stone barrier. Most of the fortunate ones found a similar defense, but there simply weren't enough rocks to go around.

About fifteen to twenty feet to my right was Jonathan Gates. Having just fired his weapon, I saw him on his back reloading for his next attempt. For some reason, the hair began to rise on the back of my neck. Something told me that this would be the moment he would deliver his verdict to General Semmes. The timing was right. But this didn't jive with the area of the battlefield where I thought I sensed the spirit of great-great grandfather Gates many years ago. That was an area closer to the Rose farm house. I was now confused. I always read that General Semmes was hit near the Rose Farm. I guess, technically, we were on the farm proper. All I could do was watch and wait. Nothing happens until it happens.

General Semmes was continually rising up to peer over his stone breastworks to determine when the time would be right for another advance. Now loaded and ready to return fire, Jonathan Gates rose to one knee and drew a bead on a lone uniformed soldier in blue as he attempted to sneak around to the rear of Kershaw's men now located deep in the Rose woods. As I observed the predicament of the two opposing warriors, it was as if time itself had slowed to a crawl. The effect was similar to when a person is in an automobile accident. The experience is so intense that one's senses absorb much more information in a short span of time. I guess the individual's heightened state of awareness receives credit for that.

Private Gates had his sights set on the core of his opponent and his finger was wrapped tightly around the trigger. He slowly squeezed down on the hammer release attempting to change the destiny of the blue clad fighter who had now taken a knee and was partially hidden behind a tree. Instead, Jonathan Gates decided his own fate.

At that same moment, under his breath, General Semmes quietly instructed his junior officers, "Let's go." Having given that order, he raised up, and like a tight rope walker ran laterally along the top of the wall to the left in search of a locale closer to the enemy. That would never occur, for at the same moment Jonathan Gates discharged his weapon sending a bone shattering .57 caliber chunk of lead through the upper thigh of General Semmes. This activity spun the commander around landing him shoulders-first on a toppled tree, his face aimed in our direction, his leg in another.

"Gates, God damn you!" screamed the general in horror. He threw his head back towards the sky in an attempt to gasp in as much oxygen as possible for his shock-ridden body. An enlisted man next to him grabbed the general by the front of the uniform, pulled him back over the wall and out of any additional harm, and screamed to anyone who'd listen, "The general! Someone help me!"

I could tell by the 180-degree twist in the general's leg that there would either be an amputation or the eventual loss of life. Unfortunately, that riddle has already been solved.

I looked over at the alleged perpetrator, Jonathan Gates, whose rifle's muzzle was still pointed in Semmes' direction. A look of shock and panic was displayed upon Gate's face. I realized at that point that I had just received the answer I sought to my question. It was friendly fire, yes, that brought down General Semmes, but the action was purely accidental, plain and simple. To be honest, if Gates hadn't gotten him, the Union soldier who was in Jonathan's gun sight most likely would have completed the task.

The amount of hate that Private Gates had exhibited in the past towards his leader was now replaced by feelings of shock, panic, and sorrow. Jonathan Gates was an innocent man, soon to be wrongly convicted and executed. In the end, it wasn't Gates' actions that decided his fate; it was his reputation.

Confusion now reigned supreme as the brigade, minus its leader, entered into a state of disorganization. Some of the men followed the intentions of their commander and started down the ravine as they were now in search of a new home with Kershaw's brigade. Their advance was less than spirited and the rebel yell came out weak and uneven.

Amongst the chargers were Rueben and Mojo. They had gotten a late start and pulled up just twenty yards out from my spot, pinned down by enemy fire. They, along with a dozen or so others, flattened in hopes that a break in the action would present them with an opportunity to join their advancing colleagues. Since no let up in the shelling seemed imminent, Mojo started to panic once again.

"Rueben!" he yelled.

"Stay down, just stay down!" shouted Rueben who was about fifteen to twenty feet away from his compatriot.

That order did nothing to placate the demolished nerves of the terror-stricken teen. He just continued to yell all the louder. Finally, with one last scream at the top of his lungs, he shrieked, "Rueben!!"

Seeing that Mojo was about to lose any and all composure, Rueben yelled back, "Just stay there! I'm coming over to you!"

His response was too late, however. Mojo, having had his senses overloaded with fear and horror, left his gun on the ground and simply stood up and looked around, perhaps in search of an escape route. He may have been confused, dazed, or possibly he had seen enough. He just couldn't take anymore.

"Mojo get down, get down!" yelled Rueben to the lad who was now in the middle of a sniveling breakdown. I don't know if Mojo at this point was suicidal, or just couldn't take it anymore and decided to leave the field to return home. That wish would be granted.

Rueben screamed at Mojo to not be a stupid fool as he crawled his way over to his friend in need. His efforts, unfortunately, would be in vain. His comrade's time was already up.

Mojo took on the appearance of a man who just walked into a hornet's nest, as the bullets began to sting his body from all angles. The first bite was to his shoulder. You could see the minie ball's exit accompanied by a spray of blood and tissue. A charge of shot riddled his knee. Mojo was forced into a genuflection as he reached for the destroyed joint. His head was now down facing the enemy. The guns of the Union infantry finally ended Mojo's fright.

What a horrible sight to see. A man, unable even to fend for himself, was put in the position to defend his country. Seeing Mojo's fright first hand and how he still faced the enemy none-the-less, led me to believe that while others may recieve the accolades, there may never be found a braver soul connected to this conflict. The fellow probably wasn't even aware of the reasons behind the struggle, yet he did his duty the best he could anyway. A man who may never have hurt a soul in his life would now be rewarded with an unmarked grave. No ceremony, no eulogy, and no tears would accompany his farewell. Probably no one would even notice his absence, but I would miss him.

Such a unspeakable sight sickened me, but like any other participant here today, there was no time to grieve. On this day, he who hesitated would be lost. Having seen all that I came for and all that I cared to, I had to find an exit to this situation. The mystique and romanticism of the Civil War was now forever gone from my soul. The sights and sounds of this conflict now appeared to me as they actually were, not as the glorified accounts I had once read.

The taste of sulfur in the air would burn as an indelible memory into my senses. As the situation transformed into a state of sheer panic, I was now aware of the yelling and screaming that seemed to bypass my ears earlier. I could also hear, to our front, both Union and Confederate officers hoarsely barking out orders in a feeble attempt to advance towards their foe.

Once again I noticed that reality was nothing like the stories portrayed by Hollywood. I never did witness a shot that felled a soldier, leaving little or no evidence of an entry or exit. A round canister ball wasn't tapered like a minie ball and that made for a difficult 'in and out' on its victims. A canister ball ended up destroying all bone and tissue in its path. To be honest, a minie ball wasn't much better. That's why there were so many amputations during that war. Over seventy-five percent of battlefield operations involved an amputation of some sort. Even Louisiana Governor General Francis Nicholls lost an arm, a leg, and an eye during the war. Nobody was immune. There was over 27,000 dead and wounded Rebels at Gettysburg. Many of their injuries consisted of shattered bones, splintered beyond all repair.

Most of Semmes' brigade made it over their granite breastworks, while a few others stayed behind to attend to the general's wound. At this point, the attendees weren't aware of the severity of the injury. They attempted to tie a tourniquet around the damaged area in an effort to fend off a great loss of blood. They also sought to prevent the onset of infection and gangrene, maladies that may have had a hand in the general's eventual demise.

However, the destruction was too far north on the leg to allow any measures such as these much success.

I was surprised to see Jonathan Gates still up on one knee. Oblivious to the fighting going on around him and the danger he was putting himself in, he obviously was still traumatized from the event. It was one thing to belittle and argue with those in your outfit. It was yet another to destroy the one you and the rest of the brigade trusted to lead you to victory or safety.

A colonel who was attending to the general looked back in Jonathan's direction and yelled, "Gates, you'll hang for this!"

Private Gates just shook his head weakly from side to side and said, "I didn't mean it. It was an accident!" But nobody was listening.

I began looking for a safe path out of my predicament as well, as if one actually existed. I wouldn't see an opening until the smoke clouds from the Peach Orchard drifted from my line of vision. When that development came to pass, cannon vapors to our front billowed in their place creating the perfect screen that I was looking for. While there was always the risk of being struck by a musket ball, my chances would never be better.

I made a southwest dash to the rear border of the grove, then hit the deck. That would be my plan, I thought, thinking fast on or off my feet. It would be foolish to attempt a complete withdrawal all at once. That would be suicidal. I would have to traverse small chunks of the terrain at a time in order to work my way back to the relative safety of the ridge.

I looked back at my former position and

saw several Southern soldiers prepping General Semmes for a trip that would lead to the unsuccessful treatment of his wound. Farther in the distance, I could see the still body of Mojo, now out of his misery, while the rest of the brigade went on without him. Rueben was nowhere in sight. I hope that meant that he was still on his feet and advancing.

Not being able to view that scene and keep my mind on the task at hand, I turned towards the Warfield Ridge area to scout out my next sanctuary on this jaunt to freedom. The open area carried only a few emerging rock formations, but a few stone fences and pockets of dense undergrowth would make for an adequate refuge. It's all I had to work with.

Once again I waited for the zone north and east of me to become shrouded by the cannon's fog. Once that scenario came to pass, I made my break. I darted for a sheltered spot containing a couple of the few available boulders. Interspersed with the rocks was a gathering of four-foot saplings that emerged from their center. This run turned out to be much longer than the previous, and protection from orchard area fire was lacking.

I must have picked the wrong time for that trip. As soon as I made my break, all hell broke loose. During my retreat, I became aware that I was in a cross fire of cannons. Running between the shell bursts, I could tell that the majority of fire was coming from the ridge of my eventual destination.

The ground shook as the Rebels' attempts to take out the orchard came up short. A blast detonated about ten yards to my left scattering me with debris. I ended up literally between a rock and a hard place. If I tried to conceal myself on the east side of the trench, I was vulnerable to the rear. If I remain on the southwest flank, Southern artillery could pick me off. On the northern edge lay the Federal troops in defense of the Peach Orchard. No area was safe, but I had no choice other than to fall back and attempt to escape from the cannon range of my own territory.

I sprinted from my shelter out across the field of oats and weeds only to discover there was no real place to hide for nearly fifty yards. Believing that I'd never make that trip in one jaunt, I just dropped down into the field next to a horse whose gallop was no more. I hoped that the carcass would hide me long enough for me to catch my breath.

As I cowered up against the steed's back, the horse's skin quivered as if trying to rid itself of a horse fly. I was hoping that it was only a reaction of nerves to my touch. I didn't need for my cover to up and leave me.

As vulnerable as I was in this spot, I felt comfortable enough to look around and take stock of my surroundings. As I hid beneath the stalks of grain, I took a risk and popped my head up above the kernels to observe this giant operation in action.

The sights were interesting to say the least, ghastly at best. As a balls of hot lead journeyed across the top of the field, it left a trail of exploding grain that almost mimicked that of popcorn being prepared. That path revealed not only the source of the shot, but its destination as well. If the reason for that artistry wasn't so deadly, a display such as that might have been considered spectacular.

My sense of near serenity was brought back to reality by the sight of a soldier attempting his solitary retreat about sixty to seventy yards to the south of my current position. He no longer possessed a weapon or hat, and looked to be elderly in appearance. At any rate, it was evident that he was much too old to be participating in a struggle that had been reserved for those of his son's generation. Despite the abundance of gunfire and shelling, he wasn't moving at what would be considered an accelerated rate of speed. I'm sure that ability left his legs many years before.

There were a several evacuating fighters nearby, so why that man caught my attention, I'm not sure. Perhaps his struggle against the elements as well as time stood out, but I wish it hadn't. As he made his way across the open field, in an instant a Napoleon's twelve-pound ordinance cleanly removed the soldier's head from his shoulders without even knocking the man off of his feet. Too shocked to realize that he was now indeed a dead man, his journey continued on for another two or three paces before collapsing in a heap on the once golden, now crimson field. Good God, the inhumanity of it all, was all I could think.

Leaving my trusty stallion, I upped once again, not being able to digest what I had just witnessed, and sprinted to another tree and rock formation I had spotted during my last jaunt. I slid in there not realizing that the area was already taken. A soldier was lying in front of a rock conglomeration minus a set of legs. A bloody glissade accompanied him to his present position.

He wasn't moving but his eyes were open. I wasn't sure if he was dead or not. If he wasn't now, he would be shortly.

When I ducked down behind the stone structure, I was stunned and sickened to find a rebel soldier, a few feet to my left, resting against the boulder in a sitting position. His left arm had been shot away at the shoulder. His uniform's sleeve was missing, along with the appendage, exposing the collarbone and accompanying muscle tissue that was dangling from its source. He turned his head towards me slightly and just stared slack-jawed. His lips would move on occasion, but I don't think that he was trying to converse with me. He may have been praying for all I knew. Two other soldiers were present. One was on my right and another to the front near my first acquaintance at this site. I guessed both to be dead as they lay face down in a puddle of blood.

I was in a state of sensory overload at this point. The term 'shocked' wouldn't do the situation justice. I was slowly being pushed towards a stage of panic. I was beginning to see how this situation got to Mojo. Trying to clear my senses the best I could, I breathed in as deeply as possible, taking in all of the airborne sulfur along the way. I decided to try and hold my position and recoup my good judgment the best that I could. I looked around and was able to see pockets of Federals and Confederates making their runs, some to and others from.

Out of the blue I spotted the fleeing form of Jonathan Gates as he made his way out of his situation using the lane in front of the Rose house and barn. He wasn't wasting much time pausing at stop off points along the way. About half way between the field and house, a canister exploded close enough to him to knock him off of his feet and send him tumbling. I waited for a few moments but didn't see him reemerge from the weeds. I thought he may have been killed. Could I have twisted up history so much that I've even changed people's destiny?

It then occurred to me that the place where Jonathan fell was the same spot I thought I felt his spirit back during my childhood. But if he had just been killed, what about his trial and subsequent execution? Was all of that made up to cover over a battlefield death?

Shortly thereafter, a Parrot ball landed twenty feet to my rear once again showering my companions and me with debris. A blanket of dirt would come soon enough for them, I thought, but I for one am not ready to be covered in the earth where I lay. "I've got to get out of here," I said to the trauma-ridden soldier to my left.

Not thinking clearly and throwing all caution to the wind, I evacuated that place with no particular destination in mind. Looking up, I noticed that the ridge was still at least one hundred and fifty yards to my southwest.

My gallop turned into a sprint as I too hit the panic stage. No wonder so many soldiers came back from a war suffering from what many people termed 'shell shock.' I'm sure if I had kept my mind focused on what I was now doing, I probably couldn't have handled it either.

I had covered over one third of my current flight when the unthinkable happened. In mid stride across the field, I was struck in the right hip by a sharp blow that knocked my feet out from under me. I lay there motionless, out of breath, and hoping that my apparent plight wasn't what it appeared to be.

My hip had taken the brunt of a blow that felt like it couldn't have come from anything other than a .58 caliber ball of lead. It wouldn't matter if the bullet hadn't hit any vital organs. If a man was lucky, an injury such as this would maim him for life. At the worst, it wouldn't be uncommon for infection to set in on this type of injury resulting in a prolonged and agonizing death. If percentages count for anything, the Union side recorded an eighty-three percent fatality rate when it came to hip amputations.

Oh God, what if I'm carrying that wound? Even if I was able to crawl to the landing zone off Emmitsburg Road, it would be a couple of days before I'd be able to return home. By then it might be too late even for modern medicine. And I wasn't about to let those butchers cut on me here on the battlefield. I didn't want to become another inscription on a granite monument. This appeared to be a no-win situation.

I reached down to my hip and found it to be warm and moist. Slowly, I brought the soaked hand up to my eyes to see the effects of the destruction, but I saw none. I didn't understand. I gradually rolled over on to my left side so I'd be able to examine the right hip. I looked down and noticed an absence of blood. The joint was numb, but I knew the pain would come later. It wasn't what I had expected. Could I have escaped the bullet's wrath?

I went ahead and inspected my person to

search for the source of the dampness. It would be understandable for me to be wet considering what I've been through, I mulled over in an almost humorous vein. Upon further examination, I found that the origin of the moisture was my canteen. A projectile had perforated the flask clean through thus preventing any further injury to me. How fortunate could a person be, I marveled. With a little luck and a few more short trips, I'll be home free. Lightning couldn't strike twice.

Being satisfied at my condition, I rolled back on to my stomach to provide a smaller target for the sharpshooters and to scout out the next area of respite. As I flattened, a slight clattering noise that sounded out of place originated from my hip region. I pulled up my camera only to discover that it too had been done in by the musket ball. Apparently the missile had pierced my canteen, entered through the back of my camera, and then lodged itself in the now shattered cavity of the lens. I guess the bullet must have been fired from quite some distance to produce this limited impact. Those things can travel up to nine hundred feet per second and were considered accurate to about fifty-to-one hundred yards. This one definitely had to be considered a stray. How many times can I luck out, I wondered.

The bullet's impact went farther than just a hip bruise though. My pictorial record of the battle—scenes never to be played out again—were lost forever. Pictures of General Semmes on his mount, a photo of Rueben, snapshots of parading troops, all were gone. Now they were part of the past forever, never to be witnessed again. While I should've been grateful for the assistance given me by the Pentax, I was incredibly disappointed. "Dammit," was all that I could say as I looked over the now useless chunk of metal.

I removed the camera and my porous canteen and chucked them aside. They were worthless to me now. I took a deep breath and buried my face in my hands as I attempted to force my nerves back into their respective sockets. While I rested there, common logic told me it would be best to let things cool down a bit before I attempted another escape.

As much as I hated to admit it, seeing the stars and stripes striving to hold its ground on the knoll of the orchard was a sight to behold. It almost brought a lump to my throat. That reminded me of all of the difficulties our forefathers had gone through to make our country what it is today. Everything has a price, especially freedom. We don't seem to appreciate that anymore, I thought.

On the other side of our now-vacated grove, I could hear sounds of mass confusion. There were cheers from the Union side as they reclaimed a piece of ground lost just minutes earlier. That was followed by a bugled charge accompanied by the infamous Rebel yell.

I watched as a canister, fired from the Little Round Top area, exploded on an incline taking out a small company of Confederates like a bowling ball taking down the pins. I'm sure that those who were dying prayed for life, while those who would survive would beg for everlasting sleep.

The screams weren't limited to only the combatants. Over and back a little ways near the Rose house, I noticed what appeared to be a mutt laying prostrate on its side. Perhaps a resident of the farm itself, he was now just another never-to-be recorded statistic. And the sight of a cavalry horse, once buffed and parade-ready, was now reduced to a screaming beast attempting to run from the fray on two front leg stumps. That was a sight I never want to see repeated, yet it was, time after time.

So this is war, I thought. How anyone could glorify a mess like this was beyond me. There was nothing noble about a soldier, a friend, an individual, lying in as many pieces as a jigsaw puzzle, unable to be assembled again. General Sherman may have thought that war was all hell, but all that I found it to be was the forced extinction of one ideal and the expansion of another. In this game, the soldiers just happened to be the pawns, and their elimination from the board could be in any one of a number of forms.

I decided that the longer I stayed out here, horizontal or otherwise, the more vulnerable I'd be to injury. The odds weren't with me and I couldn't take any additional chances. I would try a different tactic on this run to safety. This time I figured that it would be best if I took smaller chunks of turf and attempted more trips rather than the opposite. Instead of waiting for a lull in the action, I decided to fly when the lead did. I was anticipating that the guns, both large and small, would already have their respective targets sighted up and their loot spent. I was also praying that I wouldn't be one of the targets.

After a while, the sounds of battle had taken on a uniform pitch. To differentiate the sounds, I had to break everything down to sectors. When I was able to detect that the volleys were emanating from both the Union orchard and the Confederate ridge, I decided this to be the best time to make my break.

The additional distraction of Barksdale's Mississippians attempting their final charge towards the orchard about one thousand yards to my north, aided in my cause greatly. I proceeded at a pace of about fifty yards a crack, and no one seemed to care.

I made my way towards Emmitsburg Road, then huddled up next to the corner of a stone wall for protection. Once in place, I found a fair amount of soldiers already present with the same idea. Some were injured, some were assisting those in need, and yet others were milling about as if awaiting their orders. This area had been the launching site of Anderson's Georgia and Robertson's Texas Brigades' assault on the Devil's Den.

For the first time since the assault began, I got an overall look at the southeast portion of the battlefield. Dying soldiers were scattered across the ground like acorns from a mighty oak on an autumn afternoon. Some of them had yet to settle into a stationary position while others had already put down roots where they lay.

After a short breather, I decided that it was time to make my way back to the brigade's equipment pile to see if my video camera was still in its place. I hoped so, for my sake, because it was all that I had left in my arsenal of visual evidence I promised to bring back to Dr. Welles. My still camera lay in pieces on the battlefield, much like many of the participants.

As I sat against the wall, I looked around and saw stretchers full of legless men, subdivided faces, and blank stares from the somber, defeated warriors. As I gazed at those sights, it became apparent to me that the surrounding explosions didn't have the same frightening effect on me as they had just a few hours prior. How awful it is to become accustomed to something like that and barely take notice, I remember thinking. I was becoming as seasoned as those I chose to study.

As a Napoleon opened up from our sector, it barely shook my senses. I was too absorbed in thoughts of how I'd make it back to camp. I did, however, become transfixed by the rhythm of each artillery line and how the cannons seemed to be ignited, one after the other, in succession. Each cannon would jump nearly two feet in the air upon each explosion. Their detonations in sequence gave the appearance of the peaks and valleys of a wave in motion.

You could tell the seasoned gunner from the apprentice. Those who were the veterans of many battles didn't even flinch at each shot. They barely acknowledged the concussions indicating that their hearing was no longer a factor. They had already given part of their lives for their country.

I looked over and saw a rebel propped up against a blood-spattered boulder. It was the same rock that Dr. Welles used as a table for his laptop during the launch. I thought this place looked familiar. I reflected on how close I was to the launch site and how I could almost reach across the chasm of time and pull myself out of this mess. I had seen enough, but an exit wasn't to be as the tables weren't set for a return just yet. Everything in life has a schedule, but I still hoped for that time to arrive sooner rather than later.

I figured that I was now far enough from the action that my worry factor would be reduced. A return trip to camp was in order. I gathered my sore self up from the wall and began my trek back over the ridge. About ten to fifteen paces out, one of the returning injured Confederates yelled, "Incoming!"

To me, that could have meant just about anything. If I moved forward, I could walk straight into the path of the approaching artillery. If I stayed where I was, I might be a dead sitting duck. All that I could do was cover up and keep moving in a crouched position to minimize any impacting debris.

An iron sphere approached on an arch, cracked its way through the boughs above, and landed on the spot I had just vacated. The impact knocked me head over heels and placed me flat on my back. I lay there for a moment trying to make sure all of my wits were about me.

The injured fighter, now covered with debris asked, "You all right mister?"

"Yeah, yeah I think so," came my shaken reply.

"Welcome to the Confederate States of America," was his unexpected humorous return. He let loose with a cackled laugh in a most heinous manner.

"Nice welcoming committee," I said, gazing at the swath that had been cut through the trees. "You folks throw a blast like this very often?" I should have stopped at the first line.

I picked myself up, brushed off my clothes, then went over to view the scene of my near mishap. Judging from the trajectory, I guessed that the shell originated from Little Round Top, probably from one of Hazlett's batteries. They were less than three quarters of a mile away, and the range of some of those guns could extend for a couple of miles. Needless to say, we were well within range.

When I went over to inspect the area of impact, I noticed that the hollow iron ball had landed on a rock splintering the ordinance into worthless scrap. The rock didn't fare much better. The once unblemished rectangle was now in two sections. I reached down and put my hand into the heart of the ten inch deep crater. I could feel the heat that was being expelled from the remaining pieces of the ordinance. That could have been me, I surmised. If that rock didn't stop that missile, my bony figure would have met its match, and then some.

I decided that was enough of the close calls for one day. The quicker I got back to camp the better. I decided to walk parallel to the wall, westward, towards the summit of Warfield Ridge. I was able to short-cut around the danger zone by clearing the crest, then making my way north towards the camp. At least I wouldn't be visible to the enemy, even if they were members of my own country.

Haze had taken over the order of the day as the sun passed the 7:30 PM mark. I limped my way down the rise, stopping at Willoughby's Run creek to fill my canteen and clean up. Once there, I remembered that I no longer had a canteen. My best bet would be to carry what I could within. I tried to wash the sweat, grime, and smoke from my face using my shirt for a towel. I took a drink and cleared the black phlegm from my throat.

I got up from my knees and walked along the creek towards camp. What a sight the encampment was. The place looked more like a staging area used during one of those mock disaster drills, but this was no drill. It was truly a disaster.

Many of the slaves who traveled with the Army of Northern Virginia were put into service on stretcher duty. I guess those in charge figured that if anyone had to risk their skin to pick up a wounded man, that skin might as well be black. "Better them than us," seemed to be the rule.

I tramped around looking for the equipment pile. Everything that was in place before we moved out was now elsewhere. So many wagons had been brought in to act as ambulance corps along with several minor aid tents. The major surgeries were being performed under roof if possible. The area houses, barns, and churches were put to use in that capacity.

I looked around and finally recognized the equipment pile that now had been downgraded to the status of a heap in order to save space. The fact that I wasn't a soldier made me think that it would probably be for the best if I checked in with the guard before I went rooting around through all of the military gear.

"Howdy. I've got to pick up a bag that I placed here before the offensive," I said informing the man.

Looking at me in an odd way because civilians usually don't utilize the soldiers' security pile he asked, "What did you put there?"

"It was a bag, a green bag."

"Well that certainly narrows it down a bit," he returned in his Irish brogue. Much of the paraphernalia present matched that description. "What's in it?"

"I had a wet plate camera, wood, about this big," I said demonstrating the size with my hands. I followed Semmes' Georgia men into the fray. I'm writing a story on them for Harper's.

"Well, look around, lad. When you find it, let me see it."

I dug around, moving others' gear aside and down from the top. Almost every soldier carried anywhere from ten to twenty pounds on his back. After about three minutes into my quest, I located my parcel. "Here it is," I announced. I took it over to the sentry and removed the camera from the bag.

"I'm a photographer as well."

"Then why did you leave the camera here," he inquired.

"This unit is more adept at shooting portraits and short work. My longer range camera was destroyed by a round to the lens out there."

"You weren't using it at the time I gather."

"Oh no."

Handing the camera back to me he said, "You'd best be careful. You might get hurt."

"I know it." I walked on with the camera and bag, yet I wasn't sure where I was headed. There was confusion, screams, and traffic all over the valley. I had no idea where I'd bed down for the night either. All of the houses and barns were now cutting rooms and morgues, some one in the same. I'll be under the stars tonight for sure, I thought.

I decided to hike over to the foot of the ridge guessing that I would be O.K. there for the night. As the sun went down, so would the activity.

A wagon pulled into my path to drop off a load of injured Southerners. They were a pitiful sight. I watched with sorrow as the tattered and torn men were lifted out, some under their own power, some with assistance. Most of the fighters appeared in salvageable shape while the limbless remained on board for a trip to the hospital. The fellows who appeared to be hurt more seemed to complain the least. I suppose one could chalk that up to the shock factor.

As I started to side-step the wagon, I almost walked into the path of Jonathan Gates. He was progressing with a drunken gait as he was being assisted along by, of all people, Nathaniel from the chow wagon.

"Don't fret none, Misser Jon. We git you fixed up real good now," was his reassurance.

I just stared at them, slack-jawed. Nathaniel had taken so much guff from Private Gates, yet he was still willing to show compassion towards the injured man. Never has a man stood so tall, was my impression. I was seeing the best and the worst of mankind here today.

Jonathan, appearing to be suffering from a head wound, was in no shape to rebuff the assistance. He almost appeared to be grateful for the help as he leaned on his aide. As they passed by me, neither acknowledged my presence. Nate was too busy and Jonathan wasn't sure which end was up.

I watched as they made their way back to

the tents for some general aid. It would be the physician's opinion that Jonathan would live to fight another day. At this point I realized that I was over-stressed and needed some rest and relief, like right now.

I turned towards the ridge and located a place to retire for the evening. I put my things down and rolled my coat up for a pillow. I turned on my video camera to make sure that it hadn't been damaged. The last scene I shot looked fine. I switched to the record button and turned towards the camp to tape the aftermath of the second day of fighting. It shortly became too dark to video, so I shut the camera down, pulled out my bottle of black-labeled spirits, and took a long draw. "Boy, that is smooth," I said to myself, recalling the words of Rueben Langston. I hope he's all right. God only knows where he is right now.

Laying on the slight incline allowed me the opportunity to overlook the camp in all its disarray. Resting somewhat comfortably, I felt the mental exhaustion taking its toll now that I could be reasonably sure that I was out of harm's way. I decided to attempt some sleep. I wasn't the only one with that in mind. Others in the area endeavored to partake of their last few hours of sleep before one of eternity took its place.

Away from the main morass of noise and confusion were, despite the evening heat, several small campfires. A number of soldiers were huddled around them, probably trying to make sense of it all. I'm sure they weren't able to see the big picture as was I. Twenty-twenty hindsight became a valuable tool in providing me peace of mind with respect to the overall situation.

My eyes were opened several times during the night due to sporadic gunfire. As I woke on those occasions, I observed a sparse blanket of smoke and fog collecting on the floor of the valley. I gazed upward and noticed the near-full moon, now tarnished from the residual smoke that still hugged the area, moving across the sky not unlike the presentation of the host during a Sunday mass. For some, there would be no future Sabbath, yet for the rest, tomorrow would be another day.

Chapter Nine
Trading Allegiance

"Any frontal attack on ignorance is bound to fail because the masses are always ready to defend their most precious possession —their ignorance."
HENDRIK WILLEM van LOON

I didn't sleep well on the night of July second to the third. It may have been because I knew what was about to take place in just a few hours, or perhaps it was from the scenes I had already witnessed. Contributing to my lack of rest was the resumption of sunrise action in and around Culp's Hill. Upon my forced awakening, I realized that I was quite hungry and thirsty. My banquet of sour mash from last night just wasn't enough to fill the void.

I looked around and didn't see the chow wagons operating anymore. There wasn't even the smell of anything cooking in the air that I noticed. The only odors to be found were those of the scattered campfires and an occasional whiff of cigar smoke. I knew that provisions were going to be scarce from here on out. I had to do what I hoped I wouldn't have to resort to: Scavenge.

I pulled my sore body up from its place of rest. My hip had stiffened up a bit, but things could have been worse. I looked around and deduced that probably far more casualties fell on top of the ridge than in this area, so that's where I would have to go.

I was right. There were still several pockets of Confederates in the woods pulling sentry duty, so I had to move out of eye shot for fear of retribution. I didn't think those folks would appreciate a northern boy scavenging goods from one of their own. When I found myself safely between two sentinels, I began looking around. I really wasn't sure what I was searching for, but when I found it, I'd know.

With all of the scattered debris, I didn't have to look very long before I located a haversack at the base of a tree. I acted as if I was the true owner, then dug through the satchel past a bundled collection of yellowed letters from home, some family photos, a knife, eating utensils, and some various stained orders. At the bottom of the bag I found a fistful of what I guessed to be hardtack, or perhaps just old stale biscuits. One in the same, I mused. That would have to do. We beggars can't be choosers, I thought.

I wiped the dirt from my meal, and after a few bites into these 'delicacies,' I began to wonder how any soldier from either side had any teeth left in his head after consuming these over a period of time. And what about those who were minus their dental work to begin with? From what I observed of late, that was as much the rule than the exception.

Well, I surmised that this meal would have to hold me for a little while. I slipped the rest into my bag to continue my stroll so as not to draw any unneeded attention from anyone.

I picked up a stray canteen to replace the one I lost yesterday and slung it across my shoulder. A person wouldn't have any trouble finding just about anything they were looking for out here today. With the sun just beginning to rise, I could see equipment of all kinds leading from our ridge towards Emmitsburg Road, and every place in between. The ground had become a real treasure trove of rifles, pistols, and swords for any future antique collector. Yet, the fight was far from over.

I decided that it would be best if I backtracked down the ridge towards Willoughby's Run creek to clean and fill my new canteen. The stream was in fine working order because of the recent rains. I stepped across several of the creek's rocks into a pooled area deep enough to dunk my flask. I washed off and out my container the best that I could, filled it, then replaced the wooden stopper.

I saw that I wasn't alone. Several others upstream were also filling canteens, buckets, and tin cups. I tried to avoid those who were rinsing out clothing or bloody dressings. It then occurred to me that the same operation was probably going on all over upstream. That meant that the water I had just potted was probably less than desirable, but I had no option. I'd just have to take my chances.

I walked back to the main portion of the camp. Nearly all of the severely wounded had been moved out as far as I could tell. Those who possessed what could be considered a 'light injury' were reclining in various areas out in the open. There were quite a few larger tents that had been erected in the flatlands that housed both officers and those in need of comparatively minor care. I spotted the Eisenhower farm where I hear tell that General Longstreet may have been making his headquarters. The house wasn't the size or grandeur that it is today, but it was in that general vicinity.

I really wasn't sure where I was going or what I'd do, but I continued walking to feel as if I was doing something constructive. I had to burn off some of my excess nervous energy along with trying to loosen up my injured hip. That's when I came upon the black man, Nate, who I last saw helping Jonathan Gates the previous night. He looked less than his usual upbeat self as he sat and whittled on a small stack of logs. Understandable, I thought.

"Hey Nate, how's it going?" I asked as I approached and tried to make conversation.

"How's what going?"

"Well, anything. You know, life, the campaign here in Gettysburg, your hopes and dreams."

"Well Mister..." he started, searching for a last name.

"Neil. Just call me Neil."

"That's right. Well Neil, to be honest I'm real worried about this battle. I don't think I've seen so many dead and wounded soldiers in all my life. I don't like it, don't like it at all."

"You don't think the South can pull this one out?"

"I don't know. There's so many of them Union boys. Can't recall ever seeing that many before, no sir. Also, they's bunched up and holding all of the high ground."

"Oh, so you know a bit about war tactics, huh?"

Following a small cynical laugh he stated, "I've been around this war long enough to know that holding the high ground is better than trying to win it."

"True, very true. By the way Nate, why aren't you cooking today?"

"There ain't no food to be found, nothing to speak of anyway. Cain't cook nothing if there ain't none. If we be here a couple more days, they'll train something in I hope."

"Hey by the way, how's Jonathan Gates?" I inquired. "I saw you helping him last night."

"Oh he be all right. Just a bump on the head."

"A bump? I saw him go down yesterday. Looked like more than a bump to me."

"Mister Neil, anything less than the loss of an arm or a leg is considered pretty minor around here. I believe we found him lying just below the road up there," he said while pointing east.

"Yeah, that's about where I saw him fall. Nate, how can you be so civil to a guy that treats you as bad as he does?"

"As Misser Jon says it, I's just doing my job," he said with a laugh. Taking on a more somber note he said, "Oh, he's not really mean. You see, that ain't his soul talking. No, that's just what he's come up around all of his life. I believe that he must have some good in him. He mentioned that he had a wife and kids. Any man who has a family that loves him can't be all bad. Only those with the finest spirits acquire the gift of family."

Almost laughing in disbelief, I then said, "Nate, you're amazing. If you can find some good in him, you could probably find good in practically anything."

"Well, there is good in everything. It just depends on what you's looking for. If you's looking for bad, you'll surely find it. It's all over the place," he said while drawing out the word 'all.' But, so is the good. Just depends on what you's open to. Like they say, as ye seek, so shall ye find."

Running his wisdom through my head, I asked, "Nate, what do you plan to do after all of this is done and over with?"

"What do you mean, all over? You mean this battle here or the war?"

"Well the war of course, but also slavery. When you're a free man, what do you plan to do with your life?"

"Slavery ain't going to be done with," he commented with a sarcastic laugh as he returned to his whittling. "Not unless I escape or they gives me my freedom."

"Well, I mean if the South were to lose the war, you'll have to be set free won't you?"

"Not according to what some folks say. I hear tell that them people in Washington could make it so that even if the South loses the war, they might still be allowed to keep us slaves."

With a negative shake of the head I declared, "I wouldn't count on that. You'll be free some day soon, Nate. You have to plan ahead. Now tell me, what do you want to do with your life?"

"I hadn't thought of that as a real possibility. I don't know how to do nothing but slavin'. But, if I could do whats ever I wanted, oh that's something

I'd have to do some real thinking on. If I'd have my pick, I think I'd become a doctor—no, no wait, a teacher," he said as if I was granting him one wish. "Yeah, I'd want to be a teacher and teach all of the little colored children how to read and write." He dragged out the word 'all' again in that sentence for emphasis. That's the way Nate was. "Then they could become whats ever they wanted to be. You know, there ain't no one around to teach a Negro man's children, not legally anyway. They don't allow it. I'd like to do that. Then they could be the ones to go on and become doctors, business folks, and store keepers. That would make me a powerful man," he said with a nod of his head. "Them children could get a job wherever they wanted, jus' like a white man's childrens. That's probably what the folks down south are a scared of. They's afraid that we Negros would take all their jobs, and we jus' might cause we're real hungry, Misser Neil."

"I know that, Nate. Remember that if you think you can, you might. If you think you can't, you won't. Your choice of profession would certainly be a most beneficial vocation."

"Well," he said just prior to a laugh, "I know that I'm jus' dreaming, but that's what I'd like to do if I could. I's just like helping folks, that's all. That's all I've ever known."

"Nate, that's a great dream. Never stop believing in the possibility and it will come to pass."

"Yes, that would be nice. I'd like that responsibility. It would make me feel useful to my fellow man. I'd like that, but first I'd have to learn to read and write better myself. I'd have to go to school. Tain't no school wanting to teach a colored man though. Like I said, I guess they's a scared of us."

"Or they're afraid of your potential. Nobody likes competition. Give it time, Nate, and you'll be surprised. You'll see things happen quicker than you can imagine when the environment changes."

"Maybe, but if and when it's all done, I'm guessing that all I'll be allowed to be is a common work hand though."

"If, through all of your efforts, you can only become a day laborer, to paraphrase a great black statesman, then become the best day laborer that you can."

"Frederick Douglass said that?"

"Um, somebody like that," I answered. "Someone after him."

Looking at me with a bit of suspicion, Nate went on. "But even if we had those rights, I couldn't go to school. I've got no money. I'm a poor man, Misser Neil. I ain't got nothing but the clothes on my back, and they ain't worth nothin'."

"Oh but they are, Nate. They cover you up don't they? They keep you warm during the cold nights don't they?"

"Yes."

"Then see, you might think that they're worth nothing, but they're actually very valuable—to you. From an outsider's perspective, that might be just like the way white people see Negros. They might see them as worth nothing as a people, but if they take the time to look closer, they might see that mankind would be at a great loss without them. The contribution they make to society is and will be staggering. Why, what would the world be without the Negro faith, their labor, and their contribution to the arts, religion, and music? It's the variety of material that makes up the fabric of life. It's a matter of perspective. See what I mean?"

"Yes, I see what you mean. With the way you speak, I can tell that you're a writer. I just hope you take the time to let others know how we matter. I hope they hear that and use their hearts to see things through the way you do, Mr. Neil."

"It may take time, Nate, but they will. And with regard to your monetary worth, with your drive and desire, I doubt that you'll be poor long. You possess a great wealth of ambition. That's priceless." Digging in my pocket, I produced a penny from the change I received at the convenience store the other morning. "Here, consider this the first step on your journey of a thousand miles," I said as I handed the one-cent piece to him.

"What's this, a copper piece with Mr. Lincoln on it?"

"Well, it's more symbolic than anything else. It's a penny. Not a whole lot of money of course, but think of it as your good luck piece. Consider it to be the mark of your new beginning. Today you've decided which direction you'd like to go. Tomorrow you'll come up with the means with which to fund your progress. After that, your efforts will carry you along that new path in your life. When all's said and done, my guess is that the penny's worth of your effort will have increased a million fold."

"Thank-you Neil, I appreciate your support. Not too many white folks take the time to talk to me like this." Looking at the one-cent piece, he observed, "Ain't never seen a northern penny like this before."

Sensing that he was catching on to me, I asked, "What time is it getting to be?"

"Oh I don't know, my best guess would be about 9:30 or 10," Nate answered.

"Oh man, I've got to get going. I've got to try and get through the city and out the other side before the beginning of Pickett's Charge. Don't want to miss that," I said of the impending adventure.

"Why, what's so special about that?"

"That, my friend, will be the largest military assault to take place in the northern hemisphere. It was considered the 'high water mark' of the Confederacy. Thousands were killed and thousands were injured. A clash like that has never been seen since," I said as I straightened up and bowed my back.

"How does you know that? A battle hasn't even been fought yet today. And what does you mean 'were'? What gives you the right to guess what's going to happen?" Lowering his eyebrows, he asked in an accusatory manner, "Are you a spy or something, Misser Neil?"

Realizing that I had talked too much already, I walked away without responding until I finally stopped, turned, and asked, "Do you see the number on that penny. It's right under President Lincoln's head?"

"Yes, I can read that. What does 1-9-9-8 stand for?"

I just smiled and said, "That's the year that coin was minted, 1998. All the best to you, Nate." I said as I waved and walked away. I glanced back to see Nate alternating looks at the penny, then to me. I'm not sure if he put two and two together or not, but from the bewildered look on his face, I could tell the gears were turning.

I departed the valley on my trek to the Taneytown Road area. To accomplish this task, I'd have to cut through town. That would be no easy chore as there were troops from both sides occupying different pockets of the city. As I was leaving Longstreet's camp, I spotted an old discarded broom or shovel handle. I cleaned the vines and mud from it and took it with me to use as a walking stick through the woods. My hip was still suspect. I could always use the stick as a monopod for my camera when I was amongst people.

In town, if people saw me carrying both the camera and its 'stand', they would think that I was just another wet plate photographer looking for work. They'd have no reason to question me. If I didn't have a pod, the camera would look like nothing more than a wooden box. Something like that would lead to suspicion and quite possibly a search and seizure of my equipment. As stated earlier, most photographers were left alone to do their work, yet I'd be breaking new ground. Most photographers didn't venture in so close to the battle while it was in progress. Most of them were around for mop-up duty.

Stopping and looking at my nearly dilapidated map of the area, I guessed that the best route would be to follow the Pitzer Run branch of Willoughby's Run creek to get to Hagerstown Road. Yes, it would be a lot quicker and simpler to cut across Emmitsburg Road to get to Taneytown Road instead of tromping through two miles of creek bed and brush, but I'd be a damned fool to attempt the quicker route.

That would mean walking through the crossfire zone between the two enemies. Even if I bore a white flag on my stick, if the North didn't shoot me for approaching, I'd probably buy one in the back from the South for fleeing.

I moved northward along the small creek and saw quite a few injured soldiers receiving treatment, as well as several grave plots being prepared. While most of the burial sites were clustered together in large or semi-large groupings, there were also a handful of single or double plots scattered all around the area. Some of them have yet to be found even today. There just wasn't enough time to create a proper cemetery for all of the fallen. There rarely is during a time of war. Most of the dead were interred fairly close to where they expired.

Many of the still living soldiers I passed were members of A.P. Hill's unit, I deduced. They were holding down the far left flank of the South's strike line. Their boundaries extended from the edge of Longstreet's camp, up past Gettysburg's northern-most border. At this point in time, they were in a defensive holding position rather than assuming an offensive stance.

Aside from the occasional tangle with underbrush, I managed to come up on what I believed to be Hagerstown Road. I progressed in an easterly direction towards the center of town. I was looking for what is now Washington Street that would take me south, away from town, and towards my destination. Washington eventually ran into Taneytown Road, and that would lead me to the center of activity on Cemetery Ridge. From there, I'd be able to video as much of Pickett's Charge as possible. Even though I didn't have the still camera anymore, I could still provide Dr. Welles with all of the video proof he needed. I trust that this tape would be viewed more often than the famous Zapruder film taken one hundred years later of President Kennedy's assassination.

Checking my map once again, I came to what should have been Washington Street. It was the first major thoroughfare I encountered, and it appeared to stretch unencumbered in a southward direction.

I was sure that I was on the right track, for after I had walked several blocks, I noticed a large gathering of gray-shirted soldiers in front of a large building. It may have been the old Gettysburg Hospital.

As I approached, I noticed much disarray, much more than I had anticipated. I guessed that after a person had been wounded, it was only natural that he'd be brought to the closest hospital. However, due to the thousands of casualties suffered by both sides, the hospitals were the first places to fill up. Nobody told the Rebel ambulance crews, so for a period, the injured kept arriving and a pile-up ensued. Some of the transported patients were too fragile to move to one of the field hospitals, so they were here to stay until their condition changed one way or another. The only places left for the late arrivals were the surrounding yards, sidewalks, and alleyways.

It became a sickening sight. Men were on stretchers, boards, and tent canvasses if they were fortunate. The only places left for the rest were out in the open. I found that the only way to get by was for me to walk down the middle of the narrow street, and all the while fighting the horses and wagons for the right of way. Between the secretions from the horses on the ambulance crews, and day old dressings lying along the wet curbs, the air had taken on a certain heaviness. You weren't quite sure if today's air quality could be classified as foul or not. It was a matter of personal judgment. That question would be answered once and for all tomorrow.

The sidewalks had taken on the appearance of a flea market peddling a variety of injured, amputated, and dying men in all shapes, sizes and colors. I have no idea what was planned for these unfortunates when the pullout began tomorrow. While I would depart at the crack of dawn, my guess is that most of these injured and dying men wouldn't, at least not under any physical means. And to complicate matters further, rain was due in tomorrow afternoon. What would they do then?

I thought this to be a once in a lifetime occurrence that should be captured on tape. I managed to find an opening by the curb where I set my camera up on its pod. I could then shoot a sweep shot, north to south, of the unspeakable collection of traumatized and suffering men. Words just wouldn't be able to do this subject justice.

As I panned slowly in a northerly direction, I saw quite a bit more agony than my quick glances afforded me earlier. Some of the once-virile combatants had been reduced to a pile of mutilated flesh. That's the best description I can give of the scene.

If the patient was lucky, he was accompanied by a fellow soldier who would shoo the flies and gnats from his comrade's bandaged and oozing wounds with a stick or fence picket. Looking around, some of the other soldiers seemed dead, or almost so. Perhaps they were, for they possessed a blank, non-changing stare as they lay on their sides gazing into nothingness. A puddle of mucous bled from their mouths with no help in sight to deflect the entries or exits of the bluebottle flies.

Occasionally I'd see a member of the sidewalk brigade hoisted up into a passing wagon. As he was piled upon a current passenger, I could deduce that this man's time on our plane had expired.

When I zoomed the lens out and attempted to focus my attention on those to the south, all I could see in my viewfinder was a gray screen. I looked up and saw a Confederate officer standing in my path and staring back at me.

"What the hell you doing?" he asked in a less than cordial tone.

"Um, I was trying to center up a photograph for the newspaper. I was just looking for the perfect shot," I replied, hoping he didn't realize that I had been shooting all along.

"You ain't going to find it here. Ain't them fellows in enough pain without you shoving a damn camera in their faces and making money off of their misery? Give me that," he demanded with his hand extended towards my camera.

"Not a chance," I responded, trying to buy time to come up with a chivalrous way out of my predicament. I decided to use a Southern approach to politeness in an attempt to win my freedom. Fight fire with fire, they always say.

"Sir, as a member of the fourth estate, if you're unhappy with my choice of subject matter and location, I shall move on. Good day, Captain."

I tucked the camera under my arm and made my way past the officer. I expected to be wrestled to the ground at any moment, but I just kept walking and looking straight ahead. I learned a long time ago that if you act like you know what you're doing and where you're going, people tend to leave you alone. I guess it was worth it to pay attention to life's little lessons.

I walked only about ten or fifteen minutes when I was able to see the heights near the infamous angle off in the distance. They were lined with Union troops in all of their glory. Quite a few members of the Army of the Potomac bordered the immediate and extended sides of Taneytown Road. I guessed that the rest of the forces took up positions in the area of the 'high water mark' itself.

While I lost sight of the U.S. forces as I traveled up and down the street, there were plenty of officers in the vicinity. General Meade's headquarters was dead ahead. I constantly received stares from those who acted like they were in charge of something. The last thing they needed at this point was a spy of some sort amongst their ranks.

My question now was where I would make my base until the offensive began. I gazed past General Meade's picket-fenced billet and spotted a barn approximately seventy-five yards to its south. I decided that would do just fine. The barn appeared to be solid enough, so I figured that it would hold up as well as anything else in the area during the upcoming battle.

Despite the heat, parts of the road were still sloppy making me walk along the raised middle portion to get by. The lane's grooves had now become a playground for dragonflies and their comrades. The muck associated with the water and urine-filled wheel ruts had taken on an odor all its own. From what I've read, the worse was yet to come.

    I passed by the general's station and noticed a number of couriers entering and leaving Mrs. Leister's once quaint, now bustling homestead. I finally came to a stretch where I had to cross Taneytown Road to get to the barn's side, stepping over rock border fences as I went.

    There wasn't a lot of room along the street side of the barn, but that's where I decided to light. If a Rebel's ball was going to catch me, it would have to pass through two walls and who knows how many ten-inch beams. This surely would be my best bet.

    What room there was on the barn's east side had been trampled flat by all of the foot traffic. My compliments to the chef, I thought as I found the best spot to recline. The barn was already in use as a combination stable and hospital. With every passing moment, the notion of a hospital was winning out. A steady stream of stretchers accompanied by yells of pain became my scenery. There were so many injured and so little room.

    It seemed that anything suitable for a chair was already in use elsewhere, so I rolled a couple granite border stones over to a soon to be shady spot against the structure. I was hoping to escape the near ninety degree heat and high humidity.

    It was just after eleven AM when a most peculiar thing to war occurred—silence. Hardly a gun could be heard discharging anywhere. It grew deafeningly quiet. About the only sound I noticed was the ringing in my ears. The shelling had gone on so long that I had become accustomed to its earsplitting volume. It was becoming more evident to me that once a person gets used to the destructive mayhem, the farther along the road they are to becoming a lost soul. I was now able to see that in the faces of some of the long-timers. If I had a mirror that day, I'm sure I would have noticed traces of that condition in myself.

I glanced around and could see soldiers passing on the road. They just looked at each other for an answer to this odd-timed silence. While no one offered an explanation, I sensed that this could be the calm before the storm.

I noticed that there wasn't a lot of activity of any kind occurring during this stretch, at least not as much as in the preceding hours. It was as if no one wanted to be responsible for the movement that dislodged the keystone leading to an avalanche of destruction.

I took this opportunity to go up top on Cemetery Ridge and video a few scenes before all hell broke loose. I took a cart path westward that dumped me right out at my destination.

During my short walk, I passed parallel to General Meade's headquarters. Even though I was some distance away, I noticed a gathering of many of the higher ups in what appeared to be more of a social gathering than a business meeting. I'm sure that both subjects would be dealt with. From this distance, I couldn't tell who was who. There was around a half dozen or so officers sheltering themselves from the mid day sun under the shade of a tree.

As I peaked out on the summit of Cemetery Ridge, laid before me was almost two hundred cannons surrounded by over five thousand Federal troops. It almost seemed like a far-fetched plan, the Union attempting to hold the high ground against two to three times that number of Confederates. They didn't know the circumstances as I knew them.

The angle looked almost foreign to me. I wasn't accustomed to seeing that plateau without all of its monuments. The cannons were wheeled into place as I watched. The forked tree located at the convergence of the stone walls appeared to be a much smaller version of the one that occupies that identical spot today, yet quite possibly it was the same perennial never-the-less. Some of the troops, unaware of what was coming, sat around on wooden artillery crates smoking cigars and conversing, while others busied themselves playing cards or dice.

I ventured down closer to the infamous stone wall so I might set up my camera. I put a full zoom into operation as I aimed the lens westward towards the operating center of the Confederate Army. I was able to see that quite a bit of artillery had been moved into position upon Seminary Ridge. Along the wood's edge, what appeared to be a wall of gray uniforms amassed. To our right I observed Southern cannons lining up in an offensive stance. I knew my time here was limited.

Straight ahead of me I saw what appeared to be as many Rebel guns as the Union had in position on this entire knoll. I wasn't able to see what the South had planned to our left. I could make out the forms of guns, but between the high heat, humidity, and stalks, too much distortion occurred through my lens to count up any accurate number.

The silence became a bit too disquieting. I felt very uneasy standing there on ground zero. I finished up my work there and walked back to the crest where I did a sweep, first north towards town then to the south. I wanted to try and capture as much of the line of defense as I could. My ploy to appear as a still photographer must have worked. At first it was a welcomed relief not to have a blue coat walk in front of my lens, pause, then lean in to say, "Hi mom!" Then I remembered where I was.

When I was finished shooting, I walked around looking for the best place to take cover when I attempted to tape the most famous military assault in American history. Behind an assemblage of land forces, at least one hundred paces east of the present day 71st Pennsylvania Volunteers monument at the angle, and roughly seventy-five paces south of the statue of General Meade on his mount, I spotted a small outcropping of boulders. That would have to do. I strolled over to check out my future haven. It was more of an obstruction than anything else, so I didn't think I would be in anybody's way. As I looked at it, I noted that it was certainly close enough to the action, yet still tall enough to duck behind. I'm sure I'd put that to use many times over.

As I settled on the decision for my vantage point, the concussive blast of a series of explosions rattled everyone's nerves and broke the treasured silence. All present turned towards the Confederate's Seminary Ridge where a line of cannon plumes ruled the landscape. The sequential detonations resembled a steam locomotive as it chugged down the line. This was it. The pre-charge bombardment had begun.

Some shells came up short, some long, while others met their intended targets. Not bad for an initial volley. As their artillery hit the earth, dirt, smoke, and debris went flying everywhere.

The salvos that went long were fascinating to watch. You could pick up the ordinance about half way over the field and follow it towards its goal. One could watch the over shots as they passed by on their way towards a yet to be determined destination.

One shell passed fifty yards directly overhead. From our vantage point, we could tell that the round had drawn a bead on the Union general's post. One of Meade's assistants took the hit dead center, halving his torso. That's when the Federal higher ups decided to scramble for cover. Some hopped their mounts while others gravitated to the front of Mrs. Leister's Taneytown Road dwelling, trusting that the shack would actually shield them.

I also felt that it would be in my best interest if I skedaddled back to my sanctuary in front of the barn. I scampered on knees and elbows, down the path past Meade's headquarters with all that I had. I ended up losing my camera's monopod leg on the ridge. That was no loss as it had served its purpose anyway.

I made my way back down to the barn and took a seat on my stone roost while waiting out the downpour of Rebel armaments. It would last another ninety minutes, so I used that time to get my courage up and my wits together. I also used this opportunity to take in all around me.

Occasionally, a twelve-pounder would overshoot its target and land across the road from me. If the round was traveling on a high arc, the ball would just thud into the still-soft dirt. Those that came in on a flat angle would sporadically skip like a rock on a pond until a tree, rock, or dwelling halted its progress.

An incoming canister was another story. A shell such as that would explode upon impact and scatter its cargo of lead spheres as far as gravity would allow. With a couple of exceptions, I was relatively free from close calls. Due to my proximity to the Confederates, the flight of the projectiles was nearly always away from me.

Once, a ball went wide left of my location by only twenty or thirty yards. The orb created a nice pothole on the edge of Taneytown Road. On one or two occasions, I felt the barn quake from an impact of the Rebel cannonade. All in all, I believe I found the only safe haven on the battlefield, if there was such a thing. We non-combatants tend to be pretty good at ferreting those things out.

Just when I thought the bombardment was slowing, the Confederate batteries would pick up their pace. The Union, on the other hand, almost ceased their return fire from the ridge. Most of the North's reciprocation emanated from the Cemetery Hill area to the north, and the summit of Little Round Top to the south. Meade was using his right and left flanks to do the North's dirty work while saving the ammunition of his middle guns for the expected Confederate charge towards their center.

As suddenly as the Rebel aggression began, it ceased. I wasn't sure if this was just a reloading lull or whether the South was just considering it 'a wrap.'

I peeked around the side of the barn and could see the Federals backing a great number of their cannons down the slope a ways. I believe they were trying to make the Southern brass believe that there was a pullout in progress. Based on the eventual outcome, that tactic proved to be right on the money.

I was guessing that it was now about 2:30 PM. Everything was happening just as it had been recorded in the history books. Based on that assumption, I believed this would be the best time to return to the ridge and get into position to video the infamous Pickett's Charge.

I walked up the same path as before, but this time I had to hop out of the way for the stretcher crews, now loaded and on their way to the rear. They probably didn't realize that their current task was just practice for what was yet to come.

I glanced back over at the general's front and side yards. A half dozen or so fine horses had given their lives for their country. Some of the unlucky still remained moored to a tree or fence.

I approached the crest of Cemetery Ridge and found that standing space along the half-mile fortification was at a premium. Even my stone rampart was acting the part of wheel chocks for a Parrott. I would just have to wait until the troops fell in to their formations before my spot would become available.

Most of the twelve-pound Parrotts had been backed down the slope along with nearly all of the accompanying five thousand soldiers. I just decided to play it cool for the next thirty minutes or so as I tried to make small talk with those in my vicinity.

Gazing around, I noticed that quite a bit of destruction had already taken place near the angle. A dozen or so cannons had been reduced to useless iron, and like with their fallen gunners, were in the process of being dragged from the zone. It would be the scrap heap for both.

Interspersed between the stone wall and the Copse of Trees were the unattached arms, legs, and what used to be the productive minds of some of the Union's finest. That which remained along the two hundred fifty foot expanse would soon become pulp under the charging feet of both infantries.

Amongst those picking up and removing the clutter, quite a few verbal exchanges could be heard as the laborers went about their task in a mechanical manner. This banter mirrored those who were on horseback and in command. The enlisted, like those in charge, wanted a perfect battle—no slip-ups. Everyone preferred to emerge from this scrap unscathed, so they were all ears. No matter how much attention was paid to detail by those in attendance on that knoll during that hot July afternoon, a favorable outcome wouldn't be in the cards for many.

A little after three PM, a mounted officer with field glasses yelled, "Guns up and in place!" He had just spotted the Army of Northern Virginia emerging along Seminary Ridge. I managed to work my way over to the observation point I picked out earlier. Since it was now free of armaments, I realized that the placement of my barrier was a little too close to the action for my taste. Looking around I discovered there was no alternative that I considered to be better suited. There were no other rock outcroppings around which could shield me well enough to perform my tasks.

While I was sighting my camera up with the right eye, a nearby private said, "Hey mister, you're going to get run over and killed there."

Becoming as keyed up as those serving behind me I answered, "Ain't we all?" I guess I had been duly warned.

I zoomed in on my target the best that I could. The heat radiating from the wheat field made the picture appear quite wavy. That wasn't all bad, I surmised. It would give future generations an idea of how incredibly hot and humid it was during the most intense point of that day.

The columns of Rebels shifted from the safety of the timbers to the open field at a quick marching pace of time and a half. General Pickett's own men to our left numbered around six thousand. The rest of the infantry was made up from General Pettigrew's men. That division, on the far right, seemed to get out of the starting blocks a little late. Whether that delayed exit was purposeful or not, Pettigrew's forces had to move double time to catch up with the leading herd. Trimble's division trailed both detachments to the right rear. Their advancement worked so well that the plan may have been designed that way.

What an impressive sight it was seeing the more than half-mile wide parade of gray shirted Confederates as they marched in unison, elbow to elbow. With firearms slung over shoulders, the procession was atypically quiet during its approach. There was no Rebel yell this time. It was as if the higher ups, as well as the enlisted personnel, realized there was no room for error in the execution of this plan. Perhaps they sensed that the odds were not in their favor during this operation. They probably realized it would be a long shot at best.

On our rise, one of the enlisted exclaimed, "Holy shit, it's the whole damn Rebel Army." Of course it wasn't, far from it in fact. But, their collective numbers did reach over 12,000 in the line, and from my vantage point appeared to be marching roughly ten deep from front to back. I couldn't believe all that I was seeing. The charge was happening just as I had learned it, except now I wasn't reading about the event; I was a witness to history as it was being made.

In an unorthodox move, the division on our far left, Pickett's, took a forty-five degree angle inward towards the middle in order to close up the fifty yard wide gap between his men and Pettigrew's. This would unify the two fronts into one massive assault line. The Confederate objective was to concentrate their efforts towards a lone clump of oaks on our own ridge. That landmark became known as the Copse of Trees. At this point in time, that benchmark was little more than a thicket. However, the brushwood still stood out on the ridge due to its solitary location.

Pickett's tactical move, however practical, proved to be fatally flawed. For as the general's line shifted, its width provided a direct line for the Union's batteries stationed on the peak of Little Round Top. They had a straight-on shot at the Johnnies, and took full advantage of the opportunity. Despite the distance, nary a shot appeared to miss its intended destination. The men in gray began disappearing into the field of green and gold.

The Southern soldiers were dropping in clusters due in part to the configuration of their line. Gaps were opened then closed as the charge's power decreased at every step. Still, no yells or gunfire came from the Confederate infantry. The Rebel artillery was still attempting to soften up the opponent to their army's front.

From what I've read and what I could make out through my viewfinder, General Pickett rode about ten yards behind his line. To some that may seem to be cowardice behavior, but that policy was standard operating procedure at that time. An officer with experience carried more clout than an enlisted man with a rifle.

There was a suitable amount of Union musket fire even though the Southern advance was at the end of the Springfield's effective range. The Parrotts and the Napoleons that had been taken rearward during the Confederate cannonade were now wheeled back into position. The entire operation appeared quite primitive by today's standards due to the size and awkwardness of their equipment, but no one could question the deadly effects of the operation when it reached its peak potential. Some of the guns were wheeled right up to the stone wall itself. Others took up position in lines at the middle and rear, north and south.

As the Confederates marchers neared, the Federals hand-fired guns became increasingly accurate. Captured on my tape was a flag bearer who was dropped as he maintained his unit's colors. Discarding his rifle, the next in line took over that task and hoisted the banner higher than the first. The two armies eventually learned their lesson concerning that tactic, unfortunately it came too late to save scores of valuable lives.

From our side, cannon fire answered the rebel charge. A clear path of nearly three Rebels deep was carved at each detonation. One entire Union battery appeared to be withholding their fire as they awaited the perfect opportunity to maximize their impact. At this point, almost all of those cannons were loaded, or nearly so. Some of the artillerymen double loaded their guns with deadly canister. I saw one of the gunners loading his barrel with jagged scrap iron. While this maneuver was generally used as a last resort when a battery was almost out of ammunition, a shot from this collection of hardware was known to take out all in its path while leaving the rest in the general vicinity unrecognizable. It didn't do much for the cannon either.

The situation that the Federal battery had awaited finally presented itself. As the Rebels approached the fence along Emmitsburg Road, many of the soldiers became entangled amongst the cross rails. To the rear, the soldiers following their leaders continued their procession towards Cemetery Ridge despite the impediment. This caused major congestion within the line's advancement resulting in a sizable traffic jam.

The Army of the Potomac took full advantage of the situation and proceeded to open fire. That action took an obvious toll upon the charging forces, but a worse consequence was to occur. Just as the back up reached its zenith, Union General Hayes took notice and ran to the forefront. With his sword straight up in the air to draw his troops' attention, he leapt skyward and screamed with all his might as he landed, "Fire!" The Earth shook as seventeen hundred muskets and eleven cannons vomited forth their barrels' contents in the direction of the unwelcome visitors.

The roar from the discharge was so deafening that my ears cracked at being unable to process the entire concussion. Legend has it that the blast was so powerful that it could be heard from Pittsburgh, Pennsylvania to Washington, DC. Limbs, torsos, and hardware became airborne as many irreplaceable rebels realized the end to their dreams and convictions.

So many soldiers were hit at once that their yells almost became a solitary howl. When the smoke cleared, we saw that entire companies had vanished. There were now voids in the South's offensive line large enough to drive a team of horses and wagons through and not touch a living soul.

As Emmitsburg's fences finally melted from the heat of the battle, the senseless parade of saber waving and rifle bearing men resumed its advance towards the prized stone wall. One could only guess what was going through the minds of those of the rear guard who watched helplessly as their comrades fell one after the other. I'm sure they were probably hoping that the Federals would run out of ammunition before the rear became the front.

Let no one question whether the Confederates could follow orders or not. Most kept coming despite the dismal odds. As an observer, I could now see why this clash is considered one of the most memorable battles in American history. Enough gray uniforms reached the keystone fence to turn the situation into an all out holocaust for both sides. Sword waving and pistol blaring Confederates numbered twenty to thirty deep along their center that stretched from just in front the Copse of Trees to the jag in the angle.

There was shrieking and yelling, cheering and cries for mercy as the opposing teams clashed at the east/west line of division. Bayonets were used to quiet those of contradicting viewpoints. The horror became unwatchable as once naive young farm boys now became fire-eyed killers. One way or another, the lives of those who participated in this carnage would forever be changed.

Some of those who escaped the bullets wrath fell victim to their mounts. When one of the half-ton animals toppled down upon its passenger, I saw the rider's bodily contents burst forth from every orifice of his body. And on other occassions, I noted where horse and rider would disappear into a smoke bank only to have the animal emerge alone, injured and bleeding, on the other side. The opposite seemed to be an uncommon occurrence.

I could see injured fighters from both the North and the South retreating towards the rear of their respective lines; a few of the armless, or those nearly so, managed to proceed under their own power. A look of resignation and personal defeat mixed with shock and terror on the faces of those so inflicted. Some of the legless were able to hitch a ride on the backs of their loyal, able-bodied comrades. I'm sure the chauffeur didn't mind the additional protection when he presented his fanny to the enemy.

One Union man was so dazed that he was moving in a north/south direction rather than towards the safety of his line. As he ventured closer, I could see that his lower jaw had been shot away exposing the orifice leading to the man's belly. Another Union soldier to my left had obviously been blinded and was basically walking in circles giving the appearance of a ghastly sleepwalker. His journey led him to stumble over rocks and body parts as he searched for an egress from his own spherical world.

It was getting to the point where the combatants from both sides were inching their way towards my breastwork. I had to start planning an escape route. The terrain behind me, which gently sloped down towards Taneytown Road, contained few if any abutments to aid my needs. I knew that I'd never make it back to the barn.

A wagon had been toppled about thirty yards to my rear and forty yards to my right. That would provide my only hope. Deep in my soul I knew that the cart would prove to be more of a psychological barrier rather than one of a physical nature. The oak boards lining the bed could hardly stop a determined minie ball, let alone a cannon's shell. But it was slightly below the grade of the crest, plus I wouldn't be long for this world if I didn't do something quick.

I peeked around the right side of my rampart to take one last look at the historic bloodbath. I was trying to see if I could catch General Armistead performing the oft written scene in which he thrusts his hat upon his sword and leads the charge over the stone angle. I couldn't make a positive I D because of the soldiers I saw, several may have met that description. My wishful thinking was the only thing that could part the smoke and make that event a reality to my eyes. My guess is that the general's collapse was no more spectacular than any of the other fifty thousand men who fell during that three-day campaign. Through time and legend, he just garnered the most ink.

The cannon fog was getting thicker and making it even more difficult for me to pick out enough details to make a difference. I could tell however that the combatants from each side were getting closer and closer to me as they flooded into the high water mark towards my direction.

I presumed that if I couldn't see them, they wouldn't be able to see me. That's when I grabbed my camera, presented my backside to the enemy, and ran, stooped over, towards the overturned cart. I slid in next to it like a baseball player stealing second base, and then rolled over behind the wagon's bed.

While I wasn't safe by any means, I was certainly safer. I was also parched. Breathing all of the sulfur and gunpowder for the last hour or so left my throat considerably irritated and dry. I wanted a drink so bad, but I dared not lift my canteen any higher than my body. Anything with elevation on it would become an attention getter. As bad off as I was, I felt that it would be best if I just lay there, flattened in the grass, for the duration of the afternoon's activities. The cart afforded me some shade now that the sun was into its downward slide.

I was not able to soak up all of the historical significance of what I had just witnessed. I could only think of those pre and post Civil War countrymen doing their damnedest in the current day and age to eliminate each other and their ideals. They all were once somebody's cute, lovable infants. Look how far they've come, I thought.

I felt horrible for all of the mothers now made childless by this action, as well as the many wives who were transformed into widows virtually overnight. Yes, I knew that everybody here today had long since passed, but I'm in their period now, they're not in mine. When I considered that my present is somebody else's past, I guess wherever one is, that's the present. The same concept applied here on this day. This was all real, it's today. I guess my knowledge of the future didn't matter at this point. A modern era is wherever you are at the time. I pondered the ramifications of those thoughts as I finished the afternoon lying face down in a clover field in southern Pennsylvania.

It must have been around six PM when things settled down to a manageable state. Scattered gunfire was still present, now more rare than plentiful though. I was finally able to quench my thirst after first clearing the swarthy contents from my lungs. I rolled back over on to my stomach and decided to wait until I heard an 'all clear' signal from somebody.

As I reclined, I began to think of how good it would be to sleep in my own bed tomorrow night. I guess we really don't realize how good we have it today. We're relatively free from the hatred and violence that permeated today's activities. I'm afraid that we take peace for granted far too often. I guess we never know what we have until we're without it.

I heard footsteps approaching. Not knowing whether these steps were that of friend or foe, I laid motionless in the weeds until I found out one way or the other. The visitors looked around the side of the cart and said, "Hey Mister." Since I didn't move, one of the soldiers grabbed my shoulder and rolled me on to my side. Seeing that I was breathing, he asked, "You O.K., Mister?"

I opened my eyes to see two soot-covered Federal soldiers staring down at me. "Is it all over?" I asked.

"As much as it will be for now," he answered.

With that positive assessment, I rose up, dusted myself off, and assured the blue-jacketed gentlemen that I was fine. "Good. How 'bout you help us right this wagon? We're going to need it for a stretcher cart," he stated.

We three grabbed the side while another man joined us, pulling down on the opposite axle. With a crash, the cart was back on its four wheels and once again functional. As the soldiers checked its worthiness, I had my first post battle view of the area.

The scene had become everything I thought it would and more. The entire landscape was littered with crates, guns, broken cannons, and dead horses. On the human side, there was an assortment of arms, legs, and torsos, some attached, some not, around the high water mark. Stretcher crews were already hard at it checking for life, loading their burdens, and hauling their cargo to any home, barn, or whatever happened to be doubling as a hospital on this evening.

"Are you busy or can you help us out?" I was asked by one of the teenaged privates.

"Um," I said looking around, then realizing that I had no place to go and nothing to do for the next several hours, "sure, I can help you out." I placed the camera in my pack then slung it over on to my back.

"O.K.," answered the one who appeared to be in charge, "let's go to the jag. That's where most of our business will be."

He was referring to the angle. Due to the lack of horsepower at the moment, we got behind the cart and pushed it up the incline ourselves. I was on the left side as we cleared the ridge.

I could see hundreds of Confederate bodies strewn across the field of Pickett's Charge. Despite sporadic gunfire, the South's pick up crews were out as well. They were concentrating their efforts on the western edge of the field. They probably weren't sure how close they'd be allowed to get to Union territory without being taken prisoner. Those truce arrangements had yet to be issued by those in authority. It was a shame. Most of their dead and injured seemed to be piled up from Emmitsburg Road upward towards the federally occupied angle.

Those who could crawl away did. I spotted one Confederate soldier with a hip injury, or possibly spinal cord damage, crawling away using his hands to propel himself down the slope towards the South's encampment over a mile away. His useless legs and a crimson slick trailed behind him. He made his way to another fallen Rebel, took the officer's pistol from his belt and placed it to his own temple.

I think I was the only one who noticed the man. "No! Hey!" I yelled.

As the shot rang out, several Union soldiers in our area ducked for a moment, looked around to see if they were under attack, and then proceeded on. I just stared.

We weren't able to make it all of the way in to the angle. There were just too many bodies piled up around the area of Cushing's Battery to allow us any closer access. We had to start picking up the wounded from the outer edge. This allowed those following us performing the same task an easier approach for their collection of souls from the hub.

My best estimate of the number of casualties in our general area definitely numbered in the several hundreds. I'd guess that one half to two thirds of the victims displayed no apparent movement upon the ground on which they had fallen. Either way, they were now a statistic for the Civil War journals.

Many of the injured we collected sustained wounds to the abdomen or hip region. The rest of the countless many were able to evacuate on their own, thus easing our burden.

After five minutes we had reached capacity without stacking man upon man. Most were in no condition to endure such treatment. I looked over and caught sight of a soldier silently looking back at me. I thought he was dead until he actually blinked. With the absence of the epidermal rind necessary to contain his bodily processors, he was attempting to manually confine his intestines to their proper domain.

"Hey," I said to one of our crew, "this guy

looks as if he needs help right quick. How about him?"

A Yank came back to have a look at his fallen comrade. "No, he's gone. He's been shot clean through the bowels. Tain't nothing can be done for him."

"We've got to do something. We just can't leave him there to die," I pleaded.

"Damn it, this job is tough enough already without your civilian input! What do you want us to do, sew his guts back together? That's been tried. It ends up being more trouble than it's worth, and the doctors ain't got time for that anyway. What's more, it won't do him no good. It would only buy him a couple of hours at best. Face it, he's dead where he lays. All that can be done for someone like that is for us to make him as comfortable as possible. He'll probably be better off out here than in a hot stuffy barn. On top of that, they ain't got no room to store him there anyway. I'm sorry fellow. Peace. Let's get the hell out of here."

The soldier returned to the front of the cart where one of his colleagues had commandeered a horse that had been wandering free. I took one last look at the waning soldier's face. Staring skyward, his eyes seemed to display less sorrow at being left behind than upon hearing that he was untreatable. I'm not sure he fully comprehended that his next stop would be his last though. I just turned away with a wretched feeling in my gut. I wasn't able to view an individual in that condition and simply do nothing. I remembered what Dr. Welles said about helping others in this plane, but I just felt so helpless.

The soldier in charge of our crew wrestled the horse into position the best that he could. People weren't the only ones whose nerves were frayed from the events of the last couple of days. We were ordered to push the cart towards the steed's rump. While I pushed from the left side of the cart, the soldier to my right slipped and fell on our next to last pace. We both turned our eyes towards the cause of his descent. The abandoned viscera from a disemboweled fighter had wound its way around what was left of the soldier's shoe. Upon seeing that, the Union private, still on his knee, broke down and began to cry. In a fit of rage, like a small child trying to free himself from a spiders web, he let out a shriek and shook his foot violently. The overbearing stress of the week had taken its toll on everyone. Realizing that there was little time for such nonsense, the man rose once again, cursing God as he freed himself once and for all.

"Where to?" someone inquired about the destination of our load.

"Let's try down there at that barn," was the reply, referring to the Leister barn that was situated behind General Meade's headquarters. "If there's no room there, we can try a couple of the homes and barns over east of there," he said while motioning towards the barn that was my former sanctuary. "Someone will have to help."

Once the horse was tied into place using a makeshift bridle and hitch from scavenged rope, the wagon started off down towards Taneytown Road. I just stood there overlooking the field of carnage.

"Hey mister, you coming?"

"Yeah, in a minute. I want to get a few photos for the paper. I'll catch up with you all in a spell."

As they pulled out, I booted up the video camera and took long panning scenes capturing the electronic likeness of the unspeakable massacre that had just taken place. As painful as it was, I took several close-up views of the loss of life, limb, and sanity that accompanied Pickett's march to hell. If I wanted to preserve the truth, I had to report the whole truth.

Moans of the dying echoed around me on that high ground as the sun continued its decent for the day. I observed one subject still rocking side to side due to the loss of both arms. Death was a little tardy in collecting that debt on this day. Some of the fallen probably envied that man. They wished that they were as lucky. While his struggle was near an end, their agony would endure a lifetime.

I stopped my camera on the nearly disemboweled soldier I exchanged looks with earlier. The sight of him continued to burn into my soul. It was then that I decided that I had to do something. Once again, I heard Dr. Wells telling me not to interfere with history. "The hell with him," I said.

I knelt down next to the man and rested my hand upon his shoulder. Unaware of my presence at first, he finally turned and looked at me with those same weary eyes.

"Is there anything I can do for you, soldier?" I inquired.

"No, I'm O.K.," was his weak response. That was a reply I least expected to hear. The man was obviously anything but O.K. Perhaps he had finally resigned himself to his fate. "I'm not long for this world, am I sir?"

"I'm afraid that your wounds are probably mortal," I answered.

"In my pocket by your hand, there's a letter to my folks. Please write in the day and time I left this earthly existence."

I reached into his pocket and found a one-inch long stub of a pencil along with an envelope, the flap partially sealed because of the heat of the day. Inside was a letter to 'Mama and Papa.' The soldier must have been expecting the worse and prepared a letter of good-bye in advance just in case. I didn't know what to say or do.

He then took a deep breath causing his exposed entrails to elevate, shift, and then subside. "Oh, my pain is worsening," he moaned. "Something will have to give. I feel that it shall have to be me." Removing his bloody hand from the decimated abdomen, bending it back and offering it to me at his shoulder, he beseeched me, "Please pray for me. I'm on my way to meet my God, and..." he said as he began to weep, "I've killed so many of my fellow men, his children."

I held his hand tightly and spoke to him in a calm manner. I gave him the best off-the-cuff wisdom I could muster under such circumstances. "God will forgive you. He realizes that there are human considerations to life as well as spiritual ones. What was it that Jesus said, "Render to Caesar that which is Caesar's?" He meant that we had to follow man's laws while we're here in this world. Fighting for one's country is a requirement of one's nation. He realized that even in His time. My guess is that He'll be more than welcoming to you, my friend. You seem like such a decent fellow."

A frail smile crossed his parched lips as death finally eased him from his agony. I placed his liberated hand across what was left of his chest. I wiped the blood from my hand on to his shirt, then took out the letter and wrote 'July 3, 1863' and '6:30 PM' in the blank spaces provided. Then, removing the knife from his belt, I cut off a lock of his hair and placed it in the letter. I had once read that it was the custom of the day. I refolded the letter, then placed it into the envelope and finished sealing it. Even though this gallant soldier passed almost a century before I was born, he was still a very real living, breathing soul that I had the privilege of knowing if even for a brief moment. I bade farewell to the man whose existence was no more.

I stood back up and looked around as the blanket of cannon-produced dusk was beginning to settle over those remaining in need. For the thousands whose existence was cut short on that field of honor, their burial would have to wait for another day.

There was broken equipment and pulverized bodies lying about in clusters as far as I could see across the darkening field. During those three days, over twenty-five percent of the Union forces and forty percent of Confederate troops dropped near the small town in Pennsylvania they call Gettysburg. For the South, Pickett's charge alone cost them all fifteen regimental commanders and virtually all of its field officers. Two brigadier generals and six colonels also numbered amongst the Confederate dead.

When I finished surveying the damage and

later helping out where I could, I noticed that the moon was just beginning to break the horizon as night was almost upon us.

It was a strange night. While there was some individual movements taking place here and there, I never felt so alone in all my life. I felt as if my soul had already begun its journey back to my time because there was no connectedness to anyone or anything at this point. I've often heard that hell isn't necessarily the fire and brimstone that mythology would have us believe. It's more of a spiritual aloneness. If that is true, then I must be at hell's gate at this moment, I surmised.

I walked back down to the Leister barn but couldn't find the soldiers that I assisted earlier. There wasn't a lot more that I could do. I wasn't even supposed to touch anyone or anything while I was here.

I continued south on Taneytown Road, not far, when I spotted a couple of large jutting boulders on what I concidered generally higher ground. Aside from the battle, I was exhausted from my walk from earlier in the day. I wasn't used to that. A Union officer, hat pulled down over his face and his arms crossed, was already in a deep slumber as he lay against the rocks. I guessed that if this bed of rocks was good enough for him, it was good enough for me.

I set my equipment down and groaned as my body sank to the earth. I hadn't even done any fighting today and I was just as exhausted as those who had. I hoped to get to sleep early tonight so that I'd be able to rise just as early. Tomorrow will be another big day. Around here, that meant that bodies would be buried, General Lee would

Chapter Ten
Farewell and Salutations

*"Awakening begins when a man realizes
that he is going nowhere
and does not know where to go."*
GEORGES GURDJIEFF

I was so exhausted that I slept soundly throughout the night until awakened by a loud pop. My eyes vaulted wide open as the ears received the sensation. I wasn't sure if that blast was of a physical origin, or perhaps just the process of all my senses becoming awake at one time. As I became adjusted to my surroundings, I noticed that I had become somewhat dew-covered. I surmised that it was still a bit before sunrise. I knew that I had a shuttle home to catch, but I had no idea what the current time was. Dr. Welles left off one important detail when building the tether—an alarm.

    I stood up and stretched my much-abused body. What a sight I'd be for Dr. Welles, I thought. I had a three-day growth of beard, xylophonic ribs, and was sweaty, muddy, and all around just plain filthy. I could have used my hair to grease the axles on one of the wagons in the area. This certainly was one hell of an experience, I concluded, but God will I be happy to get back to reality—my reality. Exposure to something like this really made me appreciate what I had in my life during my here and now. I concluded from this three-day odyssey that there was no need to bide one's time for the promise of future contentment, nor was there any reason to desire the simpler times of the past. There is no such time. There's only the present that's bestowed upon a soul, and that time should be lived to the fullest. Aside from this junket, the future never arrives, and the past will never be again. It's always the present wherever you are. I felt that I had learned my lessons well.

I picked up my camera and bag, then weighed the best route to take to the landing zone. Trying to discern the hour of day to see if I'd have to hurry or not, I asked the sleeping Union officer next to me if he had the time. I received no response. Either this guy was a sound sleeper, or his wish to sleep forever had been granted.

When I passed in front of the soldier to confront him, I noticed a dried blood stain around the ring of his neck. I didn't see that last night due to the shadows of darkness and my weariness of being. I got the feeling that the man was in fact no longer with us. I lifted his tall, Burnside-style hat from his head to revealed little else but a set of shoulders.

I let loose with an "Oh God" as I dropped the hat, turned, and quickly abandoned the area. "I've got to get the hell out of here!" I yelled in a panic.

I stepped onto Taneytown Road and pulled out the tether. I had to jockey it around a bit to see the time readout. The tether, if I didn't explain earlier, resembles a cross between a pager and a flip phone. The readout is digital and faintly illuminated.

"Zero four twenty-four hours. Good."

In my haste, I hadn't decided which direction I would be heading. I pulled out my map to locate the quickest escape route. While I had difficulty seeing my diagram at this time of the morning, I was able to locate two possible exits. One would lead me around, then south of the Round Tops via Plum Run. That proved to be a bit too speculative and awkward. While the lane I joined up with would drop me right about at the landing zone, if I remembered correctly, that path is still very tree-lined today. I couldn't risk any more surprises in the dim morning light.

The other route would have me leave Taneytown Road at the same junction, but I'd travel west towards the Peach Orchard. That was an area of some of the heaviest fighting. I'm sure the scenery would prove to be none too enticing to the eyes, let alone the nose. However, that would be my best bet, as it were.

As I continued my walk down Taneytown Road on my trek towards freedom, my earlier suspicion presented itself to my senses. The smell of death was beginning to become a fixture in the area. The stench seemed to hover just above the ground mirroring the morning fog. No matter where I went, there it was. The odor would do nothing but increase in intensity as the day came of age.

I continued down the dirt and gravel road for about a mile or so when I came to the hollow just north of Little Round Top. There was little more than a dirt path at this junction. I believe Wheatfield Road now connects Taneytown Road with Emmitsburg Road via this route.

Just as I passed the smaller of the two hills, the journey I had taken so lightly turned out to be anything but. There were plenty of soldiers around, yet few of them knew what to make of me. With what little light I had available, I could see some of them pointing in my direction and whispering to their cohorts. Since they couldn't tell if I was friend or foe, they didn't shoot first and ask questions later. For all they knew, I could be one of their own. My strategy was paying off.

As I approached Plum Run, I heard a cry for water. The man must have heard my footsteps. He sounded so pitiful. I knew that I really wasn't supposed to do anything to upset life's balance here in this plane, but this time I just couldn't pass by. The hell with Dr. Welles.

"Hold on man, let me get you some water," I told him. I had to go into Plum Run creek to fill my canteen. I drained it last night thinking that I wouldn't need it anymore.

As I came out of the creek bed, I had to ask the soldier to voice himself once again. While the sky was lightening, the sun wasn't up quite yet so it was difficult to see who was where. For all I knew, it could have been a trap. When he once again called out, I went over to assist him in any way I could. He was as grateful as a man could be. Turns out he was a Southern man; a soldier from Texas named Jacob.

Seeing me in my outfit he asked, "Are you a doctor or a preacher man?" hoping that I'd say yes to either.

"No, I'm sorry to disappoint you on both accounts. I'm simply a photographer. What seems to be your problem?"

"I can't feel or move my legs," he replied. "I've been out here for a day and a half, I think."

"Good God, man. About all I can offer you is a piggyback ride in the direction that I'm going. Hopefully, we'll run into someone with a wagon who can get you to the help that you need."

Remembering that I had a deadline I had to meet, and I was still unsure of the tether's accuracy I asked, "By the way, I hate to trouble you, but do you have the time?"

He pulled out his pocket watch and replied, "It looks like five until five."

After I assisted him with a drink I asked, "How accurate is that watch?" I inquired.

"Oh very," he said between gulps. "It was my father's. He gave it to me for good luck."

"Good luck, huh?"

"Well, I'm still alive so I guess it's working."

"Fair enough. Let me try and get you loaded here," I said as I had him put his arms around my neck so I could right him. As I raised his back off of the ground, the man let loose with an ear-piercing shriek and begged to be put back down.

"I can't travel. Leave me be, leave me be!" he pleaded.

"Hell, I can't just leave you here, Jake. You probably have a broken back."

In his pained frustration, he waved me on as if swatting at a pesky fly and said, "Go on, git."

I could do nothing but survey the pitiful specimen as he turned his head away. As a parting goodwill gesture, I said, "Here, bite down on this." I took his bandanna from around his neck, rolled it into a wad, and placed it between his teeth. With a muffled voice I think he muttered, "What are you going to do?"

"I'm going to attempt to make you a little more comfortable. Sometimes you have to go through hell to get to heaven."

I walked behind him, raised him up slowly this time, and dragged him backwards. He let loose with muffled yells of pain, then relief, as I leaned him at a comfortable angle against a rock under a large Cyprus tree. "At least you'll be able to see if anyone's approaching to help you out. Plus, the cover will afford you some protection from the rain that's due in later this afternoon."

With tears of pain and gratitude in his eyes, he thanked me for my concern. I took his bandanna, dabbed his eyes, then placed it in his breast pocket.

"Jake, I wish I had something to offer you to eat but I don't even have that for myself."

I went over and picked up his canteen that had been just beyond his reach for the last thirty-six hours. As I placed it in his lap, he looked up at me and said, "God bless you, sir. You were an angel of mercy to stop and quench my thirst and ease my distress. I wish you all of the best, my friend."

"Many thanks, I'll need it," I returned. Speaking of which, I had to be moving on. I bade him farewell and assured him if I found anyone to assist him, I'd send them his way.

"Jake, I hope you make it back home all right."

"I wish you the same. I'll be O.K."

To continue my journey, I had to go off of the path in search of the end to Wheatfield Road. It was anything but pleasant, walking through the damp weeds, brush, stickers, and occasionally trees. Once I tripped over something cylindrical and long. It might have been a branch, or an appendage. I just kept moving.

It wasn't unusual to hear what I believed to be the groans of a dying man or movements within the undergrowth nearby. I had to convince myself that these sounds weren't those of a sniper. They may have been, but they probably belonged to those who still clung to life despite being overlooked.

I finally found my way to Wheatfield Road and moved in the general direction of the Peach Orchard. Surveying the fields in and around the Rose Farm was, quite literally, a disaster area. There were so many bodies on the farm proper that, even at this hour, crews were out digging the beds of perpetual rest by lantern light for those who would never fight again.

What I believed to be mounds of freshly turned earth dotted the orchard. There were, no doubt, many times more interments yet to come. There were still bodies lying where they fell several days ago. The closer I got to the orchard, the stronger the odor of death became. It was akin to the carcass of an animal whose life had been extinguished on a country lane three days prior. Coupled with the baking sun and multiplied by the many hundreds that fell in this region, one would have a good starting point to imagine what I was experiencing.

The Peach Orchard didn't resemble anything

like I saw a couple of day sgo. Many of the trees had been forcefully uprooted or reduced to splinters. While most of the bodies had been removed from the grove itself, some unattached body parts remained. They may have ended up buried at a later date, or perhaps not. I read one time that wild animals in the area feasted upon many of the remains.

I turned south down Emmitsburg Road and moved in the direction of the landing site about three quarters of a mile away. There were broken wheels, carts, and crates lying along the side of the road. One soldier, about seventy-five yards to my front, was slamming a crate to the ground in an attempt, I believe, to salvage the boards for either firewood or headboards for the newly planted.

Even though I was out in the open, I was still quite guarded. I was aware that even now there were Rebel snipers inhabiting the trees along Warfield and Seminary Ridges. Being that it was the general direction of my travels, it was understandable that my nerves were on edge.

I veered off Emmitsburg Road and down the lane that Dr. Welles and I traveled three days ago. My heart was pounding as I was now nearer to home than I had been in the last seventy-two hours.

I cut across the debris-strewn field to save a few valuable seconds. As I arrived at the stone fence, there were several Confederate soldiers milling about. Some were pulling picket duty while others appeared to be doing little more than keeping the sentries company. Some of those present were carrying visible wounds, while the rest appeared intact.

I sat down on an adjoining boulder and thought that I had better check the tether so I'd be sure and hit my mark at the exact second. I reached into my coat to retrieve the device and found the pocket unoccupied. "Oh come on now, God don't do this to me!" I said as I dug through my other coat pocket, then through my pants.

During the process, a Southern sentry had been watching me root around on my person and walked up to me. "You looking for a smoke, pal?"

"Oh no, I think I may have misplaced something though."

"Ha, you'll never find it out there if that's where you lost it," he said motioning towards the open battlefield. He was right. I've been from one edge of this countryside to the other. If I lost it out there, I'd never find it.

"May I ask what you're doing here, sir? You live around here?" he asked.

"No, I'm just visiting you could say. I'm, uh, supposed to meet someone here shortly."

"You picked a funny time and place to meet if you don't mind me saying."

"Yeah well, I'm not even sure if he'll show up now or not. Hey, by any chance do you have the time?"

"Yep." he said as he took out his pocket watch. "Twenty-five past the hour."

"Oh thank-you, I'll be O.K. now. Thanks."

"Well O.K., better watch your head," he advised as he walked off a short distance. I was in a panic now. There's no way that Dr. Welles would send the ATM here without a matching signal. Actually, there was no way he could.

I was almost shaking at the thought of being stranded in this time and place that wasn't my own. Well, Dr. Welles warned me that something like this could happen. I guess I should have listened. How in the hell could I have not better secured the piece of equipment that would act as my lifeline? I scolded myself. For all I know, it might have slipped out when I was cutting through the brush. Maybe it fell out when I went into the creek to fill Jacob's canteen. If it hit the water, it would short out and I'd be a goner.

As a last ditch effort, I felt down around the lining of my coat near my knees. Viola, there it was! Now, if it's only in working condition, I'll be on my way after all.

I scooted the tether upwards along the lining of my coat moving it towards the pocket. With my right hand in my pocket, I felt around until I located the slight separation in the seam.

"Damn cheap theatrical costumes," I said in exasperation.

The tether advanced up, then out to the freedom of my waiting palm. As I looked it over, I pronounced it to be in working order. It was a bit dirty, and there was a micro dent or two, but the LED readout seemed to correspond with the time the soldier had just reported. Now the question was how I would be able to pull off this departure with all of the Rebels less than fifty yards away. I guessed that my best strategy would be to act as nonchalant as possible. Was that possible? I hoped that when the ATM showed up, I could get loaded and ready to go before anyone noticed that something out of the ordinary was occurring.

I went over to my landmark boulder and

acted as if I was just resting and waiting for a friend. And to be honest, I actually was.

I looked out over the battlefield and thought of all the history I had been witness to over the last three days. The people who fought here, both friend and foe, left their indelible mark on eternity. While many of the dead would never be identified, amongst the fallen were those whose namesakes garnered many more headlines than did the soldier himself. Of those who breathed their last breath on the field in southern Pennsylvania were names such as Nixon, Patton, and Revere.

There were also survivors who went on to gain greater fame in areas other than the War Between the States. Union General Abner Doubleday was credited with inventing the game we have come to know as baseball. General George A. Custer went on to his last stand some twenty years later in a meadow far west of the Alleghenies. The waste of it all, I thought. Yet, as Dr. Welles pointed out, a person, or in this case a country, learns more from its mistakes than it does from its triumphs.

I snapped back to reality when I remembered that it was incredibly close to the launch time. I watched the readout and counted it down in my mind as the zero hour was now upon me. I would be emancipated from this carnage at last, I thought with a sigh of relief. I rose and pointed the tether in the direction where the ATM would arrive. As the LEDs read 05:29:58, 05:29:59, then 05:30:00, I pushed the button that would usher in my rebirth to the modern era.

Just as I performed that function, I remembered the 'sonic boom' that occurs when the craft breaks the time barrier. That would surely draw the attention of those in the vicinity. I'm sure that at this point, these fellows know a 'boom' when they hear one. Hopefully, their hearing would be so decimated that they wouldn't even notice the low thump.

I watched and waited for my homeward bound taxi to arrive. It dawned upon me that I had no idea how long the ATM would take to show up. It would be cutting across almost one hundred and forty years of time. I did remember that during my arrival trip, after I regained my senses, the LEDs indicated that somewhat less than a minute had passed.

I waited, then waited some more. Ninety seconds went by and still nothing. I was at a point where I had to make a decision, and right now. I was about to commit a Cardinal sin as I once again pointed the tether and pressed the button. Dr. Welles warned me not to do that. There was no way of knowing how many charges were left in the tether's power supply. I may be using the last one. I may have already used it. After another minute, it became apparent to me that something was definitely amiss. That which I had feared has come to pass.

I didn't want to leave the area just in case the ATM may have been 'held up in traffic' and would break free at any moment. I just sat down, pulled off a tick from behind my ear, and stared at the empty ground as my mind began to wander aimlessly. I began wondering if I had been stranded on purpose. Perhaps the whole CIA plot to commandeer Project Sundial's equipment was a ruse. Maybe the Feds put Dr. Welles up to finding a test subject, willing or otherwise, to prove the government's case on time travel. Who knows, the Feds might have caught up with Dr. Welles after he launched me and confiscated his equipment. Henry may have not been able to tell the authorities that human experiments had already begun. He left me to fend for myself in an era not of my own birth. There's always the possibility that the ATM had already materialized without my matching signal. The Confederates could then have seized it. There's always the chance that Dr. Welles could have been in an accident or even suffered a heart attack. That guy never did take the best care of himself. For all I knew, that S.O.B. might have overslept.

All in all, the most likely scenario pointed towards the ATM just not being able to make it back for whatever reason. The module's power cells may have discharged. I may have taken a few too many tumbles to the ground that in turn damaged the tether causing it to skip a second or so, maybe a day or two.

I knew that I was doing myself no good just sitting there and worrying about something I could do nothing about. My troubled thoughts were interrupted when a Southern fellow, sporting a heavy cockney accent, commented to me, "Hey bloke, you sit there much longer and you're likely to get your arse blown to a smither."

"Yeah, I know." Remembering Jake I said, "Hey, there's a soldier from one of the Texas brigades I spoke to over in that direction whose in dire need of treatment."

"Yup, there's a lot of that going 'round."

"Is there anyone around here who could help

him? He can't walk."

"That's Yankee territory you know. And how would you propose that we get over there and back in one piece?"

"I don't know. I just hated to leave him there. He seemed like such a decent fellow."

"They're all decent. At least, we all were once of a time."

Feeling a physical emptiness to match the one of my spirit I asked, "Sir, is there any possibility of finding some food around here? I haven't eaten in some time."

"Friend or foe?" he inquired.

"Excuse me? Oh, I guess you could say that I'm an independent. I side with no one. I was just here to photograph this whole mess," I said as I exposed the wooden skin on my camera.

"Hmmm," he said trying to figure out if I was worthy or not. "I wish you'd have asked me a mite earlier. I would have gladly shared the last of me banger with you. Um, they tossed some leftover meat out over there by those boxes. You're welcomed to anything you can find, but I doubt anything over there is fit for pigs. If you keep rooting around in there, maybe you'll find some that is."

I thanked him and made my way over to what appeared to be the remains of some sort of field galley. Why it was so close to the action, I hadn't a clue. Nothing there was worth salvaging, but I did find a pile of meat scraps lying in an adjacent crate. I figured that I could take what I need and find a nearby campfire to prepare my much-appreciated bounty.

I bent down and took hold of the rations to tear off a piece. The meat didn't feel right in my hands. It was slippery and slimy. I lifted up the largest piece and found the underside to be crawling with maggots. At that same moment, the stench unleashed from the provisions equaled that of the decaying tissues of soldiers lying to my rear. I dropped the rotting flesh and brought my hand up to cover my nose. That's when I noticed that it was impregnated with a putrid stench. I staggered over to an adjacent tree and proceeded to lose what contents remained within my withered belly. Regaining my composure, I used canteen water to free my hands of the rotten odor, and rinsed out my mouth before taking a swig from what was left in the flask. I then sat back down on the stone fence for an extended time out.

"I'm as sick as a dog, I can't get home, and I'm surrounded by dead and dying soldiers. It don't get no better than this," I sarcastically reported.

I then looked up and noticed a band of several hundred Union soldiers, sidestepping the carcasses of both sides, making their way towards the ridge. I'm not sure if they planned to capture what few Southerners they believed to be loitering about, or if they were going to attempt an all out offensive on their own.

When they made it as far as Emmitsburg Road, the trees along Seminary and Warfield opened up with a fair amount of firepower. Even though this action was a fair distance from me, I hopped behind the stones for protection.

The scrap didn't last long. The Union boys quickly found out that there was far more than just a few Rebels still around.

As the Federals retreated and the hostilities halted, I realized that I still had to figure out what to do about my predicament. When the area around the Rose house finally cleared itself of offensive troops, I thought I'd venture in that direction. I had nowhere else to go.

At mid to late morning, the majority of Southern troops must have cleared out from the ridge, for all available Union hands were out digging trenches between the Peach Orchard and the Rose Farm. I ventured on to the farm proper to inquire about the availability of foodstuffs on the Union side. My stomach that sided with no one was now emptier than empty causing my head to ache profusely.

I kindly asked the officer who appeared to be in charge about the possibility of getting something to eat. I think he took pity on me and my situation and replied, "Sure, I'll help you out. I'll just, uh, hmm. Tell you what, help those men out there for about an hour or so and you and me'll fry up some eggs I found in the barn for lunch. How about that?"

"That would be fine, sir."

"Ironic, isn't it? All of those broken men lying about in the weeds and most of these eggs survived," he said with a chuckle.

No matter how much financial credit I could qualify for at home, I was now a poor man. I was broke both spiritually and physically. I figured that I might as well make up a sign that read 'Will Work for Food.' However my proclamation, unlike those of today, would be considered honorable. There were few handouts in this time and place. There just weren't enough available resources around for that kind of nonsense.

I thanked the officer, took off my coat, and

placed it over my camera and bag for safe keeping. I rolled up my sleeves, marched over to those hard at it, and then asked anyone if they needed relief.

A mustachioed man looked up and replied, "We all need relief, man." He then looked around and said, "Hey George, you've been at it all morning. Go take a rest." Turning back to me he asked, "How long you going to be here for us?"

"Oh I don't rightly know, perhaps an hour or so. The officer over there said he'd get me some eats if I help out."

"He did, did he? George, take an hour. Make it two. We'll join you at the half."

"Thank-you, sir," the weary, heavyset man replied.

"So you're going to bury stiffs for your meal, are you? Hah! After five minutes of doing this, you won't want to eat again. She's all yours," he said as he tossed me a shovel.

There were quite a few fallen bodies in this sector, only a few of them wearing the butternut and gray from the Army of Northern Virginia. Usually an army would only bury their own dead. I could only guess that since the number of southerners was so small in our particular vicinity, we'd throw them in as well for sanitary reasons—if we had time, and in their own separate holes, mind you.

Many of the bodies had already been placed in position. We were to dig a hole, then throw the soil from the fresh crater over top of the corpse to its immediate left. That method left an abode for the next resident. And so went that process on down the line.

Since there were dozens of cadavers in this

area, the holes we dug were no more than a foot or so deep. The soil just barely covered the shoe tops of the deceased. There just wasn't enough time to do the chore as thorough as it should have been.

Problems did arise when we went to bury the dead that had been on the field for several days. Those bodies had bloated to nearly twice their normal size, in some cases, and that meant that we had to double our efforts to accommodate their maturity. Some of those dead actually burst during the burial process due to a conflict between the internal and external pressures, and thereby emitted a foul gas that increasingly permeated the entire battlefield.

Because of that situation, it was decided that the wrists and ankles would be bound with cloth strips. This technique not only kept the rigor mortis-laden limbs in their proper position, but it also assisted in the transportation of the body. No one wanted to physically handle a bloated body. It wasn't unheard of to have a corpse pop on one of the pallbearers during removal from the field.

A long pole was shoved through the two restraints allowing for safer lifting and moving during the obsequies. That kept the carriers free from flying bodily debris should the unfortunate occur.

I noticed that the longer I labored, the worse the battlefield stench became. I was hoping that I'd become used to it over time. No such luck. That smell reminded me of the fetid meal I nearly consumed. Employing that as a flashback, I turned my head to the side and gagged. Since there was nothing left to exit my body, I resumed my duties.

I noticed that I wasn't afforded the luxury

that those in the military enjoyed. Many had pieces of cloth tie strips soaked in peppermint oil and kept them close at hand. Others tied the rags around their faces like a doctor's mask. This allowed those fortunate few to work the burial detail in comfort, comparatively speaking.

While filling the holes with their contents, a box of miscellaneous body parts was occasionally dumped into the cavity. No ownership could be determined, and I'm sure that the current occupant wouldn't mind the company.

We switched jobs every three to four holes. I was now privileged to be the chaperoning escort to the expired. In this task, like the others, there were no gloves available. Unless the corpse was in exceptional shape, and few were, we used the carrying pole whenever time allowed. It was hell when a wrist or ankle binding let loose and the body tumbled to the ground. Whoever failed to properly secure their end had to stand over the body and rebind the limbs of the rotting soldier. Not a pleasant task.

As I stated earlier, most of the bodies were in fairly pitiful shape. Few of those who lay prostrate in the field escaped the repulsive results of time and battle. If they hadn't been ravaged during the fighting, the post engagement period had taken its toll. Some considered it to be poetic justice that the baking sun and the passage of time combined to turn many of the downed Rebels' skin black.

Some of the dead bodies inflated to the point where they began to squeeze their remaining bodily contents from every fissure of the being. That proved to be a veritable feast for the gnats, flies, and sweet bees. Also accompanying the distention was a phenomenon where the withered eyelids weren't able to contain their tenants. That produced a ghastly, fixed stare that seemed to be looking towards the heavens for an answer.

"I noticed that nearly every dead soldier had his pockets turned inside out. Why is that?" I asked my assistant.

"Oh, they were probably checking for some identification or something like that," he answered.

"Funny, I don't notice too many headboards being erected atop many of the mounds," I added.

"Probably a shortage of boards," answered the soldier in an unconvincing manner. It was apparent to me that others rifled through the belongings of the fallen men seeking something other than identification. I noticed that particularly amongst the Confederate dead in our sector. Looting of the fallen was another sad by-product of the war. The justification for such behavior was that the downed soldier wouldn't need any of those things where he was going. Desperation turned otherwise caring individuals into greedy scavengers. I too now live in that glass house.

When we deposited our latest cargo, we had to tuck the wrist wraps in and around the corpse's belt to keep his arms from reaching upward. What a ghastly sight that would produce after the first rain, I thought.

As we went to load the next moon-faced Rebel, I shoved the pole through the bound legs and passed it up towards my colleague to secure the wrists. We found it more comfortable to drop to one knee on this still and very humid overcast day while awaiting our call to action. With the corpse's belly nearly the size of a basketball, some of the shirt's buttons had given way to reveal the same type of dingy, almost pale green undershirt Mojo had sported. In the front, his shirt was never tucked in, and only partially so to the rear. The front of Mojo's garment drooped lower than the back because of his constant, almost habitual effort to keep it tucked in.

I released my grip on the pole, got up and stood over the body. Now hardly recognizable, it was indeed the former Mojo. His eyes now looked back with the fixed stare of death. "Oh God," I said lamenting my discovery.

The carrier manning the front of the transport turned and gazed back at the body. "Aw hell, this is a Rebel. I ain't burying no God damn Rebel! Who's lining up these stiffs anyway?"

"Sergeant, if I could, I'd like to bury him."

"You know him?"

"I knew him, at least briefly. I, uh, interviewed him," I answered. "Would it be possible for me to say a few words over his body before he's buried? I mean, I know that we're busy and all."

"Hell I don't know. I'll ask."

As we carried the body over to the hole and placed him in position, the fellow relayed my request. "He cain't go into a Union hole, sorry. You'll have to put him over by that tree."

"Sergeant, if you could give me a hand, I'd appreciate it."

"Go ahead, Clancy. It's close enough to mid day to call it a morning anyway," our lead man said as he dropped his shovel. "You do your damndest, Reverend," he said with a spread-armed bow, either mocking my efforts or mistaking my uniform for someone of a higher calling. After we carried Mojo over to the badly scarred tree, the three of them walked back towards the barn, conversing as they went.

"This is one man who'll receive his last rights if I have anything to say about it," I muttered to myself. And if anyone deserved it, Mojo did.

I dug the hole a bit deeper than military dictates and finished just in time. Blisters were starting to appear on my hands. The last thing I needed while handling the dead was an open sore. I did however make sure the hole faced east, for that was the direction Mojo was heading before the angel of death robbed the Army of Northern Virginia of one of its finer spirits. It was my way of indicating that Mojo never turned his back on his fellow countrymen.

I scooted the soldier along the ground and into the hole, bent down while pulling my shirt up over my nose and mouth, and tried to think of something religious to say. I drew a blank. That was understandable considering the diorama laid out before me in all directions.

As I began to think of the proper sendoff, the only sound that entered my ears was a half a dozen distant shovel 'chunks' as room was scooped out of the earth for another lodger. The entire area seemed to be absent of all life. No crickets or cicadas could be heard. Even the buzzards were conspicuous by their absence. If there was ever a time that their presence would be noticed, it would be now. This was a far different place than I walked into just a couple of days ago.

All I could think up to say was the following: "Oh Lord, welcome with your open arms, a brother whose name is known only to you. We knew him as Mojo, we knew him as a friend. Small in number came to this place with less, yet few gave more of his soul to his fellow man than did this child of yours."

After a pause and realizing that no additional words were necessary, I bade farewell with an "Amen." I stood up with the aid of the shovel and began blanketing Mojo for his eternal sleep.

When I finished, I paused at the front of the newly constructed mound and realized that I had nothing to use for a headstone. It didn't matter; from what I read, all of these remains would be removed from this site within ten years anyway. After that amount of time, no one will know who's who, I thought. I tramped down the earth with my foot, and felt afterwards it was a sacrilege to do so. With the sleeve of my shirt, I wiped the copious amounts of sweat from my forehead, and then moved on.

I walked back towards the barn and met up with my employing officer. "Ah yes, the breakfast man," he chuckled. "You still good and hungry for some filling vittles after going through that routine out there?" he said with a touch of jest.

"No, but I had better eat. I need something in my gut." He offered me a seat on a log and allowed me to fill my canteen from their wagon's barrel. He proceeded to crack as many eggs as an iron skillet could hold.

"Like 'em scrambled?"

"Prefer them that way."

We made some small talk to pass the time in between the interruptions. It seemed as if everyone needed his approval for one thing or another. After we finished off nearly a dozen and a half eggs between us, I thanked him profusely, and almost as an afterthought asked him if he had access to the mail.

"Yes, I should be able to meet up with them in a day or so. Why, are you expecting a parcel or something?"

"Oh no, but would you be so kind as to put this letter in the sack," I said as I handed him the nearly forgotten letter from the soldier who passed away at the angle. "It's from one of your boys who dropped on Cemetery Ridge yesterday."

Looking a bit more solemn, he replied, "Oh my, I'd be more than honored to."

I conferred my parting thanks and walked back up towards Emmitsburg Road. I shot what I hoped would be some valuable tape of the burial crews in action. Now, all I had to do is to figure out a way to get the camera and me back home.

It was closer to the one o'clock hour as I began walking once again to parts unknown. It seemed that I was always heading to nowhere in particular since becoming stuck in this dimension.

While there were still soldiers from both sides milling about, their numbers were negligible. Neither was sufficient in strength to launch an offensive nor defend against one.

I heard what I mistakenly believed to be the rumblings of a distant battle. However, judging from the darkening skies, the only cannonade that would take place would be originating from the heavens above. As I continued northward towards the Codori Farm, I noticed that the interment crews were hard at it there as well as at the Klingle place across the way. Just as I was passing their operation, silver dollar-sized raindrops began their sparse coverage.

Hell, I had to find some place to take cover. The old Codori barn was already full of spent soldiers, some dead, some still alive. I decided to cut across the infamous field of Pickett's Charge, past the angle, then on to the Taneytown Road barn. Perhaps there would be some room for me there. It provided me protection before. I'd even settle for the shelter of their outhouse at this point. We were in for a blow and I had to try and keep my equipment dry at all costs.

As I crossed over the acreage, the few bodies that remained as yet untouched produced an eerie sight. A couple of them must have met with a recent end as they exhibited no bloating to speak of. I saw one soldier lying on his side. Glancing at him, I was unsure if he was dead or alive. Upon further inspection I noticed that his canteen was to his lips, yet nothing was going in and nothing was coming out. That answered that question.

Another man had obviously experienced a longer exposure period. He was flat on his face, ram rod in his right hand and the barrel of his Enfield in the left.

I hopped the wall and moved swiftly past the now unobstructed angle; an area I thought I bade farewell to some time ago. As I ran down the now familiar path, the rain began to pick up its pace. What few people I saw out appeared to be running for cover as well.

Out of desperation, I indeed ran up to an outhouse figuring that I had breathed in worse—quite recently in fact. At least it would give me a place to rest and sit the storm out. I yanked open the door, then leapt back, for inside was a blood-soaked cringing soldier huddled up in the corner. He was absolutely terrified of me. I realized he was actually terrified of life right now, so I slowly closed the door and scooted a rock between the frame and the door to allow in some fresh air.

I continued my search as the skies began to deposit raindrops at a similar pace as the bullets flew the day before. I scaled the small stone fence adjacent to the barn, then headed south on Taneytown Road until I reached the side entrance to my sanctuary. I ducked under the overhang and reflected, while looking around, that I had gone in a complete circle this day. I dashed through the door and discovered that I had run into what was now a field hospital.

Inside was a sight that even the most schooled physicians couldn't fathom. The barn itself was dim and humid. An unspeakable stench consisting of sweat, mildew, and a bouquet of burned and rotting flesh hung like a cloud inside the structure. Soldiers were piled up in the corner like discarded toys in a child's playroom. Some were still living; their abdomens open to the dank barn air. While their organs were still visibly operating, I'm guessing it wouldn't be for long. Many of those unfortunates even showed signs that the spirit had long since abandoned its host, but the body had yet to be convinced of that fact. Those segregated cases were considered hopeless. Not a lot could be done for them in that day and time, but a caring aide had heart enough to place them there until they were ready for a final resting place. I'm guessing that few if any of those individuals possessed a known surname.

In the middle of the room was the operating

table. In this case, it consisted of a series of barn planks supported by two barrels. Standing to its side was the doctor, stripped to the waist. I would use the term 'surgeon' loosely as his job was to do little more than sew up wounds and amputate limbs. There was little time for anything else.

Occasionally, a probing finger to the leg, abdomen, or skull could extract a minie ball from its hiding place. The doctor would perform his tasks as quick and efficient as a blue-collar worker on a busy assembly line. And, that's exactly what this was.

When a useless limb was freed from its owner, the surgeon simply wiped the saw on his apron and yelled, "Next. Come on, come on!" The only time I saw the doctor wash his hands was when he began to curse because the saw's handle became too slippery from his customers' life-sustaining fluids to grip. He left the saw half of the way through a shrieking man's femur as he leaned over to a bucket to rinse the bodily fluids from his hands. He dried his hands on his apron then returned to his task with renewed vigor.

The soldiers continued to trickle in on makeshift crutches and stretchers, while occasionally you would find one leaning on the shoulders of his enemy. Most proved to be filthy and dehydrated. Those who could wait were ushered over to the barn's wall. The current occupants of that space were checked for signs of life. If none existed, a shroud or handkerchief was placed over the deceased's face alerting the attendants that this body was ready to be moved outside. In the rain, the figure was cleansed by the elements in preparation for its burial. Quite efficient, nature is.

Shortly into my stay, a Confederate soldier was carried in, and a recovering Union soldier raised up and yelled, "Get that damn Reb out of here! He ain't fit to quarter with us fellows!"

"Please, I have no where to go. Please?" begged the soldier whose drying muscle tissue was still dangling from his stump.

The doctor, noting the dispirited look on the face of the man who was minus a forearm said, "He stays. Private, find room for him. He'll be last in line. And to you," he said, pointing his bloodied saw in the direction of the Federal spokesman on the floor, "shut the hell up! If you don't like the way this hospital is run, then there's the door!" Enough said.

Screams and moans accompanied the saw as it performed its morbid concert within those four walls. For some of the tougher amputations, a crude type of chloroform was poured on a rag and placed over a hollowed-out cow's horn. The sawed-off antler was then fitted over the patient's breathing passages. It helped keep the noise level down and the patient somewhat still, but rarely was the practice sufficient.

When finished with the amputation, the doctor would either cauterize the remnant with a hot iron, or slap a dressing of grease and charcoal over the newly carved stump. I saw the fire for the irons just outside the door, down-wind, and the chloroform/ether inside. It had to be that way to keep it going during the rainstorm. I thought, oh my Lord.

Upon finishing with another nameless, faceless entity, the surgeon yelled, "Private!" In walked a green-horned Northern lad, still wet behind the ears. Due to the inclement weather, that was true not only figuratively but also quite literally. His drenched clothing carried the stain of maroon and brown from the lengthy performance of his duties.

The private worked his way over to one of the old wheelbarrows formally used to transport manure from the barn. As he lifted the cart up, I saw that it now contained discarded arms, legs, feet, and anything else that could be removed from the body in an attempt to salvage a human life.

While I stood next to a support beam, I decided to take out my camera and video what I could with the light I had available. I zeroed in on a lad who had recently received his treatment then moved to the wall to begin his recovery. He continued to fight the war from his place on the ground. He barked forth a few unintelligible orders, but spent most of the time covering up from the incoming 'bullets and balls' that rained on him from above. God forbid that a clap of thunder would occur. It was such a sad display to witness. In time, that man's body would perhaps heal itself sufficiently, but his mind would forever be plagued by the ravages of war.

"Can he be placed somewhere else?" one of the attendants petitioned.

"You tell me where," the doctor demanded, planting his knuckles on the table and employing a facial expression of bulging eyes and pursed lips.

I was continuing my recording when one of the cutters turned in my direction. He had been so busy that this was probably the first time he had taken notice of me. He saw the camera and yelled, "Out! Dammit we don't have time to pose for a portrait!" I assured him that posing was unnecessary, but that did little to change his demeanor.

"Look mister, you want to be helpful? Take the other wheelbarrow and deposit it where the private dumped his load."

Even though the rain had tapered somewhat, I guessed this to be the price I'd have to pay for my shelter. Everything here has a price attached to it, I reminded myself. I guessed that during desperate times, everything carries a cost no matter where you are. Besides, I got the impression that the surgeon's demand was an order, not a request.

I went over and took grips on the two handles. In doing so, I noticed they were tacky from an accumulation of old blood and tissue built up over the day. I squinted my face in disgust as I lifted the incredibly heavy load. Upon taking a few steps, the load shifted on the uneven floor and tipped to the right spilling a small portion of its contents.

"Clean it up," came the command from the surgeon.

"You have got to be kidding."

"Do I look like I'm in a kidding mood? Do it!"

I reached down to return the foot and forearm portion back to the barrow. I then scooped up the undistinguishable conglomeration of ferementing body innards and heaped them on top bringing about an involuntary distorted expression to my face. This had to be gut truck duty at its foulest. I shook the crimson syrup from my hands, wiped them on my pants, took grips once again, then rolled, with a head of steam, out the back door in to the steady shower in search of the dumping ground the surgeon spoke of.

Over by the fence was a bloody pyramid of gray-tinted limbs stacked not unlike a woodpile. Immediately I thought of it as a monument to the swiftness of the surgeon's blade. I pushed the steel-wheeled cart in that direction via the well-worn ruts in the mud. I tipped the part cart up and watched in horror as the arms, legs, and feet took their last tumble in their journey of life. Finally, the last foot marched its way out of the wagon followed by the accompanying sauces. "Good God, what have these people done to each other," I asked.

I assured myself that this was my last delivery as I wheeled the gut truck back for a refill. Knowing that I was on my way out, I decided to see if I could obtain one last piece of information.

"Uh, does anybody know if General Armistead is or was here?" I inquired.

Nobody said anything for a few seconds. Finally, one of the enlisted assistants spoke up and said, "He's a Rebel, right? Heard of him, you might try one of the hospitals east of here." I'm guessing that he was referring to the Spangler Spring area, or any one of the many barns that lined Taneytown Road. With the weather being what it was, I decided that attempting a deathbed interview just wasn't worth it. I'm not even sure if it was possible at this time.

If the resident doctor here was hoping to persuade me into leaving by placing me on disposal duty, he succeeded. Once again, I didn't know where I was going, but I didn't want to stay in an area where there was little room and even less of a welcome. I stopped in the doorway and pulled out my poncho. The skies showed no sign of forgiveness as the rain was really teeming down now. I had to use something to protect my equipment, so I slung my bag over my shoulder and pulled the rain gear into place.

I went around the side of the barn to the oft-acquainted footpath and started forward through the mud. I glanced back at that house of dissection that saved, yet disfigured so many. I couldn't keep from noticing the pile of discarded limbs. Lightning reflected off the saturated and now obsolete finger nails on hands that now appeared to be begging to the heavens for relief. I repeated my desperate plea, "I have to get the hell out of here."

Now I had to decide where to go and what I'd do. I too was at the point of searching for relief from the heavens. I determined that it wasn't time yet for me to retreat into town in search of a place to stay. First of all, I was sure there were no rooms available. Next, I had no money with which to secure myself lodging. I guess that if I became stranded here permanently, I'd have no choice. I've never been in that position, and I'm not sure how I'd be able to pull something such as that off, but I didn't want to think about that now. I still planned one last attempt at a departure tomorrow. Maybe Dr. Welles had to do a repair on the ATM, maybe, maybe. Maybe I'll be stuck here forever.

As I cleared the summit of Cemetery Ridge once again, I noticed the stone rampart I hid behind while videoing. It had been reduced to a pile of stepping-stones with one of the few remaining Union bodies lying next to it. I thought that if he had any money left on him, it might help me, however briefly, in my search for lodging. Just as I rolled him on to his back, a lone picket posted under a tree trying to stay dry in close proximity to the Bryan house approached. I suppose he was a look out, but just what he was on duty for is beyond me. I doubted that anyone would make an enemy assault under such conditions as these. I suppose stranger things have happened though.

A bit startled, I asked of the sentry, "How are you doing?" hoping to begin on friendly terms.

"What are you doing sir," came his official reply.

"I just wanted to come up here and see where General Armistead was dropped. That was considered a pretty significant event during the assault you know. I'm a reporter."

"You ain't going to find him looking there." I stood there, a bit embarrassed as I almost resorted to looting the body of a deceased soldier. My God, what have I become?

"I was trying to see if he was still alive. He was just lying here." I sounded like a third grader making a feeble excuse for some unsuitable behavior.

"Who did you say you're looking for, Umstead? Shoot, we took him out right over here," he said as he walked over to a muddy and still debris-strewn spot. "From what I understand, he was one of the best the South had to offer, so we took them up on their offer. Talk has it that he was one of General Scott's buddies."

Remembering where the monument commemorating General Armistead's courage is placed today I stated, "Oh, I thought that it was over there." I pointed to where a crate's lid now rested, approximately twenty feet away.

"Was you here?" he said in a rather challenging tone. "Did you see him go down?"

"Well no, during the battle I was over there. But I thought..."

"Well I did," he interrupted. "I was stationed at that corner over there," he said while pointing to the farthest ninety-degree angle of rocks. "I seen a bunch of them Rebs hop the rocks. We made sure that they didn't get far though. You always go for the color bearer or the officers. Without a leader, them boys is nothing." Changing tones, he stated, "So, unless you seen him, you can't tell me who was where."

"I suppose you're right," I stood corrected. "I only figured..." was as much as I could get out before the soldier spoke up.

"And I suggest you take your ass the hell out of this area. You don't belong here. Now git!" he shouted before turning his back to me and returning to some shelter at the Bryan house less than a hundred yards to the northeast.

"Well, I guess I'm on my own," I said under my breath. I turned and walked back down the field towards Emmitsburg Road. The soldier I spotted earlier lying on the field of Pickett's charge was still in search of relief from the empty canteen. I guessed by now his thirst had been quenched.

As I turned to walk southbound on Emmitsburg, my head began to pound profusely, and the pressure was increasing with every beat. I instinctively bent over and grabbed my head with both hands in an attempt to hold myself together. I wondered if perhaps I had been shot, but I reckoned that wasn't the case. I stayed in a crouch for some time trying to ride out this migraine, or whatever it was. I experienced a flash of lightning, but this originated from within, not from Mother nature's great outdoors. I was sure of it. My eyes were squinted shut, but I saw the flashes none-the-less.

When I managed to straighten up, I endeavored to take stock of my situation. At first I couldn't figure out where I was and why I was standing in the middle of a thunder storm. Before long, I was able to decipher who I was and where I was, but I still wasn't quite sure why. However, for some reason I knew that I was supposed to be here.

Once I became a bit more lucid, I wondered if perhaps my cellular make-up wasn't meshing with the vibration of this period anymore and was defragmenting in an attempt to return to its original composition. Or maybe it was just the stress of the day. Things were coming back to me a little by little. I still wasn't quite sure who Dr. Welles was, but for some reason his name was stuck in my craw. It would come to me. I continued on.

I struggled to maintain my path down the center of the road. That hump was the only high ground that I could find on this jaunt. The farther I walked, the worse I felt.

I was heading towards the land of delirium at this point as I passed the Peach Orchard and Rose house. I looked over and spotted the newly constructed mounds of dirt protecting those who perished during their last confrontation. The mud barricade would prove to be no match against the elements for the remainder of the season. Yet, as far as the armies were concerned, the individuals did their time and received a just payment for their troubles. The Army.

Another hundred yards up and to the right was an abandoned cart. At this juncture, my knees were wobbling and they reminded me of the legs on a table I built in eighth grade shop class. I had no choice but to accept what accommodations were available. The cart's bed was facing west which allowed it to become the perfect clubhouse. I placed what few boards I could find scattered around the area across the gaps in the bed's surface to create a nearly moisture free shelter.

As I was walking back after having retrieved my last board, my stomach hit the point of no return. Unfortunately, everything within did. All this and stomach flu too, I bemoaned. This was getting to become a bad habit.

I rinsed out and attempted to fill my gut with the water which, in looking back, may have been the source of my problems all along. I crawled under the wagon and removed my poncho. Luckily I had remained relatively dry underneath. On this cool and damp night, I was finally thankful for the coat I lugged around for the last couple of days. It was dirty and smelly, but it helped contain the body heat of my shivering body. I laid my pounding head down on my bag in hopes of obtaining some relief.

My dehydrated brain began to fill with a combination of lucid and delusional thoughts, and the two battled for dominance. What if I come up empty again tomorrow? If Dr. Welles doesn't pick me up by then, chances are he can't or won't be able to pull it off, I continued in my confused state. Maybe I could go down to Georgia and get a job at the Gates's farm. They would need the help. And me, being a father figure, wouldn't dim my chances. Good God, I could end up being my own step great-great grandfather.

What would happen if I was indeed stranded for eternity, I continued. What would become of my life? What would become of me? I guess, on the plus side, I'd know every political outcome for the rest of my natural life. I could win a lot of bar bets that way, but one couldn't survive on that. Maybe I could go back to Penn State and get my old job back. I could build a house on the same spot my current one occupies. It would be just like I was back home. Almost.

Wait a minute, I thought as I came up with a bizarre idea. How about if I put a message in a bank safe deposit box with instructions for the contents to be delivered in one hundred and forty years to Dr. Welles at Penn State the week before I left? I could then warn him not launch me back to this time. But, if I accomplished that, I wouldn't be stranded here tonight, would I? And yet here I am. So does that mean that my message wouldn't make it?

I'll be dead and buried for decades before I'm even born. I'd be able to visit my own grave. But how could I if I wasn't even born until the 1960s and wouldn't have a clue of my own demise? Would that mean that my life would become one non-stop circle? Would I be forced by destiny to repeat this journey over and over again? That reminded me of Dr. Welles's description of a ghost. I'd be an entity doomed to repeating my identical actions at the same places throughout the millenniums. I'd be born, grow up, arrive in Gettysburg through Dr.

Welles' efforts, send the safe deposit box note preventing my departure, then pass away here before the note was received. My thinking was all too crazy at this point. I couldn't make sense of anything anymore. I needed to disconnect from this world that I had journeyed to. I closed my eyes in repose.

Chapter Eleven
A Time to Live

"Life does not count by years. Some suffer a lifetime in a day, and so grow old between the rising and setting of the sun."
AUGUSTA JANE EVANS

I woke up several times during the night. It may have been raining harder or softer than the previous hour, but I didn't take notice. My body and mind were still attempting to make peace with one another on this Sunday morning.

I finally managed to slip into a sound sleep for a period until I was roused from my slumber when I felt someone going through my pants pockets. I thought it might be a branch rubbing up against me, but the act was repeated. This time, guessing that it may have come from a wayward soldier scavenging the dead, I had to decide if it would be better to play dead and let him have what he wanted, or whether I should fight for my rights. Then my thoughts went immediately to the tether. I decided to fight. I rolled over and announced, "What the hell?"

I couldn't see a face because his lantern's illumination played havoc with my bloodshot eyes, but he retreated. "What the hell do you want? Who's there?" I asked.

"Oh, I'm sorry. I thought you were dead. Neil?"

"Gates?"

"Yes. Holy mackerel, Neil." Jonathan was so shocked to discover that the target of his burgles was someone known to him that he jumped back. "What are you doing out here underneath a wagon?"

"Trying to stay dry, what the hell are you doing out here at this time of morning, trying to get me for the second time?" I asked looking through the darkness. "By the way, what time is it anyway?"

"It's around five I guess. It's the only time I could slip out of camp. I'm a marked man. Please don't say anything to anybody. I'm sorry to wake you so early. You look like you've had a rough night."

"No, no, that's O.K. A rooster couldn't have proven more dependable. You may have been right on time."

"Why do you say that? Are you preparing to move on?" he inquired.

"In a manner of speaking," I said as I gathered my stuff up. "You never did answer my question. What are you doing out here at this time of the morning, Jonathan?"

"I couldn't sleep worth a damn. I needed to talk."

As I crawled out from under my shelter I asked, "You wanted to talk to me? I find it amazing that you'd know right where to find me," I said, noting the happenstance of the situation. "I take it you've got something on your mind."

"As a matter of fact, I do."

"Well, tell it to me as we walk," I said as I attempted to reorient myself to my surroundings. In my confusion and the darkness of the previous night, I had forgotten exactly where I was. "Oh

O.K., this way," I affirmed as I located the direction of the landing zone. It all came back to me.

As we made our way back on to the road, I was grateful that the rain had slowed to a mist. My shoes were cold and damp.

"What have you got for me, Jon?" I asked.

"I spoke with Rueben Langston Friday evening," he stated.

"Oh yeah? Then he made it! Great, how's he doing?"

"He ain't doing nothing. He died on the night of the third."

"Aw God, don't tell me that. Both he and Mojo are gone." After a moment of quiet contemplation I declared, "I guess one shouldn't try and make friends around here. They don't last very long."

"The lucky ones lose a friend. The unfortunate others lose their life. The first thing they told us when we signed up was never become too attached to an encampment or a friend. They'll both change before you're ready."

"How did it happen?" I inquired.

"What do you mean how did it happen? What difference does it make? He bought a piece of lead like everyone else."

I stopped and asked, "Jonathan, why are you telling me of this? I'm just curious, but you never gave me the time of day before. The only words I ever heard you speak were your cutting remarks putting others down to make yourself appear superior."

Jonathan then reached into his pocket and retrieved a battered Bic pen. "Here, Rueben wanted me to return this to you."

I reached over and slowly took the pen from Jon. I was afraid that Rueben might have spilled the beans about me and my reason for being there. It turns out I was right.

"We never really talked a lot before, so imagine my surprise when, as he lay there dying, he requested to speak with me personally. I was about as surprised as you are of me talking to you. He told me quite a bit about you. I'm not sure that I can buy all that he said. He kept going on and on. I think he was a bit out of his mind, you know. It all sounded a bit too strange to believe," he said as if testing me to see if the whole thing was made up.

Restarting our walk I replied, "Depends on what he told you."

"He said that you and me's kin. You claim to be a descendant of mine. Ain't that the craziest damn thing you've ever heard?"

"Oh, I've heard of things a lot more weird than that in my day," I stated as we turned down the hundred-yard path leading to the landing zone.

Jonathan grabbed me by the shoulder and spun me towards him. "Hey Dammit, don't turn your back to me! Level with me; is what Rueben said about your being from the future and all of that stuff on the level? I have the right to know."

I turned and resumed my walk while replying, "Yes, it's all true. I'm not exactly sure what he told you of course, but knowing Rueben, he probably told you the truth. He had no reason to do otherwise, especially in his condition."

"Why are you here? He said that it had something to do with me. Does it have to do with the fact that I shot General Semmes?"

"For the most part it does."

"Hey, I didn't plan that you know. I didn't deliberately shoot him. I wouldn't do that to nobody."

"Perhaps, but your reputation precedes you," I reminded him.

"Yes I know, but even I wouldn't shoot somebody on purpose unless it was a Yank."

"Uh huh."

"Hey look, I know that I've made a lot of mistakes in my life, but I'm a changed man. Let me tell you, when I saw the general go down, I felt so bad for him."

"For him or for yourself?" I asked.

"For him, dammit! I mean it! I never intended for that to happen." Adapting a calmer manner he added, "Anyway, while I was recovering from my head wound, I figured that if I could feel sympathy for someone who I hated as much as I did him, then I might be able to do right by most anyone else I meet."

"That's a good lesson you learned. Sounds like you finally paid attention to someone or something other than your own selfish needs."

"Yeah, I see what you mean. I guess I've been a pretty rotten person the last year or so. But I did it all to help out my family," he said continuing his confession. "They always came first."

"Yes, but you didn't help out your family by running down all those around you."

"Hey, money can do that to a man, you know. It comes with the territory. Being involved in this stupid damn war doesn't help out none neither. But I gots a family to take care of, and I won't let no-one stand in my way of providing them with all the best that I can give them. No

Yankee is going to deprive me of that, neither will General Longstreet."

"You'd better watch it. Words like that wouldn't sound good in a court of law." Stopping, and feeling more sympathetic to his predicament, I tried to enlighten him. "Jon, when all's said and done, you'll find that life's a lot more than cold, hard cash or a hot chunk of lead. When you look back at the toll you've paid in life, it has to stand for something more than just your style of life. You've made great strides when you talked about feeling compassion for General Semmes, a man you really didn't care for. That's great, but you have to realize that you've dug a pretty deep crater here. It's going to take a long time and a lot of effort to climb out of that pit," I summed up.

"From what I hear, the military courts may end up charging me with a crime. That's why they made me stay behind. So, I guess I'm already starting to pay that price. Lieutenant's got me on burial duty today; me, some other malcontents, and the rest niggers. Some good company, huh?"

"You could improve your lot in life quite a bit if you stopped calling black people niggers."

"Well, that's what them people's called. What do you want me to call them?"

"For starters, how about just plain 'people?' They're no different than me...or you for that matter. They may lack the education you were privy to, but what do you expect? The law doesn't allow them to be schooled. That can, over time, be remedied."

"That's one hell of a concept you're speaking of," he said, adding a laugh. "It would sure as hell take a lot of getting used to. Could you imagine what the other fellows would think of me if I spouted that sort of thinking?"

"Who cares? Talk is cheap. It's what *you* feel inside that's important, not what some other people utter about you. You have to treat others by how you feel, right here," I explained pointing to my heart. "You have to be true to yourself despite others' criticism. Yourself is all you've got, Jon. It ain't easy, I know, especially not in this day and time."

"But suppose I don't get the chance to put that so-called concept into practice. I hear tell that General Longstreet was so furious at the failure of our last assault that he's looking to take it out on anyone and everyone. Word has it that if General Semmes dies, I'll be brought up on charges. I might be anyway. The way people feel about me around here, I'll end up in prison for the rest of my days. If they make the charge murder, I'll be a goner."

"Yes, that's possible. We all reap what we sow, as the old proverb goes. It's also been said that one's destiny is the house you've constructed in which you reside."

"Yes, I get the picture."

Seeing his spirits droop, I added, "Look Jon, despite what I do or don't know what will happen to you, your fate isn't carved in stone. Mine isn't either. I mean, look at me, my past is nearly a century away, yet here I am. Technically speaking, my life has yet to begin. You see, it's your decision as to what you're going or not going to do. If and when I return to my day, you'll already have made your decision. My advice to you is to not over-analyze the situation, just do what you feel in your heart of hearts to be right.

That's all anyone can ask of you. That's what makes you a complete man."

We walked over to a boulder at the landing zone and took a seat. "A toast," I said as I pulled my bottle out of the bag, attempting to lighten my load before returning home. I offered Jonathan the last swallow of the Jack Daniel's, "To new beginnings."

As the last guzzle disappeared Jonathan commented, "Boy, that is smooth. It's a damn good thing that you didn't show up earlier. You'd most assuredly have put me out of business with this stuff. Of course, seeing the predicament that I'm in, that probably would have been for the best," he realized as he chucked the empty bottle into the weeds.

As the clock wound down, I reached into my bag for the tether instead of risking another loss from my pocket. "I'm on my way home, the good Lord willing," I announced. "I wish you luck in making it home sometime too, Jon."

Jonathan perked up. "What do you mean 'sometime?' If you knew the past, you'd know if I made it home or not." Then in a panic, realizing the gist of my statement he said, "They're going to get me, aren't they? Oh God, they're going to arrest me and try me for murder, and you knew that all along, didn't you? That's why you're here, isn't it?"

After a pregnant pause I replied, "Nothing happens until it happens, you know. Like I stated earlier, it's all up to you from now on."

"For the last time, quit talking to me like I'm an idiot! Speak to me man to man. You won't deny that it's going to happen that way, will you? I didn't shoot the general on purpose! You know, you were there, you saw it all." Then, as if he received a brilliant revelation, Jonathan straightened up and spoke in a softer tone. "Yes, you did see it, didn't you? You're a witness! You can help me out here. Yes, this is great," he shouted to no one in particular. "They'd believe you. You don't have an ax to grind here. And, you seem like a decent fellow. You wouldn't dare bear false witness against one of your own family now would you? All you'd have to do is tell the truth."

"Jon, I can't do that."

In a defiant tone, Jonathan declared, "You can and you will."

"Jon, in a military court of law, they'd want to know my name, prove where I'm from, and so on. How could I tell them that I'm your great-great grandson and I'm from one hundred and forty years into the future? They'd convict you quicker than ever if you insulted their intelligence with a story like that. They'd also throw my ass in an insane asylum. Jon, you just can't risk having me there, and I really shouldn't be attempting to tear the fabric of time. I've done too much already. I just can't do it."

"OK," he said as he stood up, reached into his pocket, and produced a small caliber pistol, "if I can't go home, then you can't neither." He grabbed my hair and held the firearm against my temple.

"Hey come on, Jon. Don't be doing that."

"Ha, what could they do to me, convict me of killing a man who hasn't even been born yet? Hey, this is my life we're talking about here!" he screamed and tightened his grip.

"What's that you said about never killing anyone other than an armed Yank?" I asked. Trying to calm him down I inquired, "Jon, haven't you learned anything from all of this? Look at you; you're still so full of hate that you're willing to take down anyone who stands in your way, even your own flesh and blood. Man, you don't learn how to survive in the wilderness by passing on nothing but smooth roads. You learn more from the hardships you encounter. Personally speaking I don't think that we are here to learn how to become content," I continued my sermon. "I'm sure, in our heart of hearts, we already know how to do that. I think we're here to learn how to weather the storms. You have to look at the bigger picture rather than just your little corner of it."

My lecture had gotten through. Jonathan released his grip, lowered the gun, and went over to an adjacent stone and sat down facing away from me. I went over to comfort him, but mostly to lift the gun from the stone where he placed it. Not knowing what to do with it, I slid it in my pocket next to the tether.

Jonathan's back started to tremble as he began to break down and said, "I've made such a miserable damn mess of my life. You have to believe me; I was just trying to help out my family. I was just trying to help! I guess I ended up making things worse. I just know that the army will take me from them. What will happen to my kids?"

"If they're to go it alone, that's their lot in life. We don't get to pick and choose what kind of life we'd like to have once we're here. All we can do is to make the best decisions possible and let the chips fall where they may. I guess we can plan all that we want, but destiny always has the final say."

Standing up behind him I continued, "You know, it's been said that peoples' lives are trapped in history. I think that history is also trapped within a person's soul. We may have little say in what we're handed in life. It's how we react to what's been presented to us that defines us as a person and our worth."

I then bent down, placed both hands on his shoulders and said, "Jon, you'll forever be remembered within the family as a man who always placed his wife and children in the forefront of his life. Yes, I'll see to that. Your intentions were always the best." With a pat on his shoulders I said, "Now if you'll excuse me, I have a transport home that I hopefully will be able catch. Wish me luck."

I walked back over to the other boulder and gathered up my belongings. I checked the tether for the time. In the interim, Jonathan Gates got up and slowly walked towards the lane. With his head held low, Jon looked like a man who just lost the war single-handedly. Perhaps he may have just realized the outcome of his own personal battle.

I felt so bad for him. "God's speed, Jonathan Gates," I called out to him. He didn't acknowledge the good wishes.

Looking around, I hoped the occasional flash of lightning in the distance wouldn't affect my attempted exit. I remembered that I could always hear the crackle on the radio when a storm was in the area. I wasn't sure what that meant in terms of a disruption to the ATM's signal, but there was no room for any interference in my final attempt of a return trip.

I watched intently as the time on the tether read 05:29:58, 05:29:59, then 05:30:00. I aimed the tether and pushed the button, and held it down longer than was usual. Since this was probably my last attempt, I felt as if I had nothing to lose.

Like the previous day, there was nothing immediately following that act. However, seconds later I heard what I hoped and believed to be a sonic thump. It could have been military action from Lee's fleeing army. It may have been a residual rumble of distant thunder. But just then, I saw what I thought to be the faint outline of the ATM. I prayed that it wasn't my mind playing tricks on me from wishful thinking. In a short instant, the image became more opaque until finally the picture was complete.

"It made it!" I shouted. I was finally going home.

I walked over to the craft, removed the cowl, then placed it aside. My hand brushed the side of the craft, then paused. I noticed for the first time that the ATM's skin was a bit warm. It felt similar to metal that has been exposed to sunlight for a brief time. Perhaps it had.

As I began to load up, I noticed Jonathan Gates just standing and staring in my direction. I thought, oh what the hell, I've waited this long. A few more seconds wouldn't hurt.

I walked the twenty paces over to Jonathan and said, "You take care of yourself. Hang in there, Jon. Everything will work itself out for the best. It always does." I placed a half hug on my great-great grandfather, now a broken man. He returned it with little enthusiasm.

In a weak, grumbled voice he proclaimed, "You do the same, Neil Gates."

When I turned to walk back to the craft,

Jonathan cleared his throat and shouted to me, "You know, when you push that button, I'm basically a dead man." I just returned a glance realizing that in a way, he was right. But from this time forward, someone somewhere could push a button in history and declare any of us extinct in their time.

Softening his tone he concluded, "Hey, I know that I'm going to be all right. Shoot, if anything happened to me, you wouldn't even be alive now would you?" I just smiled and returned a weak wave of acknowledgement. I guess Jonathan forgot that he already had two male heirs, his oldest from which I descended.

While I squeezed my body into the cockpit of the ATM, it reminded me of crawling into the Soap Box Derby car I assembled back in my youth. "Boy, it'll be so good to get back home." I placed my camera and bag on my lap, then pulled the cowl over top of me and locked it into place.

"Now, let me see, I have to remember all of the pointers that Dr. Welles gave me to insure a successful trip," I muttered. I rested both ankles against the two sharp contacts. I spit on my shirt cuffs, wiped off my greasy temples, then attached the electrodes. I positioned my left wrist against its spike. I then replaced the tether to its rightful resting place, pushed the button, then completed the circuit as my right hand and neck met their prongs. I looked straight ahead and saw Jon staring back at me seemingly unimpressed by the entire spectacle. He had other things on his mind at the moment.

Breaking one of Dr. Welles Cardinal rules, I was going to wave at Jon one last time when I was hit by a jolt of power. I felt as if I was the one being executed as all color and light became absent from my vision during this period. Amazingly enough I was still mentally conscious within myself, an event that escaped my notice on the way over. I was learning something new every time I went through this process. As I passed across the spectrum of time, I felt as if I had taken a spiritual breath. I then 'exhaled' as the humming within my head and body came to a swift conclusion.

I didn't notice the bump in the landing this time around, but I felt as if I had taken a swift, metaphorical punch in the sternum as I exhaled profoundly. As I fought to clear my eyes in desperation to discover my new surroundings, the slight valley leading in the direction of the Rose house was the first scene that came into focus. Since the general terrain has changed very little over the years, I didn't know if I was home or not. While the time of day was the same, I knew that I wasn't at the place that I just abandoned because there were no bodies or mounds scattered about. The grass was green and neatly mowed. The weather had also transformed itself, for it was now dry and the sky was clear. The Sun was just breaking over the horizan welcoming a new day. I glanced towards my front and spotted a sight for sore eyes; Ed's van. I didn't see Dr. Welles however. As a matter of fact, I didn't spot anyone about.

When I unlatched, then tossed the lid to the ATM aside, I saw a head peek around from the van's open back door. It was Dr. Welles who emerged at a full trot yelling, "Welcome home, son!"

I set my things on the ground as Henry came to my aid and assisted me from the module.

"Oh my God, it's great to have you back, Neil! I was worried that...good God, what happened to you? Are you O.K.?"

"I will be," I said as I planted my unsteady feet on a drier, calmer earth than the one I just left.

"You look horrible, and you stink, too," he said commenting on my fermenting body. I believe I also brought back the residual scent of dead and decaying flesh.

"Likewise I'm sure." Then, finally realizing that I was indeed home and that four-day nightmare was over, I started to laugh and grabbed Dr. Welles' arm and exclaimed, "I made it! I made it back! Henry, you're a genius! It worked!" I then began to break slightly and started to cry. "I'm home, I'm back home aren't I?"

"Take it easy now. I don't want you to get all worked up. You just traveled across nearly one hundred and forty years, you know."

Straightening up and clearing my head I declared, "One hundred and forty years? Seems like just yesterday," I concluded with a sniff upwards and a cocky attitude now that I was victor over the elements. He walked me over and sat me down on the now familiar rock.

"Here, here, let me check your eyes," he said as he peeled my eyelids back and gave them a visual inspection. "Bloodshot as all hell and a slight hemorrhage in the corner. That's noteworthy."

"Probably has something to do with the fact that I heaved up everything I had within my gut onto God's green Earth."

"O.K. then, I'll just write that off as a bad night for right now."

Upon calming down, I looked around and observed, "A lot has taken place right here. Oh Henry, you wouldn't believe what I've been through. I've been shot, shot at, nearly blown up, robbed..."

"Wait, what do you mean 'shot'? Are you O.K.?"

"Yes, I'm fine, but I'm afraid that they got my camera."

Resigned to that possibility all along he exclaimed, "Another casualty of war, I guess, so long as you're O.K."

"Henry, I had some great shots for you. They would have kept you busy for years to come."

"Well, I'm guessing that it wasn't your fault.

You risked your neck for those. Your efforts are appreciated." As if not wanting to hear the answer, Dr. Welles gazed at the ground and asked, "Uh, how about the video? Did you manage to salvage anything from that?"

"Oh hell yes! I shot about forty-five minutes of footage for you. Let me go over and get it," I said as I stood up and flexed my back. Even the earth I stood on seemed so much calmer. "Boy, it's good to be back home," I said. "No hassles and no one trying to hunt you down."

I looked over at Little Round Top, once the scene of death and carnage from a struggle of Titanic proportions. Now it merely serves as a tourist overlook.

When I was in my third wobbly step towards the ATM to retrieve my luggage, I was broad sided and knocked flat on my face. I rolled over and exclaimed, "What the hell?" I looked up to see a familiar looking mangy mutt, his tail section in high gear, staring back down at me.

"Tramp!" I yelled as I attempted to right myself against the dog's enthusiasm. "Dr. Welles, it's Tramp!"

"I know that," he said with a laugh. "Who do you think brought him here?"

"But how? I thought he was gone for good."

"You and me both. I called my voicemail to pick up my messages the day after you left. Dr. Goodrich called and said that when he was in the Davey Lab, he heard a dog barking. He recognized the bark but thought it came from outside. When he went to investigate, he found Tramp and the missing ATM in the assembly room."

"How long had he been gone? How long had

he been back?" I asked as I buffed the dog's bristly coat.

"No one knows. I'm not sure if we ever will. Judging from all of the little 'gifts' Tramp left around the lab, according to Mel, I'd guesstimate that he had been there for some time. I figure he chewed through the nylon restraints and was running loose down there."

"Well, I guess you still have to work out some additional 'dee-tails' on this case, huh?"

With a chuckle he observed, "Oh, I can see that your sense of humor hasn't improved one iota since you've been gone."

"He looks none the worse for wear," I commented while looking the dog over.

"No he doesn't," Henry admitted as he inspected the ATM. "That's the main reason I risked going over to Mel's to pick him up. It could have been a trap, you know. Anyway, I wanted to observe him for a while. No one's sure what a trip of such duration will do to a being in the long term. That's why you're going to come with me. I'm going to be watching you as well."

"Don't worry, I won't leave little gifts around for you like ol' Tramp here."

"Yeah, I'll bet. In his phone message, Dr. Goodrich gave me a brief rundown on how he found Tramp. The last thing he said was, "Get that damn dog the hell out of my house!"

We both started to laugh noting that Dr. Goodrich didn't strike either of us as a dog lover. Sadly, he was too busy to take time out for things like that.

"Looks like you have a new best friend there," he commented on Tramp's never changing enthusiasm towards me.

"Yeah, you could say that. We have a lot in common. Tramp ol' buddy, would you like to stay at Uncle Neil's house and have a warm bed and a steady supply of eats?" I asked. "We could sit around all weekend, drink beer, watch the games on TV," I joked. I received overwhelming approval.

Laughing at my new ownership Henry continued, "I went over to Mel's house to pick up the dog. He wasn't home, but I could hear Tramp in the garage. I got him out and tossed him in the van. I didn't want to hang around in any one area for too long so I hot-footed it back here to Gettysburg."

"If Dr. Goodrich wasn't there, how did you get Tramp out of the garage?"

"One hell of a tug on the handle," he said with a chuckle. "I guess I'll owe Mel a couple of bucks on that one. What the hell, he's a renter. Good God, Mel had a five gallon bucket of water and an opened ten pound bag of food sitting there in the middle of the floor for Tramp. That's his idea of caring for a pet."

"Henry, what in the hell happened to you yesterday? Why didn't the ATM pick me up? I did everything right. I was there on time."

"You may have been but I wasn't. I parked across the way waiting for the rangers to vacate the area. I guess they were conducting a sunrise anniversary battle walk and didn't leave here for fifteen to twenty minutes. By then it was too late. I'm sorry, Neil. You must have been worried sick. I apologize for that but what could I do?"

"I understand. You know Henry, on the

positive side, I think I learned more about my great-great grandfather this morning than during any other time that I was there. So I guess things happen the way they're supposed to."

"A metaphor for life itself. Well tell me, did you find out what you wanted to know about your great-great grandfather?"

"Yes, yes I did," I said as I pulled my belongings out of the craft. "You know, he wasn't the angel I hoped him to be, but he wasn't the devil his country portrayed him as being. He didn't commit the crime for which he paid with his life, but he did, in essence, die from the sins of his own making."

"I'll be damned. Maybe that's why you didn't find more details on that incident in the history books."

"Perhaps. Maybe I ought to write a book of my own some day and set the record straight. By the way, how did you spend your time around here?"

"I played the part of a tourist," he stated as he surveyed the area. "I've been from one side of this battlefield to the other, educating myself as I went."

"Tell me about it!" I said with a smirk.

"I'll level with you Neil, I'm embarrassed to admit it but when I was at the visitor center, I did look through the casualty lists and check for your name. When I realized that there were so many unidentified bodies left on that battlefield, I came to the conclusion that my search would be fruitless regardless of your outcome."

"What, you didn't have confidence in your own work? Oh ye of little faith."

"Let's just say that I was cautiously optimistic."

"Well, if you were anything more I'd say that you were a fool. You know," I said while looking around, "future generations will look upon us with awe. I suppose the future is now though."

"Smart man. It sounds as if you learned quite a bit on your excursion. Tell you what, suppose we talk it all over at breakfast—my treat."

"Oh yeah, like I have a lot of money on me at the moment."

"Well, you look like you haven't eaten for days. How about if we go over to the hotel's restaurant and I'll buy you a mess of ham and eggs?" he offered as he began inspecting the ATM.

"Oh God, don't say eggs. I've had my fill of those things for a while. I will take a shot at the ham though. And to be honest, I'm so parched that I could down about a gallon of orange juice; the colder the better. And a stack of pancakes would..."

"OK. OK, I get the picture. Let's get this thing loaded up and we'll decide when we get there."

"Let me get my camera and bag out of the way before one of us steps on it."

"Oh yes, I almost forgot! Let me have a look at that video. I'm dying to see what you saw."

I brought the camera over to him, removed it from its wooden facade, turned it on, and then hit 'rewind'. After a minute or so I hit 'play' and handed it to Dr. Welles for his viewing pleasure. He gazed through the viewfinder for a time, hit 'rewind', then 'fast forward'.

"Well how about it?" I asked with anticipation.

"How about what? There's nothing here. Are you sure you had it on 'record' the whole time?"

"Yes! I even reviewed it a couple of times myself. The scenes were there then."

"Well they ain't there now," he returned.

"Give me that," I said as I went through the same exercise as Dr. Welles. He was right, there was only static in the viewfinder. "I don't understand, it all looked so good when I viewed it. I don't think I broke it or anything. Nobody else had access to it that I know of," I said as I rewound to the beginning. "Even the intro we made up last week is missing. I don't get it."

"I think I do. Damn it," he said with frustration and disappointment. "We were so rushed during this whole operation that I didn't have time to consider all of the variables. I totally overlooked the fact that video tape is of a magnetic property and thus subject to whatever electronic stimuli that it comes in contact with. The teleportation process involves nothing more than the realignment of an object's vibratory molecular structure. That's similar to the process the tape itself undergoes when being recorded. When you returned to this time zone, the tape returned as tape only. Its iron coating realigned itself and you, in essence, erased the tape, unknowingly of course."

"Oh geeze, don't tell me that!" I said in exasperation.

"I'm afraid that it's true. Seeing is believing. Damn it, it was so obvious, why didn't I think of that!" Dr. Welles said chiding himself.

"It wasn't your fault, Henry. You're right, the whole operation was a bit rushed, but we had no alternative. The loss of the still camera was probably the result of my rushed evacuation. At least if my 35 had survived we would have had some visual proof of the success of the undertaking."

"That is if the film hadn't been exposed the same way airport security x-rays have been known to expose a roll or two. For all we know, your film may have been ruined before you even took your first shot."

"I guess I see what you mean. Oh Henry, it's all gone. All of the proof you needed to demonstrate your project's worthiness to the scientific world. Now who'll believe your efforts? How can you even believe me?"

"Perhaps it's just as well, now that I think about it. I doubt that today's people are intelligent enough to use a tool such as this for the betterment and further understanding of mankind. They'd probably use it for their own greedy desires. That's what frightened me the most about the feds."

"You could be right. Hell, I don't even have any proof myself that everything I went through was legit. For all I know, the entire trip could have been some enormous hallucination brought about in my mind by the electrical activity of the ATM. I didn't even end up with a souvenir of any kind, other than my muddy pants and shoes, to prove to myself of my whereabouts. I have no way of knowing if what I experienced really happened. Could Rueben, Mojo, and even my great-great grandfather been a figment of my imagination? Oh God," I said in despair as I looked out over the field.

Neither one of us said anything for a spell as the disappointment sank in. We both felt as if we failed even though, in our heart of hearts, we knew what had been experienced actually occurred.

As I sat there silently looking around and not focusing on anything in particular, I glanced down at the boulder I was sitting upon and actually searched for any telltale signs of blood from the soldier I saw clinging to this spot just a couple of days prior. It was then that I noticed Tramp disappear then reemerge around the front side of the Texas memorial. He was sniffing around, I presume, to do what dogs do best. He came to a rock that sported a divide at its center. That's when it hit me.

"Tramp!" I yelled, nearly scaring the poor mutt out of his wiry coat. I ran over to the side rack of the van and pulled loose a short-handled shovel.

"What is it son," Dr. Welles asked. "What have you got?"

I ran over to the split rock that is positioned about five or six paces behind the Texas marker. I buried the shovel into the soil heart of the rock's divide.

"Hey, hey Neil, you can't do that. If the rangers catch you vandalizing the battlefield they'll throw your ass in jail—not to mention me and our equipment. What the hell are you doing?"

I ignored Dr. Welles as the first shovel full revealed nothing but dry earth. I sank the spade once more, this time jumping on the shovel's steps, and pulled up the contents. I didn't even have to sift through the soil, for the shovel itself revealed two iron chunks, remnants of a Napoleon's twelve-pounder. I reached down and picked up the two pieces and thumbed the dirt from their surface.

Now cooled by time, the rusty old segments were little more than battlefield souvenirs to the average collector. To me, they were the proof I had been seeking. What I held in my hands were remnants of the ordinance that nearly took my life some fourteen decades earlier.

I clinked the two pieces together, looked up at Dr. Welles and said with a feeling of vindication, "It did happen, didn't it?"

He smiled with satisfaction and said, "It happened just as you saw it. You would know better than anyone else because you were there. As they say, whatever was, has been."

I remained in a squat for some time gazing at the destructive pieces and thinking how meaningless they seemed today. They certainly carried the gravest of intentions in their day, but now the iron shell was in the process of returning back to the earth from whence it came. And thus goes the cycle of life for everything on this planet. Some things pass through this plane quicker than others. I hoped that the concepts and ideas attributed to that war don't become outdated relics such as these that I held in my hands. Material objects can be replaced, but ideas and concepts learned by mankind over the generations are priceless. We have no choice whether we are born or when we depart this life, so the lessons we learn as individuals, and as a country, should never be allowed to pass away. That choice is ours alone.

During my self-reflection, Dr. Welles wandered over by the van. He was still working with the videocam trying to determine if the problem was indeed of a mechanical nature. He broke my train of thought when I heard him say, "Uh oh."

Dropping the iron, I raised up, walked over to Dr. Welles who was now facing me. I could tell by the troubled look on his face that something was amiss. "What's wrong, Henry?"

Under his breath and through a barely moving mouth he said, "Look through the viewfinder as if you're scanning the horizon. Keep it on full zoom. Don't stop, but make sure you take notice of the inconspicuous grey car sitting on the shoulder of Emmitsburg. Tell me what you think."

Looking towards the lightening sky, I squinted my eye as I scanned the vista starting from Little Round Top towards the east, and circled towards the west. "We've got visitors, don't we?" I muttered as if trying to avoid being eavesdropped upon.

"We do unless the park guides have taken to wearing suits and ties while using binoculars aimed in our direction at this early hour of the morning. They're too early to be visitors, too formal to be rangers. If I was a betting man, I'd have to say those two possess an uncanny resemblance to our old buddies Holbach and Block. I just noticed them, but I'm sure they've been observing us for some time. For all I know, they may have been monitoring our every movement for the past week."

"Feds, are you sure?"

"I say we don't wait around to find out. Leave the shovel and grab the dog. It's time to go."

We left everything as it was and jumped in the van. Dr. Welles performed a flawless U-turn, dodging a rock and a cannon as we went, then headed towards Emmitsburg Road. The government vehicle was aimed south, so we traveled north. I'm sure Dr. Welles didn't think that maneuver would outwit our pursuers, but he was probably hoping that it would buy us some time for a successful run through town.

In an instant, the grey car performed a near-perfect U-turn of its own, shot up behind us, then nearly locked bumpers with our van. I peered in my side view mirror, and sure enough Dr. Welles was correct. I spotted Edward Holbach in the passenger side of the car reaching inside of his coat and producing what appeared to be a firearm of some sort.

Fearing for our lives, I reacted rather than acted. I reached into my pocket, seized the pistol I confiscated from Jonathan Gates an hour earlier, whirled around towards the tailing sedan and pulled the trigger. Being an antique, I had no idea how to operate this gun. I aimed and fired just as we entered the curve in front of the Codori farm proper. A cloud of smoke accompanied a loud crack as the gun went off striking the automobile's windshield. While the agents' car continued curving around the roadway and collided with the inset rock wall leading to the entrance of the barn we kept going.

Thanks Jonathan.

The End

About the Author

Kent Richardson is a lifelong resident of Hamilton, Ohio, and is a photographer and sports columnist with the *Venice Cornerstone* newspaper. A 1979 graduate of Miami University (Ohio), Mr Richardson as been wrting for thriteen years, and *Journey Across Time* is his third published work. He has written three screenplays and is busy on his fourth novel.

Also available form Dailey Swan Publishing

Beyond the Fears of Tomorrow $9.95
by Casey Robert Swanson

Revenge $12.95
by JH Hardy

Bones of the Homeless $15.95
by Judy Jones

Endlight Event $14.95
by John P Cater

The Black Beast of Algernon Woods $14.95
by Nickolas Cook

Deadline $15.95
by Paula Tutman

Dupers Fork $11.95
by Andrew Olsson

The Acorn Dossier $14.95
by William Beecher

The Transyvania Connection $14.95
by Garrison Walters

Widdershins $13.95
by Eve Lestrange

www.Daileyswanpublishing.com